**"FROM THE FIRST WORD TO THE LAST,
YOU'LL BE BREATHLESS AND CRAVING MORE."
RT BOOK REVIEWS**

"An action packed, keep you guessing story and a surprise ending. I recommend it to all fans of historical romance."

TARA CHEVRESTT
Author & Reviewer
Book Babe Reviews

"Great characters. Exciting adventure. Burroughs is a witty, crafty storyteller. This is the kind of book Joan Wilder [Romancing the Stone] would have wished she'd written, if she were real. Luckily Patricia Burroughs is."

TERRI EDDA MILLER
Filmmaker, Screenwriter, Producer, **"Castle"**

"[LA DESPERADA] is hands down the best love story I have ever read. The story is incredible with surprises that keep on coming. You cannot for the life of you figure out where it is going, and when you get there, it wraps with another big surprise. I was so sad when it was over, that I didn't have more of it to read. A sequel, please!"

MELANIE MAYRON
Actress, Director, Writer

"Every once-in-a-while, you come across a fellow writer who is so damned good, you want to hate them. Patricia Burroughs is that kind of writer. (Except, she is so funny and nice, you cannot hate her. Dammit.) LA DESPERADA is phenomenal: characters, pacing, story, quality of writing–it has it all, hands down. Read this book. You'll thank me."

TONI MCGEE CAUSEY
Author of the **Bobbie Faye Books**

"[Her] writing is witty, full of charm and engaging twists, her characters live and breath for you — you can't go wrong with a story from Patricia Burroughs.

MAX ADAMS,
Screenwriter, Author
Founder, **Academy of Film Wr**iting
Associate Professor, Film & Media Arts
University of Utah

La Desperada

Other books by Patricia Burroughs

The Contemporary Romances

Razzmatazz

Beguiled again

Some Enchanted Season

Scandalous

Nonfiction

Adapting Your Novel
Into an Award-Winning Script
and why you don't want to [a cautionary tale]

The Fantasies

The Fury Triad

This Crumbling Pageant [2014]

The Dead Shall live [2015]

untune the sky [2016]

La Desperada

Originally titled *What Wild Ecstasy*

Patricia Burroughs

Book View Café

Book View Café
P.O. Box 1624
Cedar Crest, NM 87008-1624
http://bookviewcafe.com

Publisher's Note: This is a work of fiction. Names, characters, places, and incidents are a product of the author's imagination. Locales and public names are sometimes used for atmospheric purposes. Any resemblance to actual people, living or dead, or to businesses, companies, events, institutions, or locales is completely coincidental.

ISBN 978 1 61138 308-9

Dedicated, with love, to:

My maternal grandparents,
for the gift of story-telling.
My paternal grandparents,
for the love of books.
My parents,
who allowed me and
even encouraged me
to be different.
My husband, Sam,
for tolerance and support,
love and laughter.

ACKNOWLEDGEMENTS

For guiding me to the many sources and resources used in the writing of this book, I would like to thank the following:

Melleta R. Bell, Archival Assistant,
Archives of the Big Bend, Sul Ross State University,
Alpine, Texas

Loretta Clark, Librarian,
Roswell Public Library, Roswell, New Mexico

Nora Henn, Historian
Lincoln County Historical Society, Lincoln, New Mexico

With special thanks and credit to
Pamela W. Renner
for clearing the smoke and polishing the iceberg.

“What men or gods are these? What maidens loth?
What mad pursuit? What struggle to escape?
What pipes and timbrels?
What wild ecstasy?”

.

——John Keats, “Ode on a Grecian Urn”

Prologue

Clay County, Missouri—1872

"MURDERERS!" THE PREACHER thundered. Torchlight illuminated his gaunt face, giving it a cadaverous quality both powerful and disturbing as he waved a tattered newspaper aloft. "You call them heroes! But they're robbers and murderers!"

His sudden rage startled even his horses, though they were long accustomed to remaining still while he delivered his sermons from the back of the wagon at any roadside where a crowd gathered to listen. Seated in the wagon, his seventeen-year-old son strained to settle the horses down again.

A low rumbling of dissent rolled through the gathering of farmers and their families, huddled in clusters in the brisk night air. A crackling voice from the back of the crowd rose above the others. "Why don't you stick to the Good Book, parson?"

The shout was echoed by a chorus of agreement.

"Leave politics to them that knows what they're doin'," cried someone else.

"Politics?" The circuit rider's voice rang out in fury. "Was it politics when the James boys robbed the Kansas City fairgrounds last week?" He brandished a ragged newspaper, waving its masthead high, just as he had brandished it a dozen times before in a dozen other crowds that same week. "The Kansas City Times would have you think it's politics! It calls the James gang highhanded, diabolically daring, knights of the round table that we should admire and revere!

"And why do you admire them? I'll tell you why! Because these robbers attack the banks that hold your mortgages and charge interest rates you cannot pay! These murderers fan the embers of the Confederate cause that you know is dead! Yes, you admire them! You revere them! These are your heroes!"

He leaned forward, his heavy brows lowering over piercing eyes that seemed to see into the very souls of all who listened. "You want the Good Book, Brother Grier? I'll give you the Good Book! Remember ye the words of Peter, the rock: 'While they promise you liberty, they themselves are the servants of corruption.'"

"Where were your shining knights when a ten-year-old girl was shot and killed in the panic at the fairgrounds?"

The old man grasped the newspaper in his gnarled, work-worn hands and ripped it asunder, scattering the torn pages over the heads of his listeners.

"I'll tell you where they were! They were holding the guns that killed her! They were riding the horses that trampled her under foot!"

A wave of shock washed over the congregation. Then, a coarse voice shouted, "You lie!"

The preacher's son whirled round in his seat at the slanderous words, his jaw set with frustration and rage. He half-rose, his fists clenched, as if daring the speaker to repeat his words.

The preacher merely shook his weary head. Days of riding his circuit, delivering his message, were taking their toll. When he spoke his voice was tired, yet his conviction gave it a resonance that carried over the crowd. "No, Brother Reynolds, I don't lie! And I can't be silenced by threats, though I've received them."

A heavy silence hung in the night, broken only by the uneasy stirrings of people forced to listen to words they did not want to believe. The preacher's shoulders slumped beneath his frayed, black frock coat, his head lowering as if in pain. Then he raised his face to them, his hard, burning eyes boring into the crowd.

"It is written, 'The innocent and righteous slay thou not: for I will not justify the wicked.' Evil begets evil, and wickedness begets wickedness. How many of our youth are taking up arms to join these outlaw gangs? How many farmers in this county, alone, are providing them refuge? How many of you here in my own congregation? And why do you do it? Because they're your heroes, your champions? Or because of your greed? How much do the outlaws pay you to hide in your caves, your cribs, your barns? To lie for them? To protect them?"

He raised one gnarled fist raised high in the air, then thundered his last, hoarse question. "At what price do you sell your souls?"

Hours later, the horses leaned into their leather harnesses, straining to pull the creaking wagon up a steep hill toward home. The preacher's body was limp against the seat; his son fought to hold his eyes open as the plodding rhythm lulled them.

The horses nickered and grew restless, raising their quivering nostrils to the sky. Stirred from his drowsiness, the boy, too, raised his face to the air and caught a whiff of smoke.

"Pa, wake up."

Reverend Bridges shifted and blinked into the darkness. "What is it, Wesley?"

"Do you smell somethin', Pa?"

At that moment they crested the last hill before descending into the creek valley where their home lay, and saw the red glow of fire. And, coming toward them, riders, all masked. The boy fought to rein his team in as the approaching horses split and galloped on either side of the wagon—all plow horses spurred on to unaccustomed speed by desperate riders—save one magnificent beast.

One of the Dougherty's finely-bred roans. It pulled up momentarily, and the hooded rider shouted, "Let this be a lesson to ya' preacher! Mind your own business and let us mind our'n!"

And then they were gone.

"Hee-yah!" the boy shouted, a sudden fear filling his veins. He slapped the reins across the horses' backs as they surged forward, bouncing down the rutted path. They pulled into the clearing moments later—moments that seemed like hours. Before the wagon came to a complete halt, the man and the boy bolted from it and raced toward the burning cabin.

"I'll get your ma and Frankie, boy—you get Susannah!" The preacher ran through the door, his son close behind.

When the boy emerged from the smoking, blazing conflagration, young muscles straining under his older sister's weight, his father was nowhere to be seen. Blood dripped from a cut on his cheek; his shoulder was seared where a timber had crashed on it, yet he didn't feel pain. The boy hesitated, his tortured eyes darting from his sister's charred, yet breathing body to the burning cabin. And then the roof collapsed with a groan, showering sparks and ashes upward as if to the heavens, trapping the cabin's occupants in a fiery hell.

"No!" the boy cried. And again, his tormented scream, "No!"

Then his sister's limp body stirred in his arms, and she began to cough, followed by harsh, wracking groans. Tears coursing down his smoke-blackened cheeks, he turned and ran, stumbling under her weight as he carried her toward the creek.

"Don't die, Susannah," he sobbed. "Don't you die on me!" His words, a litany of fear and panic, of grief and hatred, continued as he cradled her body in the cold, flowing water of Boone Creek.

"We're gonna make them pay, you hear me, Susannah?" He choked on his bitter tears. "We're gonna make those bastards pay!"

Chapter One

ELIZABETH DOUGHERTY STOOD alone at the kitchen window, staring into the distance. In that last, lonely moment before dawn, there was no beckoning world on the other side of the glass, no distinction between mountain and sky, only an all-encompassing blackness, void of moon or stars. Listening to the gentle crackle of the fire in the potbelly stove, she inhaled the rich aroma of coffee, soaking up the solitude and peace that were so precious in this hostile house.

Within minutes the peaks of the rugged mountains to the west appeared, bathed in pink and orange and magenta, honored by the sun's first rays. With agonizing slowness, the colors washed down the slopes, creeping into the valley, yet Elizabeth remained alone in the semi-darkness, as if the lonely kitchen where she waited was unworthy of the sun's attention.

A sudden movement in the rocky terrain beyond the barn caught her eye—a bobcat lurked beside a rabbit trail, its keen eyes and ears alert for the sound that would lead it to its last chance of feeding for the night.

Elizabeth shuddered and hurriedly lit the oil lamp hanging on the wall, no longer content to await the sun's benevolence, then she filled her coffee cup. She spooned white sugar from the china sugar bowl that had been part of her hope chest. A dollop of heavy cream, a quick whirl with a sterling spoon, and she turned, heading for the door.

She gasped, finding it filled with the looming figure of her husband's brother.

"Good morning, Clayton," she murmured without meeting his eyes, hoping to pass him and retreat to her bedroom without further contact.

But he didn't budge, only leaned against the door frame, his heavy-lidded eyes sweeping possessively over her, leaving her feeling defiled. His massive body, only a few short years away from corpulence, filled the door, and she squared her slender shoulders in a self-conscious effort to compensate for her own slight frame.

Five years older than Joel, Clayton's features were an ugly mirror of her husband's. How could the same dark eyes burn with passion in one brother, with hatred in the other, the same wide, full lips soften with almost poetic beauty in Joel's face, yet twist with malicious anger in Clayton's?

She fought the cold shudder that threatened to ripple down her back, fought to keep him from seeing the effect he had on her.

He straightened as if to let her pass, but when she stepped forward his hand shot out, blocking the door.

"What's the matter, Miz Dougherty, havin' trouble sleepin'?" His voice was deep and gravelly, and his head dipped closer, his eyes narrowed as his mouth curled in an ugly smile. He looked past her, his eyebrows knitting in a scowl when he saw the single plate at the table. "Where is he?"

"Joel isn't well this morning." Elizabeth made a sharp gesture toward the platter of thick-sliced ham and fried potatoes on top of the stove, leftovers from the night before. "There are rolls in the bread box. I'm afraid you're going to have to fend for yourself this morning while I see to your brother."

The sheriff finally moved, stepping toward the stove in movements surprisingly light and quiet for a man of his size. "Ain't nothin' you can do to help that husband of yours nurse one of his goddamn hangovers, woman."

She stiffened, meeting his dark gaze with her cool, clear one. "That is none of your concern."

The dog yapping in the yard drew their attention. Elizabeth walked to the window. A solitary figure was riding down into the shallow valley, his horse's hooves plowing up dust in his wake. The lanky rider dug his spurs in, driving the beast harder, pushing it on to greater speed.

The young man slowed his mount as he rode into the yard. He swung down from the saddle, almost falling when his boot heel got caught in the stirrup. "Tar-nay-shun!" he spat savagely, limping on a twisted ankle as he trudged toward the sheriff's house.

"It's Wendell," Elizabeth said. When Clayton shot her a dark look, she shook her head. "I'll see to it." He grunted and turned his attention back to loading his plate.

Elizabeth smoothed a stray wisp of pale hair into the tight coil on the back of her head as she moved across the kitchen. She opened the door and the cold morning air blew in, swirling her skirt's full folds. She pulled the door closed behind her and stepped onto the porch.

"Wendell, what brings you out so early? The sheriff's still at breakfast, and I don't think he wants to be disturbed."

"I'm sorry, ma'am, I'm here on official business. It's important, beggin' your pardon for interruptin'."

"I'll tell him." Elizabeth stifled a smile as she turned away from the eighteen-year-old deputy. These bouts of self-importance weren't unusual. The poor boy was earnest enough; he did so strive to be a good lawman. Yet he was blind to his sheriff's shortcomings, hanging on the older man's every word in his eagerness to please, so that his efforts to imitate Clayton were often pathetically inadequate.

Inside the kitchen, her smile faded as she met Clayton's impatient gaze. "He says he's here on 'official' matters."

"Damned impertinent fool," the sheriff growled low.

Guiltily relieved that Wendell would now absorb the sheriff's ire, Elizabeth stepped aside as he stomped to the door, his plate still balanced in one beefy hand.

"What the hell are you doin', botherin' me this time of mornin'?" Clayton challenged, his deep voice booming.

"I figgered you'd want to know, Sheriff Dougherty," the young man burst out. "Late last night, a stranger come to town. He's holed up in the hotel right now."

Elizabeth had her cup in her hand, grateful for an excuse to leave the kitchen to the two men. But something in the boy's voice stopped her.

"Stranger? What in the hell does that mean? That's nothin' to drag your ass out here at the crack o' dawn over."

"But, Sheriff, this ain't just any stranger. They're sayin' it's Boone Coulter."

Dougherty swung around and faced the deputy, his body suddenly stiffening. "Couldn't be," he growled. "Coulter ain't been seen for years. Hell—he could be dead for all we know." He brushed Wendell impatiently aside. "Somebody's just lettin' their imagination go wild, and I'm aimin' to think that somebody's you."

"Just a minute, Sheriff. This ain't anybody's imagination. It's all over town." Wendell followed Clayton as the older man snatched a fistful of cold rolls from the breadbox and tossed them onto the pile of potatoes on his plate.

"First, this here maid from over to the hotel comes to the jail like her tail's afire, jabberin' a blue streak about outlaws 'n such. Well, I ain't payin' no mind to the likes o' her. Reckon she wouldn't know a desperado if he tipped his hat, raised her skirt and said 'howdy'? But then one of them gals from over at the saloon decides to see if she can—well, maybe do a little pleasurin' on a real outlaw, so she moseys on over there and goes up to his room."

"Which gal?" Clayton demanded, dropping his plate on the table with a loud rattle.

"Doralee—who else? Anyways, she stays over to the hotel for quite a spell. That's when I heard about it ag'in. Folks was gettin' worried that maybe she'd got herself in a fix, and they wanted me to go over there and rescue her. I would've done it, too, you know. I ain't afraid of no outlaws—not Boone Coulter, or anybody else. But about the time I got my pistol loaded, out she came, spittin' mad. Said it was Boone Coulter all right. She wouldn't say much more, just cussed a lot. So anyways, I went down to the livery stable and looked his horses over. One of them fit the description to a 't'. There ain't no two mustangs anywheres with striped scars on their haunches like that one. Odell said that horse won't let nobody near it—said the stranger tended it hisself afore he took off for the hotel."

There was a long silence, broken only by the fork and knife scraping over the plate as Clayton finished his breakfast.

Elizabeth realized she was holding her breath. Visions filled her head—visions of gunfire, of a vicious gunslinger taking aim, of Clayton Dougherty hitting the dirt with blood spreading around him. Grasping the back of the chair, she steadied herself against the shock of truth that slammed through her: the visions brought her pleasure. With a shudder, she sank heavily into the chair.

"Did you wire Fort Davis, boy? Last I heard, the cavalry was still after him."

"Them range-riders must've been usin' the telegraph poles for firewood again. Couldn't get through."

The sheriff growled low, shoving away from the table with a violent movement. He tossed his crumpled linen napkin onto his plate, heedless of the wild plum jelly that would stain it, then strode into the hallway to the hall tree where his gunbelt and hat hung.

Wendell followed close on his heels. "What are we gonna do, Sheriff? Think we should rush the hotel and flush him out?"

Elizabeth's motions scraping the plates slowed as she listened.

"Hell, no, you idiot! Boone Coulter ain't done nuthin' to me. If the government wants him, they can catch him. I just aim to see that no trigger happy citizens or deputies stir up trouble."

His words didn't ring true. Elizabeth raised her head and listened intently.

"But, Sheriff, there's a bounty on his head—two thousand dollars!"

"Hell, Wendell, I know that." His voice sounded thoughtful, tempted.

Elizabeth's pulse quickened at the thought of Clayton going after Coulter. They said the outlaw had already killed five, six men, two of them lawmen. There were those who said he hid out like an animal in the mountains, that there was no catching him... that those who tried didn't live to regret it.

"Boy, you just steer clear of that hotel, and everybody else'd better do the same. I don't want trouble in my town."

Elizabeth rose shakily to her feet and was crossing to the sink when Clayton reentered the room. With no attempt at courtesy, he pushed past her and grabbed his mug, tossing the lukewarm coffee down his throat. Wiping his mouth on the back of his hand, he eyed her speculatively.

"Stay away from town today." He buckled his gun-belt low on his hips and left.

Peering through the kitchen curtains, Elizabeth watched their departure, the sheriff swinging his large body onto his horse with a lithe agility that belied his massive form, the deputy attempting to match his authority with little success.

Elizabeth let the starched fabric fall back into place and squared her shoulders. She wasn't in the habit of taking orders from anyone.

Especially not Clayton Dougherty.

Coulter stood at the narrow window, his tense shoulders hunched slightly as he leaned forward, peering into the distance, watching. One long, lean finger rubbed slowly over his cheekbone, idly tracing the shape of a small, dimple-like scar. The wound had healed, the memory faded, yet the scar remained.

Boone Creek... Clay County, Missouri...

He pulled the limp, worn letter from his hip pocket and pored over its cryptic message for the thousandth time. Who was this Dan P. Jennings who had written him? What did he know?

He leaned back against the yellowed wallpaper that was speckled with tobacco juice and God only knew what else. Contemplating the sweltering, close quarters that constituted a fifty-cent room—the best in the house—he massaged the back of his neck and grimaced. Strange that he should feel so calm. The vendetta was coming to an end now. Long years of deadly purpose would cease, replaced with a life unfettered by debts, and yet, he wondered... would the scars remain?

Always.

His hand dropped to the old, weathered gun butt protruding from his low-slung holster, and even though he hated what it stood for, the polished wood was a comfort to his palm. Stretching his long body out on the narrow bed, he slept.

From deep in the shadows under the overhanging roof of the jail, Clayton Dougherty studied the hotel across the street. His inquiries had revealed which room housed the gunslinger, and now he stared with fierce intensity, his breathing shallow beneath the soft rise and fall of his barrel chest.

What did Coulter want? Why the hell was he in Cavendish? Dougherty pondered the question irritably, coming up with no answers. If the outlaw only wanted a resting place, Dougherty'd provide him a place to hide—for a price. He'd padded his pockets for years that way, and felt perfectly justified. That kind of word traveled fast. Those in need of a few days respite knew Dougherty would provide it.

For a price.

But Coulter had exacted his own price from two lawmen—their lives. Dougherty was no coward, but he was no fool, either. So he stared at the window across the way and waited.

What did Coulter want?

Elizabeth paced through the lower floor of her house, her fingers trailing across the light film of dust that coated every surface. Regardless how often she cleaned, how diligently she kept the windows shut and draperies pulled, the dust seeped in. And today, just as she had found herself unwilling to prepare an adequate breakfast, she was also too restless to spend an hour wiping and polishing, removing then replacing the knick-knacks that covered every tabletop. And so, instead, she paced.

What grandeur this house represented. Not by Philadelphia standards perhaps, but it was quite unlike anything west Texas had seen.

And all designed specifically for her.

She had waited long months before following Joel to Texas, months when she had endured the choking rigidity of her family in Philadelphia for the last time. The waiting to put Philadelphia behind her had seemed to last forever, but she had endured it willingly for Joel.

Older sisters and younger, already married, had been astounded when an obligatory visit of a distant cousin from the Missouri branch of the family had become the first of many. When Cousin Joel turned out unlike the intolerable ruffian they had expected, but instead charming, refined, with a sad haunting behind his dark, penetrating eyes, they had been surprised. When Joel Dougherty's subsequent calls had become more and more centered on Elizabeth—plain Elizabeth—they had been astounded. Poor Elizabeth? On the shelf, undowered? She was a spinster, for pity's sake, destined to be shuttled from one sister to another, caring for their sick children, accepting their grudging largesse.

Until Joel Dougherty.

Even now, she could close her eyes and remember her family's reactions. They ranged from barely contained jealousy to outright relief when Elizabeth had not only become betrothed, but had landed a handsome and wealthy man as well.

When Joel had returned to Texas to prepare for their marriage, there had been an emptiness she couldn't fill. Lost in the middle of a large family of chattering sisters, Elizabeth was accustomed to being ignored. But then she had suddenly become the center of all attention, and she hated it. She had written a tentative letter to Joel, asking if perhaps the bride should not have the pleasure of influencing the plans for her new home.

He had responded quickly, smoothly, delightfully... "No."

Of all his letters, it stood out in her mind, in her heart. His first letter, his words so warm and natural she could almost feel his breath tickling against her ear as he teased her for her impatience. His first letter, so unlike the others that gradually grew more withdrawn, more infrequent with the passing of time, until her heart was chilled with apprehension.

Joel had insisted upon more and more time to prepare for her arrival. And what preparations. This house had traversed a nation, crated and bundled, piece by piece, first by train, then by wagon for the last few hundred miles. For almost a year, she had waited for him to tell her all was finished; every month, mounting with tension as she found herself the center of elaborate preparations for a Texas wedding that none of her family would witness.

Her apprehensions were never voiced. Even if there had been someone to listen, she would have kept them to herself, for with each passing day it had become more apparent to her—there was more joy in leaving Philadelphia and her family, in achieving the independence she so longed for, than there was in anticipating her marriage.

So she had quietly suppressed her misgivings, choosing instead to stoke the flames of her childish infatuation. Childish? Yes, though she had been almost twenty-three years old, Joel, her first true suitor, had inspired emotions in her that she had witnessed in her sisters many years before.

She paused before a small, oval photograph hanging in the dark, green wallpapered hallway, taken moments after her marriage to Joel. It was a picture that still stunned her when she saw it, for framed within that oval of silver was a new Elizabeth. Beneath the dignity, beneath the poise, there was beauty. Not classical features, perhaps, but the aristocratic bone structure that would be enhanced by age. A few loose tendrils wisped gently from her immaculate coils of hair, softening the angles of her face. The camera revealed a strong woman, a graceful woman, a woman perched on the edge of her wicker chair as if on the brink of some untold excitement.

Leaning against the wall, with her gray eyes closed to the reality of her life and her senses opened to the dreams, she could feel it again... the fluttering hope in her breast, the belief that things could be different. If only she could persuade Joel to abandon this godforsaken place. Thirteen months she had spent here, Joel's promises to leave growing more infrequent. What had happened to those plans they had made in a faraway Philadelphia garden, of starting anew in Denver?

She heard him even before he spoke; her eyes flew open to see Joel at the top of the stairs, his white shirt carelessly unbuttoned, exposing the dark whorls of hair across his chest. His black trousers were mussed, and a bottle of whiskey dangled loosely from one hand.

Joel descended the stairs easily, his mouth curled in a softly mocking smile. "Don't tell me. My brother left in disgust, and I am supposed to be properly chastised and remorseful."

Elizabeth moved forward without thought, ready to receive his careless kiss when he arrived at the bottom of the stairs. Then, his arm slung casually around her shoulders, she led him to the kitchen. "Let me fix you some eggs and biscuits," she urged.

But Joel only winced and dropped into a chair at the table, holding one pale hand up to shield his eyes from the sunshine now pouring through the window.

"God, no. Coffee, that's all."

Elizabeth held a hand against the coffee pot, finding it still hot to the touch. She poured the strong brew into a cup and placed it in Joel's hand, stifling the urge to argue. Similar experiences had taught her it would be useless.

"And shut those blasted curtains—my head is splitting."

She had snatched the bows loose and was about to smooth the curtains shut, but the mountains in the distance made her hesitate. "I don't quite understand it," she began slowly, "but they always seem to be luring me. Offering me something, though I can't imagine what."

Joel shook his head and laughed wryly. "It's your Anglican upbringing. Too many psalms muddling up your head. 'I will lift up mine eyes to the hills, from whence comes my—'"

"That's quite enough," she replied crisply, but even as she spoke she felt a stab of pain from his words. He had never taunted her in Philadelphia, no matter what fanciful turn her thoughts had taken. She shook herself and turned to refill her own cup.

He shrugged, apparently bored with the conversation. After draining his cup by half, he splashed in whiskey to top it off.

"And tell me, what did my dear brother have to say about me this morning?"

She dropped the pot back on the stove top with a clatter. "Nothing. He was too distracted with Wendell. I'm surprised you didn't hear all the noise the dog was making."

"Wendell was here this morning?"

"Yes." Elizabeth set her cup on the table, then dropped nervously into the chair adjacent to his. "The town's in an uproar over some outlaw who came into town last night."

Joel pulled upright, suddenly intent. His hand shot across the table and closed tightly over hers. "What outlaw?" He was hurting her, but when she tried to pull her hand away, his grip only tightened. "What outlaw?"

"I don't remember," she lied without understanding why. "What's gotten into you, Joel?" This time when she pulled, he released her.

"Think hard, Elizabeth. Surely you remember," he coaxed, seeming to relax. But beneath his velvet cajolery lurked a menace that confused her.

"Colt," she stumbled, evading him. "Coulton. Something like that."

Joel sank back, his eyes dark, unreadable, his breath coming in quick pants. "It worked," he whispered.

"What are you talking—"

And then he was standing, pulling her up with him, his hands closing hard over her shoulders. His face dipped closer, and his eyes burned with a fire that was frightening in its intensity.

"Justice, Elizabeth. It's all coming to pass. Justice…"

Elizabeth flinched away, her heart pounding. Once she had longed for his touch, but not like this. Something was wrong, and she was too confused and frightened to understand.

"Do you know this outlaw?" she asked, folding her arms across her middle, her fingers closed in tight fists.

"Know him?" Joel seemed to ponder her question, his eyes never leaving her. "What a strange question, Elizabeth. Why would I know a cold-blooded murderer?" That thought seemed to amuse him, and his mirth grew to full laughter. "Other than the esteemed sheriff, my brother, of course."

Elizabeth's hand flew to her throat, and she found it difficult to swallow. "Clayton, a murderer?"

"This isn't civilization as you know it, love. Out here, whether a man is viewed as a murderer or not is determined by which side of the law he's on. Clayton, of course, is on the right side of the law." Joel tilted the whiskey bottle to his lips and drank deeply, leaning against the doorjamb. When he lowered the bottle, he pushed away from the wall and stepped closer to her. "At least, he is now that he's sheriff." Seeing the confusion flickering across her features, he laughed again. "Surely the fact that my brother has killed doesn't surprise you."

She didn't want to ask. Yet, the words came anyway. Barely audible, but laced with fear. "And you, Joel? Have you... killed?"

His eyes flickered with a strange emotion as he raised his hands slowly in front of her. Fine, long-fingered hands. Soft, poet's hands. "Do these look like hands that could close over the butt of a pistol and pull the trigger? These eyes…" He stepped still closer. "Do they look capable of sighting a prey and marking it for the kill?"

"No," she whispered, shaking her head. And then he sought her embrace, shivering. Her hands stroked his back in an attempt to comfort. "No, Joel. Please forgive me."

"Out here," he groaned, his dark head close to hers, "it makes me less a man."

"All the more reason we should leave," she pleaded. "This is no place for us, Joel. You know that as surely as I do."

He pulled away, his face lit with wild desperation. "Of course I do. And we will leave, I promise. Don't you see? It's all going to happen, now. I'll be able to put everything behind me. We can be happy."

"I don't understand."

"No, and you never will," he responded. "Be thankful that you never will."

He swayed, then slumped against her. It was all she could do to guide him up the stairs and back to his bed. She swept his assorted newspapers onto the floor a split-second before he collapsed on the rumpled counterpane. When she would have stepped away, he reached for her, his hand grazing hers.

"Lib…"

"Yes, Joel darling," she sighed, and stooped to pick up some of the newspapers. One, a Harper's Weekly, had slid under the edge of the bed. She was reaching for it when his hand closed gently over her shoulder.

"Hand that one to me, darling."

Her fingers closed over the yellowed paper and she handed it up to him. He cradled it against his breast.

"Justice," he murmured, stroking it almost lovingly. And then, "You're too good to me, Libby."

She could only look into his ravaged face and shake her head. There were no words for answer. He drifted back into his own nightmare world, the world she would rescue him from if only he would let her. Yet, how? The demons he drank to forget were his own. He refused to share them.

And for the first time, she admitted she didn't want to. She didn't want to be dragged into his hell. Her head spun with confusion. What was happening?

Joel's voice echoed in her mind: Justice... It's all going to happen now... it worked. Then the sheriff's words: Stay away from town, today.

Blind frustration coiled and writhed within her, then hardened into hatred for the man who seemed to hold her husband's will in his powerful palm. Her restless spirit was no longer content to stay put in the dark, confining walls of the house. Her house. Her prison.

The sheriff's wishes be damned. She was going into town.

Chapter Two

A YELLOW MONGREL was tied to the hitching post in front of the general store. Elizabeth raised the edge of her tailored brown linen skirt as she stepped past it. Ignoring the puppy's pitiful whine, she entered the store and tilted her head to acknowledge Rena Mason's subdued greeting.

The older woman at the dry goods counter watched her with furtive interest. Elizabeth smiled and handed her list of necessities to Rena, then waited while she gathered them.

Walking slowly toward the far corner of the single-roomed building, Elizabeth headed toward the patent medicines and scented toiletries. Trailing her slender, gloved fingers across the rows of colorfully wrapped soaps, she appeared to consider their fragrances, occasionally lifting a hard milled bar to whiff the aroma of hyacinth, or lilac, or rose. Yet her mind was elsewhere, with her husband, with the outlaw. Strange that Rena hadn't mentioned anything about the stranger in town. She finally picked up a box of yellow soaps that emitted the strong scent of honeysuckle and carried it back to the counter where her purchases were slowly mounting.

"About the female remedy, Mrs. Dougherty. We're plumb out of Dr. Kilmer's. Have you ever tried this Hofstetter's Tonic? They say it works real good." Rena offered the dark brown bottle for Elizabeth's perusal. "It's real potent, though. You better be easy with it."

"That will be fine, I'm sure." Elizabeth pulled a snowy handkerchief from her reticule and dabbed it at the beads of perspiration forming on her upper lip.

"I imagine the sheriff'll be picking your other things up later, as usual?"

"No." Elizabeth's firm tone startled the other woman, and she hurried on, "I'll be taking them with me. If you'll have your boy load them in my buggy..."

She paused as Rena beckoned to the young boy sitting behind the counter, his cheek bulging with a sour ball. He began loading his arms to carry the purchases outside.

"Mrs. Mason, have you heard anything about the trouble at the hotel?"

Rena's face took on new animation. "That's all a body's been able to hear all day. It's hard to know what to think—what with that man supposed to be there. But if you ask me, there's no knowing for sure he is there. After all, we've only got the word of a feeble-brained maid and a—" She hesitated, waiting for the door to close behind her son before continuing. "—a harlot to go by. Now, you tell me. Are those reliable sources?" She sniffed her disapproval.

"The deputy certainly seemed sure of himself this morning," Elizabeth demurred, gathering those items of a more intimate nature and holding them close to her bosom.

"Well, you know Wendell Crutcher," Rena replied, unimpressed. Then, her expression changing, she remarked in more solicitous tones, "Of course, you have special reason for being concerned, the sheriff bein' your husband's brother, and bein' involved and all."

The bell on the door jangled, announcing a new customer, and out of the corner of her eye Elizabeth caught a glimpse of the older woman stiffening in affronted silence. Elizabeth pivoted slowly to see the cause of the disturbance—one of the "girls" from the saloon across the way.

Hands on her crimson-satin clad hips, the woman brazenly surveyed the store's contents, then dismissed them with a disgruntled toss of her yellow curls. Rena pulled a package from under the counter, her movements jerky with embarrassment, her voice tinged with disgust. "This is what you've come for, Doralee."

The woman sauntered nearer, her alert eyes sweeping over Elizabeth's stiffly erect body. How young she looked to be doing what she was doing... how old.

"I hope I'm not interruptin' anything," she drawled softly, retrieving a few coins from her reticule. Rena didn't even hold out her hand for the money. She stared at the whore until the girl dropped the coins on the counter with a wry shrug. For a moment, Elizabeth felt a pang of sympathy for her. But then the girl turned, her eyes settling on Elizabeth. Her smile was a crooked smirk, never reaching her kohl-lined eyes.

"Well, now. If it ain't Miz Dougherty. The Dougherty men always did like 'em uppity."

Elizabeth stiffened, but the girl pressed closer, her arm knocking some of Elizabeth's purchases loose and scattering them to the floor.

The girl dropped to her knees and scooped the packages up, then thrust them at Elizabeth, her eyes narrowing. "Why don't you jest tell the sheriff that littl' ol' Doralee said hello. He'll think that's real funny, I bet." She burst into peals of laughter.

She rose gracefully, her own purchase dangling limply from her fingers. Pausing at the door she cast a hooded gaze over her shoulder. With a toss of her curls she walked through the door, letting it bang closed behind her.

Mobilized by the harsh jangling of the bell, Rena shot to Elizabeth's side near the doorway, mumbling about the nerve of "some people" as she dusted Elizabeth's dark brown skirt. Yet, amid all the clucking and fussing, Elizabeth remained stoically silent, her gaze following the figure of the woman as she paused by Elizabeth's buggy and patted Rena Mason's bug-eyed boy on the head. She turned then, and the two women's eyes locked in a battle of wills. It was the whore who finally broke the contact, though not without another mocking smile.

She held her small package in her gloved hand and after a moment's consideration, she dropped it into the buggy, her face contorting with laughter as if amused by her own secret joke. She turned her back then, and strolled toward the saloon, her hips swaying an invitation to anyone who cared to respond. Even the boy stood transfixed.

"—and to think she would come right in here while you were inside!" Rena's voice rattled in her head; Elizabeth merely nodded in agreement, her pulse throbbing at her temples. Raising her chin, she silenced the older woman with a quelling glance.

Rena accompanied her to the buggy, offering profuse apologies for the incident. But Elizabeth touched her hand, assuring the woman that no harm was done. After climbing onto the seat, she pulled away, driving the buggy around a corner and out of sight of prying eyes.

She reached her trembling fingers toward the package Doralee had cast into the buggy. Disgust and revulsion filled her, yet she carefully removed the brown paper and stared at the flagon of cheap patchouli toilet water and the tin of Persian henna in her hands.

You jest tell the sheriff that little ol' Doralee said hello, today. He'll think that's real funny…

From his vantage point, Coulter could easily make out the jail across the way. He'd waited all night and half the day for some signal he might not even recognize if it came. The letter was vague, but it had said enough to get him here.

He let the curtains drop closed and dragged his fingers through his tangled hair. Standing by the open window, he heard the creak of saddle leather as a rider dismounted at the saloon next door and a pup's playful yapping as a young boy chased it down the street.

Coulter dropped to the bed; rusty springs groaned in protest. His head throbbed from the heat. Running. Always running.

Who was this Dan P. Jennings?

How did he know about Missouri?

Suddenly, like a wild animal catching the scent of a predator, he felt the cold burning in his gut. He should have known better than to trust the message. He, who trusted nobody.

Cold sweat broke out on his forehead. He launched himself upward from the bed, reaching for his rifle and ammunition in the same movement.

He was getting out of this room, this town.

"Sheriff—look at this!"

Dougherty stiffened at the sound of Wendell's voice. It took scant seconds for him to cross the room and join his deputy at the window. His thick fingers knotted into a fist, his face twisting into an ugly scowl.

The gunslinger appeared silhouetted in the hotel's open doorway, tall and lean, feet widespread, gunbelt low on his hips, and Dougherty felt a strange excitement.

He'd get him—he'd kill the bastard, collect the reward. His hand closed over his gun. A surge of white-hot satisfaction coursed through him. The gun that killed Boone Coulter.

Dougherty pushed by Wendell, out the door, on the boardwalk, his gun drawn. But when Coulter stepped into the sun, the sheriff froze. Time seemed to stand still. Sheriff Clayton Dougherty found himself staring into the eyes that he'd been trying to forget for nine long years.

Their gazes met across the dusty road, met and locked in mutual shock and recognition.

Coulter recovered first and dashed down the steps.

Hands trembling with ice-cold fear, the sheriff took aim. But just as he pulled the trigger, Wendell shouted and knocked his gun arm.

"Goddamn you! You made me miss!" His face blazing with fury, Dougherty backhanded the deputy, sending his spare frame sprawling in the dirt. He fired again, but Coulter was already on a horse and galloping away. Three, four, five futile shots at the fleeing outlaw. None of them hit their mark.

Only when he turned his gaze back to the hotel did he see what Wendell had seen—Rena Mason's boy, white-faced, with a squirming yellow puppy in his arms.

"Sheriff—the kid ran right in front of you! You would've shot him!" Wendell moaned.

Blind with shock, with desperation, the sheriff clenched his fists and staggered toward his horse. "Don't just stand there," he shouted as he mounted. "Round up a posse!"

"But, Sheriff—you said you wanted the cavalry to handle their own business. You said—"

"Shut yer ass up, Wendell," he snarled, yanking hard on the reins to turn the horse around. "I know what I said. Things are different now!" Almost as an afterthought he added, "The son-of-a-bitch stole Pete Murphy's horse!"

Within minutes the saloon was emptied, and with a posse of the good citizens of Cavendish, Texas, at his back, Clayton Dougherty took off after his prey—and only Clayton Dougherty knew the truth: He wasn't after the man because he was a murderer, an outlaw, or a horse thief. He was after the man because he knew if he didn't kill Boone Coulter, Boone Coulter would come back and kill him.

Squinting into the slanting rays of the late afternoon sun, Elizabeth snapped the reins over the roan gelding's back. Gritting her teeth, she allowed the horse to take its own pace, not caring when its speed picked up gradually from a trot to a canter, faster than was her usual custom. The wind whipping the light veil of her hat fanned the flames of rebellion in her veins. She only wanted to ride... faster... and faster...

So intent was she on her own thoughts, the unexpected appearance of a lone rider galloping up on her right caught her off guard. Startled, she jerked her head around to stare at the man leaning over the neck of his horse, apparently determined to pass her even on this narrow stretch of road.

Suddenly, she felt the gelding's reaction to the other horse. As the black began to pull ahead, her own horse strained at the bit, his nostrils flaring and lips pulling back to reveal dangerous white teeth. Try as she might, Elizabeth could no longer control the beast. He bolted—taking off at a full gallop, trying to edge the stallion off the road.

A scream froze in her throat. Bouncing wildly on the hard leather seat, she grasped the reins, pulling leather with all her strength, but the race was no longer under human control. A quick glance to the right revealed the rider of the other horse struggling as well. Their eyes met for an electrifying split-second, hers wide with fright, his narrowed with dangerous determination.

With a heart-lurching jolt, Elizabeth realized what was coming before the rider did: the trail narrowing at the curve, an outcropping of rocks jutting into the road. Clinging desperately to the reins, she watched in horror as the black horse edged closer to her own. The gelding lashed out, trying to bite, and still the rocks loomed nearer, closing space for the horseman and the buggy to pass through abreast. At dizzying speed, the boulders grew closer, the trail narrower. Heart pounding, she clutched the reins, squeezing them in nerveless fingers—

Then she heard the screaming neigh. As if in slow motion, she turned her head and saw the black slamming against the rocks, rearing up on its hind legs, the rider fighting to stay astride, as the buggy passed it and left it behind.

There was no time to wonder about the rider's safety as Elizabeth fought to control her gelding's frenzy. She pulled back on the reins with every ounce of her weight, and with the other horse no longer a threat, the gelding began to slow his gait, his withers lathered, his massive chest heaving.

It was then that disaster struck. Her left wheel struck a large rock embedded in the red dirt and the buggy careened out of control.

A scream ripped from her throat—nothing to hold onto—nothing to protect her—she felt the reins tearing through her fingers, felt herself flying through the air, then slamming into the ground with a jolt that echoed through every joint in her body.

And then, ear-ringing silence.

The sky spun overhead. She was aware of excruciating pain and lungs screaming for air, yet no sound came from her throat, no breath entered her body. For what seemed like an eternity, she was caught in a vacuum of searing, pervasive pain.

The minutes stretched out, but gradually she felt her chest slightly easing, and the dizziness subsided as her lungs received the oxygen they so desperately needed. Was that low moan coming from her? Was that animal sound her own? She raised her head and gasped at the effort, then, gritting her teeth, strained to a sitting position. Only then did she think to look for the rider whose outright recklessness had caused her accident.

To her relief, he was running back toward her in long strides. Helplessly, she waited, fighting back the burning tears that threatened to spill down her dusty cheeks. Teeth clamped over her lower lip, she watched his approach. Lean and broad-shouldered with dark hair long and tangled on his neck, his face shaded by a battered Stetson pulled low.

But when he reached her, he didn't stop, just kept going to her buggy, lying overturned on the rocky trail, its traces broken. The gelding, still wild from its brush with disaster, bucked and reared among the splintered remains and tangled reins of the wrecked buggy, his eyes rolling white as he snorted his distress. Yet the instant the man laid his hands upon the horse's bridle, uttering soothing noises beneath his breath, the beast calmed.

Elizabeth struggled to her feet, unable to stifle a moan as her legs protested the weight she put on them. Slowly, she made her way toward the stranger, unable to speak.

By the time she reached his side, he'd begun to free the horse from the overturned buggy, and turning, faced her with no indication of remorse. In fact, so merciless was his gaze, she found herself stepping back a pace.

"Stay out of my way, lady." His voice rustled over her as soft and deadly as that of a rattlesnake's warning.

Raw fingers pressed to her lips, she bit back a sob. Without another word he turned his back on her and continued untangling the reins. Only then did she realize his intent. He had no interest in her physical condition and had never intended to offer her any apology or assistance.

He was stealing her horse.

Rage boiled up in her, rage she'd never allowed herself to display before.

She reached for the buggy whip, the whip she'd never used on any beast. Whip in hand, she stood frozen, waiting until he faced her once more. With an aim more governed by anger than skill, she swung the whip in a wide arc and watched it slice across his hollow cheek, leaving an angry red welt in its wake.

His expression changed from shock to violence, as his long, lean fingers touched the spot where her whip had assaulted his flesh. Yet his eyes never left hers. As long as she lived, she would never forget the stark hatred in those eyes, and the fear that gripped and squeezed her like a vise. He stepped closer, and with a lightning-quick movement akin to that of the rattlesnake she'd compared him to just moments before, his hand shot out and grabbed hers, clenching it in his strong fingers, his thumb digging into her wrist until the whip fell from her numb fingers.

She was unable to move, and it was several moments before she realized there was no more pressure on her aching wrist, that his hands cradled hers with nothing more than a whisper touch, that it was only the power radiating from the venom in his eyes holding her captive.

Then he stepped away.

Trembling, she watched his anger fade into confusion as he seemed to comprehend her condition for the first time. "I'm... I'm sorry, lady."

His soft voice stroked over her, no longer lethal, almost pleading. His gaze went from her to the horse, then back to her again. He reached inside his shirt and pulled out a small, plain cross. His eyes never leaving hers, he lifted the chain from which it hung over his head.

Elizabeth was helpless to do anything but stand and watch as he approached her slowly, cautiously. He held the cross out, its chain dangling from his fist. She could only stare. Finally he closed the gap between them and pressed the cross into her hand, the gold still warm from his skin.

"Take it," he said. "It's all I have."

She tried to give it back, shaking her head in confusion, but he closed his hand tightly over hers, his expression intense.

"Take it for the horse, lady," he grated. "It's all I have." Then, defiant, "I'll send money back for the other one."

"The other one?"

He jerked his gaze away from her and stared over her shoulder. "That horse I was riding didn't belong to me either"

"Why are you taking mine?" she demanded. "What happened to the other horse?"

"He threw me and bolted. But you tell whoever he belonged to, I'll send the money." His eyes suddenly glittered with a new emotion. "I don't steal."

Elizabeth watched him leap onto the gelding's bare back and gallop away. Long after the cloud of dust had disappeared over the horizon, she stood in stunned silence.

She ached, she felt feverish, yet of all her discomforts, one took precedence. She didn't have to raise her wrist to see the dark bruise forming, to feel its tender throb, to remember the expression of hatred that accompanied its injury. But there was something else. The cross in her hand. The fierce pride when he had told her, I don't steal.

She felt shame—shame for raising her whip, shame for losing control. What did she care about the horse? Nothing. Absolutely nothing.

A tremor of apprehension flickered through her body

He was a madman, this cowboy who'd almost killed her. She'd never seen him before.

There was a stranger in town, Wendell had said. A gunslinger. Stunned, she clutched the cross tighter until it dug painfully into her palms.

Was he Boone Coulter? Elizabeth gazed into the purpling dusk toward the mountains. If so, he'd escaped Clayton Dougherty, unknowingly on the sheriff's own horse.

"Godspeed," she whispered softly. And for a brief moment, she envied the outlaw his wilderness, his freedom.

Chapter Three

"I'VE ALREADY ANSWERED your questions, Clayton." Elizabeth's skin was waxen in the dim light of the short-wicked lamp as she stared up at the seething sheriff, his fists clenched at his sides.

"The horse just bolted?" he repeated angrily. "You expect me to believe that story?"

"It's the only story I have." She tossed her head, meeting his glare with determination. "And it's the truth. For some reason the horse was already skittish. Then there was a rattlesnake in the road. The gelding panicked. He took off—I couldn't do anything but hold on." She raised a bruised wrist to her forehead.

"Something's not right. I haven't got it figured yet, but I will. And if you're lyin' to me, woman—" Clayton stared at her, his eyes calculating. As they dragged down her body, they flickered with something different, yet akin to his anger.

The door slammed open. Reeking of whiskey, his hair wild and ruffled, a tangle of leather reins clutched in his fist, Joel stood poised in the doorway, an anger emanating from him that was enough to startle even his brother.

"What the hell is going on here?"

Clayton backed away, but jabbed a thumb in Elizabeth's direction. "Your wife took it upon herself to go to town today against my orders. She wrecked my goddamn buggy and lost my prize high-stepper. Wendell found her at the side of the road—"

"Elizabeth doesn't take orders from you," Joel broke in, his voice a vicious whisper. "Get out of here. And don't let me ever hear you threatening my wife again."

Elizabeth tensed, watching in shock. Clayton's brows lowered and his voice took on a more menacing tone as he shot her a last, threatening look, then turned back to his brother.

"I think you might be interested to know what happened in town today."

"I've already heard," Joel ground out. "Looks like you let one get away."

"You ain't heard it all." Clayton smiled then, a cunning smile. "You want to protect your precious wife? I'll leave you to her. But I'll also leave you with somethin' to think about... Clay County, Missouri."

The words seemed to echo as a strange emotion radiated between the brothers. Then Clayton tore himself away and passed through the doorway.

Elizabeth watched his departure in silence, waiting for the door to click shut behind him before slumping against the slatted chair-back.

Joel stood stiffly by the door until Clayton's angry footfalls had descended the staircase. Then he walked toward her, the reins dragging the floor behind him. His voice still low, he pinned Elizabeth with a stare almost savage in its intensity.

"What are you hiding, love?"

"What—what are you talking about?" Her hand went involuntarily to her slender throat; the pulse jerked beneath her trembling fingertips.

Joel dropped to his haunches, bringing himself to her level. He tossed the tangled reins into her lap. "Look at them, Elizabeth. Tell me what you see?"

Confused, she closed her hands over them. The supple leather was fine and well-oiled, strong. Suddenly her fingers clenched on the leather lines as she saw what Joel had obviously discovered: the ends of the reins, dangling from her hands. They had been cut—clean, and smooth.

"Yes, dear wife. I do think you're hiding something, and the time has come to tell what really happened today."

She shot him a wary glance. "So you can tell your brother?"

"No, not for my brother." He reached out with his long fingers and stroked her cheek, then toyed with a wisp of hair. "Elizabeth darling, you're mine, not his. I won't let him hurt you."

She released a trembling sigh and leaned her cheek against his hand. "I don't know why I lied, Joel. It came out before I could stop it, and once started, I couldn't stop."

"It's all right, love. Just tell me what happened." He cradled her jaw in the palm of his hand, his thumb stroking hypnotically. "Tell me."

"It was the outlaw," she whispered.

His hand stilled.

"I was driving too fast, and then he came up beside me and tried to pass—his horse was injured too badly for him to continue." She lowered her lashes. "He stole your brother's horse." As soon as the words were out she realized her mistake. He hadn't stolen the horse. He'd given her something in exchange. Her gaze dropped guiltily and lodged on the worn gold cross nestled, tingling, between her breasts. Her breath caught in a trembling gasp, she repressed a strange tremor and reached quickly to close the neck of her robe.

Joel's low laughter brought her eyes back to his face. His beautiful lips were curled in a bitter smile. "So Boone Coulter escaped on the sheriff's prize gelding..." He laughed again, and sprang to his feet, grasping Elizabeth's hands and pulling her up with him. "I told you justice would be served, didn't I, love?"

"I don't understand," she murmured, his wild-eyed pleasure scaring her.

"What did he look like?" Joel demanded.

"Dark hair… I'm not sure what color his eyes were, but they were… frightening. Like a—" She caught her full lower lip between her teeth. She had started to say "rattlesnake," but couldn't bring the words to her lips.

"And his cheek? Did he have a scar on his cheek?"

She squeezed her eyes shut, a vivid memory of the red welt she had administered springing into her mind. "I don't know," she began. Then the picture cleared. Yes, there had been a scar. A scar now obscured by the mark she had put on him. She opened her eyes and met her husband's intense gaze. "Yes. There was a scar on his right cheek."

Ignoring her confusion, Joel pulled her to him and buried his face in her hair. "Libby, love, it's going to work. It'll all be over, at last, then I can forget. I can live again."

Elizabeth's mind raced with disconnected thoughts, her senses reeling.

And then almost as if the words weren't meant for her ears, Joel whispered, "He'll be back."

The sheriff waited impatiently for a response to his query.

He had sent Wendell to Fort Davis to find out what he could about Boone Coulter. That had turned out to be a wild goose chase. Whatever had been wrong with the telegraph lines this morning had been fixed.

The telegraph operator handed him the message, but he couldn't read it in front of the man's curious eyes. He left without thanking him and headed to the jail. Only when the door was closed behind him did he pull the folded sheet of paper out of his vest pocket and read it.

As his eyes dragged fearfully down the names of Coulter's victims, his hands began to tremble. Abner Reynolds. Walter Tankersley. B. T. Grier… all murdered by Boone Coulter.

It couldn't be a coincidence. They were almost all there, but Clayton knew what few others would. The wretched list would not be complete until one more name was added.

His own.

Though the night was deep, the moon cast its eerie glow over the rugged terrain, illuminating scrubby mesquites and knobby mounds of prickly pear cactus, casting strange shadows across the scrubland. The slow jogging motion of his horse tempted Wendell to sleep, but with an effort, he managed to keep his eyes open and trained for trouble. Not that he expected Apaches—they'd been cleared out of the area two years back. Victorio was dead. The Apaches were squashed, for good. But then again... a tremor of unease shivered down the back of his neck.

A few more hours would find him at the fort, and after delivering his message he might venture into town for a drink and possibly a night's rest. He glanced down at his badge, its polished surface flashing a reflection, even in this scant light. Women were supposed to go for a man with a badge, though he couldn't vouch for that from his experience in Cavendish. He rubbed a gloved finger over the inscription and felt a thrill of anticipation. Hell, he might not get any rest, after all. Suddenly, he didn't feel quite so weary. He kicked up his mount's speed.

A mile later, he paused. The pungent smell of a mesquite fire scented the cool night air. Someone must be camped out nearby. His horse stood still, its earlier restless movements gone with its first burst of energy. On the one hand, Fort Davis and duty, and possibly pleasure, beckoned. On the other, the chance to warm his hands over a friendly fire. Seeing a low mound up ahead, he dismounted and walked to it, intending to climb up and scout the area for the fire's location.

Drawing near, he found a startling sight in the deep shadows. A horse, dead for some hours, it seemed, one leg twisted at an awkward angle and a bloody head wound where someone had shot it, probably to put it out of its misery. Damn shame, it was, too. It looked like a fine piece of horse flesh. Nigh as fine as the sheriff's high-stepper —

Wendell leaned closer, his eyes widening in shock. It was the sheriff's high stepper.

"Gawd-damn," he muttered, then straightened. That horse had run a far piece, must have been plumb loco after crashing. He never had put much faith in high-strung horseflesh.

His hand on the butt of his gun, he made his way up the low rise in the land to scout the area. Whoever had put a bullet in the gelding's head was probably still around, judging from the smell of that mesquite fire. It seemed like they'd done the sheriff a favor, puttin' the horse out of its misery.

Then again, things weren't always what they seemed.

One way or another, he intended to find out what had happened, so he could report it.

The sheriff would want to know.

The sheriff slept fitfully, even the remnants of his drunken stupor had faded too much to give him the rest he longed for. In his dreams, Coulter taunted him, rearing on the black horse, its front hooves pawing the air, its teeth exposed in a mocking grin to match that of its rider. Only, no... the outlaw didn't smile... his visage was devoid of emotion, horrifying... empty... a nightmarish face.

His fist clenched spasmodically in his sleep, his large body's restless movements shaking the bed.

"Clayton, honey—wake up!"

He reached out with a quick backhand and felt it meet soft flesh where he'd expected something else. Giving his head a shake, he pulled upright in the bed.

Doralee was sitting beside him on the bed, studying herself in a porcelain-backed mirror. She gathered her loose hair into her free hand the best she could, piling it on her head. "What do you think about red hair, honey? Think you'd like me with red hair?"

He didn't answer, just lay back down and stared at the ceiling.

"I was gonna surprise you last night. I was gonna have red hair when you came in to see me, but I changed my mind." A low gurgling laugh sprang from her lips. "I decided to give to charity. I gave the henna to somebody who needed it worse than I do." She cast him a slant-eyed look, watching for his reaction. "Don't reckon your brother's wife mentioned it, did she?"

He jerked around on the bed, the springs squeaking with a sudden shift of weight. "What the hell are you talking about?"

Her lashes lowered and her full lips curled in a satisfied smile. "I spoke to Miz Dougherty at the general store yesterday. Her thinkin' she's so much better than everybody else..."

She eased her hand across the bed to give the sheriff's crotch a playful pat. "I guess by the time you got your share o' randiness, there wasn't any left over for your baby brother."

His hand closed around her neck and squeezed until she winced. "What did you say to her?"

"Nothin', honey. Just hello, and I gave her a little present, like I said. Wish I could have seen her face when she opened it."

Clayton flung her hand away with a snarl. "Uppity bitch. Somebody needs to put her in her place. Things have changed since she came here. And I don't like it one little bit."

Doralee took his hand and eased it between the satin folds of her robe. "What's the matter, honey? Tell me... I can fix you up, good."

The eyes he turned in her direction were bleary, red-rimmed. They settled upon her small, firm breasts. His hand tightened over one, and he felt himself still sleep-hard, and ready. "Yeah... that's just what I need," he ground out, squeezing until she flinched.

"Oooh, honey—" she moaned. "You're hurtin' me."

His hand relaxed only slightly as he tossed back the sheet and revealed his engorged member.

Her tongue flickered out, wetting her lips, but the fear still remained on her sleep-swollen features. "You ain't gonna hurt me, are you, Clayton?" She reached for his hand, to push it away.

With a quick jerk, he pulled her down on top of him, thrusting up into her. Hands tangling into her ratted mess of hair, his lips parted in a cruel smile. "You don't want me to hurt you—then, you better make me happy, Doralee... good and happy. Understand?"

He pulled her face near his, and she whimpered into his mouth, before closing her teeth over his lower lip and clamping down hard. "You son-of-a-bitch," she hissed. "I always make you happy..."

Their mouths fused, the metallic taste of blood inflaming his lust all the more.

But behind his closed eyes, the hair twining his fingers was golden brown, and the blood he tasted was that of his brother's wife...

"Ma!"

The boy's shout turned heads up and down the dusty street. Eyes trained first on his form, then followed his pointing finger to the horseman approaching from the western edge of town. "It's him, Ma! It's Boone Coulter! Wendell done went and capchered Boone Coulter!"

The deputy and his quarry presented a strange sight: Wendell astride, with Coulter thrown across the back of the horse, his wrists and ankles bound. By the time they reached the jail, at least twenty people lined the street, some of the curious craning forward to get a better glimpse, others hanging back in apprehension.

"Sure that's Coulter, Wendell?" an old man asked, scratching his yellowed hair. "Sure can't tell by the wanted posters."

"Course, I'm sure." Wendell dismounted, his quick movements belying his exhaustion, his eyes darting to the closed door to the jail. "Is the sheriff here, yet?"

At that moment, Dougherty appeared in the doorway to the saloon, his heavy-jowled face flushed. Crossing the road in wide strides, he pulled up short when he saw the body slung across the mare's back.

"What the hell have you done, Wendell?"

Wendell grinned. "Reckon I went and done caught me an outlaw, Sheriff."

Dougherty's stomach reacted with a spasm of apprehension. Recovering quickly, he grabbed a fistful of the outlaw's hair and yanked, dragging him off the horse.

Coulter landed on the ground in a heap, but pulled himself to a sitting position, his eyes narrowed, sending out lethal messages he was unable to carry through.

"So this is Boone Coulter. I have to say, I'm disappointed. I expected something better than a greenhorn who'd let a young pup like Wendell, here, catch him. But then, what can you expect from a sidewinder who'd kill two fine lawmen in cold blood?"

Coulter stared back at him, the shadows beneath his eyes like bruises, his nostrils flaring, but he remained silent.

"Don't want to talk, huh?" Dougherty circled him, eyeing him from every angle, though maintaining a safe distance.

"Somebody's gotta go on to Fort Davis, Sheriff. Somebody's gotta let 'em know. I don't figger I'm up for the ride, seem' as how I've been ridin' all night. But somebody's gotta go. How long you think it'll take 'em to get me my reward money?"

Wendell's mention of the reward brought angry glares from both the sheriff and the bound prisoner.

Backing away, he repeated, "Somebody's gotta go..."

"Shut up, Wendell. First we've got to get him behind bars." Dougherty pulled out his gun and jabbed it into Coulter's neck. "Now, you listen here, mister, you get up nice and easy, no funny business." With a jerk of his head, he sent Wendell to open the jail.

Not until the cell door had clanged shut with Coulter inside did Clayton Dougherty relax a little.

"Well, Sheriff? What do we do next?" Wendell rasped, his shoulders slumping despite his attempts to stand erect. He was fit for nothing but bed.

Dougherty looked at his deputy, and the new pride he saw there didn't please him. Besides, now that he had Coulter sitting in his jail cell, he'd prefer not to have a witness.

"Get the hell outa here, Wendell. Go get some sleep. I'll handle this."

Watching the deputy mount his horse and head home, Dougherty felt a hard kernel of tension forming in his gut. Still gathered outside the jail, the townspeople watched the deputy's departure with expressions of awe—a far cry from the skeptical opinions they'd voiced when the sheriff had appointed him.

Dougherty turned away from the door and walked back into the jail. Coulter slumped into the corner of the cell where the plank wall joined with iron bars, his face etched with fatigue, his feet and hands still bound.

"John Wesley. My, my, how you've changed." Dougherty surveyed him slowly, his ugly lips twisted in a smile. "You done your pa's name proud, I see. No wonder you changed it."

Coulter stiffened, spots of color blazing high on his cheeks, but still he remained silent. The sheriff laughed then, the laugh of the victor toying with the vanquished.

"You may as well hop on over to the pallet and stretch out." Dougherty spat out the words, his eyes gleaming with satisfaction. "I'm not lettin' you out of those ropes. Matter of fact, I don't know what the hell I am gonna do with you." The sheriff held his pistol under the outlaw's nose, close enough for him to smell the grease. "I could kill you, you know that, don't you? Kill you escaping."

Coulter's eyes were glazed with pain, or maybe fever. They seemed unable to focus on the gun, or the sheriff. His skin was ashen beneath his ruddy tan.

"I'm gonna have to kill you," Dougherty repeated, as if to himself. But the image of the crowd outside was etched too clearly in his mind. They'd seen the shape the man was in. They'd never believe he was capable of escaping in his present condition. They'd think it a ploy to get at Wendell's reward money.

The money meant nothing. Let Wendell have it, and good riddance. But the last thing the sheriff needed was to call attention to himself where Boone Coulter was concerned. Coulter's trail of murders was too obvious, if anybody started digging. And Coulter's death would bring newspapermen from everywhere, all looking for an exclusive angle to the story. And if someone stumbled across the truth...

What the hell was he going to do?

Uneasily, he slipped his gun back into his belt and moved to settle in the chair behind the desk. He propped his scuffed boots on the desktop, staring through aching eyes at the outlaw asleep in the cell.

Dougherty had worked too hard for this setup, a town of his own with people too scared of outlaws to worry much about their sheriff's private dealings, as long as he kept the peace. He had a sweet little situation here, and he wasn't about to risk it in a panic. That wasn't his style. He'd bide his time, give it a little thought. For the present, he was safe enough. There was only one other man within a thousand miles who knew about what happened in Missouri: Joel. And Joel was loyal. He'd kept that secret all these years. Besides, Joel had his own reasons for not talking, his own guilt to hide.

Dougherty studied the outlaw's body, then caught sight of a fold of paper sticking out of the man's shirt pocket. Curious, the sheriff returned to the cell and eased the yellowed page from the outlaw's pocket.

He spread it open. Jagged script, bold and firm, covered the page. He glanced at the date, two months previous. And the content... a cold fist closed over his lungs. He couldn't breathe.

The letter was vague, but the references to Missouri... and the signature, Dan P. Jennings. The same Dan P. Jennings who had been in Cavendish a month earlier, seemingly for no reason. Yet he had stayed in the hotel for a week, waiting for someone who never came.

Or waiting for Coulter, who had shown up late?

Dougherty fell heavily into his chair, the unoiled springs squeaking loudly in protest. He pulled a small hip flask out of the bottom drawer and, to still his nerves, took a swig. Now he understood. There was only one person who could connect them. He had been betrayed. Betrayed by his own blood. By his own brother.

Hours later a bewildered Wendell watched the sheriff leave, not heading toward the livery stable and his horse but to the saloon across and down the street.

"Reckon you could cut me loose, boy?"

The soft drawl caught him by surprise, and he spun on his heels, his hand poised on his gun, but the outlaw was lying on the pallet, staring at him.

Wendell crossed the rough plank floor with caution. Drawing near, his brows knit in concern. The outlaw's bound hands were swollen and discolored.

"Sheriff didn't cut you loose?"

Dead silence was his reply.

Wendell reached for the cell key hanging on the wall, then stopped. He looked back at the outlaw, then seemed to make a decision.

"All right, mister. Stand up and back up to the bars." He watched Coulter's awkward progress, not missing a flinch of pain when he fell back against the wall, pinning his hands between him and the raw siding. When he was in position, Wendell slid the knife out of his boot.

"Grab hold o' them bars, best you can. I want to see your fingers closed around them bars—if you so much as twitch, I'll stop and leave you to your pain."

Three strokes of the knife, and the top winds of rope were severed. "You take care of the rest, yourself." He backed off, eyeing the man as he struggled with the bonds. Coulter's face contorted with pain as blood rushed into his limp appendages.

Satisfied that his act of mercy had gone off without a hitch, Wendell plopped into the sheriff's chair and leaned back, imagining what two thousand dollars would buy. Suddenly, Wendell remembered the one fact that had nagged him all day. The sheriff's gelding. He sat up so abruptly, he almost fell out of the chair.

"Hey, there! Coulter! Where did you get that horse you was ridin'? That gelding?"

No answer.

"If you stole that horse, you're in worse trouble than before—you know that, don't you?"

Coulter sat massaging his fingers back to life, his back turned toward the deputy, and Wendell realized he wasn't going to get anything out of the outlaw. The gelding... he hadn't told the sheriff about it. And now he'd have to wait until the sheriff came back. He dared not leave, even with Coulter behind bars, working at the rope binding his feet together with hands still discolored from their similar treatment.

Wendell stood in the open doorway, his gaze lingering on the saloon and its forbidden pleasures. Things were sure gonna change for him when that reward money came in. He felt a pleasurable tingle and scratched his crotch. Maybe sooner.

"What men or gods are these? What maidens loth? What mad pursuit? What... what struggle to escape?" Elizabeth leaned closer to the lamplight, straining to see the words on the page through her unshed tears. Yet when she spoke, her voice was deep and clear, belying her emotion. "What pipes and timbrels? What—"

She raised her gaze to meet that of her husband.

He completed the quotation. "What wild ecstasy?" His dark eyes burned fever-bright. His day's growth of beard shadowed his hollow cheeks in harsh contrast with his pale, sallow skin. He closed his fingers around the neck of the cut glass decanter beside his bed and raised it to his lips, wincing with pleasure as the dark amber liquid poured down his throat.

"Ah, sweet Elizabeth," he groaned softly, a mocking smile on his lips. "What wild ecstasy you deserve."

"What nonsense." She attempted a light laugh and closed the leather-bound book in her slender palms.

"The very fact that you call it nonsense is proof enough," he said wryly, his grip tightening on the decanter. He held it up to the yellow lamplight, and her gaze followed his to its sparkling facets. "Tell me, darling wife, what it is in this demon bottle that entices a man to destruction? Or rather, what lack is it in a man, that he seeks his release from Irish whiskey instead of the luscious flesh of his own sweet wife?"

"Joel, no. Don't say that." She started to rise, but he was too quick for her, grasping her arm with surprising strength.

His eyes burned into her as he slurred, " 'To make delicious moan upon the midnight hours.' Isn't that what our Keats called it, love?"

"You've had too much to drink," Elizabeth reprimanded softly, prying his fingers from her arm with gentle pressure. "Don't do this to yourself, Joel."

"I should never have brought you to this godforsaken place. I knew... I knew it would never work."

"Stop it!" she cried, moving away from the bed. "I can take anything, but not your moods."

"I know, dearest." The haunted expression on his ravaged features captured her more surely than any physical restraint. "I know what I'm doing to you. You, who least deserves it. If I were half a man..." His laugh was bitter. "No, that's quite the problem, isn't it?"

Elizabeth sighed forlornly. "There's nothing I can do with you when you're like this, Joel. And so I shan't even try." She backed toward the door, carrying the lamp with her. There was already one ugly burn on the floor where, in a drunken stupor, he'd flung an arm out and knocked over a burning oil lamp. But for the grace of God, his bedroom would have gone up in flames before she was even aware of it. But she'd smelled the smoke and screamed for Clayton, and together they'd beaten the fire out.

"Elizabeth... wait."

She paused, wary. But when he motioned for her to come nearer, she couldn't refuse the pain in his eyes. She replaced the lamp on the table and sank to the spot on the bed he was patting.

"My sweet Elizabeth…" He raised his hands to her hair, and she felt the gentle tugs as he removed the pins one by one, felt the heavy burden released as her hair tumbled to her shoulders and down her back. "A vision to take to my grave…" he murmured hypnotically. "My beautiful Elizabeth."

"No." She shook her head in embarrassment. "I'm not... beautiful."

His fingers played through her hair, spreading the strands like fine silken threads, tangling them into wild disarray. Again, he smiled that bitter smile. "And that is the vision that will haunt me even beyond the grave... that I failed to show you what beauty you possess. That I failed to kindle the passions that burn in your eyes. That I failed—" His voice broke off and his hands fell away.

"I've heard enough of your melancholy speeches for one night, Joel Dougherty. Everything will be different when we reach Denver," she insisted, stroking his cheek. "When we get away from…" She broke off in mid-sentence, her eyes wide with fright, her hand suddenly frozen against his face. Then, fighting for calm, "When we get away from here."

"From my brother, isn't that what you mean?"

She couldn't stop her gaze from darting toward the closed door. "Hush. He might hear you."

"Somehow, I fear we'll ever see Denver, darling."

"We will! You promised!" she insisted desperately.

He squeezed his eyes shut, and this time his laughter was a mockery, not of her, but of himself. "Elizabeth, you are the strong one. Why couldn't you have also been wise... wise enough not to believe the empty promises of a drunken fool?"

"That's your liquor talking," she snapped, springing to her feet. "I'm leaving you alone with your ravings, but I'll be here to console you and your aching head in the morning, as usual."

"And who will console you?"

His sad taunt unanswered, she scooped the book up in a trembling hand, the lamp in the other and swept from the room. Not until her bedroom door was closed did she allow the tears to flow.

Elizabeth hadn't realized she was asleep until something startled her awake. She raised on one elbow, her head throbbing. Hearing the kitchen door open and slam shut, she fell back against the pillow. Clayton was home. She lay uneasily, waiting to hear him pass her room on his way to his own.

She felt tight, strung to the snapping point. She needed to shift her weight to relieve the tension, yet she dared not move. A long strand of hair had somehow worked its way into her parched mouth, yet she dared not spit it out.

Suddenly, a gunshot split the air.

She bolted from the bed. My God—my God—

She raced to the door joining her room to Joel's, and fumbled with the lock. Jammed. "Joel!" she cried, rattling the doorknob, then pounding with her fists. "Joel!" Frantic, she yanked open the drawer of the bedside table, and searched for the pistol Joel had insisted she keep for protection.

It was gone.

She whirled away and ran into the hallway. Clayton stood in Joel's doorway, his wide back to her, a crumpled newspaper clutched in one trembling fist. She was halfway to him when she heard his low animal moan that rose to a roar when he spun and faced her. His face was a horrid visage of pain and revulsion.

Panic seized her. "Joel!"

"Stay out of there, you bitch!" Clayton roared, thrusting an arm out to block her way. "You did it to him! You—killed—him!"

"No!" With a violent jerk, she pulled herself free and forced her way past him. "Joel…"

She stepped into the room, all black and white with stark moonlight and dark shadows... and on the bed, her husband's still form. "Joel," she repeated, as if expecting him to stir, despite the black pool around his head. The blood. The black, sticky blood.

And in his still hand, her gun.

She opened her mouth to scream, but no sounds would come. Great gulping breaths were trapped in her lungs, air laden with the stench of gunpowder and blood and death, and still the scream wouldn't come. Covering her mouth with trembling hands, she backed away, backed toward the door—

Iron arms closed around her.

The scream ripped from her throat. And came, and came, and wouldn't stop, even when Clayton's massive hands bit into her shoulders and turned her and shook her. The world shattered around her, shattered into a thousand frightening pieces. Her teeth clattered in her head as her head snapped from side to side. Yet she felt no pain, no fear, only mind-numbing disbelief.

As suddenly as it began, he ceased his assault, flinging her from him. "You lousy bitch." His voice was a hoarse growl, his cheeks wet with tears. "It's all your fault."

"The doctor," she whimpered, her back pressed against the wall. "Maybe the doctor…"

His face contorted into a travesty of laughter. "He's dead, woman! Dead! And you did it!"

"No." She shook her head in confusion. "I don't know what you're talking about." Fear clutched at her heart, and she stumbled into her room and slammed the door, locking it behind her.

"Open this door or I'll break it down!" Clayton slammed his heavy fist against it, and the door shook on its hinges. Not waiting for her response, he brought his shoulder against it, and this time the force was enough to split the thin wood.

Two more blows, and the door caved in with a splintering crash, and Clayton stood there, his immense chest heaving, his eyes bloodshot and lit by raw emotion unlike any she'd ever seen before. He grabbed her, digging his fingers into her hair and twisting it until her skin was nearly splitting away from her skull.

"He did it for you, didn't he? He never would have done it if it hadn't been for you!"

"What are you talking about?" she pleaded, choking on great, wracking sobs.

"He killed himself, you bloody fool! Killed himself because he couldn't be man enough for you!"

"No... no, he didn't..." But even as she spoke, Joel's words rang through her mind. A vision to take to my grave.

"You sail through this house like a goddamn goddess—nothing's too good for his damned Libby." He gave her hair a hard twist, pulling her face inches from his own, his whiskeyed breath washing over her. "Well, there's a man in this house who can give you what you want, bitch. A real man! Before this night is over, you'll wish you were the one dead." He bellowed and raised his balled fist to strike her—

She groped behind her, grabbed the base of the oil lamp and crashed it against his temple.

His agonized howl split the night as he jerked away, his hands clutching his face. She watched in horrid fascination as the blood spilled, and mixed with the kerosene. The fuel burned into his flesh and eyes, and he staggered away from her, hurling curses and blasphemies.

She ran toward the wardrobe, stepping on shards of glass that bit into the soles of her feet, and yanked out a heavy carpetbag. Casting an anxious glance over her shoulder, she ripped clothing from the hooks, wadding the garments into the bag. At the sound of crunching glass, she spun and gasped to see Clayton's hulking form weaving toward her.

"You'll pay for this..." he hissed.

He advanced toward her, a twisted leer on his lips, demonic laughter rasping from his throat. "You... stupid... bitch! Where do you think you'll go? It was your gun! I'll tell everyone you did it—you can't get away!"

Elizabeth backed toward the shattered door, clutching the handles of the carpetbag in her icy hands. "Stay away from me," she warned. "Don't touch me!"

He lashed out at her with a crimson stained hand, barely missing her as she climbed over the wreckage and lunged into the hallway. She staggered under the weight of her portmanteau. The hall loomed long and narrow and dimly lit, but she surged forward for she heard Clayton behind her, cursing, gaining with each heavy stride.

Suddenly, she felt his fist close over her nightgown, felt herself being propelled backward, and using that momentum she spun, the force carrying the carpetbag away from her in a widening spiral. It took every ounce of strength she possessed to hold onto it, but she did, sending it flying toward his head, the collision freeing her from his grip. He crumpled against the banister, teetering on the edge of the top step, then plunged backward into the black, yawning chasm of stairwell, his descent thundering in her ears.

Her entire body began to tremble, and she winced at a searing pain in her shoulder, yet she listened for a sound, anything to warn her that he stirred. Fearfully, she crept toward the top step. A wave of nausea swept over her, and she sank to the floor, her back pressed against the banister.

"Oh, my God..."

Tears coursed down her cheeks, blood flowed from the lacerated soles of her feet—all signs of a body still living, still functioning. But her heart, her soul, were frozen in a living nightmare of death. Moments stretched into minutes as Clayton's body lay sprawled across the bottom steps. But it was his chest that captured her attention—that massive chest, rising and falling steadily... alive.

She squeezed her eyes shut, experiencing both relief—she was not a murderer—and agony.

She was still in danger.

Chapter Four

MINUTES LATER, ELIZABETH stood at the top of the stairs, her hastily packed portmanteau in her hands, her dark cloak pulled close around her. She descended the steps slowly, stealthily, her blood racing. What if he were only pretending to be unconscious, and waiting... waiting for her...

She had bested him once, but not again. He would see to that.

She prayed the combination of alcohol and injuries would subdue his immense brawn long enough for her to escape. She stepped closer. How could she get by? She would have to crawl over him. One step above his outflung arm, she laid the carpetbag down and knelt, inching to his side.

He didn't stir. Averting her burning eyes from his face, she reached for his pockets, groping. A few coins, not much. Then she found them—found the keys. A surge of relief shot through her as she pulled the small brass ring with its four keys from his vest pocket.

His breath rasped deep in his chest Elizabeth stiffened, her fear a bitter taste at the back of her throat. Moments passed—how many, she didn't know—and finally she reached for the portmanteau and swung it over his body, cringing as it hit the carpeted floor with a heavy thud.

Still, he didn't move.

Standing in the doorway, a knife-edged pain tore through her. How could she leave Joel, unmourned, not to be grieved over—

Clayton coughed.

Choking back her tears, she fled.

Wendell drank a sugar-laden mug of coffee to keep him awake on this lonely night. The outlaw was sleeping in his cell. Wendell propped his feet up on the sheriff's desk, toying with his badge. Things were really coming together for him. And it had been so simple—so durn simple. If the truth were known, the cook at the hotel was more responsible for Coulter's capture than Wendell himself. It was the bad meat the gunslinger'd eaten on that hot day—had it only been yesterday? —that had slowed him down, keeping him from being able to get to the mountains after the gelding horse gave out.

Wendell had just been lucky enough to happen across Coulter when he was most vulnerable—taking a shit behind a boulder. Even raisin' his head and findin' a shaky Colt revolver trained at his head, Coulter'd been too sick to react other than with a muffled oath.

Yep, it was almost enough to make you feel sorry for the man. Anybody in town could've told him to stay clear of the hotel's food. One thing for sure, though. Wendell would rest a lot easier when Ernest Tucker came back from Fort Davis with a military escort for the prisoner.

Two thousand dollars... more money than he could even imagine. His palms itched, just thinking about it. His palms, and that other part of him—that part that was finally gonna get its fair share of exercise, over at the saloon. The thought of those unspoken promises brought a groan from his throat.

A soft knock sounded at the door. Wendell snapped to attention. "Who is it?" he barked in a cracked voice.

"It's me, darlin'. Doralee."

The husky voice sent a shiver down his spine. He shot up from the chair and crossed to the door, opening it a crack. "Sheriff Dougherty ain't here, ma'am."

"I wasn't lookin' for the sheriff, Wendell. I was lookin' for you."

He gulped, his Adam's apple bobbing in his narrow neck. "Is somethin' wrong? Are you all right?"

The yellow lamplight poured through the opening, casting a golden sheen on Doralee's skin and hair. She smiled, and in the dim light he could hardly see where her dog-tooth was missing. "Wendell, darlin', I just couldn't sleep. It's so hot tonight. My nightgown was plumb stickin' to me—" And with that, she let her shawl fall open to reveal a thin gown that certainly did cling, in all the right places.

"Aren't ya' gonna let me in?" she asked, leaning closer, and he caught a whiff of her clean scent. She was small, tiny almost. Not wide-hipped or heavy breasted, but what she had was more than ample.

"I can't let ya' in, ma'am. You know that. I'm on guard."

"Is Boone Coulter really in there?" She stepped up on her tiptoes, ostensibly to peer over his shoulder, but in the process she gave him a clear view down the front of her nightgown.

Wendell gulped, letting the door open a little wider.

"Yeah, he's in here, all right. That's why I can't let you in. The sight of a pretty thing like you might—well, it might make him go plumb loco!"

"Why, Wendell. Do you really think I'm pretty?" Her lashes lowered artfully, and her lips pulled into a wet pout. "I mean, really pretty? I was so proud of you, today. I just nearly busted my buttons, I was so proud." She shot a sidelong glance up at him. "You really gonna get a thousand dollars reward money?"

"Two thousand," he said, his chest swelling when she smiled and stepped closer. It was almost enough to make him forget she was the sheriff's gal.

"Wendell, honey." She dragged her finger across his wide shoulder. "When you gonna get your reward money? Real soon, I hope."

She moved closer. And closer. Until she was pressed right up against him. "You're different from the others, Wendell... you've got manners, and you're gentle... it's no wonder you aren't interested in the likes o' me."

He didn't trust himself to speak, just stood stiff as a board while her fingers rubbed up against him. Even through the thick fabric of his trousers and long-handles, he could feel her fingertips, hitting all the right places until he feared he was going to embarrass himself, right there in the street. Then she pulled prettily away, turning a wistful look into his eyes. "It would mean a whole lot to me if you'd come with me."

He looked over his shoulder at the sleeping outlaw, then back at Doralee. Without another moment's hesitation, he hastily reached for the keys and locked the jail door.

"Oooh, Wendell..." she cooed. "You won't be sorry... promise." And with that, she led him off across the street, her hips brushing against his with each step, his gait firm, if a little widespread.

Elizabeth huddled in the shadows, her cloak pulled tightly about her, watching the deputy being lured away from his duty by a pretty face and a light skirt. Any other time, she would have pitied the poor boy, but not now. Not tonight. She felt only relief that fate had conspired to remove another obstacle from her path.

Waiting until the woman's laughter faded behind the closed door of the saloon, she hurried across the street, her heart pounding, her head deep within the folds of the cloak, lest she be seen and recognized.

Arriving in front of the jail, she slipped Clayton's key into the lock with nervous fingers. When it gave easily, quietly, she ducked inside, closing the door behind her and falling against it with a trembling sigh—

And found herself staring at the reclining figure of Boone Coulter, stretched out on a pallet in the cell.

Her hands clamped over her mouth as she saw the long, red scar on his cheek, the one she'd put there with the buggy whip. His eyes were shaded from the lamplight by his hat, his hands were limp at his sides, his form so still, she wondered for a brief, unreasoning moment if he even lived. But, as if in response to her silent query, the trigger finger on his right hand twitched.

What if he awoke and saw her? He would give her away—point the finger once she was gone—maybe even do something to bring Wendell scurrying back. She seized the door handle, ready to dash through the door and find some other way.

But there was no other way.

Her eyes trained on him, she crossed to the desk, holding the keys quiet in her hand. She tried one of the smaller keys in Clayton's desk drawer. It didn't fit. Her hands trembled so, she could scarcely fit the next key into the lock. She glanced up at Coulter to find his position unchanged, then tried again. A sharp click sounded and the key turned.

She eased the drawer open, reaching inside for the cash box. Her fingers hit the handle of a gun. Gently, she pulled it out and stared at its smooth, unnotched handle. It wasn't Clayton's, or Wendell's for that matter.

Again, she looked at the outlaw. It must be his. She broke it open, finding three chambers empty, three loaded, then snapped it shut and placed it in her cloak pocket, the awkward weight worrying and comforting her at the same time.

Still the outlaw slept.

Her hands reached in the drawer again, searching, until they finally closed over the cold, heavy, metal cashbox. Thank God. She'd found it.

With trembling fingers, she inserted the last small key into the lock, and twisted. The lock snapped open, and she raised the lid to find and found—bullets.

No money. Only bullets for Clayton's Peacemaker.

"No..." She groped desperately in the drawer, finding nothing else. Frantic, she tried the other drawers, but the money wasn't there. A sob bubbled up in her throat. Without money she couldn't get away. Without money she might as well ride into the mountains and turn the outlaw's gun on herself.

Joel's image flashed before her eyes, and she pressed her palms hard against her temples. Stop it. Stop it!

Alone, without money, she couldn't survive.

Unless... again, her eyes went back to the sleeping outlaw. Her mind raced with doubts, with fears. How could she even consider such a thing? The man was an outlaw. A killer.

But Clayton would kill her if she didn't get away. In her heart, she knew the truth. Money couldn't buy her way out of town. The mail stage might get her to Marfa, if Clayton didn't waylay it first. In Marfa, there was the railroad, but only one train ran a week and there was no place to hide. And even if, through the grace of God, she made it that far, by time she got to El Paso, the authorities would be waiting for her, ready to take her back to the sheriff of Cavendish, Texas... for the murder of his brother, her husband.

There was no escape that didn't lead to death, or capture. Unless...

Coulter lay, unmoving. Even his trigger finger remained still. All of her rattling in the drawers, her clumsy search, had failed to rouse him. That's when she knew.

He'd been awake all along.

Slowly, she straightened. Slowly, she paced toward him. He remained motionless. Drawing near the bars, she stopped.

"Mr. Coulter."

His left hand reached for the hat, and when it came away, his eyes were clear, hollowed, yet unblurred by sleep.

"Mr. Coulter, I would like to speak to you."

He rose slowly, his eyes slicing down her body in a thorough, scrutinizing movement. Lean and broad-shouldered, his cheekbones slashed across his gaunt features, making his face appear craggy, sinister. Hard weathered eyes stared at her through the bars. Terrible eyes, merciless, coldly hypnotic... the eyes of a rattler—coiled, cunning and ready to strike. This was a man who would not be caught unaware...

"I have the keys to your cell in my hand. If you agree to my terms, I'll release you. Otherwise, I'll leave you here for the sheriff."

There was no curiosity in Coulter's expression, no surprise at her offer, and Elizabeth felt a cold chill.

"What terms?"

Swallowing hard, she raised her chin a notch, meeting his stare. "I'm going with you."

Without hesitating, he thrust a hand through the bars. "Give me the key."

"No." Her voice was steady, unlike her nerves. "The deputy will be back any minute. He'd raise an alert before we could get out of town."

His hands gripped the bars, knuckles white against deeply tanned skin. "Then might I ask what you have in mind, lady?"

Elizabeth backed away, unable to tear her eyes away from his. "I don't know, yet."

Something flickered in those cold, fathomless eyes, but was quickly shaded. "Let me out. I'll take care of the deputy."

They said the outlaw had already killed five, six men, two of them lawmen. "No!" And quickly recovering her composure, she repeated quietly, "No. I won't have him hurt. There's another way."

"Another way," he repeated through his teeth, then shoved away from the bars with a barely suppressed violence that frightened her to the core.

How could she be thinking of going off with this wanted killer? She squeezed her eyes shut, but behind her lids lurked an even more frightening picture—Clayton, coming after her. And with that sharp stab of fear, came a flash of inspiration.

"I've got it —wait here."

Heart pounding, she raced across the street. A glance showed the lighted window above the saloon and shadowy movements behind the curtains. Please, she begged silently. Please... don't be through, yet.

Reaching her horse, she thrust her hand in the portmanteau, found what she was after, then ran back to the jail.

Elizabeth hurried once more to the desk and grabbed Wendell's coffee mug. It was empty, save the thick, dark sludge of brown sugar that remained from his previous cup. She pulled the brown tonic bottle of Dr. Hofstetter's Female Remedy from within her cape, broke the paper seal, then splashed a generous amount of the laudanum-laced liquid into the sugary dredge of coffee.

Replacing the mug where Wendell had left it, Elizabeth once again met the outlaw's gaze. "When he comes back, ask him for coffee. He's a good boy. He won't turn you down. And he'll take some for himself. He'll be knocked out in a few minutes. I'll be waiting across the way for your signal."

He simply stared without answering, but the expression in his eyes told her he didn't trust her or her plan. Well, that was fine enough. She didn't trust him either.

She left him that way, carefully locking the door behind her. Taking her place in the shadows, she watched for Wendell's return.

It had to work. It was her only chance.

"Goddamnit —" Coulter flung the oath at the closing door, but the only response was the clicking of the lock. Hands trembling, he stared after her, then slammed his palms against the cold steel bars of his cell in frustration. What kind of game was she playing?

Quickly, he scanned the jail, eyes darting sharply to his gun, his holster, the rifles locked in the gun cabinet. If she came back, he was going to be ready. Like a caged animal, he began pacing, all his suppressed tension boiling over. But when he heard a clumsy step outside the door, he froze, then dropped silently to the dirty mat on the floor. By the time the deputy finally got the lock open, Coulter's eyes were shaded by his hat once again.

As soon as the deputy entered, a wave of cheap, cloying perfume enveloped the room. Coulter raised groggily up on one elbow, removed his hat, and squinted at the kid. Dumb shit didn't even notice he was awake. Coulter cleared his throat, and the boy jumped, startled.

Fumbling for his gun, Wendell whirled toward him. But when Coulter made no move, the boy seemed to relax. "You okay, mister?"

"Better than I was."

Wendell crept a little closer, his hand resting on the butt of his gun. "You be needin' anything?"

Coulter took his time, though his heart thudded in his chest. Grabbing the bars of the cell, he pulled himself up, each movement slow and measured. When he was standing upright, he glanced toward the coffee pot on the stove. "Any grounds left?"

"Why, why sure." Flustered, Wendell crossed toward the stove and touched his finger to the side of the speckled enamel pot, jerking it away when it burned. "Matter of fact, I could use a mug, myself."

Only a twitching muscle in his jaw hinted at Coulter's relief. He watched as Wendell poured the steaming liquid into a tin cup and brought it to him, and his stomach recoiled at the stench of the rancid mess. The deputy lifted his own mug up from the sheriff's desk and peered down into it. He tilted it slowly, watching the dark brown sludge slide toward the rim. After a moment's consideration, he frowned, and Coulter felt his blood turn to ice.

Hurry up, you son-of-a-bitch—hurry!

Wendell pulled a small tobacco pouch out of his shirt pocket and loosened the drawstring. As Coulter watched in confusion, he reached in with his fingers and pulled out a hefty pinch of brown granules, tossing them into the mug.

Brown sugar. The kid was loading his mug with enough brown sugar to make syrup. By the time the sugar mixed with the day-old brew, he wouldn't taste a thing. Coulter felt the knot of anger loosen a bit. The woman's plan might work after all.

Wendell poured the dregs of the coffee into the cup and stirred it with a tin spoon. He sipped a little, smacked his lips appreciatively, then strolled toward the sheriff's desk, a secret smile playing on his lips.

Hurry up, damnit!

But the kid took his leisure, sipping, propping his feet on the desk's scarred surface, as if in imitation of the sheriff's earlier pose. Another sip, another slow smile... he began to hum. He craned his neck to see out the window, his dreamy gaze fixed on the saloon across the street.

Coulter felt a pang of sympathy. The kid would always remember this night... the night he let a fortune slip right through his fingers because he couldn't keep his hands off a piece of female flesh. A valuable lesson, if the whelp was smart enough to make the connection. But any sympathy he felt was overshadowed by tension.

Drink it... drink it...

Wendell peered into the depths of his cup at the sugary sludge that had settled back to the bottom. Dreamily, he dipped a crooked finger into it, scooping up the sweet sugar, licking it from his hand, scooping again and again... until...

The chair slid out from under him and he crashed to the floor, his head banging against the corner of the desk. From across the room, Coulter stared breathlessly.

The deputy didn't flinch; he was out cold.

Not until his own mug dropped from his trembling fingers did Coulter realize how shaken he was. In an instant, he had the cup back in his hand and, reaching through the bars, flung it through the window. As the shattered glass tinkled to the floor, one thought hung in his mind.

The woman had sure as hell better come back.

Elizabeth stood by her horse's side, clenching the reins more in an effort to still her trembling fingers than to control her mount. Unaccustomed to the night hours, the mare was.

At the sound of breaking glass and a soft plop, Elizabeth froze. Breathless, she remained frozen for a few moments longer, then shook herself out of her fear. There was no time for fear, it was too late for second thoughts. Pulling the hood of her cloak close around her face, she hurried across the road and twisted the key in the lock, her teeth clamped over her lower lip, sweat beading on her face despite the frigid night air. Then she was inside the jail, confronting the menace in the outlaw's face. She closed the door and pressed her back against it.

"Hurry up, damnit!"

The outlaw's hoarse croak startled her into movement.

"Give me the key."

Ignoring him, she scurried to Wendell's side, peeling his eyelid back and staring into one dilated orb. The knot on his head, still swelling, seemed minor enough. Slowly, forcing calm into her voice, Elizabeth crossed to the cell and spoke.

"Mr. Coulter, we don't have much time, but I cannot let you out unless you agree to my terms."

"We've already been through that, lady!"

"I'm not a fool, Mr. Coulter. I stated my terms; you did not agree to them. Until you do, you won't get the keys."

Desperate, he shot a look at the deputy, then back at her. "You must be in a heap of trouble, lady. And I don't think you've got any more time to waste than I do. Now just give me the goddamn keys, and let's get this show on the road."

Elizabeth pulled the ring of keys from her cloak and tossed them toward him, watching as he curved his hand around the bars and fumbled with the padlock. So intent was he on his task, he apparently didn't notice the soft smile forming on her lips, nor the barrel of the gun trained on him, until he was free and ready to push past her. Then, confronted with his own weapon trained upon his middle, he stopped short.

"What the hell—"

The yellow lantern light flickered in her eyes, dancing off the hair billowing around her face and turning it to gold. Elizabeth cocked the pistol and held it in both hands. Now calm, she spoke softly. "I have just learned something very important about you, Mr. Coulter. You are not a man who makes promises easily. But I believe that when you make them, you keep them. Now I ask you once again, are you going to take me with you?"

He squeezed his eyes shut and grimaced, dragging his fingers through his rumpled hair.

"Damn it."

She didn't flinch.

Finally, he nodded. "I'll get you out of town—now, let's get the hell out of here."

"After you, sir."

Coulter cast a measuring look at the pistol. "I told you I'd get you out of town, and I work a lot better without a Colt .45 aimed at my vitals."

Elizabeth flushed, then lowered it. "I'm afraid we're going to be together for a little longer than you'd like," she began.

"We already have been," he answered, heading for the gun case.

Within minutes, they were armed and outside, the jail door locked behind them.

"Where are you going?" Elizabeth demanded as Coulter started down the street. "The horses are over here."

He kept walking. "Not my horses."

"We don't have time," she insisted, hurrying after him.

"I'm not leaving without Sage. Best damn horse I ever had."

She caught up as he arrived at the livery stable. The ramshackle building was dark, with only the soft sounds of a restless horse coming from within.

"Is there a guard?" Coulter whispered gruffly.

Elizabeth swept an anxious look from the lean-to where the stable boy slept to Coulter, his features set and threatening in the pale moonlight.

"Only a boy. You needn't bother—" she began, but he ignored her protest and eased toward the lean-to.

After casting a glance around, he slipped inside. Hand to her mouth, Elizabeth shrank into the shadows. When Coulter emerged he started toward the stable, but she grabbed his elbow.

"What did you do to him?" she demanded.

Emotion flickered in his narrowed eyes. Finally, bitterly, he responded with a question of his own. "What did you think I was going to do?"

"Is he... all right?"

"He'll wake up with a headache in the morning. In the meantime, he won't raise an alarm and bring the town down on top of us."

He jerked his elbow away and pushed inside the stable, leaving Elizabeth relieved, but strangely ashamed for having asked.

How much time had passed? How long since she'd left Clayton unconscious on the floor? Joel, dead— She bit back a sob and a shudder shook through her body.

"Please hurry," she begged into the dark interior.

"Then get in here and help," Coulter snapped, fumbling with a lantern. As the light's glow spread, he hung it on the wall beside a stall near the back.

Elizabeth followed closely, anxious to do anything to help. But as they drew near and the horse reacted to the sight of Coulter, Elizabeth realized that this was no normal reunion between beast and master.

The horse reared its brown body, its black-stockinged front hooves flailing the air.

"Damnit, Sage," Coulter shouted, grabbing a fistful of black mane and jerking the horse's head down, ignoring the dangerous hooves. Then with his free hand, he scooped some oats out of the bucket that had been just out of the horse's reach, and shoved his open palm under the horse's bared teeth. The horse seemed more inclined to take his fingers than the grain, yet Coulter's hand was steady, and the horse finally calmed enough to eat.

"Hand me that bridle," he ordered, and Elizabeth complied. In seconds, he'd slipped it over the horse's tossing head.

"Hurry," she pleaded, but the outlaw was maddeningly methodical as he soothed and gentled the wild beast.

Not until it was time to tighten the cinch strap did he reveal his own frazzled state of nerves. He jerked once, twice, over the stallion's bulging torso, then to Elizabeth's shocked amazement, Coulter hauled off and slugged him in the side. The horse stamped and whinnied, but the outlaw was able to cinch the buckle two notches tighter. The horse had been holding his breath!

Coulter's second mount was more distinguishable than the first—a white pinto with legs and underbelly of dappled red-brown, that looked as if the horse had been splattered with mud as it tore down a West Texas road. But despite its flamboyant coloring, it was saddled easily, and Elizabeth found herself being hoisted unceremoniously onto its back.

"But my horse—" she protested.

"I've had enough horse trouble already," Coulter broke in. "Where we're going, you'll be grateful for a horse that knows the wilds."

The outlaw grabbed his own horse's saddle horn and planted his boot firmly in the stirrup, but as he swung up and over, the animal bucked. Yet he held on, somehow managing to land in the saddle. Again the horse reared, but the man held firm, only the tension in his jaw revealing the strain of staying seated on the thrashing animal. Without warning, the horse shot forward, Coulter hunkering low and disappearing through the stable door before Elizabeth had a chance to react.

Fear and anger melded in her veins. She kicked hard, but even as the horse sprang forward beneath her, the outlaw reined in his mount. With silver moonlight pouring over them, man and beast paused, the horse prancing with wild impatience, the man's arm raised as if beckoning.

In a split-second, Elizabeth was through the stable door and then in the cold, black night, the wind whipping at her cloak, her hair, her very soul.

Chapter Five

THE HORSE MOVED under Coulter, covering the ground with pounding hooves, sure-footed and dependable on the uneven terrain. The cold night air braced him, revived him, stung his skin and set his blood to racing, wiping out the effect of his sickness. The horse, the night, the escape, it was all good.

Except for the woman.

He spared her a glance over his shoulder. She still rode steady, her hair streaming silver behind her in the moonlight, her horse keeping pace with his despite the heavy carpetbag she'd refused to leave, thumping on its rump. He had to get rid of her.

She hadn't slowed him down yet, but she would.

He didn't want any part of whatever had driven her to such desperation. He didn't want to know anything about her. Her frantic emotion was palpable, despite the pace, despite the silence between them, and he insisted on keeping that silence. No, he was getting rid of her at the first opportunity. He'd gotten her out of town—that was all he'd promised. For now, with the full moon over their shoulders and the risk of pursuit still strong, he had to concentrate on finishing what they'd begun.

Escape.

He trained his eyes ahead on the dark silhouettes against the star-studded sky: the Apache Mountains. Refuge. He had to make them by dawn. Another glance over his shoulder, this time to the eastern horizon and its telltale glow. It would be hard going, but he'd make it. He had to.

As he pulled his gaze forward, he caught a glimpse of her again and felt a thud of recognition deep inside. The terror on her face, carefully guarded, the wildness in her eyes, were emotions he knew all too well. She was driven by something of which he wanted no part. He had enough problems of his own, without taking on those of a stranger.

Doralee stirred; someone was pounding on the door downstairs. She fought her way out of a heavy sleep. She listened, but the noise had subsided. She must have dreamed...

There it was again.

She grabbed her robe and slung it on, stumbling down the stairs. Surely Wendell wasn't back again, though Lord knows, once he figured out what to do with himself, he was eager enough to stay all night, if she hadn't had to remind him about the outlaw in the jail.

By the time she crossed the saloon, she didn't hear anything. She unbarred the large plank door that covered the swinging doors that served as an entrance during business hours.

Nobody there.

She stepped into the night, and that's when she saw him slumping against the side of the saloon, barely able to stand.

"Clayton, honey—what happened to you?" She stepped back and pulled him inside, shoving a chair under him as he collapsed. She eyed his face with near-horror, first reaching to touch the lacerated skin, then pulling back in revulsion at sight of the dried blood and swollen tissue. "I better get the doctor."

"No. Leave it" He groaned and clasped a hand to his side. She reached again. This time he batted her hand away and winced at the movement. Again, he groaned. "My side. I think I busted a rib."

"What happened? Did somebody jump you?"

At that, he raised his eyes to her with an expression that chilled her. She backed away, her fingers working nervously in the folds of her robe.

"Let me get you somethin' for your pain."

She retreated to the bar and pulled out a bottle, not bothering with a glass as she offered it to him. He stared at it through bleary eyes, then took it and swallowed convulsively as the liquid burned down his throat. He closed his eyes and stilled himself, then in a quick movement, poured the whiskey down the side of his face. He blanched with the pain, but he didn't make a sound. Only the quavering hand that lowered the bottle to his thigh revealed his agony. When he spoke, the words were soft rasps, barely intelligible.

"The bitch is gonna pay."

Doralee felt a stab of fear. Had he somehow found out about her and Wendell? No. Nobody knew but her and Wendell. Even Wendell Crutcher wasn't that big a fool. She stepped closer and rested her hand against his shoulder.

"Let me put you to bed, Clayton. You need to rest. In the mornin' you'll feel better." She licked her dry lips and pasted on a practiced, sultry smile. "In the mornin'... I'll make you feel better."

"I won't be here in the morning," he growled, shoving to his feet.

"Clayton, you ain't fit to go nowhere. Come on upstairs with me." Her voice dropped to a husky drawl.

His eyes fixed on her then, and she backed away. Something about him had changed. For the first time, she looked at him and was truly afraid. What if he did find out about Wendell?

Heart pounding, she let her robe gape open. She wasn't sure what to do, so she'd best do what she knew how...

"Maybe I could even find a way to make you feel better tonight... right now. You wouldn't even have to move, Clayton.

Let Doralee take care of your hurtin'. Nobody knows how like Doralee."

She didn't know if he was really interested, or just too shaken to argue, but he let her lead him up the stairs.

She went about her business with no other aim than to satisfy him quickly, but he had other ideas. His fingers dug into her hips with bruising strength as she moved over him, her eyes frozen on his bloody face; his lust seemed fueled more by violence than desire. When it was finished, he had nothing left. His mouth slack, he slept.

Doralee snatched up a dress and pulled it over her shoulders. It was almost dawn and she didn't dare go out in her robe. She ran across the street in her bare feet, hair streaming behind her.

She hammered on the jail door with her fist. "Wendell! Wake up!"

Not a sound.

She hammered again, then ran to the window, and her heart froze.

Wendell was out cold on the floor; the door to the empty cell was open.

The horse plodded steadily along, but Elizabeth's joints ached and her muscles throbbed in protest. The nightmarish night was over, but the golden dawn offered little comfort. Sheer rock walls stretched upward on each side of the dry stream bed, casting the canyon in cool shadows, the sun's early rays illuminating the opposite wall with fire and gold.

Her mouth was dry, and she barely had the strength to lift her hand and pull a strand of hair from between her parched lips. She had long since ceased watching the outlaw ahead of her, had left the following up to her horse. For her own part, she would do well to stay mounted much longer.

The horses seemed to pick up their pace of their own volition, and minutes later, rounding a corner in the canyon wall, she saw why. A clear, shallow stream rushed ahead where the canyon widened, and in no time the horses were splashing through its rocky bottom. The reins fell from her numb fingers as the mare dipped its head and began noisily guzzling the creek water. Coulter dismounted and dropped to his knees, scooping water into his hands, drinking thirstily.

Elizabeth grasped the saddle horn with both hands, trying in vain to ease her leg over the horse's back and dismount. Knives of pain shot up her calves and thighs, and she bit back a moan. Her head fell forward and a tangle of hair swept into her face.

She couldn't cry. Her eyes were gritty, grainy, void of moisture, as if her body had exhausted itself of tears and grief. But not her heart. Her heart bled tears, hot and burning, and the stark black and white memories of the night before were etched as surely on its surface as a lithograph's frozen image. Joel, asleep... death's sleep... black blood...

Coulter paused and looked in her direction. For a moment his face seemed soft with indecision, then hardened as he turned back to the stream.

"Lady, you'd better drink now. Stretch your legs. We're a couple of hours away from where we're going."

"No..." The word was little more than a whimper, and as soon as it was through her lips she hated herself for the sound of it. She had intended to ask for help, but not now. Not when his jaw clenched with disgust at her weakness. She gritted her teeth and seized the saddle horn with one hand, a fistful of mane with the other, and with a monumental effort, swung down until her boots were ankle high in water, though her feet were too numb to register the cold.

She clung to the horse, ever aware of her muscles' screaming protests, even more aware of the outlaw's surreptitious surveillance. She would not break down. She would not let him despise her. She would not.

The water swirled at her ankles, soaking her skirt. Slowly, she stepped backward until she was at the stream's edge. Then she dropped to her knees on the sandy bank, and finally, finally scooped icy water to her lips. Sweet and clean and achingly cold, it soothed her. Gulp after thirsty gulp, until at last she was sated enough to splash it over her face, her arms, the back of her neck, letting rivulets of water run where they would. She reached to fling the tangle of hair out of her face; it was rough and matted to her raw fingertips. She didn't care. She couldn't care. Cavendish was hours behind her.

She had escaped.

Her gaze shot up to meet that of the outlaw's as she corrected the thought: He had made that escape possible.

"I—I don't know how to thank you."

"Don't thank me, lady." He slapped his hat against his legs to shake off the dust and raised more dust from his trousers than from the hat. "You drove the bargain. I didn't have any choice."

He turned his lean profile to the sky, squinting at the sun. His face was shadowed with unshaven beard, and his hair was pressed against his forehead, wet and dark with sweat. As he studied the sky, he idly brushed his hair from his eyes. No, not idly. Nothing this man did was idle. Each movement had a purpose, however grim.

"You'd better be thinking about mounting up again. We've got a ways to go."

Just the thought sent more pain through her throbbing muscles and shoulders. "Surely we can rest a while. I... I really don't think anyone will be following us so soon." She averted her gaze as she thought of the condition the sheriff had been in when she'd last seen him. "They probably are just now discovering we're gone."

Coulter stood up and stretched, his broad shoulders straining under the faded red chambray shirt. "We bought ourselves a little time, not much. They've got daylight to travel by. They'll cover the territory twice as fast."

"Even so, Mr. Coulter." She fought to keep the emotion out of her voice, yet still it sounded too much like a plea. "Surely we can spare an hour or two."

He turned to her then, fixing her with a disconcerting stare. When he spoke, his lips curled in a half-smile, but his voice was as gentle as a rattler's warning. "You can stay and rest, lady. But you aren't slowing me down. You'll stay and rest without a horse, without me."

"You wouldn't—" she began, then closed her mouth.

Of course he would. She was traveling with a murderer, a wanted man. He would do anything, and not think twice about it.

"Bad luck landed me in that jail. Good luck got me out. I'm not waiting to see which way my luck's running today." He took his horse's reins and walked on ahead. "I'll give you five minutes to do whatever you need to do. When I whistle, you can catch up with me."

Even as she was grateful for the privacy, she wanted to call out to him to wait, to help her mount if nothing else. No, what she really wanted was the assurance that he hadn't deserted her. A bitter laugh rose and lodged in the back of her throat. Like it or not, she was a burden to him, a burden he'd desert at the slightest provocation. She'd do well to remember not to expect any help from him.

It was almost an hour later, an hour of pain as her muscles cramped and screamed their protest at returning to the saddle, when she remembered that he'd already helped her more than anyone else she'd known.

He'd saved her life.

She refused to ask how much longer they would be riding. Instead she chose her words carefully to find out the same information, she hoped, without seeming to complain. "Have you chosen our destination?"

He cast her a sidelong glance from under the brim of his hat. For the past few miles their horses had walked side by side, still steady, though definitely the worse for wear.

"Your destination," he replied.

"Mine? You mean you aren't going with me?" Her mind was too numb to question the panic that set her heart racing.

"We're about half an hour from Fort Davis. I'll get you that far."

"Fort Davis? I can't go to Fort Davis!" This time there was no effort to hide the panic, the fear from his scrutiny. She tugged hard on the mare's reins, pulling the confused beast into a sharp turn as she tried to change direction. Coulter reached out and grabbed the horse's bridle, holding it steady before she could take off.

"Just what are you—" He broke off, and she saw him eyeing her left hand and the narrow gold wedding band glinting in the sun. "I should have known." He jerked his hand away. "Running away from your husband, bringing a whole town after me before it's over with."

She stared at the wedding ring, and for a moment she saw blood, black and sticky. Joel's blood. Maybe Clayton was right. If it weren't for her, Joel wouldn't have killed himself. Wouldn't have—wouldn't have —

She fought the memory, seizing instead on the one thought she must convey. "I can't go to Fort Davis." The words were measured, even, showing none of the emotion quaking through her.

"Lady, you don't have a choice."

She clenched her jaw and gripped the reins, blinking back the tears stinging her eyelids. "I can't," she choked, gulping on a sob. "You don't understand."

His words bit through her protest. "I don't wanna know."

"Please," she begged, her wet lashes glistening, spilling tears down her dusty cheeks. "If you'd listen, you'd understand. He—he told them I ki—"

"Shut up, lady!" He whirled on her, his face savage. "Do you hear me? I don't care what happens to you. You're going to Fort Davis!"

"No!" The scream tore from her throat, tore with all the anguish of a night of nightmares overlaid with hours of exhaustion. Tore from her in a spasm of pain and desperation. And behind the scream flowed the agony of tears, until she was blinded by them, her eyes seeing instead the dead man who was her husband, the living brother who was her death.

The outlaw stared at her with a guarded face that showed no sign of remorse, no softening of intent. A surge of determination shot through her body, and she plunged a hand into her saddlebag.

The outlaw pulled his Colt from his holster, its barrel flashing in the sun. "Sorry to disappoint you, ma'am, but I relieved you of my gun along about sunrise." Eyes as unyielding as granite, he steadied his grip, stopping short of aiming it directly at her. "You do what I say, when I say. And I say you're going to Fort Davis."

The satisfaction melted from his face when she pulled her pearl-handled derringer from her saddle bag. "Perhaps, Mr. Coulter," she said, aiming the gun at his heart, "you'd better know what I'm running from. For your own good."

This time he didn't cut her off, didn't turn away. His expression was carefully void of emotion.

"I'm wanted for the murder of my husband."

Coulter didn't flinch. His gaze went from her gun, to his, back to hers again. With a click that seemed to echo off the canyon walls, he cocked his. "You didn't murder anybody, lady. You don't have it in you."

She swallowed hard and raised her chin, peering at him through blue-gray eyes the color of the hazy Texas sky over her shoulder. "You're wrong, Mr. Coulter. I'm not afraid of killing because I'm not afraid of dying. I'm not afraid of you or anyone." Slowly, deliberately, she cocked the derringer.

"Then we're at a stalemate. But lady, you're barely able to sit a horse now. Tomorrow I'd have to tie you on. And before we get to where I'm going, you'll turn that gun on yourself and blow your head away."

At that, she swayed in the saddle, her eyes glazing with pain. She stiffened her spine and compressed her wide, full lips in a tight line.

He lowered his gun to his thigh.

Her own grip tightened. "Do you have any rope, Mr. Coulter?"

His nod was barely perceptible.

"You may have to tie me on my horse, but I'm going with you," she said, her profile silhouetted against the glare of sunshine and the red canyon wall.

"You don't know what you're asking, lady."

"And you don't know why."

He dug his knees into Sage's sides and rode off.

Elizabeth followed.

An hour later they trotted over a high slope to a small valley in the mountains, a valley deceptively green from a distance. Closer examination proved the vegetation to be scrubby and sparse.

Elizabeth slid gratefully from her horse. She wouldn't have cared if they'd been in a scorching desert. At last, they could rest. For the first time in thirty-six hours, she could sleep.

The outlaw's horse moved restlessly as he freed it from its saddle; the horse attempted to nip him as he slipped the halter from its head. Coulter stood clear of the stallion and it disappeared down the ridge in a whirl of dust and churning hooves.

"What if he doesn't come back?" she asked, amazed.

"He always comes back."

She leaned against an outcropping of rocks and loosened the laces of her high-topped shoes.

"Don't take those off."

She glared up at him. "My feet hurt."

"And come morning your feet'll be so swollen you won't be able to get 'em back on." He turned his back to her and unsaddled the mare, as if assuming she would obey.

She did.

Coulter awoke with a start. He opened his eyes to an early night sky, stars like diamonds glowing through the hazy gray aura of clouds. He had slept too deeply to be aware of what was going on around him. Now he raised on one elbow to see the mare still ground-staked nearby, the woman asleep on the ground beside him.

The woman.

Asleep on the hard, rocky ground with only a blanket for cover and a saddlebag for a pillow, yet no one could see her and not know her for what she was. The dirt and grime couldn't disguise her pale skin, milky in the night, though the sun was sure to blister it before long. Even without combs and curls, her tangled hair couldn't detract from the fine-boned structure of her facial features. She had large, wide-set eyes, high cheekbones and a narrow face. A trifle strong-featured for a woman, and rather skittish, like a thoroughbred filly. Where he was going was near-death for the tough, the scarred, the mavericks.

It was no country for thoroughbreds.

He was crazy. He should have dumped her at Fort Davis as he'd intended. He'd already gone miles out of his way to get close enough to leave her there, miles that put him at risk. She'd cost him time, and worse, safety. And now, within reach of the town, it was all for naught. She refused to go, and he didn't have what it took to leave her.

He kicked his blanket aside and pulled upright, massaging the back of his neck, his stomach gnawing with hunger. He shot another look at her. Her lips bore a certain softness, and her eyes seemed shadowed and melancholy, even in sleep. She'd never said a word about food, yet she had to feel it worse than him. Hunger was something he dealt with as a matter of survival, time and time again. He doubted she'd ever been hungry a day in her life.

Well, she'd better get used to it.

He squatted near the fire and blew the ashes, revealing red embers which he stoked with more dry wood and fanned with his battered hat. Then, waiting for it to catch, he heard a distant sound on a wisp of night air. Not the doves, the crickets, the owls—not the night sounds of the wilderness. He slipped his spurs from his boots and headed cautiously toward the source of the sound. Haunting, ghostly, beckoning from the past...

He climbed the rocky slope, catching onto low, gnarled mesquites and junipers to steady himself as he went. His heart thudded with foreboding.

Topping the crest of the mountain, he stayed low and squinted through the darkness at what lay on the other side. Instead of the empty valley that had been there his last time through, he saw a rude dwelling and outbuildings—settlers. Ranchers.

He froze.

How close had he brought them to disaster?

The night breeze lifted, and again he heard the sound that had drawn him... music. And again despite the warning in his head, he crept nearer, blending in with the dark shadows on the eastern slope of the mountain.

The music lifted, voices raised in hearty fervor, unaccompanied. Wafting toward him, first loud, then soft, as the breeze wrapped around him, pulled him closer... closer, until there was no doubt, no question.

Hymns.

Judging by the gathering of horses and wagons and bonfires in the valley below, a camp meeting. How many years, how many long years had it been?

"Ye who tossed on beds of pain.

Seek for ease, but seek in vain;

Ye, by fiercer anguish torn,

In remorse for guilt who mourn…"

The words, the memories, they hit him in the gut, a pain so sharp, so strong, it rose in the back of his throat like bile. Stunned, he missed his footing and slid several yards in a spray of small rocks, heart pounding. He clung to a mesquite branch and waited for the outcry that he'd been spotted.

But no one in the valley was aware of the silent observer high above them on the mountainside.

No one was aware of his pain.

Elizabeth moved quickly about the campsite, trying to still her fear. He hadn't left her, she knew. The horses and his bedroll were still there. But where had he gone?

Before she saw him, heard him, had any indication he was near, she felt the outlaw's presence. Hollow. Aching. Rocks crunched and she flinched, flinging her head back to see him standing still before her. His face was all shadows, gaunt and dark, as was his presence.

"I have food," she said.

He stared at her as if not comprehending. When he spoke, it was with great effort, his soft, rustling voice little different from the wind blowing through the sparse grasses.

"We're moving on."

Chapter Six

ELIZABETH WASN'T SURE how or when it happened, but her fear receded, swallowed up by her pain and exhaustion. After so many hours of riding, her muscles were numbed past feeling. After so many hours of grieving, or reliving horror, her mind ceased to grieve or be horrified. She was past hunger, past feeling, past caring.

Past fear.

Only one thing drove her forward in this limbo existence beyond pain: the outlaw.

Not that he spoke to her; he didn't. Nor did he have to prod her again. But only the night before, the outlaw's expression when her grip had slacked on the reins and her horse had stopped to graze from the tall, silver-tipped grasses had been one of disgust.

She had jerked the reins hard, desperate that he not find more reason to despise her, for deep down she knew he did. She had forced herself upon him, continued to force herself upon him, and knew he hated her for it.

The hatred of the man who wanted her dead caused her no fear. The hatred of the man who kept her alive pierced her to the core. She didn't question why, she only reacted accordingly. She gave him stale biscuits from her saddlebag, not bothering to keep any for herself, and wished that she had fresh ones to offer. He didn't thank her, but she didn't care. His acceptance was sufficient. He dribbled water into his mouth from his canteen first, then handed it to her without a word.

Again, it was sufficient.

When a cougar's scream sounded from a distant peak, no chill rippled down her spine, though the horses both pranced uneasily. When the outlaw's lead took her too near the edge of a precipice, and the distant canyon floor was lost in blackness below, she felt no qualm of fear, for the outlaw feared not.

At daybreak they topped a crest and went from darkness to light. They had reached the edge of the mountains, and the desert stretched before them for mile after dawn-drenched mile, all the way to the next distant range of mountains on the northwest horizon.

Her spine remained stiff though her eyes were bleary with fatigue. The early sunlight illuminating her skin and hair with gold, Elizabeth surveyed the panorama below them with something akin to wonder.

"It's so vast... so empty. How will we ever get across it?"

"We'll make camp on this side of the mountain and head down into the desert tonight."

She nodded, averting her face lest he see the relief coursing through her, and they headed back down the mountain until Coulter spotted a flat clearing in the junipers and mesquite.

This time when she eased from the horse, she didn't sway, though exhaustion soaked through her. She watched him as he unsaddled Sage and cautiously tried to duplicate his actions. He saw her attempts, but made no move to help.

After Coulter started a small fire, he led the horses to the meager stream they had crossed several hundred yards down the slope.

Elizabeth dug deep in her carpetbag. In her hasty raid of the kitchen, she'd been too hurried to think properly. She'd grabbed a stale loaf of bread and biscuits, a half-inch rind of bacon wrapped in linen, but had brought no skillet. She'd packed a tin of coffee and three cans of vegetables, but had no way to open them. She had food enough for four meager meals, and other than the bread, no way of preparing that food. What had she been thinking of? She clenched her raw fist and winced at the pain.

But no matter. Somehow, she was going to find a way to get into those cans without the outlaw's help. Damned if she was going to give him another reason to sneer, to threaten.

She cast an uncertain glance across the area, her gaze landing on the saddlebag beside his rumpled bedroll. Lain carefully across the top of the saddlebag were his heavy leather gloves. She slid them onto her hands, their soft texture an irritant, and yet vaguely soothing against her raw palms.

She stood stiffly, her joints aching, and began scanning the ground for a stick or tool of some sort. Time and again she struck a rock against the top of the can, but soft shale crumpled at the impact, or harder rock glanced off the edge. The sharpest sticks broke without piercing the tin. Even with the protection of the outlaw's gloves, her hands burned.

And then she saw his spurs glinting on the ground by the fire. She grabbed the heavy iron boot-piece and brought it down on the top of the can; it pierced on the first try. Again and again the spur punctured the can, until she had made a small opening adequate for pouring. The sweet, green corn smell, subtle enough under normal circumstances, caused her stomach to twist in hungry reaction. She couldn't remember her last food.

A flat rock lay beside her on the ground. She shoved it closer with her foot, almost into the fire itself, then put the can on top of it. She was at a loss for the bacon rind, for twining it on a stick wouldn't work—the stick would burn before the bacon crisped. Instead, she began hammering on the top of a can of tomatoes.

"I'll open it."

She jumped at the sound of his voice.

And without another word he knelt beside her and pried the lid open with his knife. He took his spur from her hand and frowned at a bent point. He fixed her with a hard glare. "Next time, let me do it."

Her hands were near bloody, she itched with grime, and even as she knelt on the ground her muscles cramped. Yet, she'd gotten one can open, and almost another one, and he counted it as nothing. But the corn was bubbling in its can, its aroma stronger now, more potent. Again, her stomach spasmed in response.

She pulled abruptly to her feet and slid the heavy gloves from her hands, flinching as they abraded her tender skin. She replaced them on his saddlebag and went to retrieve the bread.

Wordlessly she tore the loaf roughly in half, handing him the larger portion, then tore a smaller piece from her own and dipped it in the can. Despite her hunger, she brought it slowly to her lips, its flavor delighting her tongue, closing her eyes with satisfaction as its warmth spread through her body. Coulter ate heartily, more than his share, she noted, and it didn't take long for the corn to disappear.

She was pondering how to eat the tomatoes when he pierced one with his knife blade and lifted it, limp and dripping, to his mouth. He plucked another one from the can and offered it to her. After a moment's hesitation, she took it gingerly in her fingers.

The juice dribbled her chin and squirted when she bit into it.

He tossed his bandana into her lap. "Don't suppose you have any sugar?"

She reached for her carpetbag, then stopped, her shoulders slumping. She'd made yet another oversight, forgetting the sugar. Men on the range craved tomatoes, just as men at sea craved lemons and limes. With sugar, they were often the only sweets a cowboy had for weeks at a time.

She turned and shook her head, to find him staring at her gaping blouse. Her hand flew to close it, though her eyes were trained on his fierce gaze, feeling its heat searing her breasts as surely as if he had touched them with his hand. Her throat thick, she swiveled her back to him.

"No," she stammered. "No sugar." She fumbled with the top buttons and only then saw what had caught his eye.

The cross.

His cross was nestled between her breasts, as it had been since the day he'd given it to her. And there it had been since, undetected by Clayton or Joel. Even Joel hadn't seen her flesh exposed that way.

She jerked her head back toward him, but he had already turned his attention back to the tomatoes. The gaze that had shaken her so totally, had merely been a matter of surprised recognition to him. A slight distraction, nothing more. She felt foolish. He would laugh with scorn if he knew how totally that glance had shaken her.

His eyes met hers and for a moment they locked. The intensity of his look disturbed her. Then he raised the gleaming knife blade, the last pulpy fruit speared on its razor-edged tip. His gaze questioned silently, and her negative response was equally mute. He ate it himself, a trickle of the juice running down his bronzed neck as he swallowed.

Elizabeth handed the bandana back to him as he moved to wipe his mouth on the back of his hand. His gaze went from the scarf in her hand to her. He tossed it aside.

She stiffened, staring into his relentless gaze. And then, her spine rigid, she whisked the bandana from the dirt and wiped the juice roughly from his neck.

His hand closed over her wrist, his eyes blazing. For a moment, neither moved. Then he snatched the bandana from her fingers and finished the task himself.

"How many more cans do you have?" he asked gruffly.

"One. More tomatoes. And a rind of bacon."

His eyes sparked interest at that.

"And no skillet." Best let him know her for the fool she was, even if it brought his censure upon her.

But he only braced his hands on the ground and levered himself to his feet, scooping up the empty cans. “Don’t need a skillet. I’ll boil the bacon in these. I’m going after the mare. You’d best make your bed and get some rest.”

She thought longingly of the stream water, of clean hands and face. “Why didn’t we camp down there?”

His eyes were hooded, then. “If it’s convenient for us, it’s convenient for them, too.”

Them. Somehow she’d managed to forget “them.” She watched silently until he disappeared into the brushy trees, and listened until his sounds faded. Despite the riotous early-morning chirping of birds and the wind sighing through the branches, she felt chilled.

Were they following? They... them... nameless, faceless, with one exception. A nightmare visage, screaming as blood and kerosene burned into his face... burning hatred and revenge into him. Clayton Dougherty wouldn’t rest until he got it.

“Joel...” His name was a whisper on the wind, a tender, aching whisper. When would she be able to forget the sight of his horrible, bloody death? Instead, she fought for good memories before the liquor, before Texas.

Laughing. He’d always been laughing in Philadelphia. She would make one of her acerbic remarks, and unlike her family he’d never been horrified. He’d laughed and pulled her close. They’d shared that golden laughter, the poetry they both had loved. He’d seemed happy, then. Softer. Before Texas.

Before Clayton.

She tossed on the blanket, pulling the cloak under her chin. Why did you do this to me, Joel? Why did you leave me?

She had seen it coming... how could she not? But she hadn’t believed it. He wouldn’t do that to her, wouldn’t leave her. He was obsessed with her, with her happiness.

No. Maybe in the beginning, but not lately. He’d been obsessed by something else. Something she didn’t understand. Justice.

But what justice? And why, when he was seemingly on the brink of this long-awaited justice, had he killed himself?

A jay streaked past above her, screaming its laughter. A twig dug into her back, and the underbrush rustled with the movement of some small unseen creature. She closed her eyes to emptiness, and slept.

The sun was higher when Coulter returned from the stream again, the clean cans in one hand, the mare's lead in the other. As he'd hoped, the woman was asleep, too tired to be disturbed by the rays of sun that found their way through the sparse foliage to dapple her face. Her cloak draped over her, soft fashionable wool, not heavy enough or serviceable enough for these mountain nights. He thought of his own warm jacket and felt a moment's guilt.

But only a moment's.

She'd done it to herself, hadn't she? He couldn't start thinking about her comfort. He couldn't start thinking about her softness, her weakness, her helplessness.

The image of his cross pressed between her breasts flashed before his mutinous eyes, and he was forced to face the truth: confronted with her softness, her helplessness, he was weak. And weakness led to capture.

He had to get rid of her.

He hobbled the horse and banked the fire, his shoulders and thighs stiff with weariness. By the time he sank to his own bedroll, it was just as he'd hoped—his concentration was on sleep. Not the woman. Not what he'd seen...

In the half-sleep of the tormented, he began to plan. After he got rid of the woman, he would go back to Cavendish, Texas. Back to the man who had killed his father, his mother, his brother.

Back to the man who had ruined his sister's life.

The trail was winding to an end at last.

Wendell carried his shame noticeably, the heavy burden slumping his young shoulders and shadowing his face. Sitting apart from the other men of the posse, he drank his morning coffee and once again swallowed bitter tears. He had been duped like a fool. He had let the outlaw escape.

The mood of the posse was resentful. Men who had looked at him with awe now wouldn't meet his eye. It helped not a whit that no one could figure out how the outlaw had done it, how he'd gotten the keys. It was all Wendell's fault; it was just what they would expect from the likes of Wendell Crutcher.

But the men were no easier around the sheriff. His silence was deadly, and no one dared risk rising his ire. Nor did they dare complain that they were miles from home. They chased the outlaw who had murdered their sheriff's brother, taken his sister-in-law hostage, and stolen his horse. Honor made them follow the man.

But they were afraid.

Too many things about Coulter, about Joel Dougherty didn't make sense.

Two riders approached the small group and the sheriff rose to question them.

"There's been thirty, forty people through this valley in the past week, sheriff. Reverend Bloys held a camp meetin', and they reckon every rancher for a hundred miles showed up."

Sheriff Dougherty peered up at the rider from under the brim of his hat, half of his face swathed in bandages. "Coulter?"

The man gave his head a shake. "Sorry, sheriff. No sign of him, or anybody near resemblin' him and Mrs. Dougherty."

Dougherty peered up at the sun-washed slope west of their camp. "Reckon you men have come as far as you should have to."

Visible relief washed through the group, except for Wendell. He alone felt the tension emanating from the sheriff's body. He alone recognized that there was something more here than grief.

He alone suffered the guilt that he'd betrayed the only person in the world who'd ever treated him better than dirt.

Except Miz Dougherty.

Except Doralee.

His face twisted, and he ducked his head. He didn't know how he'd done it. But somehow, he'd messed up everything.

And the sheriff had stared at him like he was scum. Hadn't even asked him to explain. Like he knew everything...

Wendell jerked to his feet. "Let them go back, Sheriff Dougherty. I'll go with you. We'll find him, and we'll get Miz Dougherty back."

The sheriff shot him a savage look. "I'm quittin'," he snarled. He reached up and ripped the star from his vest. It hit the dirt with a plop and a puff of dust. "I'm goin' on alone."

Elizabeth awoke in late afternoon. Her legs were tangled in her long skirts, her cloak cast aside from her tumblings. Bracing her palms on the ground, she pulled stiffly to a sitting position. The sun-dappled clearing spun around her, and a roaring sounded in her ears. She fell forward, resting her forehead on her knees. After a moment, the dizziness passed, leaving her weak and cold.

She glanced up, relieved to find the outlaw gone again. He hadn't seen, hadn't witnessed her weakness.

Her head itched, as did her skin. Dare she go down to the stream alone and wash? The luxury of a bath took on fantastic proportions; the better to distract herself from the gnawing hunger that threatened to consume her.

But first she must get the tangles out of her hair. She reached up, wincing at the stab of pain in her shoulders, and touched the matted mess. That settled it. She had to at least try to comb her hair. She forced her stiff feet to propel her to her carpetbag where it rested beside a newly fallen tree. Wisps of mesquite leaves brushed her face as she bent over it and dug for her comb, finally locating the silver-backed set she'd brought all the way from Philadelphia.

Like a child in a treehouse, she perched on the fallen tree and studied the valley below. Each stroke of the brush soothed her, bringing new suppleness to stiff muscles. The soft breeze carried the dusty scent of dry earth, the sweet scent of warm foliage.

A sudden crashing in the underbrush stopped her brush in midstroke. A deer bounded into the clearing and froze. For a split-second, the deer hesitated, then bounded away, taking a new direction.

She wasn't breathing. Not until the deer's hasty descent faded away and her chest was pained to bursting, could she force herself to breathe again. She dropped the brush into her lap and covered her face with cold hands. How ridiculous, she told herself. Frightened by a silly deer. And I'm a silly woman.

The thought amused her. Thinking of herself as silly—what a luxury. A silly woman had no thoughts of impending danger or doom. A silly woman had nothing more serious to frighten her than an unexpected appearance by a deer. A silly woman squealed at the sight of a field mouse in the kitchen, fainted at the sight of a cut finger, had no memories of moonlit death hovering behind her closed eyelids, waiting to catch her off guard.

Oh, to be a silly woman.

She sat silent, still, no longer amused by thoughts of silliness.

The underbrush rustled a second time. Not crashing through this time, but a soft, surreptitious stirring, the sound of a predator. This time, she wasn't frightened. She glanced at her saddlebag and thought of the gun deep within it. Not silly, but foolish, to be caught without it. Yet she didn't move. She simply catalogued the thought for future reference: keep your gun at hand, foolish woman.

A twig snapped but she wasn't afraid because she sensed, without seeing, that it was the outlaw. Limbs bent in front of his tall form as he approached. Through gray-green mesquite leaves, she caught a glimpse of his hat, once light tan, now dark with dust and sweat. He emerged from the narrow animal trail and stood before her, several dead quail dangling from his gloved hand.

"This won't be much, but it's all we've time for."

"I didn't hear gunshots."

"I snared them." He dropped them into the dust and squatted to rebuild the fire.

She took her hairbrush in hand and started toward the carpetbag. "With some wild onions, I could make some kind of a stew. It would be very filling. I haven't any more bread, but there are the tomatoes—"

"No tomatoes"

"Why not?" she demanded, bristling.

Her challenge startled him, and his hands fell away from the fire he was fanning as his brown eyes widened in surprise. Sherry brown. She'd never noticed before, never cared.

"Because tomatoes are water, and on the desert we'll need them. Not for fancy cooking, but to stay alive." His voice was tinged with disgust.

She ignored the outlaw as he plucked the quails in silence, a task she had intended to take herself... but she was tired. So tired. And weak. She leaned her cheek against the rough bark of a sparse mesquite tree and closed her eyes. Ahead lay hours on horseback. Her thighs were chafed from rubbing, her back and shoulders throbbing from the effort of staying upright. And she was hungry. The quail he had might provide a single course for a single meal, not sustenance for an entire day....

No. She couldn't let herself think that way. The aroma of roasting quail and mesquite smoke lay heavily on the air. It wouldn't take them long to cook. She must think how good they would be, how filling. She swallowed convulsively. When the thought was almost too much to bear, she opened her eyes.

The distant report of a rifle echoed through the valley, and Coulter was on his feet, gun in hand.

Elizabeth shook her head slowly. "It's just someone hunting for their dinner, don't you think? See?" She pointed a slender finger across the valley. A wisp of smoke floated toward the sky from the opposite slope, stretching high and straight to a point, then feathering away in the breeze, unlike the smoke from their own fire that was diffused by the mesquite branches.

He turned a look on her both savage and alarmed. "How long has that fire been there? Why didn't you tell me?"

"I didn't think... I didn't think it mattered," she stammered.

He closed the distance between them, and grasped her upper arm, his fingers digging into her soft flesh. "Lady, when will you understand? When you're on the run, everything matters!" And then, as if reacting to her touch, he jerked his hand away. "Get your things together. We'll eat in the saddle."

The saloon smelled of sweaty bodies and rotgut whiskey, of chawed tobacco and heavy perfume. No current of air stirred the sweltering stench, which was both a blessing and a curse.

Doralee sat alone, her pale yellow hair a ghostly beacon in the dim corner. Late on Monday nights business was light, for which she was grateful. She dipped her finger in the dirty glass of whiskey, then raised the finger to her lips, sucking the drop off with an effort more desultory than enticing.

Yet, of course, it enticed.

The man was watching her, had been for an hour. But an evening's employment held no allure this night. Not since Wendell Crutcher had let Boone Coulter and two thousand dollars slip through his fingers, and her fingers. Wendell'd been like putty in her hands... She sighed and dripped another drop of whiskey onto her tongue.

She'd had too much, and still she couldn't forget. Damn it all, Wendell had been downright sweet. She'd set out to latch onto his money for a while, and damned if he hadn't proposed like a jackass. Like he really thought they could go off and start over somewhere else. And damned if she hadn't said yes.

She shoved the glass away and tried to stand up, but the chair slid and she fell back into it.

"Let me," a voice came from over her shoulder.

She angled around and recognized the man who'd been watching her. She fluttered a hand in his direction. "Don't mind little ol' me, mister. I can manage quite fine, thank you." The shoulder she turned in his direction was as cold as the night was warm. She blinked fuzzily. Something was familiar about him. He wasn't from these parts, but he'd been here before.

"Do you mind?" He reached for another chair and pulled it up to the table without waiting for her response. "I'm Dan P. Jennings, Harper's Weekly."

Her eyes brightened a tad. "The magazine?"

A sure smile spread across his lips. He wasn't too tall, nor was he too handsome. Black hair, black eyes, hooked nose. But he had an air about him, a sureness. It made her feel uneasy and exhilarated at the same time.

"Weren't you here a spell back?"

"A spell," he agreed. "I had an appointment with a gentleman who never showed up." His fingers closed over the whiskey glass. "Do you mind?" he asked again, and she shook her head as he drank, draining the glass in one long swallow. "Just as I thought. The whiskey they gave me wasn't the best, after all." Yet he didn't seem angry, only amused.

Doralee flicked two fingers in the direction of the bar, waiting to see the bartender preparing a couple of fresh glasses before she turned her attention back to Dan P. Jennings. What an impressive name.

"Where do you hail from, Mr. Jennings?" She smiled her special crooked smile, hiding the gap where she'd lost a tooth in a brawl.

"Baltimore. And you?"

She leaned back in her chair and tossed her curls. "A long time ago, Louisiana. Ruston, Louisiana."

The bartender arrived with the drinks, and she waited patiently while Jennings paid through the nose for authentic Kentucky bourbon. A man of fine tastes, she decided. He knew what he wanted and was willing to pay for it. Her lashes lowered in speculation. A night's employment might not be so bad after all.

"And what brings you to Cavendish this time, Mr. Jennings? Another appointment?"

He shook his head, his eyes trailing down the neckline of her dress. "I'm afraid I may have lost out on my chance of interviewing the gentleman this time."

"Interview?" Her tone was even, only half-interested. She shrugged a smooth shoulder, exposing a bit more flesh in the process. "You mean, for your magazine? There ain't nobody 'round these parts worth interviewin', far as I can tell."

"I'm afraid you're right, Miss ..." He let the question dangle.

"Doralee," she cooed, dragging a fingernail over the back of his hand. "You can call me Doralee."

"Well, Doralee, I'm afraid that I've missed Boone Coulter again."

Her hand froze over his and her lips pulled into a moist, petulant pout. "Boone Coulter. All a body ever hears about these days is Boone Coulter."

Jennings' interest sharpened. "Do you know him?"

"No." Doralee pulled her hand back and gave her curls a toss. "And I don't want to. The only way I was interested in that gentleman was to see him at the end of a hangman's noose."

"Strong opinion for someone who doesn't even know the man."

Doralee leaned forward, and this time there was no artifice, only real emotion in her voice when she spoke. "Mr. Jennings, that man was gonna provide me with a new life."

Jennings arched his heavy brows. "By hanging?"

She shrugged. "Let's just say I had a stake in his reward money."

His black eyes glittered with interest. "Were you in on his capture?"

Her laughter tinkled in the darkness. "Of course not, Mr. Jennings."

"Then just exactly how did you get this stake?"

"By doin' what I do best, Mr. Jennings." Doralee smiled, slow and easy, and slid her hands up her midriff until they rested just beneath her breasts. "And I can assure you, I'm very, very good."

"I'll just bet you are," he chuckled. "And something tells me you know more about Boone Coulter's capture than you've told me so far."

"Let's just say I'm personally acquainted with the man who did the capturing."

"Lucky man."

She arched her brows. "If it's information you're after, Mr. Jennings, you've come to the right place."

He shot a glance upstairs. "Is there somewhere we can talk in private?"

She grinned. "Like I said: You've come to the right place."

She was conscious of eyes following them up the rickety staircase. Her feet were like lead, too much whiskey, but his hand closed on her elbow and steadied her. By the time they entered her room, she'd begun to feel right pleasant.

"Mr. Jennings …" She turned to find him taking in the shabby surroundings, and the color ebbed from her cheeks.

Of course, he'd seen finer. But as he closed the door behind him, she felt a new surge of assurance. She had ways of making men forget where they were. "Don't forget to lock it. We wouldn't want our... interview... to be interrupted."

"Most assuredly not." He turned to face her, and the smile slid from his features as her dress slid from her shoulders. "You... you had some information for me... about Boone Coulter."

"I know how he was captured …" she sighed, rolling a stocking down her shapely leg. "And why he was captured." She followed suit with the other. "And I have a pretty good idea how, he got away …" She leaned across the bed to pull back the covers, giving him a prime view of her bare bottom. When she turned back, he was striding toward her.

He cupped her bare breast with his smooth hand, his palm not worn and callused like a western man's. "You know an awful lot, don't you, Doralee?"

"I surely do, darlin'," she sighed, arching against him.

"I believe you're right, Doralee. I do believe I've come to the right place." He bent to let his lips take up where his fingers left off, and together they fell back onto the bed, Doralee's sighs masking the whirring of thoughts in her head.

She might get out of Cavendish, Texas, yet. If she had her way, and she fully intended to, Dan P. Jennings wasn't going to leave Cavendish without her.

After all, she had her ways.

Chapter Seven

THE HORSES MOVED relentlessly forward, though Elizabeth could only assume that they were headed for the Guadalupes on the horizon, but she couldn't see for the night was dark, hazy, almost starless. At this pace, they'd be in mountains again the following night.

If she could last that long.

Earlier that night they had stopped for a short rest, both dismounting to stretch. The mare stood docile at her side, but the outlaw's horse chafed at the delay, and Coulter had to keep a tight hold on the reins.

Coulter had moved a distance away, to relieve himself, she was sure. She had done likewise, but not without a great deal of trepidation, aware of every restless stirring among the prickly pear and desert grasses. Diamondback and black-tail—she'd seen every kind of rattler imaginable at one time or another near her house. And she was well aware they were night feeders. This dark, moonless night was their time, this desert their habitat. She was the intruder, and terrified lest she stumble across one.

She was mounted and waiting when Coulter returned with a restless Sage prancing at his side. He started to mount, but the horse moved and he fell backward, maintaining his balance only by his firm grip on the saddlehorn. Again, he swung up, this time anticipating the horse's mood, and landed on the saddle with a grunt, despite the horse's antics.

"What's wrong with him?" Elizabeth asked as they set off. "He doesn't act like any horse I've ever seen."

Coulter took the lead, riding silently at first and she assumed he had no intention of answering. Then he spoke.

"He was wild, half-mustang, half-domestic. Somebody caught him, tried to break him the wrong way."

Elizabeth's eyes were drawn to the disturbing scars on the animal's flanks. "How did you obtain him?"

Again, the outlaw was silent. When he finally spoke, she wasn't quite sure whether he was answering her or not.

"I didn't. He's not mine." And then, softly, "He doesn't belong to anybody; and never will."

They rode on in silence, Elizabeth pondering the enigma of a man with a horse he could barely control, yet trusted implicitly. She clutched the reins, staring blindly at the creosote bushes spreading for mile after empty mile, their natural spacing like that of an orchard. But there, the comparison ended. There was nothing lush or promising about the tough, drab-looking shrubs, growing where little else could, leeching the ground of what little nourishment it offered. By day, their greenish-brown foliage offered no solace to the tired eyes. At night, they stretched into silvery-gray infinity, a creosote sea.

The aching spread—a slow progression that became so all-encompassing she ceased to feel it in her shoulders, her thighs... she only knew the constancy of pain. Until finally, in a haze of weariness and hunger, even the pain seemed distant. Even her thoughts faded, with only occasional flares of recognition. And beneath it all, the awareness of the man... a man she couldn't control, yet trusted implicitly... half-wild, badly broken... yet she trusted him.

She slumped forward in the saddle.

The mare halted abruptly; Coulter saw the woman sliding forward, then down. He sprang out of his saddle and caught her before she hit the ground, his steely arms closing around her. Her shoe hung in the stirrup. Supporting her with one arm, he wrenched it free. Her cloak billowing around them both, he stood, stunned; her limp body in his arms caught at his heart. The panic caught and robbed him of breath. He dropped to the ground, his hand trembling against her neck as he sought her pulse. It throbbed beneath her warm, satin skin. He'd pushed her too hard, expected too much.

He pulled his hand away, staring down at her body cradled against his thighs. What was he thinking of? She'd done this to herself. He'd warned her. Anger welled, blessedly submerging the panic, the fear... and his guilt.

Her body was light, fragile, in his arms. Birdlike, her shoulders and height had suggested a weight that she didn't have. Now, she looked like a broken doll.

He'd warned her.

The thought kindled him, forcing reason into corners of his mind that threatened to shatter his resolve. He'd warned her, and she hadn't listened, and hadn't he gone along with her wishes, even when it slowed him down, endangered him? Hadn't he?

He scanned the horizon for what appeared to be low storm clouds against the night sky, but what he knew to be mountains still hours away. A sea of desert, with islands of mountain refuge studding its bare expanse. Yet his mountains, his refuge, were farther still. He thought of his half-full canteen, of the one can of tomatoes in her saddlebag and couldn't stop his roughened finger from finding the dryness of her lips, rasping against their parched texture.

He'd done it to her.

She lay still in his arms, not even stirring, and again the panic welled. She was only exhausted. All she needed was rest and food.

What was he going to do with her?

He left her on the ground, wrapping her cloak about her as best he could, then crossed to his horse and grabbed his canteen. Back at her side, he lifted her head into his lap and tilted the mouth of the flask to her lips. The first drops dribbled uselessly down her chin. He took a finger and eased her lips apart, then tried again. At first, nothing, then she swallowed the water that trickled down her throat. A little more, a little more, his fingers were damp with the moisture, her moisture. Not too much... an ounce, maybe two, dribbled down her throat. Enough for now.

She coughed, a soft, choking sound, and her lashes fluttered as she stirred against him, turning her face into his middle. His stomach tightened at the contact, his hand cradled the back of her head, even as he leaned away from her. Her eyes opened, black against milky skin, glazed and sightless as her head tossed. Again his hand touched, soothed, though he dared not speak. He dribbled more water, aware that every drop he gave her now was a drop he wouldn't have come daylight when she would need it worse. Two hours till daylight, till the scorching sun.

Again, he gazed toward the distant mountains.

He lifted her high, and for once Sage didn't shy away but stood stock still as he laid her across the saddle. He mounted the stallion behind her, then pulled her into his arms. Resentment and anger and panic and emotions he dared not name warred within him.

She was making a game effort, he couldn't deny her that. But how much longer would she hold up? He had no choice; he had to seek help. A long journey lay ahead, and this time there'd be no night traveling. That meant crossing the desert by day.

And even as he felt steel-cold dread in the pit of his stomach, even as he recoiled at the very thought of taking the woman into the Diablos, he knew that there was only one place he dared go for that help. And only one man, a man even more desperate than himself, could he approach.

Miguél Obregón.

The midday sun beat down on his back, roasting the skin even through his shirt. The woman's body pressed against his, their sweat sealing them, locking them in a heated embrace closer than lovers, yet the passionate instinct flowing from him was of a different nature: survival.

The bolsóne, a low stretch of desert surrounded by mountains, spread before him. Now Coulter was forced to take the long way around its edge to avoid the low point of the basin, white with drying, killing salt. Accumulated rainwater, trapped again and again, formed a shallow lake which in time evaporated into a playa, a salt flat. Beyond the playa loomed the grim visage of the Diablos, the Sierra del Diablos, the mountains of the devil.

He approached the mountains from the wrong direction. From the northeast they were accessible by gentle, sloping foothills. But from the southwest they loomed before him, a wall of rugged cliffs a thousand feet high, grim and oppressive, daunting to the wary, stretching for miles. And in the heart of the mountains, beyond the canyons flanked by steep walls, he must seek refuge to save the woman.

In the heart of the devil himself.

The woman stirred in his arms, delirious with heat, with exhaustion. He reached for his canteen and dribbled the last drops of water into her parched lips. He, whose tongue was thick and throat was raw from lack of water, he, who had denied her his coat when it was cold, he, who had thought of no one but himself for many years, now sacrificed for her.

He stared at the playa, at the heat shimmering before his tired eyes, then the woman. Her skin was red, her hair limp, her body pliant, burning hot, feverish from the sun. At least he hoped it was from the sun, and that rest and water would relieve it. He glanced again at the hot playa, his lungs already seared from inhaling the salty air, and urged Sage toward the Diablos, ponying her horse behind.

An hour later when the sun slanted downward, Coulter found refuge in the Diablos' dark shadow. He cleared a spot on the ground and spread his blanket, then laid the woman on it. From his saddlebag he produced the last of the tomatoes, the open can carefully cushioned so that the precious juice wouldn't spill as they rode. And, though his own tongue was so thick with thirst that he could scarcely swallow, he cradled her head in his arm and tipped the edge of the can against her parched lips. Her lashes fluttered, and her mouth opened again for more. Slowly he poured a bit more and a bit more. Then he ate the last bites of tomato, fleshy and tangy and burning his tongue. And wet. Wet with life-giving moisture.

A slight breeze circulated around the base of the mountains, and their sweat-damp clothing cooled. The false coolness caused him to linger, to stretch out beside her on the blanket and close his eyes to the playa, the bolsóne, the heat.

But he couldn't.

Now the distance between them and Obregón was only scant miles. Miles that he must cross immediately, despite the sun and heat, or it would be too late.

Too late for the woman.

At midday, Coulter crested the rugged hill above the hacienda, the woman asleep in his aching arms, the mare unsteady beneath them. Sage had been released miles back; the stallion had borne the brunt of the journey with both humans on his back and deserved his freedom. He knew these mountains, had survived in them before, and would now. But for no man, not even Coulter, would he return to the hacienda of Miguél Obregón where he'd received the devil's stripes on his haunches.

The sun's blinding rays found their way under the brim of Coulter's hat. In the rugged valley below—dry and sparsely vegetated from a late-summer drought—spread the adobe buildings and rough corrals that made up La Hacienda del Corazon del Diablo.

He descended the rocky slope slowly, partially shielded by piñon pines and junipers. His approach would not be undetected, he was sure. But he was too desperate to seek another approach.

The body in his arms had been too still for too long. He pressed his spurs into the weary horse's sides, forcing her to pick up her gait.

But even as he approached the hacienda itself, he went unchallenged. Where was all the activity? Every sense was alert to danger, to the expectant quality of the air itself. Smoke rose from the chimney, horses stirred in the corrals, yet over the entire hacienda hovered the aura of death.

And then from the shadows of the long porch emerged a tall figure clothed in black.

Miguél Obregón.

From behind him, several others stepped from within the casa, filing onto the porch. Miguél Obregón's men. They were all poised with guns drawn, waiting for Miguél's response.

Coulter halted. Now that he was faced with uncertain welcome, he could go no farther. What if they were turned away?

The bandito stepped into the glaring sun. Coulter watched as he slowly approached him, his steps unsteady.

"You are here, mi amigo?"

Then Obregón's eyes seemed not to see him, but were trained on the woman in his arms.

Coulter tightened his hold on her, fighting a wild urge to wheel away and ride back into the mountains. "I need your help," he rasped, his words like grains of sand on his raw throat.

Obregón stepped closer and touched her hair, thick and matted with dust and dirt and ravaged by the sun.

Coulter tensed, and even the mare back-stepped in reaction.

"Mi amigo," Obregón repeated, his voice velvet and slurred. "It is like the first time, eh? The first time you came to me for help."

"No. Not like the first time." Coulter's gaze went toward the low, adobe house to the shuttered windows, and a mixture of pain and emotion colored his vision. "Where is she?" he whispered, for a whisper was all that would come from his dry throat.

Obregón's eyes lit with pain, his thin lips twisted in a grimace of a smile, he angled his handsome face toward the house. "She is in la sala, amigo. I am sorry... she did not wait for you. Her time of waiting is over."

"Susannah…" Coulter croaked, his arms tightening around the woman until she stirred and moaned in his arms.

"Es muerta."

Is dead.

"No…" The word, the merest of breaths, tore from him like a scream of agony.

This time, when Obregón reached out for the woman, Coulter released her blindly, turning her over to his friend, his enemy, without qualm. As he slid from the mare's back, his legs buckled, yet through sheer will-power, he straightened, standing for only a moment before starting toward the house.

Toward Susannah.

Toward death.

Chapter Eight

ELIZABETH AWOKE TO pain... to thirst... to a choking veil of incense... to voices keening a song that filled her with sadness, and with comfort. Mourning... someone mourned... and even in her daze, her soul responded. She mourned.

The keening stopped and plump arms circled her shoulders, raising her to accept water, blessed water.

And she slept, again.

The next time she awoke, it was to darkness. A low, rhythmic sound came from nearby... her eyes finally adjusted and she saw the round figure of a snoring woman seated near the foot of the massive bed, her tired face wreathed in wrinkles and sleep.

Elizabeth raised her hands to her hair, combed by unknown hands to the consistency of silk... her skin burned and stung from the sun, yet was soothed by scented oil... thirst... still thirsty... a chill shook through her body.

She rolled her head to the side to see an earthen pitcher on a table beside her bed. She raised up on an elbow, then fell back in pain. Long moments passed... the snoring woman continued to sleep... Elizabeth raised up again, her thirst stronger than her pain.

A small mug, already filled, sat beside the pitcher. Her fingers closed on its cold surface and she brought it to her lips, swallowing convulsively as the water poured into her mouth and spilled down her shoulders and breasts. When she could sit up no longer, she leaned back against the pillows and closed her eyes, her fingers still clutching the precious water.

Time passed... moments that seemed like hours. The night was deep; a candle beside her bed sputtered into blackness. The earlier scents and sounds had faded, yet the air was heavy with tension.

The sleeping woman didn't stir; the house emitted no sounds. Yet Elizabeth felt a presence, a sense of melancholy, embracing her. It was haunting, tempting, frightening. Where was she? Somehow, it seemed not to matter. Nor did all the other questions whirling through her hazed mind. Pain, thirst, these were important. The rest... nothing.

Until she thought of the outlaw.

Suddenly, she was filled with panic—a surge that sprang not from her weak body, but from the desperation of her soul. She had to find him. She clutched the massive bedpost, pulling weakly to her feet, bringing the tangled linen sheet with her, draping it around her shoulders against the night chill. Clutching the bed, the table, the walls, she made her way to the door and into the hallway, where candle nubs sputtered in sconces placed high and far apart, halos of gold in a cavern of blackness.

Drawn by an impulse too vague to name, too strong to ignore, she worked her way down the hall, her hands seeking support from the walls on either side, the sheet flowing behind her like an ethereal cape.

Forward she moved, groping through hazy darkness, though whether the haze was in the air or her own exhaustion, she didn't know. She only knew she had to find the outlaw, Coulter, her only point of stability in a world turned upside down. A chill shook through her and she stopped, bracing herself against the wall. When it passed, she went on.

At the end of the hallway, a choice. Left or right. Like an animal, she raised her face to the darkness, sensing, feeling a glow of warmth that chilled her because of the scent it carried. She turned toward it, this time walking stiffly, erectly, until she found its source—a soft illumination spilling from a partially opened door. The nearer she got, the heavier the scent, of incense... of death... of decay.

She clutched the sheet to her with numb fingers, moving forward, placing one foot before the other on a floor that moved beneath her feet. She reached the door, stepped around it, and saw the source of the glow.

Candles burned. Dozens of them flickering from every surface. Two ornate candelabras held vigil at the head and the foot of a woman... a dead woman stretched in perfect stillness, her hands folded across her breasts, her haunting profile a waxen image of deathly perfection.

Elizabeth stepped forward into the room, her eyes seeing only the woman lit by an unearthly halo. The dead woman's gown and shroud were white silk shot through with threads of gold, draping, surrounding, shielding all but half the woman's face and one hand.

That part of the face which remained uncovered already showed the gray pallor of decay beneath its waxen surface. The nearer Elizabeth drew, the more frightening the visage was, the more unable she was to pull away. If Joel had been buried, it would be like this, one half of his perfect face exposed, the other hidden. No, gone... missing... blown away by her pistol.

She didn't feel the bite of her teeth on her knuckle, nor did she taste the blood. She didn't feel the floor when she hit it. She didn't feel the strong arms that lifted her, the hoarse Spanish words that comforted her, the gentle hands that soothed her, the dark eyes that kept vigil by her bedside through the rest of the night.

Elizabeth awoke to darkness again. Yet she perceived that this was not night, but the suffused darkness of a room shielded from light. Her burning eyes easily distinguished details that had escaped her earlier: heavy, ornately carved furniture, a washstand with gilded porcelain bowl and pitcher, a large rug of deepest burgundy patterns, so dark as to be almost brown in the false dusk.

No longer were her covers tangled and disheveled. Instead, they were smooth and dry, cool against her body. Her hand went to the high neck of her bodice to find tiny pearl buttons, a pristine nightgown suitable for a young girl. Whose was it? Where was she?

Questions that earlier had never been posed formed in her consciousness now. She raised herself abruptly, her fingers digging into the bed for support as the room spun around her head. She squeezed her eyes shut until the slow revolutions ceased and the world righted itself once more. She slowly swung her legs around and down until her bare toes touched the soft carpet.

"No, no señora," a sharp voice cried out.

Elizabeth raised her eyes to a young girl, no more than fifteen or sixteen. Even as she stood there, the girl moved quickly to her side and frantically struck the soft mattress with a thin, dark hand.

"¡Cama! ¡Acuéstese en la cama!" She whirled her braided head toward the door and called out, "¡Juana! ¡Venga pronto!"

"Please," Elizabeth begged, grabbing hold of the bed post. "Please help me. Where is Mr. Coulter?"

At the outlaw's name, the girl's eyes narrowed and she shook her head as if she didn't understand.

The girl would be no help. Elizabeth scanned the room frantically, finding a white robe on a bench at the foot of the bed. She had to find Coulter. What if he had left her? She slipped the silken wrapper over her shoulders and started toward the door, her steps shaky, yet far stronger than before.

At that, the girl flew into another tirade of Spanish, leaping agilely in front of her and barring the door with her thin arms. "¡No!" Then she flung desperately over her shoulder, "¡Abuela!"

A hurried shuffling sounded in the hall, and then a woman appeared behind the tiny girl, the same woman who had slept in the room with Elizabeth the night before.

"Señora, por favor," she soothed. "Come back to bed. Let me help you."

Before Elizabeth could protest, the woman's plump arm was around her waist, steering her back into the room.

"Please... where is Mr. Coulter?"

The woman stiffened, her wrinkled face falling into a frown.

"Señor Coulter?" Elizabeth repeated desperately.

The woman shook her head and clucked again. "Pobrecita," she murmured melodically, and she forced Elizabeth onto the bed. Her brown eyes creased with concern, she stroked Elizabeth's head and barked an order at the child, who promptly appeared with tepid tea in a porcelain cup.

"You drink now, then you eat."

The thought of food brought a bitter taste to her throat. "No. No food. Please, if I could have more water…"

The woman raised the cup to her lips, and she accepted it willingly, wincing when the nauseating liquid washed the raw tissue of her inner mouth.

"That is good," the woman said. "You must rest…"

"Mr. Coulter?" she begged.

But even as she fought the lethargy, she collapsed against the pillow, the woman's soothing fingers soothing her forehead in rhythmic strokes.

"Please…" Elizabeth whispered, her eyes fluttering closed. "Please…"

Several minutes later there was a movement in the doorway, and both the old woman and the girl fell back in obeisance.

"Don Obregón." The woman dropped to a curtsy, then motioned to the sleeping woman in the bed.

His dark eyes caressed her fragile form as he stepped into the room, and the odor of his sickly-sweet tobacco came with him. He stopped short of her bed, his black clothing contrasting with the white linen that surrounded the woman. The two servants departed, leaving the room to their master.

"And who are you, querida?" Obregón murmured. "How have you come here to me, and why at this time?" His hand lingered at her temple, not touching, yet close enough to feel the radiant heat of her body. "Ah, querida, you are a mystery. I know only one thing... you are not Coulter's woman."

His sensuous lips twisting in a grim smile, he leaned closer, finally allowing himself to touch, to caress. Her hair was silken against his fingertips, sunbleached at the temples, silver and gold against her skin. And her eyes... he touched their lids, willing them to open, but they didn't. The drug he had mixed was too strong for that. Her eyes, too, were a mystery, waiting for him to discover their secrets.

She was a woman of many secrets, of that he was sure. Which was fitting, of course. He, too, had his secrets. His hand drifted down her cheek, feathered over her lips, and down her throat to find the sluggish pulse at its base. There it lingered, hovering above the high neckline, tingling to unfasten the buttons, to discover more of her secrets.

But no. He was a man of patience, of wisdom. He had all of the time in the world. The one important thing he already knew. She was not Coulter's woman. Coulter had no woman and would never have a woman.

Now, with Susannah dead, he had nothing to live for.

Susannah... her misery clutched at his heart, but he wouldn't let himself think of it. She was gone. Was this woman to take her place? The thought teased, tantalized. Even as he longed to touch her, he was conscious of innocence and danger, both radiating from her in palpable waves... A tantalizing combination. How could she be both?

"Don Obregón," Lupecita whispered nervously from the doorway, her rough skirts clutched in her young, thin fingers. "El funeral."

He nodded, straightened, his somber form towering over the sleeping woman, as his mind fought through foggy thoughts for control. He couldn't bring himself to leave her, to abandon the seductive puzzle which had presented itself in his tiny corner of misery.

"Who are you?" he whispered, again.

Again, she did not answer.

Finally, he pulled himself away. This woman must wait, for it was still Susannah's time. Later... later, he would delve into this new woman's secrets.

Low laughter sprang from his throat, sinister laughter that had caused him to be called El Diablo, even before he'd come to this devil's wasteland.

Yes, he would delve into her secrets.

He would delve into her soul.

The raw earth opened up to accept its latest sacrifice. In the absence of a priest, Obregón stood cloaked in black at the head of the grave. The group huddled around were silent, weighted down with the eerie quality of the leaden sky, the windless air. Peons clad in homespun and serapes, and others more sinister—brooding men with guns on their hips—all stood back in respect, and in fear.

Doña Susannah was dead.

Some said by her own hand, others said she simply had gambled with the deadly mescal bean once too often. The means made no difference. She was dead, and it was as if even the elements were reacting. Thunderclouds gathered; the earth held its breath for the unleashing of spirits welcoming home one of their own.

The casket, ornately carved with gilded corners and handles, a lure to the greedy and sacrilegious, lay deep in the hole, awaiting its final blanket of earth.

But Don Obregón did not fear graverobbers. No one would dare disturb the final resting place of his woman... no one would dare. For she was a woman of the spirit world, and the fear she inspired while living was only magnified by her death. The mountains would swallow her up, and she would be as one with them.

So he chanted, the Latin incantations flowing from his lips. Did he grieve her loss... or did he welcome release from her hideous beauty...

Finally it was over, and Obregón motioned the others away. When they were gone, he dropped to his knees and lifted a handful of dirt in his aristocratic hand. The anguish of his loss overwhelmed him as the fistful of earth struck the dark pine casket, hollow, thudding, final... mirrored by another thudding sound, growing louder, closer.

A rider appeared over the ridge, his horse frothing, rearing, screaming like a demon. And with the arrival of the demon rider came the first cold gust of wind rushing before the storm, and Obregón pulled upright in shock, in fear. The horse tore down the ridge, its hooves echoing the thunder from above, until it was reined in inches from the yawning grave, where it pawed restlessly. The rider stared down at the earth-spattered casket.

Obregón stepped back, though his eyes met those of the rider and didn't waver. "Amigo... I thought you weren't coming."

"Not come?" Coulter stared down at him, his brown eyes dulled by pain. "How could I not come?"

Obregón shrugged negligently. "I suppose you want to add your heretic blessings, mi hermano?"

"Don't call me 'brother'. I was never your brother. We have no bonds... no kinship. Do you call the half-life you gave Susannah reason to think so?"

Obregón's eyes glittered with malice. "And what kind of life did you offer her?"

"None. And that," Coulter returned through gritted teeth, "is the only reason you're still alive."

His angry gaze dragged slowly from Obregón to the yawning grave; his face haggard, he swung off the stallion, holding tightly to the bridle in an attempt to control the nervous beast as he dropped to one knee. After several strained moments, he pulled to his feet and mounted again.

"You are leaving, then?"

"I'm leaving." Coulter whirled away on his horse, but Obregón's shouted words caught the wind and carried to him.

"And the woman?"

Coulter rode on, letting his action provide the answer. He knew what Obregón wanted, and it was the only solution.

A welcome solution.

He'd be rid of the woman, free. Free to go after Dougherty. His anger heated to an all-consuming rage. Wasn't Dougherty the one who had ruined Susannah, all those years ago, who had made her life worse than death?

But Susannah was gone. Her pain was over. And his pain... how long would it take him to forget?

The rage tore at him, ripping him apart. He must leave this place, for it was as surely the place of the devil, as its name proclaimed.

The wind whipped against the heavy shutters, rattling behind Elizabeth's head. She stirred uneasily, her hands clenching and unclenching, fighting back the darkness….

"Lady…"

Even above the sound of rain lashing the roof in sheets, she heard the whisper, the familiar voice... the outlaw. Tears flooded her eyes as relief overwhelmed her. He was here. He hadn't left her. She reached frantically for him, but he didn't respond. She tried, but she couldn't speak. She held her hand raised between them, imploring, pleading silently. Finally, words escaped her parched lips.

"Thank God." And then, only the softest rasp, "I knew... I knew you wouldn't leave me."

But still he didn't respond.

She rolled to her side, her hair spilling over her face and shoulders like a silken veil. "Mr. Coulter..." Only his name would come to her lips. "Mr. Coulter..."

His voice was the low, rustling drawl that had haunted her tumultuous dreams. "I came to say goodbye."

"No!" She raised up, her eyes large and dark in her hollowed face. "I don't believe you." But deep down, a tiny, panic-stricken part of her recognized his words as truth, and refused to accept it. "I don't believe you."

"I can't stay here. I've got to settle some business."

"Then take me with you!" Despite her weakness, she slid from the bed and stood before him, swaying, yet determined, her arms outstretched in entreaty.

Finally, slowly, he accepted her hands in his. His coarse thumbs rubbed over her blistered palms, as if testing their strength and finding them wanting. He shook his head. "You aren't well enough. Miguél will arrange for you to leave when you're stronger."

"Miguél? Who is Miguél?" And then, "No!" Snatching her hands away from his, she braced an arm against the bed to keep from falling. "I can ride. You have to take me with you. You can't leave me here—you can't!"

Wild-eyed, she grasped the bed covers as she lurched sideways. But her hands lacked strength and fell limp, letting the sheets slide through her fingers.

Coulter sprang forward, barely managing to break her fall. One knee planted on the rich carpet, the other raised, he crouched and pulled her to him, cradling her against his chest. She lay helpless, eyes closed and skin parchment white near her temples and hairline where the sun's rays hadn't reached. He jostled her gently, one rough hand cupping her chin, his fingertips pressed against the soft fluttering rhythm of the pulse at the tender hollow of her neck.

"Come on, lady," he grated. "Wake up, lady." He jostled her again, but she didn't respond. His muscles bunched with frustration, he rose abruptly, her hair a cascade swaying and spilling almost to the floor.

He had to think straight, think about Dougherty, about Susannah—and that was impossible with her fragile body in his arms. A half-stride took him to the head of the bed. He swept back the covers and bent to deposit her where she belonged, yet when the time came to let go... he didn't.

The wind buffeted the shutters by her head, but the flame of the oil lamp burned steady and undisturbed, casting its golden glow over the woman's features, sharp angles, all of them. High-cheeked and narrow-faced, even more drawn than before. Days without sufficient food had done that. Her mouth was full and wide, bruised even. And her eyes. His chest tightened at the thought of her eyes—wide and gray and frightened.

And trusting.

That was the damnable thing. That trust. It made no sense and never had. Why should she trust him? Why in heaven's name had she turned to him? He wanted to know, he had to know. So many questions that he had suppressed welled to the surface. Suppressed, because if he knew, he might want to respond, he might feel responsible.

As he responded now. Without knowing the first thing about her, he felt more than responsible. He felt... compelled. Without understanding or questioning why, his lips were brushing hers, seeking their warmth, their solace. Her mouth was soft and yielding, startlingly so. Heart pounding, he pulled away.

"Who are you?" he whispered.

Her hand moved, fell over the edge of the bed, the wide gold band slipping to cover her knuckle. A frown creased Coulter's forehead. Her husband. She was accused of killing her husband. His gut clenched at the thought.

She couldn't have done it.

But if the man had needed killing, he would have gladly done it. Done it for her.

The thought staggered him, assaulted him with the full force of its hideous truth. He, who had put killing behind him. He who had convinced himself those days were behind, was faced with the ugly fact: The thought of killing still sprang all too easily into his head.

The woman stirred. And as she stirred the wedding band slid off her thin finger and hit the floor.

He stooped and picked up the ring and placed it on his calloused palm. He stared at the minute inscription inside, too small to see in the dim light. He stepped closer to the lamp and read: Joel to Elizabeth, August 18, 1880.

Joel. Joel Dougherty's wife.

"No." He backed away from the bed, blinded by emotion.

"What is wrong, mi amigo?"

The voice, low and sibilant, came from over Coulter's shoulder. He spun, his hand on his gun butt, and found Miguél leaning negligently in the doorway.

"She cannot travel, that is certain. You must leave, that is equally certain." The tall, dark man shrugged and smiled, his eyes hooded. "I will explain all when the time comes."

"After what you did to Susannah, you really think I could leave this woman with you?"

"And what did I do to Susannah?" Obregón lounged easily in the doorway. "Provide her an escape from her monstrous fate? Give her the illusion of beauty, where she had none?"

"She was a virtuous woman until you touched her with your evil, Obregón."

"Ah... virtuous, indeed. Until I awakened her true nature."

Coulter reacted, but Obregón stilled his anger with a cool stare.

"Do not talk to me like a brother, Coulter. Talk to me like a man. What did I give Susannah? Mescal? Peyote? Opium?" A low, mirthless chuckle escaped his lips. "Escape? Forgetfulness? Freedom from pain?

"And love, amigo. Do not forget, I loved her. You loved her as a brother, but I loved her as a man. Susannah stayed with me because I gave her what you couldn't. I looked at her without remembering, without guilt. Yes, her scars were... unpleasant. But for me, they were nothing more. For you they were a constant reminder of what you wanted to forget."

His gaze slid past Coulter to the woman on the bed. "You have no more to offer this one than you did your sister." Miguél shoved away from the door jamb and planted his booted feet wide, his eyes challenging Coulter to disagree. "You too have your scars, amigo. Only your scars are on your soul."

Obregón closed the distance between himself and the outlaw's stiff frame and passed him by, stopping beside the woman.

"Ah, querida," he murmured softly.

"Don't touch her." Coulter's arm shot out to bar the woman from Obregón. Eyes like burning embers, he spun to face his old friend, his old enemy. "Leave her alone, Miguél. Just leave her alone."

"And you, amigo?" Obregón met his gaze without rancor, though his eyes gleamed with secret pleasure. "Will you leave her alone?"

"My only thought for days has been to leave her," Coulter spat out. "What are you saying?"

"Then this is your opportunity. This is your chance to rid yourself of such an... unpleasant burden," suggested Obregón, his voice thick with mockery. "If that is what you really want."

Coulter shoved his hand through his hair. In the lamplight, he saw not her, but Susannah. Susannah, whose promise he had failed to keep. Susannah, whom he had let down once too often.

Now at last he knew where Dougherty was. Now he knew how to get his revenge. His hand closed over the woman's wedding band until it cut into his palm.

He slipped the ring back on her finger.

Dougherty studied the dry terrain, the distant mountains to the south, west and north. That goddamned Coulter could be anywhere, and Dougherty wasn't fool enough to think he could track him, not without food and drink, not when some of the finest trackers in the West had already tried and failed. A couple of times he'd felt close, close enough to smell the bastard. But he hadn't seen a sign or felt the outlaw's presence in days.

But that was all right. Let Coulter hide out for now. Dougherty had time on his side. Eventually, Coulter'd have to come back out of the mountains, because this time he wasn't alone.

His breath quickened and nostrils flared. She thought she'd outwitted him. She thought she'd gotten away.

But she hadn't.

His lips curled in a cruel smile of anticipation, the tender scar tissue at his temple stretching, smarting. He hadn't left Cavendish empty-handed. He had a plan, and the means to carry it out. He had plans for the bitch from Philadelphia. She'd never run far enough or fast enough to get away from him.

Chapter Nine

ELIZABETH LAY PROPPED against the pillows, the cool morning breeze from the open window caressing her skin, teasing her with unfulfilled promises. She had already learned how ephemeral its promises could be—how quickly they turned to a furnace blast in this land. The thunderstorm had taken its toll; the hard-baked dirt was now a wash of red mud; the scent of the earth was raw and fresh. A bouquet of late-blooming wild flowers beside her bed still glistened with moisture.

A rustling of skirts drew her attention to the doorway and the old woman, her rounded shoulders stooped over a large silver tray laden with dishes. "Señora," she smiled, though her eyes remained sad. "You are awake."

Elizabeth stared at her with fixed eyes. "He is gone, isn't he?"

"No, no," the woman responded. "Don Obregón is here. He desires to speak with you, when you are refreshed."

"I was speaking of Mr. Coulter."

The woman stopped short, then seemed to recover. "I do not know."

She laid the heavy tray on a table and uncovered a dish of steaming meat, the smell of onions and peppers causing Elizabeth's stomach to contract with hunger.

"You eat, no?" She held the plate out for inspection. "I am Juana, and I am to take care of you, to put meat on your bones. You must eat."

She nodded. "Maybe a little."

"Good. You will like it, you'll see. Doña Susannah said it was too strong for her stomach." The woman's face took on a distressed cast and she crossed herself. "Doña Susannah did not eat enough. And you," she raised her brows as she glanced at Elizabeth's body, "you need more meat. This menudo will give you back your strength."

Doña Susannah... the dead woman... silk and gold, incense and decay...

The cold breeze chilled her, and she reached for the shawl that had been draped across the foot of her bed when she awoke that morning. But the warmth it provided did little to ease the chilling of her soul.

"Señora would like coffee? Or chocolate? Or tea?"

"Coffee will be fine, thank you." If only the woman would leave. She knew nothing about the outlaw, and her endless chatter about the dead woman... Elizabeth took the mug of coffee into both hands, seeking its warmth.

Where had Coulter gone?

"When you finish, I will bring your combs and other things. You must look your best when Don Obregón sends for you."

"Who is this Don Obregón?" Elizabeth demanded.

The woman's eyes popped open wide in disbelief. "Señora, look around you." Her arms spread wide, encompassing everything. "Everything you see belongs to Don Obregón. He is the patrón of the hacienda."

"Then he can help me make arrangements to leave?"

The woman's face became guarded. "Si, Señora. If he so desires." And with that, she left Elizabeth alone, closing the heavy door behind her.

Elizabeth ate a few bites but her stomach quickly rebelled. She pushed the rest aside and stood up tentatively. Her knees didn't buckle; her legs felt strong. She crossed the room to the blackwood framed mirror hanging on the whitewashed wall, and stared at the reflection within. Her eyes shone blue against her sunburned skin, its top layer already peeling away. Her hair gleamed—someone had brushed it free of its mats and tangles. But it seemed lighter in color, less drab, brighter.

She lifted her hair off her back and shoulders and twisted it haphazardly on her head. But then her eyes caught a gold flash in the mirror and stopped, startled. The gold chain at her neck... she had forgotten about it. She dropped her hands and her hair spilled back down over her shoulders as she reached for the plain cross nestled between her breasts. Whoever had removed her clothing and bathed her had left her this. Coulter's cross.

Her hand closed around it, and her eyes met her reflection in the mirror. A sharp pang struck her. Coulter wouldn't have left her here unless this place was safe. Perhaps he had left instructions for her with Don Obregón. Perhaps he could answer her questions.

When Juana returned, Elizabeth had already coiled her hair into its customary style, and had washed her face gently with the water supplied for that purpose. Her skin glowed with a soft sheen of oil where she had patted Juana's healing unguent on it.

"Señora, you must wait for me. I would do that for you. I take good care of Doña Susannah."

"I am quite capable of caring for myself, thank you," Elizabeth broke in. "My bag, and my clothes. Where are they?"

"Oh no, Señora. You are still not well. You needn't dress. Get back in bed. Later, when you are rested, Don Obregón will come to you."

Elizabeth stiffened and raised her chin a notch. "Please inform Don Obregón that I do not entertain gentlemen in my bedroom."

Juana's dark cheeks colored a deeper shade and she clutched her apron in her hands, but her eyes were mutinous. "If you insist, Señora. But Don Obregón will not be pleased."

"I owe my host a great deal of gratitude," Elizabeth concurred. "But not access to my bedroom. If you'll give me my things …"

"Lo siento, Señora. I am sorry." The woman's hands fluttered helplessly. "They were burned by accident."

"Accident?" Elizabeth demanded.

"The cook is very superstitious. With Doña Susannah dying, and then you coming... You were so hot, so sick. She insisted we burn your clothes."

Her hand closing over the cross at her breast, Elizabeth only sighed. "What am I to wear?"

"We have many, many beautiful dresses." Her face brightening, Juana crossed to the massive wardrobe against the opposite wall. "Doña Susannah was small, but some of her things might fit you." Her black eyes swept down to Elizabeth's ankles, exposed beneath the voluminous folds of the white nightgown. "You are taller, but your body is no bigger."

Of course. The nightgown had belonged to the dead woman. Elizabeth took a step backward as Juana swung open the wardrobe doors. She didn't want to wear the dead woman's clothes. But eyeing Juana's stout figure, she accepted the truth. She didn't have a choice.

Above hung over a dozen dresses of every hue. Below them lay stacks of undergarments and shawls. More shawls and mantillas than Elizabeth had ever dreamed of one woman owning. Juana's deft fingers whipped through the clothing and pulled out a white silk chemise.

"You would like this?" she asked. "It would fit."

She longed to have silk next to her bare skin again, or to wear the rose dress Juana fingered. She had had a dress that shade once, a lifetime ago in Philadelphia, but never one with such flounces of lace and frippery. Her eyes slid resolutely to the next dress and paused. A rich forest green, its creamy lace trim was lavish, yet subdued. Much more fitting a widow.

Juana pulled the dress out of the wardrobe. “It is lovely, si? So pretty with your hair and your eyes ...” She shook her head and clucked her tongue, again. “Your poor skin. You must stay out of the sun, Señora”.

“But I did,” Elizabeth answered defensively, thinking of the long nights on horseback, the days sleeping. She touched her cheek. “This must have happened after I ...”

She broke off, ashamed to put her weakness into words. No wonder the outlaw had left her. No wonder he had no patience with her. She had proven him right, in everything.

“Señora, let me help you.”

Wearily, Elizabeth allowed the woman to remove her gown and help her with her chemise and pantaloons. Cool and white and clean, they slid over her skin. But when the woman came forward with a small bustle and corset to go over them, Elizabeth waved her away. “I have no need for that nonsense. Please, if you’ll just help me with the dress.”

Without voluminous petticoats and the wire bustle to hold the skirts away from her body, the front of the gown brushed her toes, compensating for the difference in height between Elizabeth and the dress’s original owner, though several inches of the train dragged the floor. After the deprivation of the last days, Elizabeth’s already slim waist fit easily into the tight-fitting gown. But as the woman fastened the long row of buttons up the back of the dress, Elizabeth stared down at the bodice in dismay.

“What’s wrong with the neckline of this dress?”

One shoulder was covered with the dark fabric, making her flushed skin appear pale in contrast. But the other shoulder was almost bare, the neckline riding low, exposing much of her right breast. Only the soft lace flounce saved it from being too daring.

Juana stood before her, stiff and silent, her old eyes shuttered. “Nothing is wrong with the dress.”

Elizabeth immediately felt a stab of chagrin as she realized her error. “I’m sorry. It is a lovely gown. I simply am not accustomed to Spanish styles.”

Juana’s eyes flickered, but she remained silent.

"And something for my head?" Elizabeth riffled through the jewel-toned array, pulling a sheer lace mantilla free. "Is this how it's done?" Standing before the mirror, she draped it over her head, carefully arranging the folds to cover her bare shoulder. When she turned to face the woman, she still got no response.

Elizabeth felt a sharp twinge of irritation. Enough was enough.

"Where is Don Obregón? I must see him at once."

Juana merely nodded and led the way.

The growing dread built in Elizabeth as she followed Juana down the hallway. Not dark shadows, this time, but the sconces high on the wall were a reminder of her first trip down this passage. And as the old woman turned to the right in front of her, her throat constricted.

She had been here before.

Miguél Obregón sat quietly in the dark sala, the smoke from his cigarette wafting upward, pervading the air with its heavy, sweet scent. He sat easily in his chair, his leg flung over the arm rest, one hand holding a goblet brimming with burgundy.

The crimson oriental carpet at his feet had been added for Susannah, as had assorted other European touches: a Bavarian porcelain shepherdess on one table, a French still life on the wall. He had humored her in these things. But now she was gone, and he longed to rid the room of its outside influences. He was proud of his Spanish heritage, and even his Irish, remote as it was. He owed his height to his Irish grandfather, but his fire, his desires were of his Spanish blood.

Strange companions... the woman and Coulter. Whatever had brought them together remained a mystery, as well as what had brought them to him.

Obregón's long fingers toyed with a hand-rolled cigarette. No matter. He would find out all he needed to know, and more.

The sound of stiff, rustling petticoats signaled Juana's arrival. He swiveled slowly in his chair and faced her. But having led the woman to him, Juana bowed and left. The new woman stood alone in the doorway—wearing a dress of Susannah's.

She cast her gaze about the room in confusion. No, in recognition.

She remembered.

Elizabeth stepped forward into the room. The room was shadows, pools of darkness. No flickering halo of golden candlelight. No cloud of incense.

No waxen figure of death.

Only a few rays of sunshine broke through the shadows, due to the wide verandah that shaded the windows and filtered the light. Her eyes began to adjust to the dim light.

Her breath lodged in her throat at the man rising from the shadows. His ebony hair swept back from a high forehead, exposing a sharp widow's peak. His eyes blazed a burning black against his pale skin.

Obregón extended a hand. She didn't speak as he grasped her hand securely in his and his head tilted down toward hers. Trapped, she felt a flood of memory. She wanted to withdraw her hand, but couldn't.

"My guest... allow me to introduce myself. I am Miguél Obregón." He bowed low, and when he rose, his eyes gleamed despite the dim light. "Señora, por favor... your beauty astounds me."

She could taste her fear. She had heard his voice before... but where? Her breath was shallow, her pulse fluttering. She swallowed hard, but couldn't speak.

He took her by the elbow, his forehead creased with concern, his voice silken, seductive. "Señora, you are not well. I should not have allowed you to leave your bed."

"Nonsense." She tugged her hand free, amazed and grateful that her voice revealed nothing of her trepidation. "I have survived far worse than traversing the corridors of your lovely home."

"Of that, I am certain. And you have my deepest admiration, Señora... " His dark brows arched in question.

"Dougherty. I'm sorry, I should have introduced myself. My name is Elizabeth Dougherty."

His facial features became immobile, and in their very lack of emotion exhibited shock as his eyes riveted on her. "Please, be seated." Again his voice retained its charming tone, was smooth and clear.

Elizabeth took a seat at his bidding on the hard, upholstered chair. He crossed to a table and lifted a decanter of ruby-colored wine. His movements were smooth, deliberate, as he refilled his own goblet and filled a fresh one for her. But behind his smooth facade she could sense his mind working. But why? Why should the name Dougherty mean anything to him?

The sheriff.

She should never have told him her name,

"Some wine, perhaps?" Obregón bent forward, the stem of the fluted crystal goblet held deftly between his fingers. She stared at him, and a smile played about the corners of his lips. "Wine, to strengthen the blood, querida."

Querida. There it was again, that voice, that tremor of recognition. Elizabeth took the goblet from his fingers. Despite her protestations to the contrary, weakness was invading her legs, her arms. She sipped the wine, shuddering as its warmth spread down her throat, her shoulders, and throughout her body.

"It had been such a long time since I had a comparable wine," she remarked. And suddenly, for the briefest moment it was Joel's eyes she saw, not Obregón's. Her fingers tightened on the stem and she turned her face away. It seemed a very long time ago.

"Señora Dougherty." He gave his head an impatient shake. "Forgive me, but we should not be so formal. I must call you Elizabeth. You will allow this?"

Her name was a caress on his lips, and she closed her eyes to it. She felt, rather than saw, him take the seat beside her. She forced herself to turn to him, to meet his gaze, wondering what secrets he was hiding so well behind his calm expression. "Don Obregón, did—"

"Miguél. You must call me Miguél."

"Don Obregón." She continued without faltering. "Did Mr. Coulter leave any message for me?"

His eyes flickered in surprise. "Message?" He seemed to ponder her question, though it was simple enough. "No, he did not. You must understand, when our friend Coulter left, he was... distracted. He felt compelled to leave you in my care, a charge for which I am very honored."

"When will he return?"

Obregón shook his head sympathetically. "I am so sorry. This must be very difficult for you. But I would not count on Coulter to return at all."

She felt a flush of embarrassment creeping up her neck and was grateful for the mantilla and the darkness. Her position in this house was anything but comfortable. What little dignity she could muster was all that she had to sustain her. But even as she was grateful for the mantilla's shield, she flinched when Obregón raised his hand to its folds, so near her cheek she could feel the heat from his touch graze her skin.

"Please," she said, edging away from him.

"Shhh ..." His expression was transfixed, his eyes taking on a strange glow, as his fingers continued tracing the folds.

Frozen, she could only watch as he adjusted the folds to cover more, until all that was exposed was the right side of her face.

Coulter's voice sliced between them like red hot steel. "Get your hands off her!"

Obregón pulled back, but it was Elizabeth who leaped to her feet, not from guilt, but awash with relief.

"My God," she whispered, her fingers pressed hard on the stem of the glass to stop their wretched trembling. "You're still here."

Coulter simply crossed the room to her side, tearing the covering from her head. His face was contorted with suppressed rage; she had never seen him so before. His clothes were clean, his face shaven, he bore all the elements of civilization. But those hard, piercing eyes... never had she seen them so deadly. The white shawl hung limply from his clenched fist, and for a moment her eyes searched his and saw the torment, the anguish.

Then, just as quickly, he confronted Obregón. "What do you think you're doing to her?"

Obregón stood slowly, but if he was distraught at Coulter's abrupt appearance, he did not let it show. "Amigo," he said smoothly, his voice bearing a slight taunt. "You have returned?"

They faced each other, Coulter rigid, Obregón seemingly relaxed. Yet beneath the surface of Obregón's calm lurked a tension that seemed as potent as Coulter's. The silence sizzled between them, then with a languid motion, Obregón indicated the wine on the sideboard.

"A glass perhaps, to take the dust from your mouth?"

Coulter's gaze shot from the decanter to Obregón's glass, and finally, to Elizabeth. He snatched the glass from her hand. He sniffed it, then lowered it to his side, his voice deadly. "I warned you."

"Mr. Coulter," Elizabeth broke in, "it was only a little wine."

"This time, maybe." Coulter's hard eyes drilled into Obregón's. "This time."

Elizabeth backed away, grasping the back of her chair for support. Whatever was between them, she was somehow at the center of it, yet she didn't know why or how. Clutching her skirts in nerveless fingers, she stepped toward the doorway. But before she could make her exit, Coulter was at her side.

"Señora Dougherty, I look forward to continuing our conversation later," Obregón said smoothly.

Without another word, Coulter caught her elbow in a viselike grip and steered her, perhaps not gently but at least considerately, into the hallway.

"I need to talk to you," he said, releasing his hold on her.

She caught her lower lip with her teeth to still its trembling. "I'm not as well as I thought," she murmured. She placed a hand on his arm to steady herself. "But I want to talk to you, as well. My room," she began, raising a pointed finger, but he cut her off.

"I know. I remember."

"Of course." She felt a stab of embarrassment. Of course he would remember her begging him... humiliating herself. Her head angled toward him. His face was rigid, his slanting cheekbones stained with angry color. He had returned. Because of her? She pulled her eyes away from him. She dared not ask.

Clutching his arm for balance, she found herself not resisting, but leaning into it. So strong. He was so strong. And she needed that strength. A strange emotion coursed through her.

She needed him.

She must save her own strength. She must recover. Because whether it be this night, or the next, when the outlaw left again, she must be with him.

Obregón watched from the doorway behind Coulter and the woman, observing their progress down the hall, a new cigarette in his fingers, his red-rimmed eyes narrowed in speculation. He raised the cigarette to his lips and sucked in hard, holding the smoke in his lungs. Then he exhaled it slowly, slowly, waiting for the pleasure, watching the outlaw and the woman disappear around the corner. A strange alliance: Coulter and Dougherty's wife.

How and why were imperative for him to learn.

A mystery, indeed.

Chapter Ten

ELIZABETH DROPPED HER hand from Coulter's arm as she entered the bedroom a few paces ahead of the outlaw. Keeping her back to him, she shook out the folds of her skirt. She could feel his presence, feel his eyes on her back.

"How sick are you?"

She pivoted to face him, and when she did, she caught him staring at her neckline. "I am much better," she managed, then added a clipped, "It is so kind of you to ask."

But his manner offered no kindness as he crossed to the table in the long quick strides of a man accustomed to horseback and impatient with the feel of the ground beneath his scuffed boots. He examined the tray that was still waiting, though its contents were as cold as his voice. He demanded, "Why haven't you eaten?"

"I have eaten a bit, but the meat was greasy, and spicy, and my stomach wouldn't tolerate it," Elizabeth returned stiffly, even as she remembered her stomach's hungry reaction when first she'd seen the food. She would have eaten it, had she not been distracted by thoughts of the outlaw's leaving her. But such thoughts only stiffened her resolve not to let him know.

"Sit down," he commanded.

Elizabeth glared at him as he approached her, a large chunk of meat speared on the heavy silver fork. "What are you doing?"

"You're going to eat, lady. You're going to eat and get your strength back, so we can get the hell out of here."

She was caught between protest and release, as the impact of his words struck her. He wasn't going to argue about it. He was taking her with him.

His jaw rigid with determination, his rough palm closed over her bare shoulder, he raised the fork to her lips with his other hand. In that moment she was certain that if she didn't submit, he would force the food down her throat.

A split-second before the meat touched her lips, her hand closed over his. Eyes icy, she met his glare, venom with venom. "I am quite capable of feeding myself."

Satisfied, he released the fork to her and stepped back.

She sank into a straight-backed chair and chewed the cold meat. Through sheer will power she managed to force the bite down, swallowing too quickly, her eyes stinging from the heat of the seasoning.

The outlaw lifted the table, tray and all, and set it down in front of her. She grabbed the coffee and drank deeply, her eyes squeezed shut until she could breathe again. She rested the cup in its saucer with a shudder, then resolutely cut another bite of meat. By the third bite, she came to a startling conclusion: It was cold, it was over-seasoned, it was tough—and she was too hungry to care. Her body, long denied sustenance, trembled with reaction. More coffee. It too was cold, but neither did it matter.

She took a tortilla and folded the meat into it, and was relieved to discover that the addition of the bland bread muted the flavor of the spices. She had finished half the plate when she raised her eyes to find Coulter watching her every move with grudging approval.

Fearing her stomach would revolt if she continued at such a pace, she took the linen napkin and patted her lips. And lest the outlaw be too cocky she remarked idly, "It was the wine, I believe. It settled my stomach so that I could eat."

He stiffened at that, his intake of breath sharp.

"Don Obregón assured me it would strengthen my blood," Elizabeth continued placidly, "and as that's a belief my own grandmother ascribed to, I agreed to share a glass with him. Besides," she fingered the necklace at her neck and peered past him, "it was a very good vintage. Better than any I've had since I left the East."

Coulter's eyes narrowed. "You're familiar with wine?"

"Quite."

He reached up and rubbed the back of his neck, though his eyes still remained wary, "There was nothing wrong with it?"

Confused, she shook her head to the negative. "It was a very fine vintage," she repeated.

Strangely, he seemed relieved, his wide shoulders relaxing imperceptibly. "If you're sure... you think the wine really helped?"

"Really, Mr. Coulter, where is all this leading?" she demanded in exasperation.

"Where it's leading is to us getting out of here," he growled, "by any means possible."

Elizabeth's shoulders slumped with remorse. "I'm slowing you down incredibly, aren't I?"

"Maybe." He eyed her speculatively, his gaze settling on the band of gold on her finger. "Maybe not."

"What do you mean?"

"I mean, I want to get out of the Diablos as quickly as possible. After that—"

"The Diablos?" Her cup fell to the tray with a clatter. "Is that where we are? My God, why have you brought me here?" she breathed.

"You didn't know where you were? Do you know who Miguél Obregón is?"

He stepped closer to the window and indicated the vista through it with a sharp thrust of his hand. "The Hacienda del Corazon del Diablo."

El Corazon del Diablo.

The Heart of the Devil.

Don Obregón was the dreaded El Diablo.

"I see you do know something about our host." Coulter's voice was hard, mocking. "Then maybe you'll understand why I don't trust him. Why you shouldn't trust him either."

"Then why are we here?"

"You were sick. I had no choice."

Then the dead woman was La Diabla.

A chill passed through her as she thought of those burning black eyes, of the woman in gold. But La Diabla was supposed to be grotesque, a monster. The woman she saw was anything but that.

"Did you know her?" she whispered. Then, reading the confusion on his face, "Doña Susannah. The woman who died."

He turned to face the window, leaving her only a quarter-profile to study for his response. "I knew her," he replied in a dull voice.

"She was very beautiful."

"Was." Then he faced her again, his head angled cautiously. "You saw her?"

She nodded mutely, her lashes lowered over the soft ridge of her cheekbones. "The first night I was here. I was looking for you. I thought you had left me …" She twisted the napkin in her hands and swallowed. "It was night, I didn't know where I was, and I was confused. I was searching for you, but I found her, instead."

She raised her face to him then, her eyes as dark and haunted as his. "It was very difficult for me. I realized for the first time, by seeing her, hearing the mourners, I... I remembered Joel... my husband." She inhaled deeply, a long, shuddering breath, then rose, leaning heavily on the table before her. "I think... I think I need to rest now."

She stepped forward, then faltered, meeting his eyes and seeing a pain that mirrored her own. He stood awkwardly, scant inches away from her.

Strong. He was so strong. She needed his strength. A lone tear slid down her cheek. She made no move to hide it, to wipe it away. She didn't avert her eyes from his, didn't shy away from the wariness she saw there.

Coulter stared at her, at her quivering chin, her glistening eyes, the crystal streak her tear had left behind, and felt his anger kindling. How could she look at him like that, as if she expected more from him, more than he'd already given her? Couldn't she see he had nothing for her? Couldn't she see that he had his own troubles?

She wrapped herself in her own arms as she sank to the bed; her chin dropped to her chest; her shoulders trembled.

He backed away from her. She had no right to expect his comfort. No right. And he had no right to give it. No right to care. No right to feel her pain as keenly as he felt his own, sharp and knife-edged in his gut, until he was beside her without knowing how he'd gotten there, taking her in his arms without knowing why, feeling her soft trembling against his body.

Not caring that it wasn't right.

His hands stroked her back, awkward hands that didn't know how, that were at once too hesitant, too rough, yet straining to comfort. It wasn't like before, when she'd lain so still, her pain a separate thing all her own. Hers was an emotion so raw, so close to his that they merged into one. And as he held her, his eyes stung with memories of Susannah, of a young and beautiful Susannah before the fire, before the scars, before their lives had changed forever.

His shirt was damp with her tears; his eyes were blinded by her hair; his arms were filled with her agony. He gave her what he didn't have to give, and burst with the desire to give more.

They sat on the edge of the bed, their bodies twisted into one another, two beings searching a solace that hovered just out of reach. Moments dragged long, neither of them sensing when her trembling stilled, when his hand climbed to press the back of her head against his hard chest as they rocked gently in the age-old rhythm of comfort. And finally, there was no division between the comforted and the comforter. Her fingers stroked and soothed his chest. The soft perfume of her filled him with solace. Pain receded into numbness, then into an elusive solace, until they were perfectly still.

He did not know where to move, what to do. Instincts failed him. She made the first move, averting her face and pulling away slowly, slowly, until they no longer touched, only their shadows joined between them.

"You must excuse me, Mr. Coulter." Her voice was weak, a mere fluttering in the still air. "I must rest, now, or we'll never make our departure."

He rose stiffly, uncertain. "Is there anything I can do?"

She sat up straight, resting a slender arm on the bed post. Her hand went to her breast. When she lifted her face to him her eyes were dark and enormous. "Mr. Coulter, you are a man of honor. A man of your word. I can never repay you for what you have already done… You came back for me."

The way she'd planned it, Doralee figured, reclining on her disheveled bed, she'd made it nigh impossible for Dan P. Jennings to leave her behind. She gasped and tugged a handful of his hair as he got a mite too rough in his attentions. He immediately gentled, and she settled back into her daydream...

He'd already stayed in Cavendish three days longer than he'd planned. He could say all he wanted about waiting for the results of the posse—she knew enough about men to know that having free use of her bed had made the stay a great deal more pleasurable.

Dan P. Jennings would leave, but she was going with him. All the way to New York City.

Riders, maybe a dozen of them by the sound of the clatter, passed below Doralee's open window. Her fingers ceased their twining through Jennings' hair.

"What's that commotion?" he muttered, his bristly mustache whisking against her nipple, where only moments before his lips and tongue had been paying their respects.

She tugged the sheet up over her bare breasts and leaned over the bed, craning her head for a view of the street below. "It's the posse come back."

The reporter's head shot up immediately, joining hers at the window. "Have they got him?"

Doralee scanned the tops of the hats, all familiar, one more so than the others. "Wendell's down there, but I don't see Boone Coulter." She hesitated, then frowned. "Nor the sheriff, neither. I don't see Clayton." She gazed up at Jennings. "What ya' reckon it means, sugar?"

"Maybe Coulter killed him." Jennings grabbed his trousers and started pulling them over his sturdy legs. "I may get my story yet, even without the gunslinger's interview."

Doralee's full lips set in a hard line. Damned if she was going to watch Jennings walk out the door to get his story, and maybe forget her and decide to leave. Damned if she'd let him get away with thinking the story ended here in Cavendish "dust-hell" Texas.

She played with the frayed edge of the sheet, adjusting it across her breasts. "Sure, honey, you'll get a story all right. But if Coulter did kill the sheriff, and I don't know no man who needs kiln' worse, don't ya' reckon an interview with the killer would be worth even more to you?"

Then as if his answer meant nothing to her she yawned and stretched across the bed. Certain that he was watching, she closed her eyes and arched her back, slowly, slowly, the sheet edging down lower until only the swollen tips of her breasts held it up. One more languid stretch, and the sheet slid free, exposing her rosy nipples to his hungry eyes. From beneath her lashes, she watched him, saw him hesitate, then grit his teeth and continue buttoning his trousers.

She smiled. Sure, he was going downstairs after his story. She'd never expected any different, after all. But he'd be back. And she'd be ready.

She watched through half-opened eyes as he scowled and began slapping her talcum powder off his black vest. That was expensive powder he was cursing. He'd liked it well enough when she was smoothing it on his fanny. It wasn't her fault he'd jerked and knocked it out of her hand, spilling it over the bed and half the floor. Come to think of it, at the time he hadn't even seemed to notice.

She trailed her fingertips down her midriff, idly circling her navel. It was too hot for writhin' and squirmin', anyway. What she really needed was a cool sponge bath and a nap.

She stretched again and yawned. And, just in case Dan P. Jennings was getting too cocky for his britches, she added with a soft sigh, "Tell Wendell I said hello. He's such a sweet boy."

Her eyes popped open as the springs squeaked in protest and Jennings fell across her. "I'm not delivering any messages to your deputy sweetheart," he grumbled, filling his palms with her breasts. "And you won't either if you know what's good for you." His dark brows lowered. "Do I make myself perfectly clear?"

"Perfectly," she responded with a pleased and surprised smile. Her hand slid down his body, finding the thick evidence of her effect on him already exposed and ready for action. As he ground into her flesh, it occurred to her that she had vastly underestimated her powers. She made a little noise that was half-whimper, half-sigh just for his benefit, but her mind was already thousands of miles away.

New York City was going to be an adventure indeed.

Evening spread its mauve cloak over the rugged mountains, softening their contours, bathing them with purple velvet shadows. Elizabeth stood at the corner of the verandah against a rough cedar post, its sharp scent filling her nostrils with thoughts of memories on horseback following the outlaw's lead.

She damned her weakness to the point of denying it. If he was ready, she was ready to put this place behind her. Nights on horseback and days hiding seemed less dangerous than the underlying tension at the Hacienda del Corazon del Diablo.

She had many questions, yet when she awoke that afternoon Juana was nowhere to be seen. The thin girl, Dulcita, who spoke no English, had appeared. Since Elizabeth spoke no Spanish, her questions went unanswered.

A masculine voice broke the silence. "It is beautiful, is it not?"

Elizabeth straightened, smoothing the folds of the deep green skirt. "Very beautiful, Don Obregón. You must be very proud."

"Ah, proud indeed. No one knows the luxuries of the devil's heart." His hands swept across the vista of mountain and deep blue sky, stars already shimmering in the cloudless sky. "Nature enjoys her tricks, her secrets."

"I don't understand."

"You don't remember the face of the Diablos." He moved closer in the twilight, his features profiled against the sky. "They are harsh, forbidding, ugly to those who fear the unknown. White men pass by and shiver with fear. But not Miguél Obregón. I wondered that first time many years ago, when I first fled Mexico, what about the Apache? How do they live there? And I came into the Diablos to discover their secrets." He laughed then, a coarse, husky sound, too close to her ear.

"I was not the first white man here. I found that another had come in search of refuge. Our amigo, Coulter."

Elizabeth felt on the brink of what she longed for. Answers. At last, someone to give her answers. Though her intuition told her to excuse herself and leave the dark verandah and its master, her need to know more about the outlaw was stronger.

"What do you know about our friend Coulter?" Obregón asked softly, and in his words were a taunting, teasing quality she didn't like.

"Very little," she finally admitted.

"The Mexicans know. The Apache did, until Victorio's defeat in these very mountains." He smiled, his teeth a gleam of white in the heavy dusk. "The U. S. Cavalry did me a great service, ridding the mountains of the Apache. Now, I alone control them."

"The cavalry doesn't bother you?" she asked. One of the most notorious outlaw encampments, and they remained undisturbed by the law? It made no sense, no sense at all.

He shrugged, an easy elegant motion of his shoulders. "I am no problem for the Americanos. My prey were the followers of Diaz, in Mexico. Their riches were enough for my humble needs, for the current time, at least."

"Forgive me if I don't share your idea of 'humble needs'."

Obregón laughed again, bracing his hand against the post above her head. "Querida, you are an enticing mystery. And I must warn you, my passion is mystery. If there is a secret, I must know it, I must understand it. Your mystery... it intrigues me beyond reason, at a time when I thought never to be intrigued again."

"Your wife," she murmured. "I feel remiss. I haven't offered my sympathy."

"Wife? No querida, Susannah was not my wife."

Elizabeth could not move, caught between the post behind her and Obregón in front of her; her heart pounded, her blood raced at a frantic pace through her veins. His face dipped lower until she could feel his words brush over her, smell the strange, distinctive scent of his breath.

"She was my possession."

A shudder rippled down her body, but she pressed on. "Who was she?"

"Who was she, or what was she?" He seemed to ponder the question, eyeing her speculatively in the dim moonlight. "She was many things to many people."

Circles. He talked in circles. He meant to tease her, to taunt her with pieces of the information she was becoming desperate to know. Her mouth dry, Elizabeth forced herself to speak. "And what was she to Boone Coulter?"

"Ah, querida, do I detect an interest beyond friendship in your question?" He moved close to her again, cupped her chin in his hand, and she flinched for his palm was icy cold.

"Listen well, querida, if you so need to know. Susannah was the only person in this world who mattered to your Boone Coulter. The only one he ever loved." His fingertip found the frantic pulse at the base of her neck, and she knocked his hand away.

Obregón shrugged, dropped his arm and faced the mountains. "You must be careful, Elizabeth Dougherty, in these mountains. You leave your window open, and spirits will come in. They are not called the Sierra del Diablos for nothing."

"What do you know of spirits?" she asked, clutching the heavy shawl around her shoulders.

"I know how to control them, how to make them do my bidding. Through them, I know how to possess... and that is what happened to Susannah. I thought she, too, could control, possess. She attempted to do the ceremony of the red bean. It killed her."

"What are you talking about? What is this ceremony?"

"A ceremony of the Apache. The red bean. The mescal bean."

"You mean... peyote?"

His chuckle rustled in the darkness, sibilant and sinister. "Not peyote... stronger. More magical. More deadly."

Elizabeth stared at him. "I don't understand how... why she would even want to do such a thing."

Obregón shrugged. "You are very sensible, querida. Sensible and beautiful and mysterious. I do not expect you to understand."

"I have been told that I am sensible before." she asserted, cupping her elbows in her hands and turning her shoulder toward him.

"But not beautiful? I do not believe that."

"My husband claimed so. That is the way of husbands, I believe." And she hadn't believed him either.

"Ah, yes, so sensible. Perhaps we will discover what lies beneath your sensibility, Elizabeth Dougherty"

"I think not." She pushed away from the corner post and moved to pass him. To her relief and surprise, he allowed her to go.

She was in her room before she realized that Miguél Obregón had raised more questions than he had answered.

Doralee descended the stairs three paces behind Jennings, her chin raised to best show off her long, slender neck. They drew the usual resentful glances, some from sullen men who had been waiting for her attentions since the reporter's arrival in Cavendish, and some from the girls who had been waiting for his.

She didn't care a whit that he constantly walked ahead of her, not bothering to perform the simplest courtesies. She knew well enough the courtesies he was capable of when they were alone. It didn't matter that after the first night he hadn't paid her a cent, for on that first night she had charged him triple the going rate, and could almost taste the riches to come.

All that mattered was that Dan P. Jennings of Harper's Weekly told her that no one in all of his experience could hold a candle to her charms, her talents or, what was the word, her proclivities. She smirked her special smile; those New York men would never know what hit them. They'd be at her feet, begging for her attentions. The price Dan P. Jennings had paid that first night wouldn't buy a minute of her time once she got to New York City.

When they reached the bottom of the stairs, Jennings cut to the left and pushed through the bat-wing doors, and headed toward the Western Union office. Doralee sat at her customary table in the corner, tempering her desire to be seen with her off-limits demeanor.

Minutes later the doors swung again. She glanced up without much hope that it would be the reporter again. It wasn't.

It was Wendell.

He stood there, all gangling six feet of him, and stared at her with a look so hungry, so pitiful, she felt an affection stirring in her breast she didn't know she was capable of. But letting him know wouldn't do either of them any good.

"Well," she said, adjusting her bodice to cover her cleavage, "go ahead and take a seat if that's what you're aimin' to do." She cast a quick glance at the doorway. "Just don't plan on stayin' long if you know what's good for you."

"I ain't gonna sit down, Doralee." He clutched his dusty hat in front of him, hiding that part of him that she'd initiated into manhood so successfully. Three times. "I just want you to know, I'm releasin' you from our agreement. I just can't expect you to wanta hook on with the likes o' me."

"Well that's real gentleman-like of you, Wendell," Doralee whispered, biting the inside of her gum to keep from laughing.

"I just wanted you to know," he repeated awkwardly, his gaze averted from her face, her body, or any place near her.

She couldn't encourage him, that was for damn sure. She'd found greener pastures she hadn't even begun to graze. But the poor kid was so pitiful. She heaved a sigh, and out of long habit, allowed her bodice to gape the slightest little bit.

"Wendell Crutcher," she said, and he dragged his eyes from the knothole in the floor to her face. "Wendell Crutcher, you'll make some girl a fine husband, and that's why you deserve a fine girl. Not somebody like me. A real sweet little ol' girl who'll treat you right and appreciate you." She allowed a knowing gleam to creep into her eyes. "And believe me, she'll appreciate you. You've got a lot to appreciate, sugar."

He blushed to the roots, and this time it wasn't a blush of shame. His eyes shot down to her chest and right back up to her eyes, then down and up again, as if he couldn't decide where they should light.

Then he faced her square. "Miss Doralee, you're wrong about some things, I know. But the biggest one you're wrong about is yourself. And if there's anything I do, it's gonna be prove myself to be worthy of you. I aim to redeem myself, to you and to everybody else. But most of all, to you."

He turned on his heel and strutted away, pushing through the doors and squinting in the sunshine.

"Wendell Crutcher, you're going to be the death of me, yet," she muttered.

But Doralee couldn't help noticing that the boy who'd dragged in through those doors and the boy who'd walked out were two different boys. He'd come in whipped, and he'd walked out determined.

It hadn't exactly been her goal, but it was damn sweet being somebody's inspiration.

Chapter Eleven

THE RAIN OF the previous night had weighted the day with muggy heat. Now it was night again, and the mountain air was clear and cold. The bedroom was chilly, causing steam to rise from the porcelain hipbath.

The heavy, jasmine scent of the perfumed bath water filling her senses, Elizabeth leaned against the back of the tub, the water sloshing gently around her. Despite the strange aura of fear at the hacienda, this was a luxury she couldn't regret. She palmed the slick bar of French-milled soap and stroked it over her body, in long, smooth strokes, strokes to soothe as well as cleanse.

The bar slipped through her fingers and into the water, and she let it go, rubbing her hands together until a lather built, then smoothing her arms, her shoulders, her breasts. Her body felt different, finer, more fragile. Yet her breasts were still ample, almost too full for her small frame.

A sudden gust of wind rattled the shutters and stole through the cracks, circling around her. Her entire body reacted, lips trembling, shoulders shuddering, nipples tightening into hard buds. She cupped the water and poured it over herself, each handful splashing warmth over her icy skin. Cool air, hot water...

her body didn't know how to react, except to revel in sensuous pleasures long denied.

The water was as cold as the room when she finally stood, sleek and dripping, and reached for the soft flannel bath sheet to wrap around herself. It clung to her, soaked in places from her wet skin. She looked down at herself... and saw bones. The sharp contours of her shoulders, her collarbone, her hips illuminated in amber candlelight and umber shadows. She had none of the padding men desired to soften her angles into curves. Her hips were slim beneath the damp flannel, though her waist drew in wasp-like, even without corsets and bindings.

She thought of Joel's caresses, which had eventually dwindled to nothing. Of Obregón's taunting lures, which would lead no farther. What did it feel like to be desired? How did those women act, what did they say, how did they move... the ones that men paid for? She thought of Doralee and her brow creased in a frown. Perhaps her sisters had been right in their girlish teasings after all.

Elizabeth Cooke, they'd giggled, wasn't the kind of woman men took to their beds. She was the kind of woman men entrusted their own daughters to, to train in the ways of proper womanhood. How strange that it was the women who failed at womanhood who were most prized by such men for rearing gentlewomen.

She gave her head a restless shake and retrieved her nightgown. Why such morbid thoughts? She had long since ceased to worry about those people, the ones like her sisters who prized a perfect dimple more than a well-formed phrase. She hadn't had a place for such worries in her head for a very long time. Was this an indication that her real problems were sliding from her weary shoulders?

The bath sheet slid to a pool at her feet, the nightgown quickly replacing it, but the thoughts remained. It had been days since she and the outlaw had escaped Cavendish. Days in which Joel would have been buried and a posse gathered. Days in which the sheriff's wrath would have grown with his frustration, his longing for vengeance. How long would he follow them? She allowed a breath of hope to flare in her heart. Surely he wouldn't think to seek them in the Diablos, would he?

She had to find Coulter. No hesitation stirred her breast as she flung open the shutters and stepped over the low window sill.

The hacienda was not yet silent, though no one was in sight on the verandah or in the courtyard. Snatches of music and raucous laughter floated toward her—hot laughter on a cold breeze: men's laughter, and a woman's cry. She glanced anxiously right and left. Where was the noise coming from? The wind whistling and moaning overhead distorted it.

She plunged into the shadows to the left. Better to seek Coulter from the shadows, than cross the brightly moonlit courtyard, a surreal mosaic of light and shadow where she might be detected.

She edged along the wall, her back plastered against it while her eyes darted about. Her fingers felt an outcropping from the adobe, another window. Her ears strained to listen through the closed shutters... no sound came from within. Coulter's room? No. Obregón would not give the outlaw the room beside hers.

She moved on to the corner. And arriving there, the sounds of revelry increased. She paused, undecided, then crept forward, peering cautiously around the building.

At once, the source of the music and laughter appeared. Too close, a large bonfire. A celebration of some sort, perhaps, for the fire was ringed by four men, one sprawled on the ground with a guitar, the others dancing in the firelight. And in their center, a female form, swaying to the guitar's violently undulating music.

Elizabeth started to go in the other direction, away from the risk of discovery. Yet she remained still, watching, realizing that she was in no danger from these people, for they were too caught up in their own activities to be aware of her.

And watching the woman, Elizabeth allowed herself to be caught up with them. She had never seen anything like it...

The woman's slender back was turned toward Elizabeth, her body's languid movements at odds with the music's pounding rhythm, her hips swaying hypnotically. One of the men stepped forward and cupped them in his hands. Elizabeth felt a surge of dismay as he crouched low to the woman's tiny form and pressed himself against the dancer... and still she moved, now more slowly, rubbing against him, not caring that the other men watched, circling closer, the music slowing, keeping time with her body's rhythm.

The man threw back his head and howled, a drunken, laughing howl that seemed to break the spell, but only temporarily, until another thrust himself forward and pulled her away from the first. He too tried to press himself against her, but this time she struck out, her hand slapping his face with a smack that Elizabeth heard even above their noise.

The other men's approving shouts echoed, and the woman backed away, then stopped still.

From the shadows, Don Obregón stepped forward, holding a small, carved chest in his long, pale fingers. The music stopped and the men circled closer, the guitarist slinging his instrument aside and joining them.

Obregón approached the woman, firelight dancing over his sinister smile. From the box he lifted something small, something pinched between his thumb and forefinger that Elizabeth couldn't see. He held it upraised, and even the man who moments before had seemed consumed with sating his lust with the willing woman now seemed transfixed. They all stared at Obregón, until he lowered his hand and approached the woman.

She was waiting for him, her mouth gaping open, her tongue extended before he arrived. She closed her lips around his fingers, sucking and licking to remove all traces of the drug. For that was what it must be, Elizabeth realized. Obregón smiled, opened the coffer again and gave each of the men a portion. Last, he took some for himself.

Then, with a careless snap of his fingers, he indicated for them to continue. The guitar player dropped to a boulder wedged into the hard ground and began playing his instrument again; the rhythm accelerated, pumping into their veins with its turbulent power.

The woman's black hair hung to her waist, stopping just short of her clinging skirt, and she raised her arms languidly, lifting her hair off her back, rotating slowly, slowly, until she faced the shadows where Elizabeth was hiding.

Elizabeth covered a gasp with her hands, unable to move. The woman's blouse gaped open, revealing small but womanly breasts bobbing gently with her movements, and even as she moved a man reached out and grabbed one, squeezing it with one hand as he rubbed his groin suggestively with the other. But it wasn't the crudeness that shocked Elizabeth, though that was certainly enough. It was the identity of the woman herself.

Dulcita.

Her childlike features, so deceptively innocent, contorted with lust. Her lips full and slack, her eyes closed, she pressed forward against the man's hand, turned into his embrace, and began her rubbing movements, against his leg, against his groin, against his hand as it fumbled between them and loosened his trousers to slide down his thighs. He tried to lift her to him, but she spun wildly away.

Teeth bared, she whirled to face Obregón. Flinging her hair out of her face, she advanced toward him. He stood still, his eyes narrowed as he watched her advance, her small breasts cupped in her hands in invitation. She stopped inches away from him, her chin outthrust in confidence.

But Obregón merely glanced down at her exposed flesh, then shook his head. He stepped back and leaned his slim, black-clad hip against an outcropping of rock, folding his arms across his chest. With a flick of a finger, he motioned them to continue.

Dulcita stared sullenly, her hands massaging her breasts as she eyed him. But this time when hands grabbed her from behind and pulled her into a rough embrace, she was ready.

The guitar stopped, all activity suspended as they recognized that the preliminaries were over. Dulcita spread on the ground, her hips undulating to her own inner music, her head rocking back and forth as she reached out. The man covered her, her legs wrapping around him, the others watched, waiting their turns.

And from his spot on the periphery, Obregón, too watched, his eyes glazed with the drug, with desire.

Elizabeth tore herself away, her heart pounding. Bile rose in her throat, and she gulped at the cold air, plunging headlong down the verandah, back to the safety of her own bedroom. But as she climbed through the window to her room, the absurdity of her situation struck her. Safe, here? Under El Diablo's own roof? Never.

She dashed toward the wardrobe to get dressed, to prepare to leave—and slammed into a hard, masculine chest. Before she could react, strong arms locked around her in an iron grip. She threw her head back to scream, her panic welling up to a fever pitch, but swallowed the sound before it escaped her lips.

Coulter.

He gave her a rough shake. "Where have you been?" he demanded.

But so relieved was she to see his familiar hard eyes glaring down at her, his clean, sharp features bathed in moonlight, his blessed strength towering over her, she collapsed against him, gasping, not caring that his sizzling anger was directed at her.

"I said, where have you been?" he repeated harshly. His hands closed over her shoulders and he pushed her away. "Who were you with?"

She opened her mouth but was unable to speak, her body trembled, her teeth chattered.

Coulter yanked a blanket from the bed and wrapped it around her, his hands rough, his expression gentle. She sank to the edge of the bed.

Finally, she recovered herself enough to respond. "I wasn't with anyone. I was alone. I was looking for you." Then she saw the gaping wardrobe and the confusion of skirts and petticoats he had obviously ransacked. Her head snapped up and she demanded, "Why are you in my room?"

"Looking for something that's mine."

She clutched the blanket around her shoulders, her eyes trained on a flounce of white lace at his feet. Searching for something of his, in the dead woman's things. She pushed aside a tremor of emotion she dared not examine.

"I certainly hope you don't intend to leave this mess for me."

He seemed startled, and glanced from her to the scattered clothing, to her again. His hard eyes seemed to bear a trace of embarrassment, perhaps even guilt.

Her words were even, measured, belying the underlying emotion. "Did you find what you were looking for?"

He nodded.

She followed his gaze to the small, rectangular bundle wrapped in coarse fabric on the floor beneath the window. Then, stabbing in the dark, "You were going to leave, weren't you?"

"I can't stay here." His lean hand reached to massage the back of his neck. "Neither can you."

Relief flowed through her and filled her with warmth. "Tonight?"

Coulter rose slowly, then gave a curt nod. "That's why I'm here."

"But how," she demanded. "How will we get out? Won't there be guards, and—"

"I know the ways, ways they don't even know. I know these mountains better than Obregón." His face consumed in shadows, his voice changed, more gravelly and pained. "I've come in and out of this encampment plenty of times without Obregón knowing."

To see Susannah.

He didn't say it; he didn't need to. Elizabeth didn't need to ask. After a moment's hesitation, she raised her chin. It was none of her concern.

"You need some clothes." His gaze took in her thin gown, transparent in the soft glow. He swallowed, and she couldn't miss the flicker of reaction that played across his face. Then he tore his attention away and began rummaging through the wardrobe.

"There's gotta be something in here you can wear. Susannah had some riding things."

"I think I can handle that myself," she said, pushing past him. "If you'll just step outside a moment, I'll dress and—"

"All right, but don't do anything to attract attention. We won't be leaving till later." It was too dark to see, yet she was sure he was blushing. "I'm sorry about the mess. Do whatever you must with it. I'll be back for you in a few hours. They'll all be dead to the world. No one will notice then."

She nodded and Coulter grabbed the carpetbag and headed for the window, a look of deadly intent on his features, the heel of his hand rested on his gun butt. She followed after, heart pounding, blood racing.

He afforded her only the most cursory of glances. "You should try and get some sleep!"

His soft footfalls had disappeared before she finally closed the shutters and bolted them.

Obregón stood high on the slope of the mountain, his eyes taking in the hacienda spread in the canyon below. From his vantage point the campfires of his men were mere flickers of gold against a black backdrop. His gaze lingered on one campfire in particular. He thought of Dulcita's swaying hips, her conical breasts, and felt a swelling in his loins.

There was a time when he would have joined them in their game. Sweet young flesh such as Dulcita's had assuaged his lusts before, but since Susannah he had found no appeal in such brazen overtures. And now, with Susannah dead, he felt his need growing. He had not touched a woman in a very long time...

But his needs were more selective, now. Dulcita and her kind served his purposes by servicing his men. Though she left much to be desired as a servant, her talents with his men more than paid her keep.

All but him. A restlessness crept through his veins, and he found that his thoughts filled with visions of the new woman,

Elizabeth. Unlike Dulcita, her sensuality was latent, but the fire was there, waiting to be stoked, to be stirred.

Like Susannah's had been.

Susannah had left a raw, gaping hole in his life that waited to be filled. Coulter didn't understand, couldn't understand. But what could one expect? Coulter suppressed his feelings, his emotions; he was incapable of understanding what Susannah had gotten from Don Miguél Obregón.

It didn't matter if Coulter understood. Between them, he and his Susannah had shared a sweet dream that none could destroy. A dream of normalcy. She was his Doña, he was her Don.

Now she was gone.

But fate had given him another woman, not Susannah, but perhaps better. He could be patient. He could get past her reluctance, create a need in her that matched his own. He had done it before.

The restlessness stirred relentlessly in his blood. He plunged his hands deep in his pockets and stared down at the hacienda. Perhaps, a small portion of peyote... yes, on this night, he felt the need for those sweet dreams...

He moved catlike down the slope, slipping into the hacienda unnoticed. As he moved toward his room at the end of the dimly-lit passage, he paused outside a closed door.

Susannah's door.

No. He shook his head. Elizabeth Dougherty's door.

He placed his hand on the door handle, long, pale fingers against the heavy black iron latch. She would be asleep. Perhaps...

But, no. He ran his fingers through his hair, sleeking the heavy locks out of his eyes. It was too soon... too soon.

He walked on, more slowly this time, to the next door, his door. He slipped the key in the lock and turned, entering soundlessly. He scratched a match against the door frame, but the tiny glow did little to illuminate the inky blackness. He touched it to the wick of the oil lamp on a massive oak desk by the door; the glow spread, revealing his sanctum.

He crossed the polished wood floor, gleaming beneath his feet, no rugs to muffle the staccato sounds. With thick adobe walls, his noises never carried, and even in the cold of winter, he found the sounds of his pacings soothing to his ears.

His bed, an immense, baroque four-poster of Spanish design, had already been turned back for him, its brocade coverlet amply padded with blankets to warm him. Above the bed, the draped portrait reminded him how lonely night could be. La Diabla, Only half her face and body were visible; the silky black drape hung loosely from the top of the frame, revealing only half of its allure, as if a careless hand had attempted to snatch it away and only half-succeeded. But half was enough.

The image etched in his mind was gold-tinged alabaster, pure, still and frozen in death. But it seemed to come to life on the wall above his bed. Hair like spun moonbeams, her features an exquisite blend of pale beauty, yet the dark secrets behind that perfect face...

Susannah.

Muerte.

And gone with her, some of the power he had possessed so successfully for so long.

He extracted a key from his vest pocket, and unlocked the low, ornate chest beside his bed. He raised the lid high, and its well-oiled hinges voiced no protest. His hand lingered over the jars and tins that lay across its bottom, coming to rest on a plain, metal tin without decoration. With a pleasurable sigh, he opened the tin, revealing its treasure of dried gray buttons, the fruit of the peyote cactus, the source of living dreams.

He fingered one lovingly. The woman, Elizabeth, would soon be ready for what he had to offer her. He would not have to wait much longer.

Only long enough to rid himself of Coulter.

He frowned. Even with Susannah, he'd never had to consider that before. Coulter had saved his life... but Susannah had been different. She had no other options, and Coulter knew it.

This woman, Elizabeth Dougherty, she might spur Coulter on to fight. And in a fight, Obregón knew one thing for certain: the only way to defeat Coulter was to fight without mercy, without honor.

Disturbing thoughts, and he didn't want to be disturbed. Already, his pulse quickened with tension. A quick decision, and he dropped the button back into the tin and snapped it shut. Instead, he reached for a brown bottle of his own distillation. He lifted it to the light; the liquid sloshed pleasantly inside.

Yes. Tonight was special. Tonight he was saying goodbye to one and preparing for another. Tonight, he would drink the extract of the drug, savor its extra strength, bathe in its power, ready himself for the morrow, whether it be the consummation with the new woman...

Or the death of his friend.

He lifted the bottle to his lips and drank, then carefully replaced the cork stopper, replaced the bottle, and locked the chest. Soon... he slid the long, razor-sharp dagger from his supple, cordovan leather boot and thrust it beneath the mattress, then stretched out on the bed, and waited.

What seemed like hours passed, though he knew time's deceptions from past experience. Even with his eyes closed, there was no feeling of difference, no suspension of reality. His inner tension wound tighter, tighter, as if in straining for forgetfulness—the mescal was rebelling and refusing him dreams.

He squeezed his eyes tighter, but the mescal colors eluded him. No sparks of stars, no streams of crystalline shimmers, no films of delicate purples and pinks...

He couldn't see them, because Susannah was not there to share his dream.

He was no longer able to hold his eyes shut, and found himself staring at the underside of the canopy. Yet it wasn't the canopy, but instead the sky... a sky without stars. It was black, and deep, and heavy, so heavy that it pressed down upon him, robbing him of his breath, of his soul. Desperate, he thrust his arms up to push it away, but felt nothing... no sky... only cold night air, as if he were cast off alone in a dark, starless, skyless eternity of emptiness.

Finally, he managed to turn his head to the side, and the emptiness melted away as his eyes rested on the lamp, its flame of molten gold filling the room. No stars... but light... magical light... light that didn't burn, just glowed and shimmered and vibrated with each of his breaths.

He inhaled deeply, and the flame sprang toward him. He exhaled and it flew in the other direction, yet even so its illumination never varied. Again, a breath, and it sucked toward him so quickly he jerked to keep it from singeing his face, his hair, and suddenly the flame was no longer benign, but a raging inferno threatening to consume him in its cold fury...

He forced his eyes shut, taking great heaving gulps of air into his lungs, feeling the cold flames sear into him, tasting their acrid smoke, every nerve in his body prickling in heightened reaction.

Then they were upon him, the stars, a hailing maelstrom of light, flashing in dizzying quantities. The universe rocked. He clutched at the bed. His groping fingers dug into the blanket, then found his own thighs, and the pressure was reassuring. The world calmed as if it had never tilted from its axis. Like gentle rain, the stars shimmered over him, an endless stream of softly shining sparks, trickling over his body.

The bed beneath him rocked gently, erotically... and he saw it all again, through the clear film of magenta, the men, the woman Dulcita offering herself to him, and he throbbed, awakening to a turgid awareness that he needed that release, needed her red lips upon him, her clutching muscle around him, needed her .

Nooooo... The low groaning protest came from within, from without, vibrating through him like the buzz of bees as his head flung from side to side in protest, in denial. He didn't want Dulcita. He wanted Susannah. Elizabeth. Susannah. Elizabeth.

His throat dry, parched, burning, he rolled over slowly, reaching for a decanter of wine from his bedside table, raising up on one elbow in a room that refused to return to normal. He splashed the wine into the waiting goblet and raised it to his lips, stopping halfway when his gaze rested on its churning contents.

The red fluid swirled, spinning into a tight vortex of luminescent fire... no, not fire, it was heavy and dense, a richer, deeper red than any he'd ever seen. Peering into the depths of the swirling cauldron, he saw not the bottom, but an endless coil, a glimpse of forever. He might have remained captured by its image for hours, had it not occurred to him what he was peering into...

Blood.

A swirling, sucking cauldron of blood.

It reached out to him, pulling at him, clutching him, tormenting him. It was Susannah's... living... throbbing... pulsating.

He clutched the glass in unsteady hands, feeling her life throbbing through the stem of the glass, pumping into his fingertips.

"What do you want?" he rasped. The silence in the room was eloquent; she was there. He felt her presence as surely as if she breathed his air, flowed through his veins, filled his nostrils with her violet scent.

He cradled the glass against his chest, a soft crooning sound escaping his lips. How could he replace her? No wonder she didn't speak to him. He thought of the woman in the next room and a spasm of remorse shook his body.

"Forgive me ..." he whispered, tears that he had thought himself beyond shedding dropping into the wine, into her blood, blending as his heightened body throbbed to blend...

She filled his hands, boiling out of the goblet and over his wrists and onto his thighs... and now she was speaking, whispering the impassioned love-words that tormented him past all capacity for thought, into a realm where he only felt her wanting to live again... to exist with him again in their world of living dreams... wanting to fill a human form again... a perfect human form.

The world stilled, the glass in his hand was merely a glass, the wine only wine. He eased it back to the tabletop, fearful of spilling a single precious drop.

She had spoken, his Diabla.

The mystery was revealed to him, the new woman's presence clarified for him.

He closed his eyes, and let the fires dance behind his lids... calm... calm... resting, preparing.

Soon.

Chapter Twelve

ELIZABETH TOSSED RESTLESSLY in the bed, the sheets tangled around her legs. Despite the cold, she was hot, anxious. Her ears ached at the effort to hear a sound outside her window, the sign that the outlaw had come at last.

When the footsteps sounded, they came not from the window, but from the hallway. Slow, heavy, they approached the door... then stopped.

The door pushed open, allowing a wedge of muted yellow light to spill into the room.

Her muscles tensed to spring up, but she didn't. For after that first quick reaction, she realized it wasn't Coulter.

It was Miguél Obregón.

Frightened, she dared not breathe; she lay very still, waiting for the door to close again.

It did. With Miguél Obregón inside the room.

For what seemed like a very long time, he stood there in silence. She wanted to move, wanted to demand an explanation for his presence. But something about him stilled her urges. Instead, she waited like a rabbit frozen under the coyote's nose, feigning sleep, praying he would leave.

He moved closer to the bed, his movements careful, too careful. He walked like a person who weighed each movement, straining to keep them natural. She had seen Joel move so when he'd been drinking too much.

He was beside the bed now. That same sweet smell clung to him, reminding her of pipe smoke. He reached toward her, and she forced her eyes closed, forced herself to remain still as his fingers feathered through the hair that spread across her pillow. His fingers drifted closer to her face, brushing against her temple.

She couldn't help it. She flinched. Her eyes flew open and she caught her lower lip beneath her teeth.

"Querida," he whispered, and somehow she knew he was not speaking for her ears.

He bent closer, his fingers lifting the chain at her neck. The cross dragged upward, grazing the skin of her breasts, catching on the lace, and finally pulling free. He bent nearer, nearer, until his lips were grazing her chin as he examined the golden emblem, his hot breath gusting against her neck. Locked in fear, she couldn't move; even her heart seemed to cease its wild pumping. Cold and frozen, it was as if she were dead to everything but the fear that wrapped itself around her, through her, choking off the life itself from her body.

He pressed nearer, his lips dragged against her neck, then, nipped her with his sharp teeth, the pain as welcome as it was unexpected; it released her.

She sprang up then, but her scream was trapped behind his hand as he pressed his palm across her mouth, the other hand pinning her to the bed.

"Quiet, querida. We wouldn't want to attract our friend Coulter, would we?"

She twisted, flailed him with her free fist, but his strength was more than she could fight.

"I will not hurt you, querida," he whispered, his lips brushing against her temple with each word. "That is not my goal. I will show you ecstasy, I will give you heaven. I will not hurt you."

Gasping for breath, she ceased her struggle, but only because she recognized its futility.

"You will listen to me?"

She refused to answer, not giving any sign that she would agree, knowing he could feel the frantic pounding of her heart against his chest. Yet he seemed impervious to doubt. He removed his hand from her mouth. Before she could scream, his dulcet words silenced her like no others could:

"Coulter will die."

He smiled at the horror on her face. "I see I do have a hold over you, Elizabeth Dougherty. But I cannot let you misunderstand. I am simply telling you that if you scream, if you bring Coulter in here to save you, I will kill him." He struck terror in her with each measured, emotionless word. "Mark my words, querida, I can and I will."

"What do you want from me?" she asked, her chest heaving beneath the thin gown.

"That is so simple. You are no shrinking virgin, Señora Dougherty, whatever you might have one think. You know what I want from you, and you will come to me. And when you do, you will find that I can offer you delights beyond those of our friend Coulter, of your husband, of anyone on this earth. For what I offer you is not of this earth, but of another realm."

"I will kill you myself for this insult," she whispered. But she dared not speak loudly, and his smile told her he knew it. She did not believe him when he said he would not hurt her, but she believed he would kill Boone Coulter.

He released her and walked to the window. "I owe my friend so much. Twice, now, he has brought me... what he did not want to lose."

"What... what makes you think he will allow this?" she demanded hoarsely.

He shook his head sadly. "Perhaps because he did the first time. Perhaps because I will kill him if he doesn't."

"He is stronger than you."

"I have my ways." He smiled a thin mirthless smile. "I am not afraid of blood."

"And you think he is?" Elizabeth scoffed.

"I think he lost his taste for blood a long time ago, and only one thing could rekindle it."

"Susannah?"

He didn't answer, but his attention suddenly seemed more keenly focused on her, attention that chilled her with its intensity.

"I believe you are the one who will die, Miguél Obregón," she forced conviction into her shaky voice.

"Let us hope we don't have to find out." Obregón faced her, his back to the window, his silhouette rimmed with silver moonlight. His face was as black as night, as fear, as death. "I would not want to kill my friend. But I will if I must. You see, querida, they do not call me El Diablo for naught."

"But why, why do you want me? I am not worth this killing you speak of. I don't understand!"

"Ah, querida... that is the mystery, is it not? The lure, the temptation. I did not understand either, the allure you have for me. And that is why I wanted you." His words snaked around her, soft and seductive, his breath sickly sweet as he leaned nearer. "But now, now I know. Now the time has come."

Each breath was a labor, as Elizabeth's chest tightened with dismay. But she couldn't let him see, couldn't let him feed off it. Instead, she turned her face away from him. "I'm sick. I must rest."

"The time for rest is over, querida," he breathed softly. "You have regained your strength. I can feel it." Again, his hand flickered out and brushed her face.

She cringed, a slight reaction that blew through her body like a leaf on a gust of wind. Coulter would come, but she didn't know whether to be glad, or terrified. Coulter was stronger. He wouldn't let Obregón touch her. He would save her. But Obregón said he would kill him.

No, Coulter would win. Or would he?

Obregón's hand closed over her wrist, his touch so gentle, it was like a lover's. A chill ran up her arm.

"Come with me. I will not hurt you."

She shook her head violently, her hair tumbling into her face. Her heart beat in desperation as she lay still, waiting for his next move. No, she thought desperately. Don't let him see your fear. There was no way to slow the pulse beneath his fingertips.

"Ah, querida," he smiled. "Your fear has not quenched your fire. I like that very much."

"I want you to leave, now," she said, a strength in her voice that her body did not feel. "Leave my room."

He laughed, shaking his head slowly. "Bluster becomes you, Elizabeth Dougherty…" His voice faded. "Dougherty. Señora Dougherty. Ah, the mystery again. And yet, there is no mystery… only fate, playing with us like dust devils on the desert."

He held out both hands. Her gaze darted to the shuttered window. Four heartbeats. Nine heartbeats. Twelve heartbeats. She stifled the scream threatening to tear from her throat if she didn't move. Unable to remain still any longer, she sprang from the bed and flew to the window.

His hands grabbed her hair, pulling her back with a jerk that snapped her neck. Before the stinging had ceased in her scalp, the ache in her neck even begun, his fingers were caressing her shoulders, and he pushed her gently before him toward the door. Like a rabbit who had been plucked by the talons of a hawk, she was consumed by fear, yet almost unable to recognize it.

"No, no querida. You cannot get away. I have something to show you, to share with you." There was no mocking laughter in his voice now, only a chilling seductiveness.

She walked ahead of him, her heart clamoring in her breast. Should she scream and fight, Coulter would surely come. But how many others? Outnumbered, Coulter couldn't save her. Their helpless state in his horrifying camp was becoming all too clear.

So she walked down the hall steadily, slowly, Obregón's fingertips light upon her shoulder, his intent heavy upon her mind. She had no choice but to appear to submit, and wait for an opportunity to... to what?

The door ahead was open, the room filled with a ruby glow. Obregón pushed her over the threshold. "Señora Elizabeth... this is where you belong."

She opened her mouth to deny, but no sound came, for he had moved to stand before her, one long hand outstretched toward the bed behind him, the wine and candles on the bedside table. Her mind groped for something, anything that might save her.

"Don Obregón, first we must talk... the mystery... I have my questions, too."

Her name was a breathless whisper on his lips, but he made no move toward her. "Ah, Elizabeth, I can answer your questions. I can solve your mysteries... Come, querida, and I will tell you all."

He took her fingers in his, the softest, demurest of touches. With slight pressure, he pulled, and she followed, until she stood before a heavy chair beside the massive stone wall. There was no fireplace, yet the wall radiated heat. As she sank onto the hard leather surface, her hands gripping the dark oak arms, she felt her trembling subside.

He crossed to the bedside table and lifted a goblet of wine. "Will you join me?"

She shook her head.

He shrugged elegantly and sipped deeply from the goblet, his eyes closed in near-ecstasy as he slowly exhaled. "You will grow to appreciate my wine cellar, querida."

He lifted the bottle loosely in his hand and walked toward her. Her pulse skipped an erratic beat as he dropped to the ottoman at her feet. Close. Too close. Not really threatening... but still too close. His gaze wandered toward the portrait and hers followed.

She focused her eyes on Susannah's likeness, its rich colors glowing with life, the blond woman seeming to meet her gaze with calm defiance. Finally, she found her voice. "She was very beautiful."

"There are many kinds of beauty. You, too, are beautiful, Señora Dougherty. A beauty no doubt that Sheriff Dougherty recognizes and covets."

Her breath caught in her throat. She fought for it, fought for calm, as he was calmly watching her reaction. She gave her head a confused shake. "You know Clayton?"

This time, he was the one to react. His entire body went whipcord tense. "I made it my business to learn about you. I know of your husband's death, of the sheriff's pursuit of you... but I do not understand one thing. Why are you with Coulter? I do not believe he kidnapped you like they say. Not our friend... you see, I have pursued the mystery as far as I can. And still, I do not understand. Why... how did you end up with Coulter? What strange trick of fate has brought you here?"

She didn't answer.

"Why did he bring you? What use for you could Coulter have if not to lure Clayton Dougherty out of his den?"

She didn't move, yet her reaction must have been apparent. Boone Coulter and Clayton Dougherty? The outlaw was running from the sheriff, not luring him. She rubbed her aching temple with cold fingertips. How had she allowed herself to be trapped by the ravings of a madman?

Obregón leaned closer and studied her carefully, his eyes seeming to savor each detail of her face. She refused to flinch away from him, yet her very stillness betrayed her frozen fear.

His eyes narrowed with intensity. "It seems, querida, you have as much to share with me as I have to share with you. I wonder which of us will be the more surprised. But first, I must convince you that your Coulter is a lost cause. He has been nothing but the shell of a man for many years. And now, with Susannah gone, it would not surprise me if he has no will to live left in his veins."

His words nailed into her heart without mercy. Her nails dug into her palms as she fought for calm. She didn't care about Coulter. She didn't care, as long as he got her away from the madman before her. She didn't care.

"So brave, Elizabeth. And so foolish. Do you think he has any use for a woman?"

"I don't care about his needs," she grated. "What matters is that I have a use for him."

Obregón's eyes flared in surprise. "My respect for you grows, querida."

"You don't understand my situation at all." she continued, gaining strength with each word. "I am not being used by Coulter, as a lure or in any other way. He is being used by me."

"You are most certainly correct, señora. I do not understand. I hope that you will explain for me this situation."

"It is none of your concern."

"And you care nothing for Coulter's past." He sipped from his wine, relaxing, fascinated.

"His past is nothing to me." And as she spoke the words, she recognized their truth. "His past has never meant anything to me, only what I see in his eyes, read in his face, of his present. In those eyes I saw the strength of a rock when the very earth beneath my feet seemed shifting sands."

"It is such a shame that our friend did not have your admiration at a time when he needed to be lifted out of the depths of his hell. For Señora Dougherty, you possess the very strength and courage and loyalty you are finding, however mistakenly, in Boone Coulter."

She fixed him with a level gaze. "I have always been a strong woman. But I live in a world where such strength isn't enough."

"Then you live in the wrong world, querida." So quickly she hadn't the time to elude it, his hand slid toward her and closed over her arm, softly, yet insistently.

Before she could react, he had pulled her to her feet. "I can show you a world where you don't need strength, a world of dreams and illusions that mean more than life itself... a world of color and sensation. A world to make you forget whatever it is that haunts you in this one."

She shook her head, the trembling wracking through her body again, but his fingers closed over her chin and held it still. "Do not turn away from paradise, Elizabeth. Do not turn away from me."

"No!"

"It is Coulter, isn't it?" he demanded angrily. "You reject me because you harbor a longing for the outlaw. Admit it, you little fool!"

"You're mad!" She shoved forward, but his grip dug into her arm.

"No, I'm not crazy, querida, though you aren't the first to tell me so. You are the one who deludes yourself." He shoved her ahead of him toward the bed, toward the beautiful Susannah's watchful gaze. "First you want to know of Coulter, then you tell me you don't need to know. You don't want to know. Perhaps you are right, querida. You don't want to know. You are afraid to know the truth."

His fingers dug into her arms. He shoved her forward, and when she struggled, he circled her and jerked her from the front. "Look at the truth about Susannah and tell me it does not matter!" Without releasing her arm, he snatched the drape away from the portrait. The silk slithered to the bed and melted into a pool of black. She gasped.

The face that had seemed perfection, was revealed as half ecstasy, half agony... the entire left portion of Susannah's face was twisted with vivid red scars.

"My God," she whispered, the words choking breaths of horror.

Obregón's responding laughter was bitter. "Do not call on God's mercy, querida. God abandoned this hacienda long ago."

She squeezed her eyes closed and tears scalded the back of her lids.

"Yes," he corrected harshly, then spun her to face him. "Yes, that is my Susannah. That is La Diabla, and now you think you know why. You look at her and judge. But you are wrong, do you understand me? Wrong!"

He grabbed her delicate shoulders in an iron grip and shook her hard. His eyes were black with anger, with passion, with pain.

"You do not know her! You cannot judge! You see the scars, and you are disgusted, but I tell you she was beautiful! Inside, she was beautiful, and she never deserved what your husband and his brother did to her!"

"I don't understand," she pleaded, but her words fell on deaf ears.

His eyes were trained on the portrait, and he released her with a sneer. "You think," he continued, his voice a low murmur, "you can trust Coulter to be your strength, but you are a fool. He too has scars, but his scars are on the inside, where you cannot see."

She inched backward, her arms folded around her middle, her icy fingers locked over her elbows in a desperate grip. What other horrors could this place hide?

"Señor Obregón, please, do not keep me here any longer. There is no reason ..."

Again, his anger kindled. "There is every reason. You must know that your husband and his brother destroyed my Susannah, that one of them left her to die in a blazing inferno, and the other took what remained of her heart and crushed it in his hands, leaving her to an existence without life. You must know that your Coulter has mercilessly and methodically hunted each man responsible for her pain, and killed them one by one, until all that remained were your husband, and his brother.

"Tell me, Elizabeth Dougherty," he continued, his voice rising. "Tell me who is living, now? Has Coulter finished his vendetta, or does it continue? You are the lure to bring the last of those villains to their deaths."

"No," she moaned, as he drew closer, his red-rimmed eyes boring into her.

"What is the matter with you Señora Dougherty? You cannot accept the truth? That you are being used by a cold-blooded killer to lure in his prey?"

"No!" she screamed. "Not my husband! He didn't do anything! He was incapable of the things you say! He was gentle, and kind to me always! How dare you defile his memory!"

"Tell me, did Joel Dougherty die a dreadful, lingering death? Did Coulter make him die in agony, as Susannah lived in agony?"

"He didn't kill Joel." Her knuckles were white, the pulse throbbing in the tender hollow at the base of her neck.

"How can you be sure?" Obregón pushed, his brows arching in disbelief. "Because you do not want to believe it is so?"

"Coulter was locked in a jail cell when my husband took a gun and put it in his mouth and pulled the trigger and blew half his face away!" Her throat was raw with emotion, with tears. "He killed himself!"

"Then he did not suffer enough."

"He suffered. You must believe me," she whispered, her eyes wet with moisture. "He suffered every day that I knew him, only I never knew why. I still do not know, because I don't believe your lies."

His eyes flamed. "Tell me how he suffered."

"Never." Her angrily upthrust chin and glaring eyes defied his will to glory in Joel's pain.

His hoarse laughter filled the room. "Ah, fate. Ah, mystery. If only his miserable soul could see us together, how he would suffer. If only I could make him suffer as he made my Susannah . . ."

He raised the wine bottle to his lips and drank deeply. "I am tired of waiting, querida. The time has come for me to teach you the rest of my secrets." He reached out to touch her, and she flinched, bringing more laughter to his lips. "If only he could see."

"No!" She spun away and he grasped her, but caught only the edge of her gown, the fabric ripping away in his hand, exposing a shoulder, a breast. She sprinted forward; her hands closed over the heavy brass door handle, and she pulled, jerked, but it didn't give.

Locked.

Chapter Thirteen

ELIZABETH WHIRLED, PRESSED her back against the door and stared at Obregón, his eyes lidded, his lips taut.

"You cannot run from me."

Her gaze darted around the room at the stucco walls, the heavy wall hangings, and she choked back an angry sob. But wait. There was a window. She'd passed it when she'd gone out in the night looking for Coulter. It must be behind one of the hangings.

Obregón crossed the distance between them and reached for her. Before she could protest, his lips were upon her neck, his hands closing around her waist, and she could tell that he was driven by some savage emotion, propelled by more than wine and desire.

"No!" She pounded at his shoulders, but to no avail. She felt herself being pushed farther and farther backward, until her thighs struck the bed, and then he was bending, forcing her down.

"Querida…"

Her throat vibrated under his rumbling endearment, and she shrank away, but not far enough, for again, his mouth sought the sunburned expanse of her neck, gliding a course downward to where the reddened skin turned to white and the gold chain rolled beneath his lips as he followed its length.

Her fingers yanked his ebony hair and his head raised; behind his smoldering black eyes burned a fervor of possession that would brook no resistance. "The time has come to teach you the dreams ..."

Her hand swung out and slapped him with all the force she could muster. "Get off!"

But his mouth closed over hers, his taste sickly and sweet as he pressed savagely until her lips opened beneath his.

The heels of her hands dug into his shoulders and she pushed, but to no avail. Bitterness welled in her throat.

She twisted beneath him and he shoved her back against the pillows, pinning her down. His fingers dug into the hollows beneath her jaw until any movement was excruciating.

A low sound crept from his throat and his body pressed hers against the bed, flattening her breasts beneath him. She felt his arousal against her thighs. The fingers at her throat pushed deeper, bruising, threatening to cut off her air. Still his lips ravaged her face, his breath heavy and cloyed with smoke.

She choked and he pulled away, leaving her gasping for air. He bestowed her with a lingering gaze, then lifted the crystal goblet of blood red wine from the table. He uncorked a small brown bottle with his other hand and tilted its lip to the goblet. A thin stream of dark liquid poured into the wine.

"These dreams are for you," he murmured. "For both of us." His patrician features angled upward toward the portrait above their heads, then lowered back to her. "It is meant to be."

"No!" She yanked away from him, from the cold goblet he was pressing against her lips. She struck out to fling it away, but only managed to swat it. Dark stains splashed on her white nightgown, the liquid streamed down the hollow between her breasts.

His eyes flared with shock, then with rage; he set the goblet down with a jolt.

She twisted and churned, but only her head had the freedom of movement, and she was helpless to do anything but watch as he bared his teeth and dipped his head closer, finding the well of wine between her breasts, and tongued it into his mouth.

And then he was sliding up her body, his lips seeking hers, and only when his tongue pressed her lips open did she realize his intention.

She clamped her teeth closed, but still the acrid taste of tainted wine trickled in. She strained to spit it out, but then his tongue was plunging deep into her mouth, choking her, and her eyes filled with burning tears as she swallowed convulsively and the liquid burned its way down her throat.

"Now you will know, querida," he growled against her. "Now you will share the dreams. You will give me back what was stolen from me. What was stolen from her ..." His eyes raised to the portrait above her, and in bulging veins at his temples seemed to throb with an unearthly desire. "It is meant to be ..."

Again his head dipped down, his tongue stroked her damp skin, but this time as she fought the small gold cross jabbed into his mouth, a cut on his lower lip filling with blood. For a long moment he seemed too stunned to react, then as the blood dropped onto her bare breast, his lips twisted in a savage grimace.

With a violent curse, he seized the gold emblem in his hand —

Something within her burst.

Before Obregón could snap the chain from her neck, Elizabeth's hands were at his head, thumbs on his temples, pressing with all the strength she had.

The cross fell from his fingers and his hands closed over her wrists. In a split-second he had broken her grip.

But not her spirit. Not her fear. Not her soul.

She twisted away and lunged again, reaching wildly for something, anything, to use as a weapon. Her hand struck the corner of the bedside table. She was aware of stinging pain, but continued groping down the side of the bed; her fingers grazed a cylindrical metal object jutting from beneath the mattress, closed over it; she yanked it out and raised it up, and lamplight glinted off its razor-edge.

A knife.

Her fingers curled around its smooth hilt, and she plunged it downward with all the strength she possessed.

A blow to her hand shot a shaft of pain up her arm and the knife clattered to the floor. Long, lean fingers closed over Obregón's shoulders and ripped his body from hers.

She saw her rescuer.

Coulter, his face twisted with rage, smashed his fist into Obregón's jaw and sent him sprawling backward against the table. The lamp flew through the air and crashed in the corner, exploding in a ball of harmless flame as the liquid spread across the tile floor. Up the adobe wall, and extinguished itself. Obregón got up, staggered forward, and again, Coulter struck. And again, until he crumpled to the floor.

Elizabeth sprang from the bed and dove for the knife. But Coulter's voice stopped her.

"No, lady... don't do it," he gasped.

"But, why…" She trembled, panting for breath, confused. "He tried to …"

"You don't want to kill him. You'll carry his face with you the rest of your life. You'll never escape him then."

In a flash, she saw the faces of his victims in the pain of his hard, cold eyes. Never to escape...

His arm closed around her waist as her knees buckled. She fell against him, relief sliding through her like quicksilver. He pulled her firmly against his body and she succumbed, his strength throbbing through her anew.

After a few moments, he released her. He yanked a sheet from the bed, his movements fluid and economical. He ripped two lengths of linen from the sheet, bound Obregón's wrists and ankles, then lugged him onto the bed. He towered over the don, staring down at him. His words were soft, pained. "Mi amigo... mi hermano…"

And then he grabbed her arm and pulled her toward the door, his brow creased with concern, his golden-brown eyes riveted on the ragged, stained nightgown she clasped to her. "Come on. We're gettin' out of here."

She stopped short. "But the lock... how?"

"I have Susannah's key."

She inhaled deeply. "Thank God."

Elizabeth and Coulter were no sooner mounted on horseback and riding out of the silent hacienda, than the stars above began to whirl in a kaleidoscope of dizzying, terrifying color. The earth seemed to rock with each of the mare's steps. Eyes frozen wide, she stared ahead, sheer willpower keeping her upright, until the hacienda was behind them, and the high, sheer walls of the canyon surrounded them as they followed its winding way.

"Mr. Coulter."

His head snapped around at the sound of her voice.

"Wait."

He reined in his horse, though it stamped impatiently at the delay. She drew beside him and offered him her reins in her trembling left hand; her right clutching the saddle horn seemed all that kept her astride. "You'll have to take them." And lest he think the worst, she was compelled to add, "It isn't my weakness, I assure you. It's the effects of something he made me drink."

"What?" he demanded, seizing the reins and reaching for her arm. "What did he give you?"

"Not much," she assured him, shuddering at the memory. "Only a swallow, but I need both hands to hold on ..."

"No, you don't." He held out his arms to her. "You'll ride with me."

"But that will slow us down. They'll be following."

"I'll worry about that. You're riding with me."

She went into his arms willingly, the world spinning when for a split-second she was suspended between the horses, only his strong grip keeping her from falling. Then she was in front of him in the saddle and his hard chest supported her back.

The Diablos rose above them, sheer walls of rock, flanked with flowing ripples of earth worn down by centuries of hot winds. What had Obregón said? The face of the Diablos... and she was reminded of the dead woman's face. She had seen two sides of the Diablos, two sides of their tortured master.

As they covered the miles, her mind wandered between dream and nightmare, but never did she forget Coulter's presence. His strength.

She was at rest.

The first rays of sun spilled softly over the salt plain when they emerged from the Diablos. Elizabeth stirred in Coulter's arms. Her own muscles were cramped from her position, how must his feel?

But when she started to pull away, his arm tightened around her. "Aren't you tired?" she asked softly.

"I'm used to it." His gloved hands tightened on the reins, and she felt his thighs move behind her as she spurred Sage to a faster pace. The stallion sprang forward, seemingly undaunted by its extra load, moving beneath them with seductive grace.

Ahead of them, the towering mountain, El Capitan, thrust skyward, walls of limestone, the southernmost tongue of the Guadalupe range of mountains. A beacon dominating the northern horizon, the golden mountain heralded a new challenge.

But with the sun on her shoulders and Coulter at her back, Elizabeth felt equal to any challenge.

Chapter Fourteen

OCCASIONALLY THE WOMAN shifted against him, but for the most part, she slept. She needed sleep. She needed rest. Guilt ate at him, guilt at pushing her too far, too soon. Guilt at taking her into Obregón's lair. Guilt at letting his own grief for Susannah sweep all thoughts of this woman out of his mind.

But it wasn't guilt that made him keep her in his arms.

They'd be at the foot of the Guadalupes soon, and he knew of a secluded spring there at the base of the escarpment. She wore one of Susannah's high-necked white shirts, loose-fitting and full-sleeved. And no matter how he tried not to, he couldn't keep his eyes away from the open neckline, from the dark stains on her skin. Each glance was a stabbing reminder of what Obregón had attempted, what Coulter had almost been too late to stop. Each glance strengthened his resolve to get her to the spring where she could erase Obregón's touch from her flesh. Each glance taunted him with a knowledge about himself that he couldn't deny.

It wasn't guilt that made him keep her in his arms.

They would spend the night in the highlands, then descend into his canyon refuge tomorrow. There, she would get the rest she needed. And he... he would continue as he had for as long as he could remember, denying himself such comfort. Only now, it would be harder.

Now that comfort had a name: Elizabeth.

The sun was almost directly overhead when they arrived at the spring. Elizabeth had long been riding the mare. Coulter had made no objection when she'd finally bestirred herself to change mounts.

Kneeling at the edge of the spring a few yards away from the horses, she cupped the cold water in her hands and drank, then bent closer to the water's smooth surface and buried her face in it. Stinging and cold, it shocked her senses, braced her, revived her, until she was forced to come up for breath, gasping and even laughing at her foolishness.

She, who couldn't even swim. She, who'd never liked water much, finding ponds and streams pleasant to look upon if one wasn't forced to get too near. She was laughing like a child at the clean, cold feel of water on her skin, trickling down her shoulders, soaking the tendrils of hair that framed her face. The desert had taught her a new respect for water.

Again she splashed water over her, cupping it and pouring it down the front of her blouse, rubbing it over her neck and chest, shivering as it slid between her breasts.

A spray of pebbles skittered down the slope and landed in the spring in a series of wet plops. She raised up and saw the outlaw, his canteen in his gloved hand. She folded her arms across her damp, cotton-covered breasts.

A deep flush spread up his neck; he jerked his gaze away. He dropped to his knees, drank, filled his canteen.

If he hadn't stared at her quite so intently, if he hadn't seemed so frozen in place, she might have thought that he had been merely on his way to fill his canteen. If she hadn't seen the hungry, aching expression in his dark eyes.

But she had seen it. She had read his hunger. She had responded to it. Her skin flushed red.

She looked down at herself for the first time and saw the flecks of blood on her breast, the dark residue of wine between her breasts. She clasped her arms tighter, hiding her shame from him.

He rose from the ground, and she sensed his strain as he looked past her at the horses, heading toward them without a word. Just as he passed her, he stopped. She stared up at him, a brooding silhouette against the midday sun.

"Here." He shoved a thick, red handkerchief into her hand, then continued toward the horses.

After a moment's stunned silence, she soaked the fabric and rubbed her skin clean. He'd noticed as well.

Coulter stood high above the campsite, his booted feet braced wide on the uneven ground. The night winds tore at him, whipping his hair into his eyes.

It was hazardous moving around the mountain with nothing but moonlight to illuminate the way. But somehow, the chance of disturbing a rattler seemed less dangerous than staying at the campsite with the woman only yards away.

He was a fool.

He should put the feel of her body, soft and pliant against his, out of his mind. And he told himself firmly, desperately, that if it were only the glimpses of female flesh that haunted him, he could handle it well enough. Even the sight of her washing, laughing, water sparkling on her lashes like diamonds... he'd never seen her laugh before. Not even smile, that he could remember. He could put it out of his mind. He could refuse to think about it.

But he could not stop thinking about the bruises on her neck, nor the fragile contours of her face twisted in pain and anger and fear, nor the horror of what might have happened to her.

He could not forget those things.

So he stood high above, leaving her to sleep in peace, if there was peace for either of them. Let the night wind howl through the peaks above him. Let the stars mock and taunt him. She wasn't his to possess. He didn't deserve her.

A long ago story flickered into his memory. For the first time, he doubted his father's biblical teachings. For the first time, he knew without a doubt, that it wasn't Eve who had succumbed to the lure of the forbidden fruit.

Finally, he could stay there no longer. He, too, needed sleep, if he was going to get her to the canyon tomorrow.

Elizabeth awoke to find herself alone.

The stars were a shimmering blanket against the black velvet sky, with only a crescent moon competing for their brilliance. There was no fire, for they'd eaten jerky and hard, dry tortillas on horseback. No fire to warm her, no fire to cast its feeble light on the empty bedroll opposite her.

She raised stiffly on an elbow. Where was he?

She scanned the clearing, but nowhere was his tall, lean form. Not a shadow moved, other than the wind. The ground was hard beneath her, and twigs and sharp-edged stones cut into her, even through the bedroll and her clothes.

Her attention stayed on the empty bedroll.

Surely he must be as tired as she, even more so. Where was he? She lay slowly back down and stared up at the sky. Her body's most urgent need for rest satisfied, now she was restless, empty, aching.

She wanted the outlaw beside her. Not only because she was afraid, but because she was... confused. She covered her eyes with the back of her hand and forced herself to breathe deeply. She must sleep.

Closing her eyes brought back the nightmare of Obregón. If only... if only... if only Coulter were here to hold her again. Tears clogged her throat as she remembered the feel of his hands stroking her back, their strength pressing her head against his chest.

She curled into a tight ball, her hands crossed and clasped over her shoulders, her breasts full and aching beneath her arms, her body shaking with silent tears. A gnawing need for his touch grew deep within her. If he were here, she would surely shame herself. If he were here, she would ask him to hold her again. A soft sob escaped her lips.

She hadn't heard his approach. When first he touched her shoulder, she jumped, rolling over to face his crouching figure with her eyes wide and large and black in her delicate face. Her lips parted, half-cry, half-gasp.

"Are you all right?" And when she didn't answer, he asked again, "Is something wrong?"

All of the somethings that were wrong flooded over her, and she reached for his hand, still on her shoulder, and closed her fingers around it.

He stared down at her hand covering his, her shoulder bare where her blouse had slipped from it. His hand was pinned, pinned between her body and her palm.

"I thought you needed... something," he whispered hoarsely.

I do... But she couldn't say the words, couldn't bear to hear his refusal. His hand moved—he was pulling it away—and she couldn't stop herself from squeezing it harder, holding it still against her. Even the merest of contacts was precious... too precious to break.

She closed her eyes and would have swayed, had not the ground been under her. And yet, even that hard ground seemed to quiver beneath her. Touch me, she begged silently, with eyes that fluttered open and pierced his with their longing, with her hand clasping his in desperation. Then, raising her face to his despite her shame, Don't make me say it. Don't make me ask.

At first, it seemed little more than her own pulse. He seemed not to move at all, his gaze meeting hers in pained silence. Then, there was no denying the sensation of his thumb stroking her collarbone, softly, tentatively.

She was afraid to move lest he stop, yet every part of her strained toward him. The strokes continued, feather-light, as if he were fascinated by the sheer sensation of her skin. She understood. Each touch of his calloused thumb against her shoulder drew a stronger reaction, until she couldn't restrain the impulse to turn her head toward him and press her lips against the back of his hand.

He pulled away as if stung.

Her humiliation spread its heat across her skin.

She raised up slowly, her hair in disarray around her face and over her shoulders. He was pulling away; she could sense his withdrawal. She reached for his hand again, and he flinched.

"No." His voice was tight, strangled. "You don't know what you're doing."

"I do," she whispered. "Oh yes, I do."

She raised to her knees facing him. He didn't move. She reached for his hand, and this time he didn't pull away. She cupped his hand in both of hers and raised it to her lips, pressed a kiss against his palm, felt him react, placed his palm over her heart. Her nipple swelled beneath his hand and she drew in a quick gasp. He felt it, too. It was in his touch, the sudden change, the sudden charge of electricity as his palm moved ever so slightly, scraping against the smooth texture of her blouse, the hard imprint of the crest of her breast.

His entire body was rigid, as if every sensation in his body was concentrated in the center of his palm... its slow circling against her hypnotic to them both. She clamped her teeth over her lower lip, fighting the moan that threatened to erupt from deep within her.

Her fingers went to the buttons of her blouse; his hand ceased its movement. She unfastened them one by one, her eyes never leaving his.

He swallowed, the contours of his face lean and shadowed, highlighted by only the most gracious of moonlight that revealed as much of his expression as her heart, near to bursting, could bear.

She read his pain, his torment, and knew what she was doing to him, if not why he reacted so. She raised her chin in challenge.

She was selfish enough, in need of his comfort enough, not to care. She knew without understanding why, that he was poised on the brink of turning away from her. But she could see in his face that if she offered herself, if she parted her blouse for his hungry eyes, he would never find the strength to deny them both what they so obviously needed and wanted.

But her fingers fell away from the blouse, and she knelt before him still covered, only a whisper of skin evident through the parting of fabric, and with the wind howling through the peaks above them and the blood slowing in her veins... she waited.

When he moved, it wasn't to part her blouse. His hands rose slowly, brushing her hair away from her neck and shoulders, and as he gazed at her throat, she saw his eyes flinch with pain. When he bent closer, it wasn't her mouth his lips sought, or her breasts, but the dark bruises on her neck... soothing, tender kisses he bestowed on them. And she filled with a tender aching unlike any she'd ever known.

His hands framed her face with a gentle hesitancy, this outlaw of hers. His lips were tentative, trembling, as was his entire body, as was hers. Each movement was slow, deliberate, almost painfully so.

Her throat ached with words of tenderness and love she dared not say. His name quivered on her lips but would not come. Instead, her hands mimicked his, stroking his hair away from his eyes, his temples, as his lips worked their magic on her skin.

And then, when she thought she could bear it no longer, he trailed his lips upward. She flung her head back, baring her jaw to him, angling her cheek toward him as his lips dragged over the tender expanse of her skin.

She leaned into the sensations, into his body, her hands holding his face to hers just as his held her. His lips fused against hers, her body melted against his, with a passion born of a lifetime of need.

Between them, the soft fabric of her blouse slipped open and his coarse shirt abraded her breasts, sending sensations shooting through her body.

He felt it too, and his hands feathered the swell of breasts exposed between them, stroking. His touch spoke of longing, of fear. Her body responded to that knowledge, with the delicacy of his touch upon her skin, with the fragile emotion quivering between them.

She turned toward him and their lips met again—she gasped and pulled back and met his startled, hungry expression, then his mouth found hers again, fusing, tasting, exploring, learning to kiss all over again, as if neither had experienced the act before.

His hands spanned her back, and she felt him easing her down onto the hard ground, only the thin bedroll to protect her, but she no longer felt the twigs, the stones, for she was lost in a world of his creation.

His head dipped lower, lingering inches away with his warm breath dusting her breasts with moist heat. His fingers found a swollen peak, explored its smooth texture, then he cupped the full weight in his hand as his lips covered it.

She arched into the feelings, the sensations of his wet suction, his tongue playing across the hard tip, then circling to drive her beyond bearing. She pressed the back of her hand to her lips to keep from crying out, and he stopped, and she could breathe again.

He began his tender torment on the other breast, suckling, seeking to nurture, to be nurtured, and this time she cried out.

He broke the contact leaving her cold, empty, shivering. His face, starlit contours and night shadows, was dazed, stricken. "I hurt you."

She could only shake her head in denial, fighting for words to tell him what he was doing to her. Finally, her lips would move again, she recovered her voice. "Mr. Coulter," she whispered, "If you truly want to hurt me, leave me as I am now, aching with my need for you, and I swear I will die …"

His jaw clenched and she saw the emotions warring within him. "I should. For your sake, I should leave you …" He bent closer, his lips brushing hers, his words a mere whisper. "God forgive me. I can't."

Joy flooded through her. She rose to meet his kiss, sliding her fingers into his hair and pulling him down with her. He shifted his weight and covered her surrounding her with warmth where there had been cold.

Again, his hand found her breast, his lips found her throat, and she surrendered herself to the exquisite agony he evoked with the slightest touch. But it was more, far more, than that. For in his embrace she felt a yearning that equaled her own, a need that surpassed mere desire.

His hand slid lower, and as his fingers probed beneath the waistband of her split-skirt, she reached down to help him unfasten the cumbersome buttons. On a stifled moan, she fumbled with the closure.

He raised up, allowing her hands the freedom they needed, but as the button sprang free, his lips found the tender skin beneath her breasts, his tongue traced their contours, and her hands fell limply to her sides. It was as if he was determined to explore every inch of her, chart each contour, memorize each throbbing spot on her body... or was it that it only took a brush from his lips to start any part of her throbbing?

He slid the skirt from her slender hips, revealing the lace-edged pantaloons. As his fingers found the knotted bow at her waist, the traitorous thought sprang unbidden into her mind. The sheer, lacy confections had been Susannah's, as had everything she wore.

She bit into her knuckles and tasted blood. His Susannah. Was that what she was giving him? A night to ease the pain of losing the woman he really loved?

She opened her eyes and stared into the heavens, suddenly black and empty, as if even the stars were swallowed up in her anguish. Something within her quaked, died a little.

But no. She wouldn't allow it.

If that was what she was giving, let it be hers to give. In a movement almost savage, she shrugged the blouse from her shoulders, flung the skirt into the darkness, and sent the pantaloons flying after.

When she faced Coulter again, it was with the only thing she possessed that hadn't belonged to the dead woman: her body.

She saw the confusion on his face; he knew something had changed, but she would never explain what that something was. It was enough to know that she didn't care about the other woman, about the past that haunted him. She reached out to him, and he took her in his arms, his hands roaming her bare skin, but it wasn't enough. She slid her hands down his body and felt him hard, ready, beneath his trousers. And if he had any doubts, her hands and their movements erased them.

She had unfastened men's trousers many times before... how many times had she undressed Joel when he was too drunk to do it himself? Even in the dark, her fingers were swift and sure, but not ready for the hot, throbbing flesh waiting for her there. Her lips parted beneath his in an involuntary intake of air.

Then his fingers were parting her thighs, probing, finding her moist and ready for joining. The tip of his forefinger hesitated, then grazed her nub of turgid flesh, and it pulsated in response; she spread her legs wider and opened herself to him, tears filling her eyes as he explored, stroked, and she caressed him as well, felt him quiver at her touch as she quivered at his.

He groaned, and she captured the sound with her lips, straining closer for a more complete oneness. She opened her arms to him, wanting to take him into her, body and soul, seeking to heal, to be healed.

Then she was lying on the ground, and he was poised to enter, his hands braced on either side of her. She tensed for the pain that didn't come.

He hesitated for but a moment, then pushed in, his entrance slow and gentle, a moist friction that left her gasping for breath. But even as she longed to succumb to the mindless glory of it, she forced her eyes to stay open and watched his head arch back, his eyes close, his lips slacken... and her glory was multiplied.

She rose to meet his next stroke, and this time he was the one to gasp. His eyes met hers even as his hips continued moving, agonizingly slowly, and she moved beneath him, her own body's rhythms quickening their pace. Each stroke gained force, gained momentum, until it seemed that all the impulses in the universe were concentrated in the tender, throbbing point where her body melded with his.

It wasn't enough until the explosion of sensation that wracked through her body, sent her hurtling through spasms of sensation beyond her experience. She cried out, reached out, and he responded, taking her into the strength of his embrace, wrapping his arms around her as she moved against him, his body tense... and then it was his cries that caught in the wind, his body that shuddered against hers, her arms that held and anchored.

The cold breeze wrapped around them, the doves sounded their calls, the trees whipped above them, but none of it was equal to the wealth of feelings coursing through their bodies, their hearts, their souls.

Two single beings united as one, and for a moment complete.

Coulter's breath on Elizabeth's shoulder was slow and even.

Not a word had passed between them afterward, but then, there were no words to express the tumult she had experienced. And Coulter... she couldn't begin to imagine his reaction. Now, he slept, and she lay in his arms, watching, wondering...

He was the strong one, the one she had relied on. She couldn't fault him for that. And if she was now cold and empty in the knowledge that it was Susannah who claimed his soul... she could find no fault that was his in that either.

Above them, a star streaked from north to south so quickly that she doubted for a few breathless moments she'd seen anything at all. And then another star, and another, blazed a white trail across the blue-black sky, and she knew they were real.

She thought to wake him, but didn't. His head nestled in the hollow of her shoulder, his lips brushing her breast, each breath a warm benevolence washing over her skin, as the starry tears of Saint Lawrence rained above them.

It would be hours before she slept.

Chapter Fifteen

COULTER AWOKE TO the scent of jasmine, to the unaccustomed warmth of a body beside his. He reached instinctively for the pistol at his side; his hand closed over warm flesh, instead. His eyes flew open... and reality seemed stranger than the dreams that had filled his sleep.

Dawn had already pinkened the sky, casting its glow over them both. Never had he seen anyone so fragile, so awe-inspiring, as the woman in his arms. Her cloak covered them both, but her skin was cold when he brushed her hair away from her shoulder. Only where they were close were they warm.

Her eyes were shadowed, the purple bruises on her neck evident even in the dim light. There were bright pink abrasions on her shoulder; he reached up, touched his coarse beard, and felt a pang of dismay. So delicate...

He leaned closer and her hair with its sweet scent brushed against him. He touched her lips; they parted against his finger. Still, she slept. He drew a deep, shuddering breath. He couldn't stay here beside her.

Not without touching her again.

She whimpered as he slid from her embrace. He reached for his trousers, his gun. And he thought he had known guilt before.

It was her own whimper that wakened her.

She felt him pulling away. She didn't allow herself to stir as she listened to his movements. Then she felt him smooth the cloak over her, felt his hand brush her breast, by accident, it seemed. Then his hand followed the contour of her breast again, lingering for a brief moment that seemed an eternity, before finally withdrawing.

She rolled to face him.

The merest whisper of a mark remained where her whip had lashed him, leaving the older scar exposed, a small, hooked scar, white against his burnished skin. The scar Joel had asked her about. Where had he gotten it? Had her lips touched it, smoothed away the pain she'd inflicted? She couldn't be sure... and needed to be sure. She needed to touch his face and wipe away the lines of care.

"I want you to know... about last night," she whispered. "I'm not sorry."

Their eyes locked, and unsaid words hung quivering between them. Even the wind held still, breathless, waiting for his response. Finally, she dropped her gaze, unable to bear what she saw in his face.

"I am."

"Indeed." She squeezed her fingers together to stop their trembling, locked her jaw tight, dared her eyes to betray her with tears. The smile that found its way to her lips was brittle, but very, very brave. "Mr. Coulter, a gentleman would never have said so."

His laughter was bitter. "You should have never expected me to act like a gentleman."

"And for that, I am eternally grateful." The smile slipped a little, was less brave, less brittle, less a smile. "I have had my fill of gentlemen who are not gentle, who make pretty speeches but only follow them with hurtful actions." She dropped all pretense of smiling. "Say what you will, Mr. Coulter, but your eyes, your touch," she blushed, then forged ahead. "They tell a different story."

She watched him yank one boot on, then the other. He rose and snatched up his shirt and blanket. He wore only his brown trousers, and for the first time she saw the dusting of dark hair over his chest. He spun toward the stand of scrub bushes where the mare was hobbled.

"I knew of your reluctance, Mr. Coulter." He paused, his back to her. "I know of your regrets. Just be sure that they are of your own making. I refuse to allow you to heap guilt atop of whatever else you are feeling, at least not guilt on my account."

He seemed to be at war within himself, his muscles bunched across his back and shoulders and his forearms knotted and clutching the blanket and shirt in a life-and-death grip. It took him a long time to finally turn and fix her with a glare calculated to chill.

"You're nothing like any lady I've ever heard of."

Her laughter bubbled to the surface, and she pulled the cloak higher around her shoulders and shook her head. "Mr. Coulter, I don't believe I've been a lady since the night I let you out of jail."

The expression on his raw-boned face indicated his disbelief.

Anger flared within her. "What do you know of ladies, Mr. Coulter? Embroidery and lace, sonnets and sachets? I will tell you what a lady is, what she learns at her mother's knee, what she has drilled into her from the day she is born."

She pulled upright, her hair tangled about her face, and locked her arms over the dusty cloak to hold it over her bare body.

"A lady endures, whether it be poverty or a pitiful, drunken husband, or even simple loneliness. A lady doesn't question; a lady molds herself to the desires of her husband, follows him wherever he goes, and stands by helplessly as she watches him kill himself with drink and despair, and a lady… through the very act of her weakness, is stronger than anyone can ever imagine a lady would ever have to be."

She stumbled to her feet, not caring if the cloak covered her, not caring if the outlaw spun on his heel and left her, or... She fought for her breath, refusing to think of the other.

He stared at the ground between them, and she knew she had moved him, and she knew he was unconvinced. "You learned your lesson well. Since the night you released me, you have endured, you have suffered, you have been stronger in your weakness than any man I've ever known."

He studied her then as if measuring the distance between them and finding it too wide to breach. "You can't deny what you are, any more than I can change what I am."

She tossed her hair out of her face, the blood singing through her veins, anger giving her strength she thought had ebbed away.

"How dare you stand there and preach to me? As if you have any idea what I am, what I've been through, and why! I have endured for myself, I have suffered because of myself, and I have been strong because there was no alternative." Her eyes blazed with fury. "For myself, Mr. Coulter. I have done it all for myself, even what happened between us last night. I did not submit, or offer myself, simply to repay you for your kindnesses—which have been many—or your strength, which has been my salvation. I took what you did not want to give, because I needed it to survive."

Coulter's eyes narrowed. The change about him was slow but distinct as he hooked his thumbs in his waistband. His trousers shifted a little lower on his hips, dragging her gaze lower still, and she found it difficult to breathe. "It seems to me, you're just like the ladies I remember. You use people for your own benefit, and lady, I don't like being used."

He took a step closer, and she wanted to back away, but didn't. "You've broken all the rules that kept me away from you."

The hand that eased around the back of her head, slithering through her hair, pulling her so close to him that she couldn't breathe for the nearness. He had none of the gentleness she remembered. "You teased me last night, and you think you got exactly what you wanted, but you listen to me, and listen good."

His eyes were the eyes of the rattlesnake, cold and deadly. His lips found hers, crushing them, and even then he didn't relent until she was swooning against the hardness of his body.

She pushed against him with all her might, but the cloak between them slipped down and she felt his chest hot against hers. She clasped the woolen barrier more fiercely, more desperately.

"Isn't this what you wanted, Lady Elizabeth?" he sneered. "Is this what you need to survive?"

"No —"

But he wasn't listening. His steely arms wrapped around her, his hands roaming down her back, lower, lower, until he was cupping her against his maleness, and she choked back a sob because, God help her, she was responding to the savagery in his kiss. His hands kneaded, massaged, and as she pressed forward, his hardness rubbed against her, even through the cloak... and then his tongue stroked her lips and she gasped, and it entered, thrusting deep in her mouth, and now she despised herself... for wanting more.

"You broke the rules, Elizabeth Dougherty," he rasped against her ear. And in his voice she heard the burning embers of rage, and of passion, and of devouring need. "Tell me to stop. Tell me this isn't what you want."

She attempted to twist away, her hair tumbling into her face. "Why are you doing this to me?"

"Because this is what you did to me."

"That's a lie!" She met his gaze straight on, refusing to back down. "I offered you as much as I took, Coulter. I didn't take without caring."

His face dipped closer to hers, his words scalding her with their intensity. "Lady... what the hell made you think I didn't care?"

He shoved her away and left without another word.

Coulter returned to the clearing a few minutes later with Sage at his back, and found the woman gone. The stallion dropped his head to tear off a switch of tall, tough bunchgrass. Coulter left him to graze, grabbed his gunbelt and climbed the incline toward a stand of pinoaks. Her trail was easy to follow. She'd made no effort to scuff over her tracks, and the underbrush had obviously been disturbed.

He topped the incline and stopped, tensing, for she was there. She sat atop a boulder staring back the way they had come, the heels of her boots resting on a worn-away indentation, her knees clasped in front of her.

His gloved hands clenched at his sides. No, not again.

He stooped and picked up a small rock, then sent it skittering across the ground. She flinched, turned, saw him, and her expression changed.

Tension radiated between them, as it had since the first time they met. Only this time the tension was different, stronger. This time, the tension pulsating in their gazes was ripe with knowledge.

"Mr. Coulter." She turned away from him again, her back rigid, her eyes trained on the distant mountains. "The world is so big out here, Mr. Coulter... the sky so vast. If I hadn't already traveled that desert, I would think the Diablos were only a short distance away."

Her words rang out clear and pure as crystal in the sharp air, and he knew from the first word that she had chosen to disregard all that had passed between them.

Still every inch the lady.

She raised her hand to shade her eyes. "How far have we come?"

He stood stiffly, not following her gaze. Instead, his eyes refused to stray from her face. "I think the question is, how far are you going?"

"I don't even know where I am." Her voice had a huskiness in it he hadn't noticed before. "How can I possibly know where I'm going?"

"We're a few miles from the New Mexico territory."

"How far from a train or a stagecoach line?"

"Two days to Seven Rivers."

Her shoulders moved, but she didn't look at him. "Then... then I suppose that gives me two days to decide on a destination, doesn't it?"

"I'm not going to Seven Rivers, lady." He shoved his hands in his pockets and faced her, his shoulders wide and immobile.

"But if that's the closest town —"

"I'm not going to Seven Rivers," he repeated.

She stiffened, her chin rising a notch. "Might I ask why not?"

"I'm known there."

Color crept up her neck. She smoothed a stray hair from her face, avoiding his eyes. "I'm sorry. I had forgotten ..." She shifted away from him and slid off the outcropping, grabbing a boulder for support as she skidded on the gravelly earth.

"They don't know me by name, but I go in for provisions occasionally. If I show up with a woman, it'll be noticed." His eyes swept over her, judging, remembering. Especially a woman like you. "Whatever stage you get on, there'll be someone to notice. Somebody who'll remember."

"I see." She swallowed nervously, and he couldn't draw his gaze away from her throat. She had buttoned her blouse higher today. But it didn't do any good. He remembered, too well, what was beneath.

"If not Seven Rivers," she asked, "then where?"

She expected him to have an answer. Frustration balled in his stomach and knotted in his trembling fists. "Lady, you're asking me the same question I've been asking myself ever since the night you stuck a gun in my belly and told me you were going with me."

She smoothed her skirt, and if he hadn't been watching her so closely for so many days, he might not have known her to be distressed, possibly even ashamed. But he had been watching. He knew.

"I had no idea what I was asking when I forced you to bring me with you." And then she angled her head toward him, and her lips were full and moist.

A tremor passed through him as he remembered their taste.

"Mr. Coulter, I had no idea where I was going, only that I couldn't stay."

He thought, staring into those large, gray eyes, that there was no one on earth who could understand that feeling more than he. How could she have ever thought that he, of all people, could help her?

But he said nothing of these feelings, for on their heels, sprang up new ones, the old questions. What was she running from?

He studied her for a moment, considered asking, but backed away from it. First things first... to get to the cabin.

He snatched his shirt from the ground.

"Get ready to ride."

The passage down the mountain and over the ill-defined trail took an hour and a half. Here and there, wildflowers bloomed among the rocks, some pinkish or white, but most of them were yellow butterweed. Coarse, lush grasses gave the air a delicacy and freshness that should have lifted her spirits, but didn't.

A wild turkey, startled and infuriated by their sudden appearance, ruffled its feathers and took a threatening stance; Coulter reached for his rifle, then let his hand drop to his side. The bird had second thoughts, and flew low and comically into the underbrush. That too, should have lightened her mood, but it didn't.

I am known there.

Where wasn't he known? Was there ever a time when he wasn't running?

Her mind was filled with questions. Had Obregón spoken the truth, or had he lied? Were Coulter's murders an old vendetta? And Clayton and Joel... how were they involved? She shivered.

She glanced over at Coulter, his hands, so sure on the reins of the high-spirited, half-wild stallion, and she thought of their touch on her skin. Watching his lips curl around the mouth of his canteen, she thought of their power to ignite fires within her that only he could quench. Watching his shoulders move beneath the dirty chambray shirt, she thought of their starlit contours as he moved above her...

Her own fingers tensed on the mare's reins, and her mind, worked feverishly, trying to erase the images so indelibly marked there. But how could she forget, when the very air around them reeked with the scents that had surrounded their love-making? Warm earth, sweet-scented firs and pines... even the heavy scent of horses, lightly lathered from the heat, drew a pang of recognition from her.

Watching him ride ahead of her, she knew a hunger that scared her with its intensity. But when her horse stumbled and he glanced back, his chilly gaze made her uncertain.

The very first day she'd met him, she had slashed his face with her whip, and she had seen such anger in his eyes she believed him capable of anything, including murder. Yet he hadn't harmed her, not really. Later she had seen something else in his eyes, a pain, a vulnerability that she didn't understand. Something that had reassured her when she was afraid, convinced her she was safe with him.

She must decide soon, very soon, upon a destination.

But first she must know the answers to the questions Obregón had raised. She had to know about Coulter's past. She knew without doubting that whatever he chose to tell her would be the truth. Her only concern was that he might choose not to tell her anything at all.

He had been painfully honest with her about his feelings about what had happened between them. Surely he would at least tell her about Joel and Clayton. She had to know everything about him, because every passing moment convinced her that she when she told him she wouldn't need him again, she was the one who had lied.

She prayed that he would come to her in the night again.

Chapter Sixteen

AT FIRST WHEN Sage trotted into the dry stream bed, Elizabeth thought the stallion was seeking water from the memory of an earlier trip. But as they followed the course of the bed upstream, she realized they were entering yet another canyon, and as the stream bed wound its way inward, she finally found herself surrounded on all four sides by steep canyon walls. The vegetation grew sparser up the sloping walls, until the walls were nothing but sheer rock, dotted with black caves and caverns.

The dry bed was strewn with smooth, round rocks, white and gray and brown. The horses skirted its edge, surefooted, impatient, slowing only when forced onto the rocky surface by shrubs or trees, which became more plentiful and larger as they progressed deeper into the canyon. Soon Elizabeth heard what they must be following: running water.

They rounded a curve and suddenly the stream was there, shallow but flowing. The horses splashed in ankle-deep and drank. Coulter pulled out his canteen, sloshed it judiciously, offered it to her.

She sipped, confused; the warm water was no substitute for the abundance beneath them. She gazed longingly at the clear stream, imagined it flowing around her while handing the canteen back to the outlaw without a word.

He wiped the back of his gloved hand across his lips. “If you want to stop for a while we can. But we’re only a couple of miles from my cabin.”

The effect of his words was like magic. Two miles... her shoulders and back ached a little less, her throat seemed less irritated. “Then why are we waiting?”

Even the horses seemed more quickly satisfied than usual, and in minutes they were pressing forward, deeper into the canyon, past shrubs and foliage that grew steadily denser, trees that grew taller, until the sky was only patches of blue between the arching tree limbs.

For a while the stream gurgled beside them, then it disappeared beneath the ground again, leaving only its earlier legacy of rocks to mark its bed. A half mile farther, it reappeared again.

“That’s a maple!” Elizabeth couldn’t resist riding closer and plucking a tender leaf. “Does it turn red in the autumn? We had a maple in our garden at home.”

And a small iron bench had been beneath it. The bench where she and Joel had fallen in love over a volume of his precious Keats, with red maple leaves dropping around them, on the page, in her hair, in his. She rubbed the supple, leathery leaf against her cheek. Reminders of home were few; the reminder of Joel should have hurt more than it did.

She felt the outlaw’s eyes upon her.

The leaf fluttered to the path.

She didn’t want such reminders after all.

Coulter reined in his horse. She drew nearer, ever aware of his intent gaze upon her, until she was close enough to reach out and touch his arm. His eyes didn’t leave her face, but she sensed a new tension in him. Finally, she forced her attention beyond him.

And caught her first glimpse of the cabin.

He held back, so she urged the mare forward. The structure was crude, without apparent thought to grace or form, yet it was graceful and well-formed, the encroaching foliage of trees and bushes softening its edges and casting it in cool shadow.

It was not only a place for hiding; it was a place of peace.

She swung her leg over the mare's back, and gasped as pains knifed up her thigh. She grabbed the back of her leg with one hand, clinging to the saddle horn with her other. The mare sidestepped nervously, and Elizabeth's left boot caught in the stirrup, leaving her right leg dangling, and in pain.

"What's wrong?"

She bit back a groan, damning herself for her weakness. Coulter seized her by the waist and she felt herself being lifted and swung through the air. He lowered her to the ground with an unceremonious plop.

"Are you all right?" he demanded.

"It's my leg," she said. "It's cramping."

"For God's sake," he said in disgust. "Is that all?" He stooped over and grabbed her by the arm, yanking her to her feet.

"What—" She winced, trying to pull away from him.

"Stand on it, lady," he growled. "Walk on it."

"Get your hands off me!" She wrenched away from him and dropped back to the ground, gritting her teeth, digging her fingers into the cramping muscle.

He towered over her, his fists on his hips, his expression uncompromising. "Lady, if you want it to go away, you're going to have to walk on it. But if you want to suffer, then just sit there and cramp. I don't have time for your nonsense."

"Nonsense!" Elizabeth struggled to her knees, anger boiling in her blood.

"You heard me, lady! If you can't make yourself useful, then just get out of my way."

"How dare you speak to me that way?" She was on her feet now, the anger a delicious release from the tension she'd endured all day. "It's not my fault my leg cramped! You don't have to treat me like I'm an albatross around your neck! I'm perfectly capable of pulling my own weight!"

Feet planted wide, he jerked a thumb toward the horses stamping nervously behind them. "Then get on that mare and do it! Take care of yourself. Get yourself to Seven Rivers, or wherever it is you think you're going. You've been nothing but a thorn in my side since the first day I laid eyes on you!"

"When you stole my horse," she reminded him

"No!" he thundered. "What I gave you for that horse is worth five times, a hundred times more than that ridiculous piece of horseflesh!"

"Then take it back. I don't want it." Her voice cracked on the bitter words and her fingers closed around the chain at her neck. As she pulled, the cross lodged between her camisole and her skin. She pulled harder; she winced as it left a long scratch in its wake before coming free. She pulled it over her head and flung it at his feet.

He had stooped to snatch it out of the dirt when she planted her booted toe over it. He raised his face to her, jaw clenched, anger etched in every line. "Move your foot, lady."

Her pulse throbbed four slow times before she finally eased her foot off the necklace. "Just in case you've forgotten, Mr. Coulter," she said, meeting the iron in his gaze with the fired steel of her own. "If it weren't for me, you'd be swinging from the end of a rope."

"Would you like me to remind you where you'd be if it weren't for me?" He rose and took another step toward her, his eyes narrow and deadly "You'd be Obregón's whore, just like Susannah!"

She gasped. "Never!"

His fingers dug into the tender flesh of her shoulder. "You think you're so goddamned high and mighty? You think you're so above everybody else? You think you're better than her?"

"If not submitting to that animal's lust makes me better than her, then hell yes, I'm better than her!"

His face went white beneath his burnished tan. "You bitch."

Her hand shot out to strike him, but his blocked it. He captured her wrist in his hand, and for a moment she thought he might crush it in his anger.

Then as the reality of what was happening poured over her, she asked in words barely audible, "Why... why do you want to hurt me? What have I done to make you want to hurt me?"

His hand relaxed on her wrist, but his voice was tight with venom. "I don't want to hurt you." He flung her arm away from him in disgust. "Don't ever, ever tell me you are better than Susannah."

"What is she to you?" she demanded. "What kind of hold does she have over you? She chose Obregón, not you!"

"Shut up, lady." His jaw clenched; the veins at his temples throbbed with his anger. "You don't know what you're talking about."

"Well, for God's sake, tell me then! Tell me what I'm supposed to think! What kind of woman could she be, if she chooses someone like Miguél Obregón over you? What kind of man are you to keep seeing her, even when she lived under another man's roof?"

"She was my sister, damn you! My sister!"

"Your... your sister?" He wheeled away from her, leaving her reeling from the shock. She could hardly encompass the thought, so alien was it to her. "Oh, my God."

"Are you satisfied? Do you really need to ask me what he could give her that I couldn't? Do I have to spell it out for you lady?"

Her expression mirrored her shock, and she reached out to touch him. "My God, forgive me. I didn't know."

"Keep your pity to yourself," he snarled. "I have no use for pity, yours or anyone else's!"

"I'm so sorry ..."

"Get away from me!"

Chin upraised, eyes glittering, she stood her ground. "You lied to me, Mr. Coulter. Maybe you lied to yourself. But you did want to hurt me, and you do want to hurt me, and I won't allow you to do so. Is that clear?"

"You won't allow —who do you think you are? You think the world is arranged for your convenience?"

"We're not talking about the world, Mr. Coulter. We are talking about you."

Coulter dragged his fingers through his hair. "I can't take any more of this," he muttered. "Just leave me alone."

"Gladly." Stiff with her anger, she turned on her heel and uncinched the mare's belly strap. Only when she was stooped over and straining did it occur to her—her muscle cramp had quite disappeared.

Damn him. Damn him for being right. Damn him for being —

"Lady."

His voice, sharp and impatient, came from directly behind her. She rose slowly, raised her eyes to him... slowly. "Yes, Mr. Coulter?"

The lines of his face were harsh, weathered. His fishhook scar showed up white against his ruddy complexion. His eyes glowed amber-brown, as his head dipped down. Her breath lodged in her throat, but for the life of her, she couldn't sidestep or dodge.

He placed a hand on either side of her head, and angled her face toward his. His fingers dug into her hair, dislodging a tortoiseshell comb that tumbled to the ground. Her lips parted in expectation.

"You want to know why I want to hurt you?" he grated. "Because I hate what you're doing to me."

"Do you really, Mr. Coulter? I don't believe you."

His lips captured hers in a kiss so brutal it brought tears to her eyes.

Her fists pounded against his shoulder as she writhed in his embrace, pounded in frustration, pounded the rhythm of his tongue as it stroked her lips, then insinuated itself between them and found hers... and the pounding became the pounding in her head, her veins, as even her own traitorous pulse took up his offending rhythm... stroking, pounding, stroking...

His fingers worked against her scalp with the same insidious rhythm that permeated her body, until it seemed every fiber of her being throbbed with it. His hands, his lips, even his body forced the lifeblood through her in a rhythm of his own making.

Her fingers clutched fistfuls of his shirt, soft and warm and damp from his skin, and they were no longer striking out, but pulling him toward her, as she met his tongue with hers, filling and being filled.

There was a melting sweetness in her core, a treacherous and desperate response that cared not that he took without asking... only cared if he stopped without taking.

Then his hands slid down, bringing her hair tumbling with them, down to rub restless circles at the small of her back, the pressure firm, then releasing, then firm again... to the never-ceasing rhythm that flowed from him to her and back again.

A groan rose from deep within her, escaping into his kiss, and his hands slid to her upper arms, then skimmed to the soft, full swell of her breasts. Her groan deepened; his kiss deepened; her breasts swelled under his hands until they ached with the remembered need of his touch against their bare, quivering skin, his fingers, his lips...

And then, as if remembering as well, his lips tore away from hers and he was bending lower, until his mouth found the hardened crest of her breast beneath the thin fabric of her blouse. His suction was wet, hard, and then his teeth were scraping the fabric, adding disturbing new sensations to the pulsating chills shaking through her body.

Her head fell back, her eyes closed and lips parted, and she submitted to his demanding passion, not hesitant and tender as the night before, but filled with a powerful need that transcended his anger, even fed off it. Her body filled with the seductive narcotic of his making, even as her eyes filled with the wine-colored, sunset sky.

She felt herself spinning, swaying, buffeted by forces beyond her control, as his hands tore her blouse open and off her shoulders, and the camisole too, slid down, and her breasts were bare and succulent and exposed, throbbing as she watched his face, his lips coming closer, the lean angles of his cheeks hollowing even more as he suckled passion from one aching nipple, then the other.

If these were the acts of hatred, then no woman was capable of surviving the rapture of his love.

Her knees buckled and she was sinking, his arms tightening around her as she fell against him. And then she felt the ground beneath her knees, then her thighs, and then he was lowering her to her back, and she found the breath, the will, to speak, though her voice was little more than a grating whisper.

"Please, Mr. Coulter... this time... don't you have a bed?"

Then his arms were beneath her again, lifting her, clutching her body to his, and he was crossing the ground in long, powerful strides. One blow of his booted foot against the wooden door sent it crashing inward, and then they were inside the cool, dark interior of the cabin. Before her eyes had time to adjust to the darkness, he was stretching her onto a bed of furs, silky soft against her bare back.

"Do you really hate me, Mr. Coulter?" she whispered as he bent over her, the rigid planes of his face undisguised by the soft, gray shadows.

His jaw rigid, his frame stiff as he surveyed her body stretched beneath him. "I hate what you're doing to me."

"And what am I doing to you?"

"You're making me need you. And I can't need you. I can't need anybody. It's the only thing that has kept me alive ..."

"Hatred has kept you alive."

"Maybe hatred gave me a reason for living. But being alone has kept me alive."

"Tell me this, Mr. Coulter," she asked sadly. "Is that kind of a life worth living?"

"It's the only life I had, and it was enough." And then, though she told herself she couldn't be seeing what she thought she was seeing, a diamond hard tear fell from his eyes, and with an angry mutter, he bent low and the hot breath of his words seared into her ear. "Until now."

"And so you hate me? Say it. Go ahead, say it—I hate you, Elizabeth."

He didn't answer.

Instead he unfastened the gunbelt from his hips and dropped it to the hard earth floor. His fingers didn't falter at the fastening to his breeches, nor did he flinch from her steady gaze as he slid the trousers down his lean hips, revealing the hard evidence of his arousal. He seemed neither proud nor arrogant, only relentless in his aim to finish what had been begun between them.

How can you let him, knowing how he little he feels for you? Have you no pride?

But she refused to believe, could not allow herself to believe he hated her.

He began the slow removal of her clothing, dragging the split-skirt over her hips, down her thighs... then the pantaloons. In the false night of the dark cabin, she could almost close her eyes and imagine the magic-kissed starlight of the night before.

But no. This was different.

For this time she was determined to make no move to help him, this man who despised her for making him throb with the lifeblood of passion, to crave her most human and elemental touch. This time, he would not be able to say she had made him do anything. This time, no matter how the need spiraled within her, she would not allow it to escape her lips...

She would not, she vowed as his palms spread her blouse open again, his eyes devouring her. Strain tightened his jaw until she could see the pulse in his neck, at his temples, as he fought with himself... and lost.

She waited for him.

And won.

He knelt at the foot of the crude bed, and she stifled a gasp behind her hand when his teeth nipped her thighs, gentle little nips, teasing little nips, higher, and higher still. She clamped her legs together to still their trembling, but they parted willingly enough under the firm pressure of his hands.

His fingers brushed aside the moist curls, dark against the smooth texture of her skin. He probed, found the swollen flesh of her femininity, stroked; a finger glided inside, and she felt herself tightening around him a small, uncontrollable spasm of pleasure, as if that most private part of her instinctively was trying to pull him in farther, begging him to fill her.

His eyes were filled with black desire, leaving a scalding trail as they dragged from her helpless gaze, to her quivering lips, to her full breasts, to the place where his finger disappeared within her. He pulled it out in a quick half-stroke; she couldn't stop the short gasp that escaped her lips, and his nostrils flared and she read the burning knowledge in his eyes, the knowledge of his power, his control over her.

Again, he moved his hand against her, within her, and this time she couldn't help it, she writhed against him, silently begging him for more.

Never relinquishing his hold on her, he bent over her and his tongue brushed the tip of her breast. Again, she drew in a short gasp, then clamped her lower lip beneath her teeth as he withdrew from her, but before she could utter the cry of protest, his fingers were feathering against the kernel of her desire, then circling, pressing harder, until she thought she would explode under the sensations.

She couldn't breathe; the short pants escaping from her lips provided no relief, no oxygen, and would have been cries of desperation if her voice hadn't been trapped deep inside her, with all her blood, all her moisture, concentrated under his hand, ready to spill over at his next touch.

The touch that didn't come. She searched his face, fighting for air, her body taut with the need for him. And what she saw in his eyes confused her.

"Now you know …"

She shook her head in frustration.

"Now you know how it feels to be driven past reason."

She found no triumph in his gaze, for he too was driven past the point of reason... beyond the point of control. The toll of his own denial was beaded over his lips in sweat, heaving in the lungs that moved his chest up and down, pulsing in the veins that wrapped his manhood.

Her arms reached up and wrapped around his neck and pulled him down over her, and her wide, full lips parted beneath his. Her body rocked against him... all thoughts of defiant submission swept away in the tumult of her response to him.

She closed her hand around his silken smooth heat, and guided him to her threshold, reveling in the sensations that preliminary contact wrought. His tip pressed into her, then withdrew, and she whimpered in the darkness. It pressed again, a little farther, a little harder, and her moisture spread higher up his shaft... then he withdrew again, and this time she sobbed her frustration. She curled her arms around his neck, moved against him, felt the muscles in his neck bunch beneath her wrists as he tensed, then tasted the exultation as he could control himself no longer and thrust into her.

She squeezed her eyes shut, tightened her sheath around him, unable to breathe or think or reason until his hips started their slow, grinding rhythm, demanding a response she was only too willing to give. His movements were steady, relentless, as he sought his release and hers, and her hands slid down his body to his hips, her fingers digging into the hard muscles as she planted her feet in the furred bedding and angled herself higher to accept more of him into her body.

She arched against him, felt that tender, private part of her swelling against him, and his mouth upon her breast, suckling with the same rhythm that thrummed in her core, until she consisted of nothing but their suckling, driving, grinding rhythm... coiling tighter, and tighter.

And when it came, the explosion of contractions that wracked through their bodies, she locked her arms around him, tears streaming down her cheeks, and his lips fused to hers, and they knew the rapture of shared release.

Her hair clung to his damp chest, their limbs intertwined. Their breathing had finally slowed.

Coulter stared straight ahead; the woman's eyes were closed. His mind whirled, it raged, it tortured with accusations—but still couldn't dispel the sense of utter and complete peace that permeated his body, that flowed from her gentle palm resting on his hip, her thigh pressed against his, her cheek against his chest. Peace, dangerous peace, radiated from her body into his.

He was afraid.

And so he stared into the deepening gloom, but instead of darkness, he saw radiance. The radiance of the woman beside him, her strength, her fragility, her beauty.

His fear grew.

"Mr. Coulter ..."

He turned his head to find her wide, gray eyes staring up at him.

"Mr. Coulter, to avoid future misunderstandings I want you to understand something... I'm still not sorry."

"Lady." But his grumble had little venom behind it. She was watching him expectantly, waiting for him to admit the same. He shifted uncomfortably, but her hand only found a more comfortable spot at his waist.

Minutes passed, but he couldn't answer, couldn't let himself examine the unspoken question between them. He waited for the pain to darken her eyes, for her to pull away. But it didn't. She didn't.

A slow smile spread across her lips. "I'm hungry. Is there anything here besides beef jerky?"

He heaved a great sigh, oddly relieved, but he felt a pang of regret when he untangled himself from her hair, her arms, her legs. He had pulled on his trousers and had his boots in his hand when she rolled over and faced him, her eyes already heavy with sleep.

"Mr. Coulter, this wretched beast I'm lying on didn't have fleas, did it?"

"I've slept on it for years, without a bite," he muttered.

"Thank God." She shut her eyes. "Thank you."

He awoke her to eat, but she fell asleep again soon after. She turned her back to him and coiled into a ball, and he tossed the remains of dinner into the fire, so as not to attract animals in the night.

Then he could no longer put off the quandary of where to sleep. He considered a bedroll on the floor, or perhaps even outside the cabin. But not for long.

The rope bedframe creaked under his weight as he slid onto the bed and took the edge of the quilt to cover himself. She remained still, though he wasn't certain that she was asleep. Somehow he managed to find a position on the narrow bed where their bodies shared heat without touching.

When Elizabeth awoke hours later, his body cradled hers, his arm circled her, his breath warmed the back of her neck.

And she knew peace.

Wendell had ridden all day and half the night, and he realized that he was still a good hundred and fifty miles out of El Paso.

Though once his mind would have been filled with silken thighs and perfumed bodies, now he had no room for such thoughts. That's what came of being a man. He figured it was time to set aside his frivolous ways and tend to the job at hand.

Problem was, at the moment he was having trouble deciding what the job at hand was.

Was his first responsibility as the interim sheriff—glory be, he did love that title—to go after the gunslinger and Miz Dougherty?

And had the gunslinger really kidnapped Miz Dougherty?

Had to have. She sure wouldn't have left willingly with that slippery sidewinder.

Wendell had stopped feeling ashamed. In fact, he'd finally gotten pretty doggone mad over the whole affair. Somebody'd made a fool out of him, and he aimed to find out who and deal with them right and proper.

Like a man.

Thinking of it that way, it seemed to make more sense. The sheriff hadn't made him look like a fool. The outlaw had. So's it only made sense that that's who he should go after: Boone Coulter.

His stomach gurgled at the idea. But that reaction was from hunger, most likely, certainly not fear.

Then again, he wasn't thinkin' like an interim sheriff. He was thinkin' like a man with a grudge, and an interim sheriff had no business letting his grudges get in the way of his law-keeping. He was thinkin' like a man who had watched his blond angel board an El Paso-bound stage on the arm of a man who had money, and learning and high falutin' airs Wendell Crutcher didn't have and probably never would have.

He was thinking like a man who was out to prove himself to Doralee and win her back. A man who was hell-bent on being able to look himself in the mirror without shame.

He was after Boone Coulter. He'd gotten him once; he could do it again.

If Sheriff Dougherty didn't get him first.

The Apache Mountains and Fort Davis were to the southeast. The Sierra del Diablos were to the north. El Paso was west. Chances were slim that the outlaw would've hung around in the Apaches. The odds were slimmer still that he would have gone near a busy place like El Paso. The Diablos were out of the question. He might've headed north over the desert and cut back into the mountains in New Mexico.

Tarnation, he could be close to Colorado by now, if he'd stayed on the flatlands.

But Boone Coulter didn't stay on the flatlands. He was at home in the mountains, like a mountain cat, hiding, waiting for night. He only came down to strike, and then disappeared again.

Six times.

Not from the Diablos. Surely even Boone Coulter would have skirted them. Even he would be afraid of the stories.

Doralee would have to respect a man who went into the Diablos, and lived to tell it.

But only a sure 'nough fool would go into the Diablos.

Chapter Seventeen

DORALEE PROPPED HER elbows on the edge of the wrought iron rail and surveyed El Paso's bustling San Jacinto Plaza with a practiced eye. There were men everywhere. Soldiers from Fort Bliss: not much money but what they had would definitely be easy pickings. Railroad workers: less money, less clean, hardly worth her time unless she caught the eye of a foreman or better. Businessmen: prime targets for a working girl of her talents, if she weren't otherwise involved.

She sighed and cast a sidelong glance in Dan P. Jennings' direction. He was writing with a pencil in a small notebook. He had a small container similar to a cigar case filled with pencils, and he spent an inordinately long time sharpening them with the small, gold-plated knife when he wasn't writing.

But now he wrote. And wrote. And wrote. She sighed again. It was strange calling for a man, scratching out words for a living. Downright boring, if the truth were known.

Of course, the places he'd been hadn't been boring. Not to hear him tell the story at least. But she hadn't been with him when he'd interviewed that crazy man, Emperor Norton, in San Francisco, and hadn't been with him when he'd interviewed

Brigham Young in Salt Lake City, and wasn't even sure he'd actually interviewed the Duke of Clarendon in London, even though he claimed he did.

Right now he was in El Paso chasing an outlaw who probably never intended to give him an interview in the first place. And here she was with him, on the chance that he might be soft-headed enough to keep her with him until he finally gave up and went home to New York City, or moved on to another story, which was pretty damned risky in itself. If chasing stories had brought him all the way to Cavendish, Texas, the man was crazy enough to go anywhere.

She turned her attention back to the bustling square below. Was she really willing to pass up a sure shot at some real money just to tag along with Dan P. Jennings until he got tired of paying her way, and maybe dumped her in some place worse than where she'd already been? She was on the horns of a dilemma.

She tapped her toe to the rhythm of a mariachi band playing somewhere beyond her sight. Several male voices were raised in near-harmony; a guitar played; people clapped along. She touched her hair thoughtfully. Yellow. A definite asset.

"Doralee."

She glanced over her shoulder, surprised. She had him figured for another thirty minutes of pencil scratching at least. She smiled and twirled a fat curl around her finger, hoping to wipe away the slight frown that creased his black brows.

"Were you needin' somethin', sugar?"

"The way you're hanging out that window, I'd be inclined to think you were advertising your wares—if I weren't so confident that I've kept you too occupied to consider looking for somebody else."

"Why, Danny, whatever do you —"

"Come over here away from that window, Doralee."

She straightened slowly, patted her curls, and adjusted her neckline to cover a bit more cleavage before turning to face him. It wouldn't do to seem too eager to please the man. She crossed the bare floor toward him in what she hoped was a demure fashion.

But Dan wasn't in a demure mood. No sooner had she reached his side, than he slid his hand up her back and pulled her down on his knee. "Talk to me, Doralee."

"About what?"

"About yourself."

"You know all about me," she began, but he interrupted by placing one of his fingers on her full lips.

"Not that you're from Louisiana. Lots of girls are from Louisiana. And not that your grandaddy had a peach orchard. There's plenty of girls with that kind of story to tell."

"There's nothin' else to tell, sugar," she edged nervously. This was a different Dan; he'd never looked at her quite so intently before, like he really was interested in what she had to say, not just what she knew.

His lids lowered until it seemed that all of his fierce attention was aimed at her, and her cheeks burned at the touch. "I want to know why you are what you are."

She tried to stand up, but his hands closed over her arms, and she was captive in his grip. "I reckon there's plenty of other girls with that kinda story to tell, too."

"But not your story, darling. Yours is the one I want to hear."

"It's none of your damned business," she muttered, all pretense at coyness dropped.

"What if I aim to make it my business?"

"What are you talking about?"

"I'm talking about a trip that seems to be wasted. I don't like wasted time, or wasted money, and there's been a lot of both this time out. Unless …"

"Unless what?" she glowered rebelliously. At least he'd chosen a decent enough place to dump her in.

"I've got an idea for a story, an interview, that's never been done before."

"And what might that be?" she sighed. More talk of stories, for God's sake. As if she really cared.

"An interview with a harlot."

"What?" This time when she shot to her feet, he made no effort to stop her.

He was watching her closely, making her nervous.

"My paper pays big money for stories... of big people. I can't guarantee that they'll pay much for this one, not because it's not good enough. It'd sell papers like there's no tomorrow. But because you're nameless, and would have to remain that way, they'll claim your story isn't worth much."

Her cheeks were burning. "Why are you sayin' these things to me? What have I done to you to deserve this?"

His low, throaty chuckle sent a ripple down her spine. "Doralee, you haven't done a thing to me that wasn't pure heaven, and I don't offer such praise lightly. That's why I know you'll be a big success in New York, if you ever get there."

The "if" set an alarm jangling in her head, so loud, she almost missed his next words.

"But you give me your story, and I guarantee you'll be able to waltz into New York City and have the wealthiest barons in the country, in the world, at your feet."

She felt a tingling sensation, the closest she'd ever had to ecstasy from a man, coiling deep in her body. It was as if he'd reached into her mind and pulled out her dream—and offered it to her on a silver platter. This idea made her want to sit back down, and his knee was still the closest thing around. "Tell me more ..."

He caressed the back of her neck. "I want to know why you are what you are."

She sat there for a long time, eyes closed, his fingers rubbing slow circles on the back of her neck. She didn't want to think about it, didn't want to remember. "I ain't never told a soul before."

"It's all right, Doralee. There's no hurry. I've got all day... all night."

His voice was so soothing, not hard and gruff like sometimes. "My ma died when I was ten years old," she whispered. "The first time my pa had his way with me, I was twelve."

His fingers stopped.

"You mean, he …"

She nodded.

"Go on." He sounded so sad, not at all like she would have expected. He pulled her closer and never had a man's arms felt so good. "I think your story will make us both a lot of money, Doralee. If that's what you want."

"The way I see it, that's the only thing good ever come out of my old man—whatever money this story'll get me." She sniffed, steeling herself for the coming ordeal. "I was thirteen when he started comin' to me every night, and I ran away from home …"

Jennings sat alone at a small, round table in the noisy bar. This was his kind of establishment. It smelled more of cigars and cigarettes and cheap perfume than of sweat; not like most out here in the west, smelling of sweat, both man and horse. A redheaded whore, pretty enough, had been giving him the eye for half an hour. Ordinarily, he wouldn't have been so slow to respond.

But tonight his mind was on other things.

He nursed his whiskey, keeping a careful watch on the swinging doors. The message he had received had been cryptic, and poorly worded, but it had been specific on one point: 8:00 tonight.

It was now a quarter till nine.

Maybe it was a wild goose chase after all. This whole damned trip seemed to be nothing more. He drained the glass, considered ordering another, then decided to hell with it. He'd just as well leave.

He scraped the chair backward across the rough wood floor but stopped when a massive form filled the doorway. He relaxed back into the chair and raised his empty glass at the bartender. Waiting had paid off.

The whore filled his glass, dipping low to show off her ample bosom. He'd always had a weakness for redheads. He paid her double the price of the whiskey, but declined her offer to go upstairs.

Before she headed back toward the bar, the newcomer closed his beefy hand over the whore's. "Leave the bottle."

She did as she was told and was about to leave when the man squinted up at her. "Don't go too far." He took the chair opposite Jennings.

Jennings sat back in silence and waited. This was the game the way he liked to play it.

"We've met before."

Jennings nodded. "Sheriff Dougherty, you're pretty far out of your domain, aren't you?"

Dougherty opened his jacket to show a vest without adornment. "I ain't sheriff no more."

"Run out of town, I presume?"

Dougherty didn't rise to the bait. "Resigned for personal reasons."

"I heard about your personal problems. Please accept my condolences over your brother's death."

"Murder."

Jennings arched his black brows. "Really? I wasn't aware anything had been proven."

Dougherty's smile was cruel. "Not yet. That's what I aim to do."

"I wish you luck, but I don't know how you expect me to help you." Jennings took a short drink from his whiskey.

"You can tell me who called you to Cavendish in the first place."

"Really, Sheriff, I can't see that any of this matters any more. A phantom summons. The proverbial wild goose chase, as they say. I must admit, I am surprised to cross paths with you in this fair city"

"I have my reasons for being in El Paso. Business."

"At the newspaper office?"

"They agreed to take on a private job for me, a little printing I need done. Had to come all the way to El Paso to find a press that could handle it." He trained his black eyes on Jennings. "That son-of-a-bitch kidnapped my brother's wife. I aim to get her back, no matter what the cost."

Jennings noted the deep lines etched around the sheriff's mouth. Something told him it was some emotion other than concern that had put them there. "Your fraternal loyalty is admirable, I'm sure."

When Dougherty smiled, it was grim, mirthless, yet Jennings had no doubt the other man was savoring some secret pleasure.

"By the time I get through, those two won't be able to set foot in any town in the southwest without getting caught."

Jennings, suddenly dry-mouthed, tossed down the rest of his whiskey. Damned if he was going to offer his assistance.

Dougherty shrugged and curled his thick lower lip under the rim of the shot glass to drink. "When you came to Cavendish, what were you expectin' to find?"

Jennings shook his head. "That's my business. But I assure you it had nothing to do with your brother's death. Funny thing, a few folks around your town seemed to think he might have taken his own life. I wonder how those kind of ugly rumors got started?"

Dougherty's thick neck colored; his cheeks were already so ruddy, it was hard to tell the difference. "I hope you aren't implyin' my brother wasn't in his right mind."

Jennings shrugged. "I'm just repeating what I heard."

Dougherty's fist clenched and unclenched on top of the table. "You heard wrong."

"Maybe the sources were wrong."

"That's why I'm here, mister." Dougherty edged closer to the table, and bent his head nearer the reporter. "I want to know who... who called you to my town in the first place."

Jennings fixed the sheriff with a steady stare. "I wouldn't tell you that, even if I knew."

"What? You don't know?" Dougherty bucked back in his chair. "You're lying to me. You wouldn't drag your ass over half the country for a story, less'n you had a pretty good reason to believe a story was there."

"This is all the reason I ever need," Jennings tapped his nose, "the scent of a good story. The information I received had the ring of truth to it. That was good enough for me. And for my editor."

"Your editor? What does he have to do with it?"

"Sheriff Dougherty, I'm authorized to pay a goodly sum of money for Boone Coulter's own story. I don't mind telling you, I expected to meet him in Cavendish last month. He never showed."

"But why in the hell Cavendish? Nobody's even heard of Cavendish! Why did he want to meet you there?"

Jennings shook his head and smiled wryly. "Sorry, sheriff. You've just about reached the limit of what I know, and you have reached the limit of what I'm willing to divulge."

"You son-of-a-bitch! Tell me the rest of what you know!" Dougherty caught the reporter's shirt in his hand and yanked him forward. "Tell me who sent for you, or I'll nail your ass to the wall!"

Jennings' eyes flared, but otherwise, he showed no distress. "Release me, or I'll have you thrown in jail, Mister Dougherty."

"People around here know me. They won't believe you, no matter what you say," Dougherty growled, his whiskeyed breath too close to Jennings' nose for comfort.

"Then they don't know you very well, do they?" Jennings knocked the sheriff's hand away from his shirt, then eased his chair away from the table. "I have a companion waiting for me, sir. I hope you find your evening's entertainment as pleasant as I will find mine."

Dougherty's color deepened, his brows lowering ominously, but his voice was low and even. "Reckon I know exactly who that companion is. Trashy little thing, ain't she?"

"We obviously aren't talking about the same lady, sir."

"If you're talkin' about a lady, we obviously ain't. Could've sworn I saw that little tramp Doralee from the whorehouse back in Cavendish hangin' on your arm when I spotted you this afternoon."

The reporter merely tipped his hat and then made his departure, pushing through the crowd near the door, aware of Dougherty's eyes following him. Out on the street, Jennings paused and watched through the plate glass window as Dougherty, still scowling, allowed the redheaded whore to coax him up the stairs to the cribs.

Jennings headed up the street to his hotel, whistling a soft tune under his breath. If the sheriff's reaction was anything to go by, and his "nose" told him it definitely was, there was definitely a story here. All he had to do was to be patient.

And Dan P. Jennings knew how to be very patient, indeed.

Especially when he had such a lovely companion to help him pass the time.

Chapter Eighteen

ELIZABETH WAS ALONE in the one-room cabin. Motes of dust floated in the thin rays of sunshine that found their way through cracks in the boarded window. The fireplace was empty and cold, and despite their night's tenancy, the cabin appeared uninhabited, musty, as if it had been vacant for a long time.

Clutching the blanket to her chin, she remembered... remembered the dark passion shared on this very bed. She raised to a sitting position and found her clothes neatly folded at the foot of the bed.

Shivering in the early morning chill, she slipped out of the outlaw's flannel shirt, slid the camisole over her head, and thought of his hand smoothing and folding. Again, she shivered.

She finished dressing quickly, and coiled her hair into a tidy knot atop her head. There was nothing left to be done but emerge from the cabin; she heard his movements outside and smelled the coffee he had obviously chosen to prepare over an open fire.

She held back. She wasn't ready to face him. She rose slowly and walked through the small cabin, her fingers trailing over the rough log walls, skimming the crude rock hearth. She stopped, however, when she spotted the small, rectangular bundle on a stool in the corner.

The bundle he'd taken from Susannah's room.

Susannah, his sister. She still reeled from the shock, from the dismay. It was no wonder Coulter had hated what Obregón had done to Susannah. And yet, the tormented man in the Diablos had loved Susannah, Elizabeth couldn't doubt that.

So many questions filled her mind. She knelt before the stool, and began picking at the string that bound the parcel. The knot came loose and the coarse burlap fell away, revealing a book, its leather cover and a goodly portion of its pages charred away by fire.

A Bible.

Breathless, she turned the crackling pages, searching, and finally finding the center. The family register. The Rev. Micah Bridges... Lydia Coulter Bridges, and their children.

Susannah Wesley Bridges.

John Wesley Bridges.

Francis Asbury Bridges.

Bridges—was his name really Bridges? Coulter was his mother's but Boone... there was no hint as to its origin. Quickly, she scanned the dates, her brow knitting in a frown. The youngest son would be thirteen years old. Susannah, twenty-nine.

Born in 1854 in Tennessee, John Wesley Bridges... Boone Coulter... was only twenty-seven years old.

She couldn't conceal her shock. Those eyes, those merciless eyes, lined with harshness. How could he be so young? He was only three years older than she. Young, dear God, Boone Coulter's crimes went back for a decade... he was merely a boy when he killed his first man.

She closed the Bible, rewrapped it in the cloth that covered it, retied the string that bound it, and rose stiffly. She returned to the bed, wrapping her arms around herself in confusion.

Then, before she had steadied herself for the coming encounter, a shadow fell across the doorway—Coulter. He seemed caught off guard by finding her awake and sitting on the edge of the bed. One hand cradled a tin mug of steaming coffee, and she wondered that it didn't burn his skin. The other held a speckled blue tin plate.

He had to stoop slightly to enter. He stooped, straightened, and she found herself unable to meet his eyes. She busied herself with putting her things away, shifting her brush from one side of the bag to the other, fumbling with things already in order while he placed the plate on the table.

Even as he crossed the room toward her, she didn't look up, though her hands withdrew from the bag and fell to her lap.

"I brought you something to drink."

She accepted the mug, and it was hot, but not unbearably so. She tipped it to her lips, and their eyes met over the top of the mug, his searching, hers cautious.

Then his hands, rough and dark by comparison, covered hers around the mug, and he squatted down before her.

"Don't be afraid of me."

Her head tilted in question. "I've never been afraid of you."

"I remember." The corner of his mouth curled in the slightest smile.

Dear God, she thought, and something melted inside of her. She wanted nothing more than to lean closer and touch her lips to his, to the corner that smiled. Such a tiny smile, almost hidden in his rigid features. Here in the dimly lit cabin, the weatherworn lines smoothed away, his face seemed almost young. Even the eyes, with their wry glint, seemed less hard, less hostile.

"You aren't afraid of much, are you?"

She smiled, then. "Of course I am. I'm not that much a fool, I hope."

He shook his head slowly. "Never that, lady. Never a fool."

This time it was she who shook her head, and exasperation tinged her voice as she replied, "Lady? Still, after all that's happened, no name at all? Aren't we a strange pair... Mr. Coulter."

"It fits you, that's all." And then, he added, "Elizabeth."

She savored the sound of it, the soft, rustling sound of her name on his lips. And yet, she found herself unable to respond in kind. She forced her tone to be natural. "Somehow, Boone doesn't seem to fit you at all."

His face clouded over. He stood up and paced away from her, then stopped, studying the earthen floor. "I guess... I guess I've been Boone Coulter too long to be comfortable with anything else."

"And you're comfortable with Boone Coulter?"

His hands closed into his fists, and when he turned to face her, his tone was hesitant. "The things I've done... I'm more comfortable doing them as Boone Coulter than as ..." His voice faltered.

She took a deep breath. "John Wesley Bridges?"

His body went stiff; his head snapped up and he pinned her with a piercing gaze. "What are you talking about?"

Her cheeks flaming, she raised her chin. "I read it in your Bible."

His chest rose and fell with his short, rapid breathing; his cheeks took on a ruddy color. "You had no right."

"I only want to understand." she pleaded softly. "You're not what people think you are. I just want to understand why you ..." She couldn't finish the thought.

"You want to know if I killed all those men." His voice was carefully void of emotion, deadly calm. "You want to know if I'm a murderer."

She couldn't answer. Somehow, she hoped beyond reason, clung to a feeble wish that he was the victim of some terrible misunderstanding.

His laughter was bitter. "I did. I am."

She waited for the pain; it didn't come. The shock was not at his blunt confession, but at her own lack of concern over it. "There must have been a reason."

"A reason for murder?" He laughed again, a frightening sound. "Lady, there's always a reason for murder." He faced her in the darkness, "You want to know why? No. What you really want is a piece of me."

She wanted to say, no, you're wrong. But she couldn't. Because maybe, just maybe he was right.

"When you broke me out of jail, you took your chances. You probably got more than you bargained for... but no more than you deserved. And you don't deserve any answers."

"That's where you're wrong!" Elizabeth shot to her feet, her eyes snapping with anger. "Maybe I don't deserve any answers about how you got there, but I most certainly deserve to know what my husband had to do with it!"

He took a step closer, his voice suddenly smooth, measured, chilling. "It's really very simple. A long time ago, my sister fell in love with a young buck who had money, and a name to go with it. His name was Joel Dougherty."

She recoiled as if she'd been slapped.

"I don't imagine he told you about his first betrothed, did he?" Reading her reaction, he laughed mirthlessly. "Of course he didn't. It wasn't a very pretty story. After our cabin got torched by some of our fine neighbors in Missouri, Joel Dougherty decided he couldn't be burdened with a wife whose body was half-covered with scars, even though his own brother was responsible."

"My God... no ..."

"Those names you saw in that Bible? They're all dead. My ma, and my pa, and my baby brother Frankie were all burned alive." He stepped even closer, his face like stone, only the expression in his eyes revealing his suppressed anger. "And just in case you decide there's anything else you deserve to know, John Wesley Bridges died with them that day, so do us both a favor and don't go trying to find him:'

"I am so sorry," but even as she spoke them, she knew them to be useless, useless words. Her hands clutched the mug in a desperate grip. "Sometimes... sometimes it seems this will never end."

He paced restlessly toward the door. “It’ll end soon enough. My job’s to see you get away before it does.”

She stood, her breath caught in her throat, but she vowed not to let him see her consternation. “And you?”

He shrugged. “I always get away.”

She went to his side, raised her hand to touch the corners of his eyes, to smooth away the lines of pain. He could pass for ten years older... or, as vulnerable as he was now, perhaps even years younger...

But not the eyes... Obregón was right, despite his twisted mind. Gazing into Coulter’s eyes, she saw not years, but scars. Whatever had happened to Susannah, had happened to him, too. Whatever had happened...

But she couldn’t ask. It was a distance between them she dared not try to cross again. To see his eyes shuttered away from her again was an agony she refused to risk. Not now.

“The years have been hard on you,” she said simply.

He didn’t answer.

She dropped her hand to her stomach and forced a smile. “Have you eaten, yet?”

He nodded. “You’d better get yours before the bugs carry it off.” His words were casual; his tone wasn’t.

She moved to the table, and felt his eyes burning into her back. Some kind of bright yellow scrambled eggs waited for her there. She briefly wondered what kind, then decided she’d rather not know.

She took her place on the makeshift stool and began eating without benefit of utensils, lifting lady-like pinches of egg to her lips, then sipping at the coffee. Once, when her fingertips were poised at her open lips, she caught his eyes lingering on that innocent motion, and suddenly it wasn’t innocent at all. With Coulter’s eyes on her every move, she felt an eternity pass while she tried to swallow.

She couldn’t eat any more, and pushed away from the table to stand. Her fingers were greasy. She found the flannel shirt on the bed and wiped her fingers on the soft corner.

He shoved his hands in his pockets and stared at his boots. Then, as if shaking off a bad feeling, he scratched the back of his ear and raised his eyes to hers. "How'd you like to take a cold bath?"

"I have rather mixed feelings about it. A bath would be lovely, but cold?"

There it was again, the expression on his face that said he didn't recognize her light tone as teasing. "There aren't any servants here to haul water up and heat it for you, and I guarantee you I'm not going to do it myself."

"A cold bath would be wonderful," she sighed, more than a little exasperated. "If you can lead me to enough water to cover my ankles, I swear I shall die a happy woman."

Coulter gave her a sharp look, then a grudging smile. "Head upstream a ways and you'll find a spot good for bathing."

Elizabeth gathered her things and minutes later, she was alongside the stream again. Along the banks, maple and walnut dominated the other trees—surprisingly, for they were totally unsuited to the desert environment that surrounded the canyon.

She quickly came to a spot where the water pooled above a small, splashing fall of water. In this oasis, even the sawgrass surrounding the pool grew lush and dense and green. She dropped to sit on a fallen log, her bare feet burrowing in the soft, warm earth. For the moment she was content to simply gaze at the peaceful scene, softly lulled by the buzzing of water-bugs darting to and fro across the water's busy surface.

The buzzing grew louder.

Suddenly, the air was filled with the drone of insects, and she felt panic tightening in her chest, welling in her throat. She leaped to her feet, and found herself in the center of a buzzing, vibrating vortex of orange and black bees. Arms crossed over her face, she stood frozen in terror, eyes pressed shut, waiting for the assault.

And was assaulted by laughter, soft laughter, and she found herself not hiding in terror, but lowering her arms, peering through the cloud of bees.

Coulter stood a few yards away, shaking his head in laughter.

"This is not amusing," she snapped.

"They don't sting."

"That's easy for you to say. They aren't attacking you."

"Lady," he chuckled softly. "If you'd just look at yourself, you'd know two things. One, they aren't attacking you either."

She had to agree. One after another of the bees broke formation and plummeting straight into the ground through small, deep holes near her feet.

"Two, you're standing on top of their burrow."

"Oh!" She leaped several feet toward him, and to her dismay, his arms were opened and ready to catch her. Just as he'd predicted, the bees didn't follow, but continued into their earthen home.

His chest shook against her stiff body, shaking with quiet laughter. "They don't sting."

"You didn't tell me there were bees here!"

"They could be anywhere, lady. Anywhere that's shady, and has soft dirt. You just happened to sit down in the middle of them." He opened his arms and released her, and she felt oddly bereft.

"Why—why did you follow me?" She made a great to-do of smoothing her skirts and hair, trying to hide how flustered she still was.

"Because you hurried out before I could tell you which pool to bathe in. You stopped too soon."

"This one seemed pleasant enough," she demurred.

"Pleasant enough," he agreed.

"But if there's another ..." She couldn't refrain from casting a wary glance at the smaller, though still teeming swarm of bees.

He laughed again, a sound that sent ripples of warm pleasure skimming up her spine. "Come on along, then."

She followed him along the trail, farther upstream, for the moment distracted from the surrounding lushness, absorbed by the new lushness that seemed to burgeon within her body. A certain off-guard look, a small quirk of smile, a low chuckle, and there it was, bubbling inside her, leaving her both weak and filled with life.

Was he aware?

For if he was, he would surely shy away, the wary shield would cover his features again.

She concentrated on his back, straight and strong in front of her, on the easy swing of his arms as they reached out occasionally to push aside a low-hanging branch, and his hands, caressing a glossy leaf a few seconds longer than mere function required.

The tension she'd seen in him was still there, but muted, banked beneath the surface, a slow-burning heat all too ready to flame into life... but not now. Not in his mountain-canyon oasis.

He stopped ahead of her and turned, waiting for her to join him. And there, standing at his side, she recognized paradise.

"Oh, my ..."

Recessed into the side of the canyon wall was a rocky grotto, and before it a glassy pool of emerald water, surrounded by a dense growth of luxuriant green maidenhair ferns. She caught her breath, half-expecting to see darting fairy-lights among the conical limestone deposits in the recesses of the grotto, some dripping moisture from above, others jutting magically from the ground.

"Why... Mr. Coulter..." Words wouldn't form. There were no words to describe the effect of such green ecstasy to her sun-ravaged soul. "It's... it's like a corner of heaven."

Coulter's eyes were shadowed, his tone somber. "It's the closest place to heaven I'll ever know."

She didn't want his somberness to ruin such a moment for her. She stepped away from him, holding her skirts high to trail the toes of one foot in the water. She stooped to pick a stalk of blue blossoms, lifted it to her nose, and promptly sneezed.

"Bless you ..."

She turned slowly.

The expression on his face dispelled all the shimmering joy of the moment, but replaced it with a substantial new emotion as he spoke. "This... now... is the closest to heaven I'll ever be."

She moved toward him, meeting him halfway. His hands went first to her hair, tugging the combs out and letting it fall free, spilling down her back in a sun-streaked skein of silk, snagging on his rough calluses, clinging like sheer strands of a golden-brown web.

His fingertips traced the high angles of her cheekbones, the sharp line of her jaw, the slender column of her neck. "Lady Elizabeth... you make it heaven."

It was the morning of their fourth day in the canyon.

Elizabeth sat on the corner of the bed, watching Coulter add wood to the fire to heat the fat for their first meal of the day, several small squirrels he had shot only an hour earlier. He'd already skinned and dismembered them; they had only to be fried.

It was easy to sit back and watch him, to be caught up in the idyll of their tenuous existence. Neither had spoken of the outside world. But the outside's shadow remained, ready to sneak in at the first unwanted moment.

Moments like this one.

In the previous days, she had explored the canyon with this man, marveling at the bat caves, tasting the tart fruit of the prickly pear, scraping her fingers along the rough bark of the alligator juniper.

Together, they had run their hands over the smooth white bark of the madrone, and in the spots where the white had peeled away, the satiny new red bark beneath. Glossy green leaves, bark colored like fruit and cream, red berries that carpeted the ground beneath the low trees... the madrone tree appeared to have sprung from an enchanted forest.

Together, they had explored; together, they had avoided the inevitable.

And so, on this cool, foggy morning, with wisps of mist trailing through the canyon floor, she tried again to push the tension aside and live one more day, without fear, without worry—two people isolated from the world.

But on this morning, such desires were impossible to fulfill. She felt it present in the room with them as surely as the crude walls and earthen floor—the awareness that idylls, by their very nature, were brief

She felt a nagging doubt. "Do you always find someone so... accommodating, to help you in your escape?"

"I never had to escape, before."

She was determined. "But you had help avoiding capture, I suppose."

"I don't depend on anybody's help for anything." He turned to face her. "Is that the answer you wanted?"

Of course it was. But it wasn't enough. She gazed thoughtfully over his shoulder, her fingers smoothing a tendril of her hair back into place. "Surely there have been other women."

His lids lowered, hooding his eyes from her. "Surely."

She shifted her gaze and nibbled her lip. Maybe she really didn't want to know any of this—but she did. She certainly did. "Many, I presume."

His eyes were steady when she finally met them. Steady, and dark with some remembered pain. "A few. But that was a long time ago."

Enough of that, she thought, unwilling to push further. And then she addressed the subject which, really, was of more importance after all.

"If we can't go to Seven Rivers, where can we go?"

He slung a stick into the fire with more than necessary force, sending a spray of sparks onto the floor. He stamped them out before answering.

"I've changed my mind. I'll take you to Seven Rivers. There's enough traffic through there that we won't be noticed. Besides, once you're on the stage... it'll be over. You'll be safe enough."

Elizabeth twisted the gold band on her finger. "A place where I can sell some jewelry to buy a ticket?"

He nodded, avoiding her eyes. "Where to? You've decided, I guess."

"I had thought Philadelphia, but now I think it best if I go to my sister in San Francisco. Clayton would never know to look there."

He seemed to accept her answer. How little he knew...

"It's very pleasant there, this time of year." She prattled on about her sisters, their "lovely" families. He went about the business of cooking, a business she'd never liked, one of many distasteful tasks she'd been relegated to in the years when it had seemed she would spend her life assisting her sisters and their wretched families...

She wondered how many bald-faced lies she could tell this man, and have him accept them without question. Accept them because he wanted to believe her, wanted to believe that her life stretched before her, a ribbon of loveliness for her to return to, a suitable life for a lady.

The spurt of self-pity died as quickly as it had come. For her, life stretched without excitement, without the independence she had come to value so much... without love. For him, life would be more running. Even his time here was shadowed by the knowledge that ranchers were moving in, encroaching on his wilderness. He was little more than a squatter on this land. Coulter would be on the run, again...

And the very least she could do for him was let him believe she would be at peace with her own family.

"Have you ever been East?" she asked, the wedding band rubbing a raw spot where she twisted it too hard.

The squirrel pieces hit the hot fat with a loud popping and sizzling. "I'm not cut out for civilization."

She thought to argue, but didn't. Certainly, she couldn't envision him in morning clothes or a business suit, working at a bank with her brother-in-law, or as a grocer or tradesman.

"In Philadelphia the winters are quite cold, and the summers hot ..." She forced a laugh. "At least, they seemed so before I came here. I've never been to San Francisco, though."

"You'll be happy to see your family again."

"I will be... content."

Oh, the lies...

The fire was dying in the fireplace, providing the only dim light; the sweet smell of burning wood and roasting venison permeated the small, one-room cabin. The woman was asleep on his bed, only a pile of deerskins spread over a narrow rope mattress, but soft enough. She was covered with a blanket.

Her hair was no longer pinned tightly, nor was it a flow of tangles. Instead, it was braided long and sweet-smelling on her back, and standing over her Coulter thought she looked of nothing so much as a young girl. In sleep, her chin didn't rise up with pride; her eyes didn't crimp at the corners from the glare of the sun; her jaw didn't clench with strain.

Instead, her lips fell open softly, invitingly, and for the first time in many, many years, he wondered how it would be to be seventeen years old again, this time with nothing more on his mind than to steal a kiss from those wide, tender lips

For years he'd been so obsessed with Susannah's tragedy, he'd never considered the other lives, unknown to himself, that would be affected. Elizabeth's marriage to Joel had been doomed from the start. And the idea of her under the same roof with Clayton Dougherty... his hatred stirred anew. But for the grace of God, she would even now be subjected to his monstrous desires. As long as there was a danger of Clayton Dougherty finding her, she wouldn't be safe in Philadelphia, in San Francisco, anywhere.

Clayton Dougherty had to die.

A stirring sounded in the bushes outside the cabin's slatted window-opening. He straightened silently, reaching for the pistol on the crude table. Two stealthy steps brought him to the doorway, where he pressed himself flat against the wall and waited to hear more.

It came again, too clumsy and heavy to be the normal sounds of night creatures. Gun raised, Coulter edged closer to the door—

and lowered it when he recognized the hulking giant hovering at the edge of the clearing. Before the bird-call signal had stopped, Coulter was already speaking.

"Lucius?" he asked hoarsely.

"Johnny!" the giant boomed, and closed the distance between them and wrapped him in a bearhug, despite the deadly pistol now wavering dangerously near the newcomer's head. "Put that firearm down, Johnny, and tell me what you're doin' here!"

"Shhh…" Coulter extricated himself from the man's grip and cast a wary look toward the bed.

"Lordy, lordy... you done brought a woman in here?" The man peered tentatively over his shoulder, but Coulter grabbed his arm and steered him back out the door.

"Let's get outside where we can talk."

Without the soft glow of the fire to illuminate them, the two men were alone in the black night.

"What are you doing here this time of night?" Coulter asked softly, dropping to his heels and leaning his back against the rough log wall of the cabin.

Lucius strained as he hunkered beside Coulter on the ground. "I was down near the Prescott range this evenin', saw ol' Sage up on the north ridge along about sunset. I figgered I'd drop in on ya' fer a spell."

He reached into his shirt pocket, and from the sounds, Coulter knew he was pulling out his pouch and papers, then rolling a cigarette. In the dark. And he probably wouldn't spill a shred of tobacco.

"Didn't mean to disturb ya' none "

A match flared, lighting the man's grizzled face, only his eyes dark, surrounded by fuzzy white beard and hair. He raised the match to his cigarette and sucked in; it caught and he shook the match out and tossed it aside. "Didn' know ya had company."

When Coulter didn't take the hint, he flicked the ash off the end of his smoke and asked him point-blank, "Who is she?"

"Somebody in trouble. A woman I brought out of the Diablos."

"Diablos! Mm-hmmm." He smoked in silence for a spell, then flicked ash off the end of his cigarette. It landed on the ground, still burning; he patted the toe of his boot over it before it could spread into the dry grass. "Well, don't reckon you'll be offerin' me a place on your floor."

Coulter leaned his head against the wall and sighed, his eyes closing in frustration. "Not on the floor. You're welcome to sleep out here. It's too late to be moving on."

"Don't want to be in the way, Johnny ..."

"You won't be. Just don't go scarin' her with that ugly face of yours before I have time to let her know you're here."

Lucius reached a gnarled hand to his beard and scratched it thoughtfully. "Might be needin' a shave, now that you mention it. This here face ain't all that ugly cleaned up."

Coulter moved to stand.

"Heard some strange things from down southwest o' here."

Coulter stopped, forced himself to relax. "What kind of things?"

"That gunslinger's been at it again. That Boone Coulter feller. This time he's really done got himself in hot water. Done killed a sheriff's brother and kidnapped the dead man's wife."

"You don't say." So that was why he'd come. To warn him.

"Yep. I do say. Take a pretty damn fool kind of idiot to do a thing like that, wouldn't you reckon?"

"If that's what he did."

"Ya don't have any reason to doubt it, do ya', Johnny?"

Coulter sighed. News had traveled faster than he'd anticipated. "On a night like tonight, Lucius, I guess I'd believe just about anything." Coulter stood up, then. "I'm going on to sleep. Find yourself a place to stretch out, and I'll be seein' you in the morning."

"Think I'll move closer to the water. I allus did like the sound of water. Ain't enough of it 'round here for nuthin; may as well enjoy it while I can."

Lucius lumbered to his feet and headed through the underbrush toward the stream. He paused and turned back. "Fact is, I reckon there ain't much reason to hang 'round these parts much longer. I figgered I'd better let ya' know 'bout that gunslinger bein' on the loose, case anybody comes this way a-lookin' fer 'im."

Coulter waited until his noises had settled, then reentered the cabin.

The woman was facing him, her eyes huge and black in her face. "Who is that man?" she asked, a tremor in her voice.

"Name's Lucius. He's kind of a hermit. He wanders through here two or three times a year."

"He called you Johnny."

"That's the name I'm known by around here, what few people know me at all. Johnny, that's all, no last name."

She rolled onto her back and stared upward, not meeting his eyes. "They're saying you kidnapped me."

"And killed your husband, so it seems."

"Clayton knows better."

"If he told that story, he had a reason."

"Plenty of them."

"Go back to sleep. There's nothing to be done about it, now." But she didn't move, and as he tugged his boots off for the second time that night, he found himself asking, "How'd he explain such a thing? I was locked up in jail."

"You've quite a reputation, you know. I suppose people would believe just about anything. Besides, the citizens of Cavendish aren't in the habit of doubting Clayton Dougherty. And with poor Wendell on duty... I did so hate making him look foolish. Bringing you in was the best thing that ever happened to him."

"That's his bad luck," Coulter grunted, tugging the other boot free. "He'll have to find another murderer if he aims to redeem himself. I have no intention of giving him another chance at me."

I wouldn't let him, Elizabeth thought.

But a new, cold fear closed over her heart. Now, not only Wendell, but a dozen others like him... all after Boone Coulter, for the glory of gunning him down... and now she was serving as the beacon to guide them.

Coulter had the enamel coffee pot in his hand, ready to toss the remains into the fire when she stopped him. "I'm awake, aren't you? Maybe we could drink the last, get warm ..."

He shrugged. "Guess so."

"And your friend outside? Would he care for some?"

Coulter seemed exasperated, but finally nodded. "I imagine he would, after riding for hours and probably no dinner."

"Why don't you take him some?"

Coulter filled a tin mug with the steaming brew and headed out the door. Elizabeth waited until he was out of sight, then frantically searched her carpet bag for the bottle.

Hands trembling, she splashed a large dollop of Hofstetter's Tonic into Coulter's mug, then topped it off with coffee, strong enough to stand alone after sitting by the fire for hours. She dropped the tonic bottle back into the carpet bag, then returned to the table to wait.

"Please forgive me," she whispered as she bowed her head over his mug.

"Lady..." The word was soft, not a title, not a label of gentility, but an endearment. The hand on her shoulder, the fingers in her hair, endearments without words. "What's wrong?" he asked, and when she turned into his embrace, his arms closed around her without question.

He smelled of outdoors, cool and crisp and evergreen, a hint of smoke from the fire clinging to his flannel shirt. His arms were her anchor, his face nuzzling hers her balm, her torture. Could she do it? Could she?

Wendell, Clayton, others... after Boone Coulter... and she was the beacon to guide them.

I won't let them.

"Lady ..." His lips found hers, and she knew a moment's doubt. Melting, sweet torment flowed through her veins as she leaned into his body, meeting his kiss with a desperation that sprang from her guilt.

Then, she pulled away and reached for the mug, and pressed it into his hands. “Here,” she said.

He sat at the table, his eyes devouring her with a hunger that transcended the physical... and drank.

She loosened her hair, sat on the bed, combed, brushed, combed...

Until he slipped forward in the chair and fell facedown across the table.

Tears streaming from her eyes, she pulled him from the chair, breaking his fall before he could hit the floor, struggled under his weight. There was no way she could get him into the bed. Sobs wracking her body, she shoved a folded blanket under his head, covered him with another, kissed his unresponding lips....

“For your own good,” she whispered, her tears falling onto his face like gentle rain.

“Please... forgive me.”

Chapter Nineteen

WAKE UP… HAVE to wake up… Coulter's eyes clammed shut against the pain… his head throbbing. He lifted his head, and the whole universe quaked around him. His fingers grasped the blanket that covered him. Cold… so cold… a chill racked through his body.

It was dark, still night. The frogs croaked so loudly they were vibrating through his ear, his head, his mind… dizzy… light-headed. His hands trembled. His face wet with cold sweat, the dizziness began to subside.

He wanted to get up, but couldn't. He felt his head gingerly… no knots, no swelling, no wound. What was the matter with him?

Elizabeth… where was she?

"Laa …" A croak, nothing more. He raised his head slowly, closed his eyes.

"Laa… dy?"

Not loud enough. She didn't hear. He breathed deeply.

"Lady? Answer me!"

His face contorted in pain as his own voice rang through his head. Still… no answer… He steeled himself… braced his hands against the floor… not strong enough. He opened his eyes.

Where was she?

The bed was empty. Her carpetbag was gone.

And then his eyes rested on the mug overturned on the floor.

With dawn came a cold, steady rain, pelting Elizabeth's face. The mild summer storm gusted with chilling winds. But her wet body was no colder than her heart, the gray dawn no more dismal than her soul. Once again, she was running.

Only this time, instead of Coulter's familiar back and Sage's restless gait, the immense form of the mountain man preceded her. She followed on the mare, keeping pace with the plodding rhythm of the mountain man's horse.

This time she was running not for her own life, but for Coulter's.

Soon the rain stopped, the wind died, and the mare picked up her pace and pulled alongside the lead horse.

"Reckon we've been in New Mexico fer a good couple 'a hours."

At first, she didn't hear the mountain man speaking to her. Then, huddled in her sodden cloak, the rim of its hood dripping in her face, she managed a nod.

"Wetter year than we've had in recent mem'ry. Ain't complainin' though. Never complain 'bout rain less'n it sweeps away yer missus and kids. Then mebbe you've somethin' to complain about." He spat at the ground. "Mebbe."

She forced a smile, another nod, and his wide-mouthed grin made it worth her while. She hadn't realized how accustomed she'd become to the outlaw's long silences, until confronted with a man whose desire to communicate had been stifled for weeks, maybe even months.

"How long should it take us to get to Seven Rivers?" she asked numbly.

"A couple of days, mebbe longer. Now we're on the plains, the goin'll be easier. The wet'll slow us a mite. Yep, mebbe longer."

He angled his face up at the sky, and the dark clouds overhead. "Then agin, mebbe not."

This brought a little laughter from her cold lips. "Do you ever give a straight answer?"

"All m' answers are straight, ma'am. It's m' mind that wanders here and yon. No sooner do I reckon one thing, another comes along to distract me." He kicked his horse to pick up the pace a little. "Jest like last night... when you ast me t' help you git to Seven Rivers, I figgered it was a good move. Johnny's done been through too much to risk it all fer somethin' I kin do jest as well. He's a good boy, Johnny is, no matter what he's done."

She aimed a startled glance in his direction, and found him eyeing her as well. What did he know?

"Now that I've done helped ya', I'm wonderin' if I hadn't done went and made a mistake."

She swallowed the lump in her throat. Johnny. Coulter. Outlaw. Gunslinger. Murderer. Lover.

"It had to be done."

"Yep, I reckon yer right, all right. Jest didn't seem right leavin' him there, sleepin' 'n all, and havin' him wake up 'n find us gone. I wouldn't wanta be the one to explain why, that's fer dadgum sure."

"Nobody has to explain why, Mr. Merriweather. He'll understand."

"Gee, haw, but if that don't beat all! Ever' time you call me that, I feel like lookin' over m' shoulder to see who the gentleman is that's sharin' my name!" His cackle was muffled by the wind and rain, but audible and comforting to her ears nonetheless.

"You've a mighty fine seat on a horse, fer all that yer a lady, 'n all." Again, he met her gaze, and this time he came right out with it. "You're Elizabeth Dougherty, ain't ya'?"

Her mouth opened, but she didn't speak. What did he know, and what did he just suspect? And what would he do with the information if she confirmed it? She stared straight ahead, and he seemed to accept her reticence, easing back into his rambling conversation.

"Yep, a nice seat on a horse. Like you're born to it. Not as good a rider as m' first wife, who could outride the wind itself, if the mood struck her, which it did, from time to time."

To the sound of the old man's voice, she drifted into sleep. Not the sound sleep of the comforted. It was a fretful rest, at best. But better that than awake, and remembering Coulter's face when last she saw it... unlined in sleep, bathed in the soft glow of tallow-light…

At peace.

Coulter stumbled out of the cabin, eyes wild, his tone of voice frantic. "Elizabeth! Where are you?"

He staggered to the place where the mare had been secured, found the rope, the tracks. He followed them. His throat was raw, his head throbbed. She had walked beside the mare, walked this way along the stream. Here she had mounted.

Another set of tracks... another horse?

Lucius?

"Lady!"

His voice rocketed off the canyon walls, echoing into infinity.

In a few minutes he returned to the cabin, a new rage building within him, feeding off his fear, his confusion. He'd follow... she couldn't leave him. Not now. He wouldn't feel safe until he put her on that stage himself. What protection was Lucius if they came across Dougherty?

He whistled sharply between his teeth; Sage didn't respond. This was no time for the stallion to act up.

What time was it? He examined the sky, gray, rain to the south, no sun. How long since she'd left?

He whistled again, and this time, to his relief, the horse responded with a distant neigh.

Elizabeth and Lucius had ridden out of the rain into the heat, into the dusk, into the night, dry-camping the first night. Another long day's ride, and they finally neared their destination.

Seven Rivers was a scattering of lights a mile away in the black night. As they rode, sometimes the lights disappeared altogether. Then they'd climb a rise and there they would be, a little closer than before. But with the town of Seven Rivers came a new problem: the renewed threat of discovery.

She paused on a hilltop, holding her weary mare back. The sweet smell of gamma grasses and sage filled her with a pang of regret. If only he were here at her side... but no. She mustn't let herself think that way.

What had he taught her? Being alone had kept him alive, and now she understood why. Alone, you had no one else's needs but your own to think of.

But that wasn't so, was it? She was very alone, despite the mountain man's presence. Yet her every action was geared to one thing alone: Protect Boone Coulter.

What if he came to Seven Rivers to find her? I am known there... Whatever stage you get on, there'll be someone to notice. Somebody who'll remember.

"Perhaps I'd better stay out here on the prairie until morning, and then you can bring me some food and help me arrange for my passage."

"No need'n that, little lady. Nobody's gonna recognize you if you do as I say. Us comin' in at night's a blessin'." Lucius tugged a wrinkled, grimy bandana from his pocket. "Tie this here 'round yer head."

Elizabeth accepted it with tight lips and gritted teeth. That disgusting thing on her hair?

Lucius got off his horse with a loud grunt, then squatted to scoop up a handful of dirt. "Yer already a sight full o' dust, but too much of ya' is still showin' fer them that might know ya'. Rub this on ya' some. That's it. On yer face, and a lot on yer britches, er skirt, er whatever that thing is."

Elizabeth rubbed the dirt into her split-skirt, and with misgivings, on her cheeks and neck. Then, with a heavy heart, she tied the bandana over her hair.

"Give me that coat yer wearin', and I'll put it up. It's too fine a thing fer a rancher's wife, and that's what we're aimin' t' make ya."

She shrugged the cloak off her slender shoulders and handed it to him. "Do rancher's wives often ride through the cold of the night with nothing but a thin shirt to protect them?"

Lucius cackled with glee. "Think y' got me there, eh? Well, lookee at this!"

He pulled a Navajo blanket from his satchel. It was as old and dusty and disreputable as she felt.

"Ya' look mighty fetchin', ma'am. Mighty fetchin' indeed." He cackled again. "Now, here's the other thing. When we git into town, don't ya' open yer mouth fer nuthin' or nobody. Ain't no way to dirty yer voice or yer fine way o' speakin', and that'd attract attention faster 'n wearin' a goldurn sign!"

He seemed quite pleased with himself over that bit of wisdom. But beneath her irritation, Elizabeth accepted it for what it was, the sage advice of one who knew better how to get by in tough scrapes than she.

"Ain't much we c'n do 'bout that mare, so it'll have to do."

"What do you mean? What's wrong with her?" Elizabeth demanded, more offended for her faithful mount's sake than her own.

"Too sassy lookin', splotchy horse like that. Too easy to remember. Take ol' Jaspar here. He ain't no differ'nt lookin' than most. Nuthin' there to hang a mem'ry on. Oh, well, like I said, ain't nuthin' we can do 'bout it. Jest lift that purty chin o' yourn up and think o' this be in one o' Maude Thunkart's clean beds afore long. Bet you'll be glad fer that, won't ya?" They picked up their gait. "Less'n you've taken a likin' to sleepin' out under the stars. Lotsa folks do, ya' know. Not women folk usually, but ya never know—why lookee at that! Fallin' star. Must be a good omen. Less'n it don't count on account o' the Tears of St. Lawrence 'n all."

Her head shot up, but it was gone. A tear, he said. She remembered the first time she'd seen that sight, and her eyes filled with them.

"Ever' year this time, sky's jest full o' them shootin' stars." Lucius cocked his head toward the sky. "Should be jest 'bout over now. So mebbe that one does count fer luck." He spat. "Mebbe not."

They could hear the town now. It must be a boisterous night at the saloon. No sooner had they started down the main street of town, than a body came crashing into the street from what was surely the local "watering hole."

Elizabeth reined in the mare, but Lucius plowed on ahead, his dull-witted mount's gait steady as ever. "Git outa my way, varmint!" he shouted when the man on the ground reached toward him. "Don't ya' be botherin' the missus, either, less'n you want to be gelded right here in the dirt!"

The man squinted up at Elizabeth in the darkness. "You can keep yer scrawny, dried up ol' hag, ol' man. Ah ain't that randy, yit, 'n hope I never am!"

Her knuckles white on the reins, Elizabeth kicked the mare's side and sped up to catch Lucius, only to find him laughing like a fool

"What's so funny?" she demanded.

"Ain't nobody gonna recognize ya' around Seven Rivers, that's fer durn sure. Ol' Lucius is gonna git you on that stage, yet!"

Her thanks were grudging, at best. "I'm not going to parade in broad daylight like this."

His mood altered immediately. "You'll do as I say, ma'am. You'll dress as a squaw and stink like one too, ifn I say so, and ifn ya want my help. Much as I like a purty face, ain't but one reason I'm here with ya', 'n that's to keep my Johnny boy outa trouble."

Of course. Was there anything else that mattered? She raised her chin and stared him straight in the face. "Then I can only hope you don't see the need for me to dress as a squaw, Mr. Merriweather, for I don't think I could bear stinking like one."

Lucius cackled and gave Jaspar the sharp of his heel. "Come with me, ma'am. I'm takin' ya' to the best bed ye'll find this side o' Lucien Maxwell's mansion in Cimarron."

"Mr. Merriweather, I've reached the point where a blanket on the hard ground will suffice, as long as you can assure me there are no rattlers or bears wanting to share it with me."

"Gee-haw, ma'am. I swear and declare, this goddurned territory'll lose somethin' rich when it loses you."

A pang of bittersweet pride trickled within her as she followed him toward the promised bed. She'd picked a fine time to toughen up: the night before she left this godforsaken land forever.

Coulter's head throbbed less, but he felt weak. Sage was wilder than usual; he scarcely had the strength to control him.

Why are you following her, man? Damn it! Let her go!

But he couldn't because of Clayton Dougherty.

Dougherty wouldn't stop until he caught her.

A loud screeching penetrated Elizabeth's dream... and for that, she was grateful. Grateful to awaken to the shaft of morning sunshine spilling through lace curtains replacing the dream of a dark midnight ride that never ended. A dream in which she repeatedly kicked the mare harder, only to stumble and fall farther and farther behind the outlaw.

Yes, the sun casting the bed in gold, the screeching of unoiled wheels passing outside the window, the verbena and lavender scented bed linens were welcome, reassuring. Not only was the bed a soft feather mattress, but the room also was redolent of lemon oil and strong coffee.

The rag rug's bright splash of color was as welcome a sign of civilization as any Elizabeth had seen. Lucius Merriweather had been right. A night in a decent bed had done more for her aching muscles than she would have ever believed.

If only her soul was as easily soothed, her guilty conscience as easily appeased.

For with the nightmare had come the certainty that wherever he was, whatever he was doing, Coulter would never understand why she had left. To have ever believed otherwise was as foolish as she'd ever been.

But it didn't change her resolve. In three hours a stage was leaving, heading west. And Elizabeth Cooke Dougherty was going to be on it. Not for herself. Dear God, not for herself, but to protect Boone Coulter.

Alone, he'd survive.

A knock sounded at the door. She raised up and realized that she had no robe or wrapper. She held the covers up over her upper body and called, "Who is it?"

"Miz Thunkart."

"Come in."

The door swung open and the short, round mistress of the house entered bearing a heavy tray. "Did you sleep well, Miz Cooke?"

Elizabeth's stiff smile faltered for a split-second, then recovered. Cooke. She'd almost forgotten Merriweather's plan. "Wonderfully well, as a matter of fact."

"I've brung you some breakfast. I'll bet you haven't had any good, sweet white bread in many a day, have you, dearie?"

Elizabeth could hardly answer, her mouth filling with water at the aroma of hot bread and butter, eggs that most certainly came from a chicken, bacon and drippings gravy, and on the tray beside the coffee sat a tall, cold glass of milk, water beading on its side. She swallowed convulsively, her stomach contracting at the sight of so much when she was accustomed to so little.

"I don't imagine you get such wholesome food out on that ranch of yours, do you? Not many have good milch cows, what with all the range steers roaming the territory."

She placed the tray on the table near Elizabeth's bed and stood back, her plump fists on her hips. "But my Henry told me, he said, 'Maude, I won't never take you farther than a milch cow can walk,' and he kept his word, bless his soul. My Henry's a good man, Miz Cooke. A good man, indeed."

"You are very fortunate," Elizabeth sighed, tipping the cold milk into her mouth. "I haven't had milk this good since ..."

"Jersey milk. The best. That's why we don't usually have to let rooms, because I can sell the milk and cream and get prices that are downright robbery, if you ask me. But there you are. When others were pamperin' their wives by bringin' out pianos and sideboards and family pieces, my Henry was pamperin' my cows."

She waved a red, work-worn hand around the room. "The rest followed later, when we had the money to pay for it, and a place to put it. First things first, I always say."

Elizabeth toyed with the egg, a sudden discomfort dulling her hunger. "About the room, Mrs. Thunkart. It's perfectly lovely. You'll never know how much it meant for me to stay here last night. But I'm so sorry." She forced herself to meet the woman's eyes. "I haven't any money to pay you, not yet. If you'll only trust me until I can find a place to sell some jewelry—"

"Why, don't be ridiculous, Miz Cooke! I never intended you to pay for this room. When Lucius Merriweather told me you was in a bad way, I was more than grateful to help. If it weren't for that ol' goat Lucius, my cows wouldn't have made it. For that matter, neither would I." She bent her stout frame over to dust the corner of the already gleaming washstand. "Don't let me hear you say another word about paying me. It's a gift of the heart, that it is."

Her eyes misty, Elizabeth could only nod her thanks. A gift of the heart...

"Now, you'd better hurry, dearie, or you'll never make that stage. When it rolls in, it won't stop longer than it takes to change horses and drop off the mail, and pick up anything that needs pickin' up. You might end up waiting for hours for that contraption to get here, but it won't wait one second for you if you ain't ready to hop on as soon as it rolls to a standstill."

Elizabeth dug into her breakfast with renewed appetite. Who knew how long it would be before she got more food, much less a meal such as this one?

As she was forking the last bit of egg into her mouth, Maude Thunkart returned, her arms filled with clothing. "Now, I know there ain't much here for a woman as tall as you, but if there's anything you can use, I'd be more than happy for you to take it. Lucius told me the bad spell you and your old man have been having. It's nothing to be ashamed of, you know. We all have to struggle when we first get out here. For some of us the struggle's harder than for others."

"All of this, for someone you don't even know?" Elizabeth murmured, overwhelmed.

"I know you, Miz Cooke. You, and a hundred others like you. I look at you, and I see myself a few years back. There's nothin' to be ashamed of. You need a rest, dearie. Nobody knows about these things better than me. But after you go back home for a while, you'll find yourself hankerin' for this place again. Oh, I know you think right now if you never see another cactus or Injun or steer, it'll be too soon. But you just wait. Your heart's with your man, even though this country has a way of blindin' you to that. Now, you take yourself a pretty dress, 'cause we don't want your family to think your man couldn't care for you right and proper. Folks back East just don't understand, do they?"

"You are so very kind," Elizabeth whispered.

After the woman had left her alone, she rose slowly from the bedside and walked to the oak-framed mirror over the washstand. She had made a concerted effort before retiring to clean the dust and grime from her face and body.

Now, she splashed cool water across her face in an effort to wash away the feeling of foreboding that wrapped her in its dark embrace. She met her gaze in the mirror. Dark shadows ringed her eyes.

Shadows of guilt, shadows of regret, shadows of grief because she had left him.

Chapter Twenty

A HALF HOUR later Mrs. Thunkart announced the arrival of Lucius Merriweather with a disapproving sniff. Arriving outside the sitting room door, Elizabeth heard the woman fuming at the mountain man.

"... all the nice dresses I offered her, and she took the worst looking one of the lot. What will her family think?"

When Elizabeth entered the sitting room, Lucius inspected her critically from beneath his bushy brows. Finally, he nodded. "It'll do. Ya' ain't stylish nor fancy. Nobody'll look twice at ya', an' as long as ya' keep that head under that bonnet, ya' won't have to mess with any strangers botherin' ya'."

Elizabeth had to agree. The dress was blue calico, faded by too many washings and sun bleachings. As it had been made for a much shorter woman, she had to shun all petticoats but one, in order for it to drop to a decent length. At her neck she wore a brown scarf, knotted in the western style, and the sunbonnet in her hand was a dull yellow.

The nondescript attire gave her anonymity. Short of a total disguise, she could do no more to insure her safety than she had done. She looked every inch the faded, tired ranch wife forced to go back home for her health.

The woman pressed a dry, lined cheek against Elizabeth's smooth one. "You take care, dearie, and remember what I said. You'll come back, and when you do, I want you to stop by and see me. I want to see those cheeks rosy and good health, and your handsome young husband on your arm, you hear?"

Elizabeth could only nod and reach for her carpetbag, but Lucius grabbed it instead and escorted her out.

When they were standing in the blinding sunlight, he cocked his head down at her. "Stage is due 'round about noon. Reckon we'd better head in that direction, jest in case it's early."

"Please, Mr. Merriweather. First, I need to find someplace to sell some jewelry."

He nodded toward the main street, a block away. "Reckon I know jest the place. Feller over at the mercantile deals in joolry purty reg'lar. He'll give ya' a fair price, or I'll know the reason why."

"What would I do without you?" she murmured softly.

"You'd be here anyway, with Johnny at yer side, and him riskin' a whole peck o' trouble," he huffed. "And that's the goddurned truth of it, ain't it?"

Her cheeks burned. "I'm afraid it is."

Immediately remorseful, he patted her shoulder as they walked along. "Don't ya' fret none, ma'am. Yer heart's in the right place; I knows that well as I know anything. Else, why wouldn't you have jest let the boy bring you in?"

But as she walked numbly at his side, she was forced to admit the truth. Her heart was in a canyon in the Guadalupe Mountains, with the hardest, yet kindest man she'd ever known. San Francisco seemed a very long distance away ...

"Whatcha got to sell, ma'am? Ya'd better let me handle it fer ya', else you'll give it all away with that fancified way you have a talkin'."

Wordlessly, Elizabeth pulled the band from her finger and handed it to him.

"Yer weddin' band? I cain't let ya' sell yer weddin' band!"

"Mr. Merriweather, it's all I have to sell. And please, believe me," she said softly. "It has little meaning for me any more."

"But —"

"Mr. Merriweather." She met his stunned gaze without hesitation. "This is an absolute necessity. Do you understand that?"

He nodded his head sullenly. "Reckon I do. It jest don't seem right, is all. If I had any money, I'd—"

She covered his large, hairy hands with hers. "Believe me, dear friend, all of the money in this territory and the state of Texas combined couldn't do for me what you have done, through your simple kindness."

His cheeks turned fiery red beneath his salt and pepper whiskers. "I'll git as much as I kin fer it."

"But first ..."

"What is it?" he demanded gruffly. "I'll help ya' however I can."

"Do you have a small knife?"

He pulled a small, bone-handled pocketknife from his trouser pocket. "Will this'n do?"

"Very well." She took the ring from him and held it close to her face, angling it to see the inside surface. Then, with a hand not as steady as she'd like, she took the tip of the knife and began scratching the inscription.

"Let me—" he insisted.

"No, Mr. Merriweather. This is something I would prefer to do myself." And even when the knife slipped and nicked her thumb, she refused to give up until the task was completed. Finally, she handed the ring back to him, along with his knife.

"It wouldn't do to have my name inscribed for all to see," she said firmly.

"Reckon not, but what do I say when he asks me about it?"

She met his gaze without faltering. "Tell him that the owner didn't choose to have her husband's words to her worn against another's skin."

He nodded silently. "Don't suppose nobody could find fault with that."

"I don't suppose;' she agreed.

And so she stood aside, the picture of fortitude, while Lucius Merriweather took on the job of haggling over the price.

"What kind of jewelry would the madam care to dispose of?" The storekeeper at the mercantile eyed her disreputable dress with a doubting eye. Obviously, he didn't think a woman of her station could possibly possess anything worth his time.

His smug look was quickly replaced by pity when she slipped the wedding band from her finger. He accepted it wordlessly, weighing it in his palm. "Heavy gold. Looks real enough."

"Of course it is," Lucius blustered, his eyes lit with the pleasure of a true haggler.

The shopowner held it up to his spectacled eyes. "What's this inside? All these scratches?"

"Nothin' you cain't smooth off."

"Hmm…" He weighed it in his palm again, eyeing Elizabeth sympathetically. "It's good gold, but even at that, not worth an awful lot."

Fighting words, for a man the likes of Lucius Merriweather.

Elizabeth withdrew outside to allow the men free rein. When Lucius arrived at her elbow a few minutes later, she could tell by the smug expression on his hoary features that he had done himself proud.

He pressed a bill into her hands; a ticket for the Albuquerque stage. "I only wish I could have got ya' a little extry…"

"Oh, Lucius, you've given me everything," she said, clasping his hands in hers. Her heart felt as if it would break, but she refused to let him see it.

As she took her seat on the bench outside the mercantile to wait the stage, she prayed the stage would come early.

Coulter rode into Seven Rivers shortly before noon.

Pushed beyond his limits, the stallion still kept going, as if he were feeding off his master's determination and fear. But riding into town, they were a worn, bedraggled pair, the horse lathered, yet wild enough, ornery enough to sidestep disdainfully when a dog ran too close to his sharp hooves and the rider dirty, unshaven, narrow-eyed and sullen.

More than one set of eyes followed them as they made their weary way down the main street past El Gallo, the saloon, the small church, the stable.

Coulter dug his spurs into the stallion's sides when she saw her familiar figure in front of the mercantile.

Standing in the doorway, hand raised to shield her eyes—he wasn't too late.

He swung off the horse before it stopped and tossed the reins around the hitching post despite Sage's angry rearing. Abruptly the woman turned and he stopped, chest heaving, staring at a stranger, a dark-skinned, ebony haired stranger.

She frowned past him, and beckoned to a man in a mule-drawn wagon.

He wheeled, pushed past a child with a hoop, and entered the store. She wasn't there, but Coulter moved forward, single-minded, toward the clerk, ignoring a woman standing at the counter.

"The stage... when's it due?"

"There won't be another one until Thursday," the man responded, measuring out a length of calico, an arm's length from his nose. "You missed it by a day."

Coulter swayed forward, bracing his hands on the counter. He shook his head as if to clear it. "Missed it... Did anyone get on it? A woman alone? Tall, pretty. Dressed like that woman back there, black skirt and white shirt?"

"Only one woman got on. She wasn't alone, though. A man saw her off. She lives on a ranch some hundred miles southeast o' here. Name's Cooke."

Coulter shook his head again. God, where could she be…

Cooke.

"A man was with her? What did he look like?"

"Big fellow. Looked like he hadn't seen a razor or a bar of soap for that matter, for a month of Sundays. You know, a mountain man."

Coulter closed his eyes. It was her. It had to be Elizabeth. And he was a day too late.

"Where is that stage headed?"

"Albuquerque."

He was exhausted; he had ridden Sage almost into the ground. But strength surged through him, renewed him. He had no time for weakness.

He had to catch her.

Chapter Twenty-one

VAST BANKS OF thunderclouds piled up on the horizon as the stage headed north, running parallel to the mountains on the west, to the Pecos River on the east. For a day and a half, they had been underway, stopping only to water the horses and relieve the weary passengers. Soon they would angle in toward the west, to follow the Hondo River into the Ruidoso valley, to the towns La Junta, Lincoln, Fort Stanton.

Elizabeth shuddered. No one should recognize her, yet how could she feel safe stopping at a federal fort?

The early part of the journey had been uneventful, despite the attempts of the "gentleman" across from her who tried unsuccessfully to make her acquaintance, and the woman beside her who had failed to learn her situation and destination.

Had Coulter tried to follow?

The leather seat was hard beneath her, and she regretted the absence of a soft bustle. Any padding would be preferable to a single petticoat and thin calico. A few more miles passed, and the "gentleman" snored, his mouth gaping open. Perhaps he'd allowed himself one too many nips from his flask, Elizabeth speculated.

Miles and miles passed: miles of flat, grassy land separating her and Clayton Dougherty. She was almost free.

She would catch a train in Albuquerque. A frown marred her fine-boned features as she remembered that she had no money to pay for it. Her jaw clenched at the thought of begging money from her family. But despite her pride, she knew she had no choice but to wire home for money. She ticked off the list of her sisters in her mind. Whom to ask?

Still in Philadelphia were her three older sisters. Dorothy could certainly afford it, but would lord it over her for the rest of her days. Grace would never say a word of recrimination, but would begrudge the money all the same. Edith's large family could ill afford the expense, even if she wanted to send it.

Since her destination was California, the obvious choice was Anna, sweet Anna. Angelic of nature, she would be the first to give, but her domineering husband would be the last to part with a cent.

Elizabeth fretted, her mind going in circles over the same impossible choices, when all she wanted was to return the way she had come, return to Coulter. But she mustn't. She couldn't.

The coach rocked violently over the uneven road. She closed her eyes and tried not to see the memories that lurked behind her lids, waiting to drag her back into the maelstrom of regret.

She awoke to thunder, to the frantic emotion bursting within the close confines of the stagecoach. Her eyes flew open. The man across from her reached into his boot and pulled out a small derringer and she realized it wasn't thunder—

It was gunfire.

The stage was being robbed.

"Goddamn the insolence of these robbers!" The woman beside her tugged at her rings helplessly, trying to get them off her pudgy fingers as the stage jolted to a rocky halt. "Goddamn!" she repeated, then yelped as a diamond and ruby ring finally slid free. She shoved it down her blouse between her immense breasts.

Elizabeth's own hand flew to her breast. The cross. Surely they wouldn't take that. Her fingers groped for the familiar chain, and then she remembered. She no longer had it.

"We ain't got no payroll!" the stage driver shouted from atop the stage. "What are you botherin' us, for?"

A shot rang; a chunk of wood from the driver's seat landed in the dirt outside Elizabeth's window.

"Lordy, my hands is in the air! Ain't nothin' on this stage worth shootin' me over!"

Another voice joined his, apparently the guard. "You got the wrong stage, mister. Star Line went through yesterday."

Craning her neck, Elizabeth saw the mail bag land in the dust ahead of them, and glimpsed the shadow of a restless, prancing horse dancing at the front of the stage. She couldn't see the horse and rider, but a rifle barrel was clearly aimed at the stagecoach from a biscuit-colored boulder twenty feet above the road. There were at least two robbers.

"If this is the stage to Albuquerque, I've got the right stage."

The voice startled her. It couldn't be...

"Everybody out!"

She fumbled with the door while the woman fell back against the seat, moaning. Half-climbing, half-falling, Elizabeth stumbled from the stage, clinging to the door.

Then she saw him, Boone Coulter, sitting high and proud on Sage's back. Her mare was tied to a scraggly juniper a few yards away.

Their eyes met and locked, and for a moment, the world stopped around them.

How could you? his asked.

Forgive me, hers pleaded.

The sky was foreboding, the absence of sunlight around them surreal, even the birds had ceased to cry as they raced ahead of the storm. A cool wind gusted ahead of the storm, whipping her skirts around her, carrying the sweet, fresh scent of grass and dirt with it.

Then the gentleman was standing beside her, taking her elbow to support her, stepping in front of her. "Leave the ladies alone, you son-of-a-bitch. Take what you're after and get the hell out of here!"

"Drop your weapons," Coulter ordered, his low voice barely audible, but deadly in its intent, "and spill your ammunition." He watched them as the two men broke their weapons open and emptied bullets and shells into the dirt. The shotgun and rifle followed, but the man in front of her didn't move.

"You too, mister. Don't make me shoot you. I aim to kill."

Elizabeth jerked her arm away and strained to see around him, and saw Coulter's eyes droop, his shoulders seem to relax—false signals. There was nothing loose about him; she could feel his lethal danger radiating from him as palpable as the storm in the air.

The gentleman smiled slowly, raising his hands above his head. "No guns, mister. I travel light."

Blood pumping in her veins, her eyes frantically scanned his loose-fitting jacket, tight trousers, white shirt. The derringer—where was it?

A sound behind her drew her attention. She whirled in time to see the woman with the derringer in her plump but steady hand, taking aim through the window. She cocked the gun.

Elizabeth sprang forward and slammed the woman's hand against the side of the coach. "You fool! He doesn't want your jewels!" she cried, trying to twist the small pistol from the woman's grip.

It fired, the bullet going wild into the dirt. Elizabeth twisted harder and the woman snarled and cursed as the gun came free and fell to the ground. The gentleman moved as if to dive for it; another shot fired and the derringer went flying as the outlaw's bullet found its mark.

"Don't shoot!" Elizabeth cried as she scrambled after the bone-handled derringer and scooped it up. She held it in front of her in a desperate grip. "Everybody stop it!"

She glanced over her shoulder at Coulter, oblivious to the shocked stares of her traveling companions. "What do you want?" she gasped. "Are you crazy? Why did you follow me?"

"Are you coming, or not?" he asked, his voice husky.

Everyone else receded from her view. She only had eyes for him, his rangy form framed by the black and gray scud clouds racing across the sky behind him. A fork of lightning split the air and thunder crashed right behind it.

Sage reared, front hooves flashing through the air, but the outlaw seemed unthreatened by the violent reaction. His strong thighs clung to the beast's back, and with one hand on the reins, the other outstretched with the pistol still in hand, he calmed the horse.

"I haven't got all day," he shouted to her.

He was crazy. Risking everything to fetch her back like a runaway child, a lost animal... she hitched her skirts up and started running toward him.

The wind caught in her bonnet and snatched it from her head; it bounced on her back as she flew forward. He leaned off the side of the horse, one arm outstretched to catch her in his strong embrace. She slammed against Sage's side, her cheek pressed against Coulter's steel thigh, her hands clinging to him. Her nostrils were filled with the scent of horse ridden hard, of leather, of man, and she reeled at the glory of it.

"How?" she gasped. "How did you find me?"

"I've been following—I cut ahead to find a place to set up."

She shot a glance toward the rifle among the boulders, high on the cliff. "Who's up there?"

At first he didn't answer, then a smile quirked the corner of his mouth. "Nobody," he whispered. "Just a straight stick."

She wanted to laugh; she wanted to cry. He'd come after her.

And then, her head whipped around and her gaze darted to the mail bag.

She started for it, hesitantly at first, then with determination.

"What are you doing?" Coulter shouted from behind her.

She tried to lift it and found it heavier than she'd expected. She slid the small derringer into the deep pocket of her skirt, then using both hands, raised the mailbag again.

"Lady, drop that thing and come on!"

Money. Now she could escape anywhere without begging funds, without risking humiliation, without waiting for responses from those who might not even respond...

"Elizabeth!"

She clutched it to her breast and ran toward the mare.

"I said leave that thing there! I didn't come here to rob the stage!"

"We're not robbing it," she panted, lunging for the horn and stirrup and hoisting herself precariously into the familiar saddle.

God, it felt good. The mare whickered and pranced a few steps. Elizabeth tossed her head and flashed a defiant smile. "We're borrowing it."

"Lady, if you don't drop that bag, I'll shoot you myself," Coulter grated.

But her mind was already racing ahead. With money, they could make it, she knew they could…

Never releasing her grasp on the mailbag, she fumbled within the interior of the handbag dangling from her wrist until her fingers found the flat, metal surface of her calling card case. Several came out in her fingers, and she rode closer to the stage.

"Damn it, lady!" Coulter jerked the rifle to his shoulder trained it on the guard's chest. "Don't touch her, or I'll kill you."

She held the cards out toward him, and the man cringed backward, his hands held high in view, his gaze darting from her to the outlaw. Disgusted, she flung them at him. The wind whipped most of them away, but one landed at the feet of the driver.

"Please," she said as evenly as if paying a social call, "give these to your superiors as my I. O. U. I can assure you, you'll get everything back, including the money. Just consider this a loan. And please," she added sweetly, "that's my carpetbag right behind you. If you'd just give it to me …"

She smiled as the guard scrambled atop the stage and wrenched it free from the other baggage. Again, Coulter's voice snarled a warning as the guard carefully handed her the carpetbag.

Eyes bulging and jowls quivering, the heavyset man stared at her for what seemed an eternity, then finally read the card in his hand. His face smoothed in surprise, his mouth falling open. "I heard about you! You're the one who was kidnapped by Boone Coulter." He looked over her shoulder at the outlaw and blanched. "Sweet Jesus."

The guard pressed back farther from her, the gentleman's face turned deathly white, and the woman's hands fluttered against her breast as she took a step backward.

Elizabeth tossed her head, hatred for Clayton Dougherty welling anew in her breast. "Remember what I tell you, sir, and relate it to the authorities in Albuquerque. The sheriff of Cavendish, Texas is immoral, and a liar, and a murderer! As for me, I was not kidnapped. I was an accessory to Boone Coulter's escape. I let him out. He is innocent of the murder of Joel Dougherty, my husband ..." She broke off, trying to regain her composure, then burned back with more calm than she believed possible.

She kicked her heels into the mare's flanks and jolted forward. She bent over the horse's neck, her grip on the mailbag never faltering as she raced up the rocky trail. A bolt of blinding lightning, a crash of deafening thunder made the horse try to shy, but she kicked again, driving her unmercifully.

She threw a glance behind her and saw the outlaw's stallion closing the gap between them, and out of long habit, the mare gave the stallion the lead. No matter. She'd had her way; now she was willing to follow.

The rain splashed over them, yet it did nothing to dim her spirits. She bent to dodge low-hanging branches, yet when one caught her on the shoulder, she didn't even feel its sting, though its fresh evergreen scent stayed with her. She raised her face to the rain, letting it pelt her, washing away the remains of her earlier despair.

They climbed higher into the mountains, slowing as the path grew slippery. Thunder crashed around them, but still they continued, for there was nowhere to stop. The rain continued without slacking, and thinking of the narrow passes below, she wondered at the safety of the small stagecoach. A crashing boulder, a landslide, a flash flood—the dangers were many. What if the stage didn't make it through?

She felt a twinge of guilt. Her fears for their safety weren't only for the people on board, but for her brazen message. Her spirit exulted at the defiance of it.

Let Clayton Dougherty try to explain that.

Yet, watching the outlaw above her on the trail, she knew a moment's dismay. Was he angry with her for what she'd done?

Through her efforts to shoulder her share of the blame, and yes, the credit, she had put them in greater danger. She had not only compounded their crimes, she had pinpointed their location beyond a shadow of a doubt.

She deserved his anger, and yet...

Her chin raised in defiance and she flung the sodden hair from her face. Her legs were strong, her back straight, her shoulders squared.

One thought above all others rang through her mind in jubilation.

She was weary of running; she was ready to fight back.

Chapter Twenty-two

COULTER SWUNG OFF the stallion's back in an easy, fluid movement but didn't release the reins. They moved forward cautiously, man and steed, following the narrow trail as it wound closer to the edge of a precipice. The stallion shied, tried to backstep, but Coulter gave his lead a yank and muttered under his breath.

By the time he'd taken a dozen more steps, Elizabeth felt the stallion's fear, tasted it in the back of her throat.

The loose rocks and gravel, now rain-slicked, were more treacherous under foot due to the encroaching darkness. How far did the cliff plunge on the other side? A hundred feet? Two-hundred?

Her nervousness transmitted itself to the mare. She pulled the leather reins tight and squeezed her tired legs to keep the horse still.

"This is it," Coulter called, and Elizabeth didn't know whether to be relieved or alarmed. He eased back toward her, following Sage's lead now, as the horse reversed his tracks. Only when they were back on solid ground did she allow herself the luxury of breath.

"This is the place," Coulter repeated, stroking the stallion with his gloved hands, crooning beneath his breath to calm the nervous beast. "We'll be safe in this cave until morning."

"Why didn't you leave Sage here with me?" she asked. "Isn't it dangerous taking him with you on that ledge?"

"He isn't going to be too happy with me for the next few days," Coulter replied, fishing a narrow rope from his saddlebag while holding the stallion's bridle. "I can't let him run tonight. He's gonna be meaner 'n hell when it comes time to ride him in the morning."

Elizabeth dismounted cautiously, leading the mare to a piñon pine where she could secure her for the night. More than once during Coulter's struggles with the stallion, she was grateful for her more docile charge. But probably because of her own inexperience and Coulter's sure hand with his mount, they finished rubbing the animals down at about the same time.

Coulter heaved the two saddle-bags to his shoulder and lifted the carpet bag in his free hand. "Come on. Let's get in there while we can still see where we're stepping."

The rocks crunched under her feet and she was paralyzingly aware that one false step, one slip, could be disastrous. She repressed the urge to cling to Coulter's shirt, clutching her own skirts instead, holding them high so as not to risk tripping over them and falling.

The trail narrowed; she leaned away from the open precipice, her breath caught in her stomach as she clenched her teeth and followed the outlaw's heavy, crunching footsteps. Occasional rocks would skitter away, some sliding over the edge and bouncing into the distance, others falling free through the air to a landing far below.

Coulter stopped ahead of her. He faced what appeared to be a rock wall, craggy, but without an indentation sufficient to be called shelter, much less a cave. He cast her a cursory glance, saw her close behind, and nodded his approval.

"Come on. From the looks of the sky, we've got more bad weather coming. I want us in and settled before it hits." He edged around the rock barrier onto a narrow ledge, no wider than ten inches, then he disappeared from her view.

Elizabeth froze. Sure enough, she heard muffled thunder in the far distance. But the distant storm was not nearly as threatening as the possibility of plunging to the unseen canyon floor below.

His voice called out to her, but she didn't move. She heard muffled movements, saddlebags and carpetbag being dropped, then he reappeared. She couldn't see his face distinctly. But she heard his voice and felt his suppressed anger, and it had more impact than any reassurances he might have made.

"You did this to yourself, lady. We wouldn't be hiding out here if it weren't for your pig-headed foolishness."

She moved forward without thinking, torn between fear and anger of her own. Reaching the rock wall, she dropped her skirts and hugged the wall, edging slowly toward him, finding the path smoother, less treacherous beneath her feet.

She stepped once more and felt the difference in the air as she hovered inches from the edge of the precipice. Her hand groped the edge of the wall, her palms scraping over its rough surface as she felt her way around.

And then her hand was encompassed in warm, abrasive strength as he grabbed it and pulled her into the cave. She knew a moment's breathless panic as she rounded the edge of the mountain's wall, felt the earth falling away from her, and then she was inside the darkness. She stood pressed against his wide chest while she gathered her wits. The cave was black behind him, its size indistinguishable. But the floor beneath their feet was solid, and she felt secure.

He placed his hands on her shoulders and turned her until her back was against him, and there, spread before them, was an explosive sky, heavily laden with clouds, mostly black and rolling, except for the western edge of the horizon which was grayer, pinker, until it disappeared in a red glow where land met sky in a jagged line of black silhouettes.

They were so high. No point of land seemed near, and the canyons below were already swallowed up by night. Distance seemed not to matter. The wind picked up, buffeting the mountain as if to topple it. But the mountain, as it had for centuries, stood solid in its path. It was the wind that circled, swirled, altering its path around the mountain.

Elizabeth closed her eyes, leaning against the outlaw's strong chest, their damp clothing becoming a warm seal between them. Air gusted around her, around him, but they were safe, protected by the rock mountain, hidden inside it.

Again, the distant thunder rumbled. The clouds lit up in the distance, revealing the thunderstorm's rolling fist, illuminated from within, thrusting heavenward against the black sky. The glowing line at the horizon twisted into a narrow ribbon of red, the sun's wicked smile as it abandoned them to the night, to the storm, to the elements that threatened from all sides.

"We can't stay here. We have to move out in the morning and just hope we can get out of here before somebody tracks our trail."

"But you never get caught," she whispered desperately. "They won't find us."

"Lady, we didn't leave an invitation to follow us before. We also didn't add a Wells Fargo reward on top of everything else."

"Are you so angry with me?" she asked softly.

His body was rigid behind her, and when he spoke, she felt his tension. "You left me."

"To protect you."

He snorted his laughter. "That makes a hell of a lot of sense."

"And now I've endangered you past reason."

His hands on her shoulders were tense, yet his fingers moved gently against the ridge of her collarbone. "I've been in danger before. It's you I'm worried about." His arms slid around her waist and he pulled her more closely against him. "I guess it's time."

"Time for what?" she asked quietly, soothed by his nearness.

"Time to tell you... everything. Since it may get us killed, and I guess you deserve to know the truth." He feathered a light kiss against her neck, soft and yearning, then released her. He paced restlessly away, and finally dropped to the ground, sitting alone, facing the distant storm. "What do you want to know first?"

Names tumbled in her mind as she watched him. Susannah. Obregón. Joel and Clayton. None would form on her lips. "Everything—from the beginning."

"You think that will be easier? It won't. But that's the way it is. … Two words described my Pa, I guess. He believed. He was a Methodist circuit-rider. He traveled hundreds of miles on horseback with nothing more than a little food, a Bible, and a gun, shouting the gospel to those who'd listen. If he was lucky, folks would put him up for the night and feed him. If he hadn't been so hard-nosed, he'd have never slept out, never gone hungry, never been murdered by those that couldn't abide his politics."

"Murdered!"

"Yeah. Burned alive for standing up against the outlaws in Clay County. The James Gang. Others."

Burned alive. Her heart lurched in her breast. She closed her eyes and sank to the cold floor of the cave, tugging her damp cloak tighter around her. "Jesse James murdered him?"

"No." He shook his head. "The outlaws didn't do that, back then. They would have just moved on to hide out on somebody else's farm... instead of the Dougherty's."

"Dougherty's?" She pressed her knuckle to her lips.

"Clayton Dougherty's old man was as mean a son-of-a-bitch as he is. Money, power—he had it all. And a son to carry it all on."

"Two sons."

Coulter shrugged. "Only one that the old man had any use for. Joel was too much like his mother. Even as a kid, he was soft. Old Man Dougherty finally stopped trying to do anything with him. He had Clayton. I guess he figured that was enough."

Elizabeth lowered her eyes. How well she understood.

"The Doughertys always liked fine horseflesh, and there weren't many people in those parts after the war who could afford more than a broken-down mule. Most people figured they got their money playin' both sides against the middle during the war. They did a good enough job of it afterward, selling a few horses to officers stationed around us, even while they were hiding fugitives from the government. But when my Pa kept stirring up trouble for them, they decided to teach him a lesson. They knew we didn't have any money, just some land we squatted on to scratch a living out of the soil, me and Susannah and Ma. Pa was hardly ever around to help and Frankie wasn't old enough yet.... Maybe they didn't expect anyone to be home that night. Sometimes when the prayer meeting was close by, we all went with Pa. Susannah would sing. Like an angel. Men would come to hear her sing 'Whispering Hope,' and they would leave believers.

"But not that night. That night, only me and Pa were out. Frankie was sick. Ma and Susannah stayed home to care for him. When the riders came, there were no lights, no sign of anybody home. They torched the house."

"No. Dear God, no ..."

"We didn't get back in time. I got Susannah out. Pa died with Ma and Frankie. They told me later that Frankie wasn't even burned. He was dead in his crib... from the smoke. I heard it said that I saved the wrong one, that Susannah would have been better off dead."

Scars... she squeezed her eyes shut, but couldn't rid her mind of the woman's beauty, her horror.

"It wasn't your fault," she breathed.

"I was seventeen. Old enough to see the trouble coming, too young to stop it. Boy enough to want to run and run and run and never look back... man enough to want to kill every bastard in the group that torched our cabin that night."

"Six of them ..."

"No..." His voice faltered, then he seemed to force himself to continue. "No, there were more than that. Most of those men were talked into something they didn't fully understand. But I found out who was responsible, the ringleaders. Abner Reynolds, Walter Tankersley, our closest neighbor, B. T. Grier."

"Clayton."

"Clayton Dougherty."

"But they say you killed six men."

"I didn't kill B. T. I killed the others, though. Always fair fights. I called them out, and they had ample opportunity to get me first. But I was better with a gun than most men. Word got around that I was a hot-headed young kid, pretty good with a gun, and when that happens, it seems like everybody's gunning for you, wantin' to prove themselves by bringing you down. One night I was jumped by two men in Kansas. I killed one, winged the other. It was three months later before I found out that I'd killed a U. S. marshal. After a time I realized the only way to stop being put in a position to defend myself all the time was to stay away from people."

He didn't offer any more, and she could imagine the rest all too clearly. Always running, always alone...

"Clayton Dougherty disappeared after the fire. Everybody knew why, but nobody could prove it. I imagine his old man sent him enough money to get by. I guess he always assumed Clayton would come back once things calmed down.

"Our nearest neighbors were the Griers. Without Pa or Ma, I was the one who had to handle everything. Right after the fire, when Miz Grier came and took Susannah home with her, I was thankful. I wouldn't go with her, though. I slept out for five nights, between the ashes of the cabin and their graves. When I finally went to see Susannah, she didn't know me. The doctor wouldn't give her anything for the pain. Said she was already too weak, it would kill her. The screaming tore her throat up so bad, she almost lost her voice.

"I couldn't bear it. I couldn't stay around. I was eaten up with hate, and wanting to kill those bastards with my bare hands. I guess I was almost crazy with it. That's when I found B. T. Grier by the burnt out cabin. He couldn't live with this guilt any longer. He stuck his shotgun in his mouth and blew his own head off.

"When he'd already thrown his torch, and the others were about to ride off, he heard someone screaming inside. He called out to the others, but they wouldn't stop. He left with them.

"But later when Susannah was living at his house... You see, the others could get away from it. B. T. couldn't. There were those who said I killed him, and I didn't stop them from saying it, because I hated him so bad, I wanted people to think I had. I was just a kid, some said. Couldn't have done it. And those who thought I had were glad they didn't have to deal with it.

"Miz Grier never felt the same about Susannah again. Another family took her in. One without guilt, I figure. It was while she was at their house that the doctor told us the rest. Susannah was going to have a baby, Joel's baby. I went after Joel; he wouldn't even see her. He'd been drunk for weeks, ever since the fire. Couldn't live with what had happened to her. Couldn't live with her. Said he loved her... but he was too yellow to stand by her and prove it."

Elizabeth's throat ached; her chest was so tight she couldn't breathe. "What happened... what happened to the baby?"

"Born dead. The midwife said it was the most perfect, beautiful baby she'd ever seen. Too perfect for this earth, maybe. Susannah almost died having that baby."

"Old Man Dougherty paid the bills... and I wanted to run. And I wanted to kill them all. But by then, Joel had taken off after Clayton. Nobody heard anything out of them after that. I guess even the old man knew that folks would never let them come back. A number of our neighbors moved after that. After the war and all, it wasn't unusual. But some of them had more reason than most, like Tankersley and Reynolds."

Silence stretched between them like the night, heavy and vast and dark.

They said I saved the wrong one.

She shuddered within her blanket, wrapped her arms around her knees and buried her head in them. How must he have felt, this man, this boy, to have everything ripped from him in one tragic night. Everything except the burden of his sister, and the guilt.

"Did they call you John?" she asked softly.

"My Pa called me Wesley. Everybody else called me Wes."

Wesley. Such a soft name. Such a hard man. It didn't fit. The boy he must have been was too painful to imagine, and gone forever. She tried to picture him and couldn't. Her heart knew an overwhelming grief.

Instead, she pulled his body against hers gave the only thing she had to give. "I would have loved John Wesley Bridges. I know that as well as I know the sun will rise. But not more than I love Boone Coulter."

"No," he said harshly. "You don't understand. You don't know."

Her fingers dug into his shoulders, her tears wetting her face even as she fought for words. "Don't tell me what I know, Coulter. Don't you dare tell me what I know."

"But I've—"

"I will not listen! I love you."

He shook his head.

"I love you!"

"You can't!" he shouted, tearing himself out of her arms.

"Don't tell me I can't! I do, and you can't change that! Don't you understand? You can tell me every horror you've ever committed, and you can go and do more! You can hurt me, you can put me through hell, but you can't stop me from loving you!"

She stood before him, trembling with rage.

"Don't preach at me!" he shouted, his fists balled at his sides, his body rigid.

"Then don't tell me not to love you," she whispered. "It's all I have left in the world."

"Then I feel sorry for you, lady. That ain't much." He turned on his heel and grabbed his saddlebags, emptying one side of his of its contents. "You need to get rid of those wet clothes before it gets much colder," he grumbled. "Spread them on one of the rocks behind you."

She nodded, knowing he couldn't see her response, yet not wanting to risk answering only to have her voice tremble or break. His words wounded, but she didn't, couldn't believe them.

She unfastened the buttons of the calico dress to her waist, then several beyond. So practical. No buttons up the back for a woman who more often than not had no other hands to help her. The dress clung to her damp petticoat, so she shrugged the undergarment from her shoulders as well, pulling them down her hips together. Finally, she stood in her camisole and pantaloons, shivering.

She flung her outer garments over her shoulder and stepped into the blackness, her hands groping blindly. She stifled a curse when her left hand struck the wall, but used her throbbing fingers as a guide, sliding them over the cold, damp surface to the pile of rocks Coulter had told her about.

She spread the garments over the craggy surfaces then turned to face the opening to the cave, where only a trace of light remained.

The cave wall curved sharply beyond the opening, providing a deep recess safe from the elements. She could barely make out Coulter's form huddled in that recess, could barely hear his movements; but then a match flared in his hand, and he ignited a small pile of firewood and dry shavings he'd brought in his saddlebag.

She watched, shivering, as he coaxed the fire into a red and gold glow. Small, it wouldn't last long, but its temporary comfort was priceless. She moved closer, holding her hands out to warm them, then chafing them over her arms to stimulate her circulation.

Coulter busied himself with preparations for a crude, meager meal of jerky and coffee. He spread a blanket on the floor of the cave near the fire.

"Can I help?"

He raised his eyes and started to respond, but his voice broke in mid-syllable. He pulled his gaze hastily away, and the small tin coffee pot clattered against the cave floor.

Elizabeth glanced down at herself, at the loosened camisole string and the shadowed cleavage that the flickering light exposed. The aureoles of her breasts were dark against the sheer white fabric which was still damp. She wrapped her arms around herself.

"Oh, God, woman, what you do to me."

She closed her eyes against the sight of his head hung low, his wide shoulders weighted with the burden of her safety and her foolishness. Her lips trembled, but not with cold. Her knees weakened; her eyes stung; her heart pounded. She couldn't respond to him, couldn't speak. She could only stand there before him adding to his despair. She was worrying about love; he couldn't see past survival. They were hiding like animals, and it was only a matter of time until they were hunted down like them.

What had she done to them?

And what had he done to her that she so willingly had flung her name and her life to the wind to be linked with him in the minds of those who would carry the tale, thus sealing her fate with his?

It was then that she understood what she had really done.

They would never be joined in any other way, certainly not the ways of society, or even the roughest civilization. She would never wear his ring, or his name. But because of her flamboyant act of desperation, their names were linked.

Elizabeth Dougherty and Boone Coulter: Outlaws, partners, lovers.

San Francisco, Philadelphia, any corner of the earth would be empty, meaningless without him. If he were destined to die under a hail of bullets for his sins, then she would be beside him. For without Boone Coulter, she had no life ahead of her, only an existence.

And she had learned at his side, at his touch, that mere existence was no longer enough.

Chapter Twenty-three

COULTER CROUCHED BELOW her, his eyes filled with her beauty, her heartache, his arms aching to surround her. A tear trailed down her cheek, and she drew in a quivering breath, closing her eyes to him.

What could he offer for her beauty, beyond more heartache? He choked on his words, their jagged edges trapped in the raw, tight confines of his throat, words that would open his heart, his soul.

He couldn't look away from her, from the firelight dancing erotically over her body, from the agony etched on the sculptured features of her face. Her refinement was untouched by the wilds of nature, both men's and earth's. If it weren't for the pulse throbbing delicately at the base of her throat, her breasts quivering beneath her arms, she might have been a statue. Throbbing, quivering with her private pain, she was a goddess brought to life.

No mere man could possess goddess a without paying the price... his life.

Kneeling at her feet, he knew the truth as he'd never known it before. At last, he'd found something worth that ultimate price.

To hold her in his arms, to take her pain as his own, to be surrounded by her loving, quaking flesh... to taste of life, no matter how fleeting before going to death's black embrace.

It was more than he'd ever hoped for.

He rose slowly, reached for her, and as his fingers clasped the soft flesh of her upper arms, her lashes fluttered, her lips trembled. He pulled her gently to him and she moved without responding, holding herself removed in spirit if not in body.

"You deserve better than this... than me." She tried to shake her head against him, but he caught it with one hand and held it still against his shoulder. "You do... you do."

He wanted to say so much, to tell her she was the sun and the moon and the stars, but those were words he couldn't form. Instead, he held her, worshipped her in silence. And then, when words must be said...

"Elizabeth... I want to love you."

Her body jerked imperceptibly at his words; her eyes opened, black in her pale oval face.

"Sir, I want your love..."

His head dipped closer and his lips parted a split-second before finding hers. When their mouths touched, it was forgiveness he tasted, and passion...

And love.

Her body pressed against his, stealing his warmth, moving against him, and their friction stoked the fires of their bodies to create new warmth, His hands roved restlessly over her contours, one sliding down from her slender waist to cup her and pull her closer against him, the other sliding up her midriff to find the fullness of a breast.

His tongue slipped between her lips, seeking the moist passion that waited there, mirroring the act their hungry bodies longed for. As his hands moved over her, his lips touched her with his fire, he felt her respond tenfold. His touch was not practiced, but he burned with his desire to fulfill her, his need to be fulfilled. Yearning, demanding, giving...

With his hands, he pleasured her, one finding a swollen nipple and rubbing it with gentle friction, the other kneading her bottom, seeking, coming close to the center of her femininity, yet not close enough.

Feeling her tremble against him, he stretched her out on the blanket, cradling her head on his arm, his hands following the curves of her body as he soothed and gentled and loved, explored the spots that brought gasps to her lips and moans from her throat. He would pour a lifetime of loving into one night, perhaps their last night together...

He probed, unable to pierce the fabric barrier, yet feeling her dampness. A tiny gasp of pleasure escaped her lips, and his own response surged, swelling his staff beyond what he was capable of bearing.

Yet he could bear it, could bear anything, if it prolonged their joining, dragged the long moments of night beyond the dawn.

He pulled the loose drawstring of her camisole and it slid down her shoulder, catching on the tip of her breast. A whisk of his fingers exposed the throbbing crest to his hungry lips, and he nursed the hard tip as she arched against him, undulating her body in time to his sucking rhythm. Her moans were his glory, her hands fluttering helplessly against him, his victory

And then, her hand brushed against him with its startling feather touch, pulled away, then returned to press against his maleness, to mimic the rubbing motion he'd used on her, and it was he who trembled at the shock of her touch, he who arched into her hand in intense pleasure, he who groaned and pulled away.

"Please," she whimpered. "I want to touch you ..."

"No," he rasped. "Not if you want to finish what's begun."

But she wouldn't listen. Instead, she guided his hand to the waist of her pantaloons. As his hand touched the warm silk of her stomach, she sighed against him. Even as his hand sought, hers slid into his trousers, and when his dragged past the tight curls at the juncture of her body, her sigh broke off and became a quick gasp; her fingers closed around him and he couldn't breathe.

"No ..." he grated.

"Let me..." she insisted hoarsely. "Let me know everything there is to know... I want it all..."

He knew her fear and understood it. She sensed with him that what awaited them might be the end of everything. She too knew that this night might be the last passion they'd share.

Her hand touched him, rubbed him with a hunger that matched his own. It was a hunger to know, to give, to taste the wine of loving as it might never be tasted again. Her fingertips stroked the pulsing veins, following their trail to his throbbing tip, up and down the length of him, driving him insane.

At first, he couldn't move for fear of responding too much, too quickly. Then he felt her flesh moving against his hand, and desperately concentrated on his own exploration of her body, remembering the way she had responded in his cabin, the touches that had made her cry out, the strokes that had pushed her to the brink.

He trained every mental impulse on the feel of her as he found the tight opening, teased and tormented until she was quivering and open to him, then slid inside and felt the silken sheath tighten around his fingers, tightening even more as she arched to meet his strokes.

When he thought he would explode if her hand moved again, that she would dissolve around him and into him without ever their joining, he pulled away, choking, fighting for air, for sanity, for the stamina to complete their lovemaking without haste.

Her garments came off like cobwebs, drifting palely into the darkness. His own movements were quick and efficient, and then they were facing each other as they had come into the world, no defenses, no camouflage, only their selves to offer.

He dropped to his knees, then pulled her down with him, wrapping his arms around her, holding her close, their heartbeats so close and fast, they seemed to feed off each other.

As he tipped her head back and captured her lips and made them his, he knew a strange new force within him. Her hands pressed against his chest, and he felt a welling of emotion that choked him, robbed him of breath and reason. He knew he would possess her, again and again, before this night ended, and that, when it was over, he would get her to safety despite the price.

He knew the price, and it made no difference.

He would be fighting for, instead of against.

He would be living a brief ecstasy, instead of dying a slow agony. "You want everything..." he grated.

"Everything ..." she repeated.

"I'll give you everything I have to give, and more ..."

At his unspoken signal, she leaned backward until she rested on her elbows, her body stretched before him.

He planted his hands on either side of her and bent low to capture first one, then the other nipple between his lips, laving them with his tongue, feeling her respond to his gentle pulls, to the rasp of his teeth against their pebbled surface, and then broke away and let the cold air wash over the moisture he left behind, and felt her shiver beneath him.

Then it was her lips against his chest, her tongue against his nipples, and he understood how completely she wanted to share his pleasure, his pain.

His hand smoothed down the flat expanse of her belly, and he felt the twin sensation of her hand on him. His lips followed after, dragging a trail down her flesh, and he opened her legs and heard her gasp and felt her thighs tense as he blew softly over her femininity, hovering a breath away from the taut flesh, finally capturing it in the most intimate of kisses, and she cried out, her fingers threading helplessly into his hair as his tongue traced her contours and ignited spasms of sensation that he felt quaking throughout her body.

But when he pulled away and rose above her on his knees, poised and throbbing to enter her, she stopped him. It was her slender hands that pushed his shoulders to the ground, her long legs that straddled his thighs, her hands that stroked his aching member. Transfixed, he allowed her the freedom of his body, as he'd had the freedom of hers.

She leaned forward, and in the soft fireglow he saw her lips part and felt her breath hot upon him. Her tongue darted out as she moistened her lips, and then it was he whose fingers clutched the blanket as the earth shook beneath him, her lips surrounded him, her tongue swirled around him, until he had to push her away harshly or not be able to complete the act as he knew he must.

He grasped her hips and guided her onto him; she slid on easily, tightly, and the expressions playing across her face showed him her passion matched his... moving up and down his hard length, her breath coming faster and faster, and his only thought was to hold out longer, until her face twisted in ecstasy, her wide lips moist and open, and he exploded within her as she moved... filling her with his seed, his passion, his love.

She collapsed, falling forward on his body, and her hair was a veil over them both. He cupped her bottom in his large, rough hands, squeezing gently as she continued to sheath him with her still-quaking flesh, until he was spent and empty.

No, not empty. For he was filled with his love for her. She rested; he felt her pulse slow to sluggish regularity.

He too waited, but not for sleep.

He waited to love her again.

The fire was spent, not even an ember glowed. Elizabeth stirred drowsily, reaching, finding the space beside her empty. She pulled the rough blanket around her bare shoulders, sat up, finally saw the outlaw's black silhouette framed against the starry sky in the cave's entrance.

He stood without moving, his shoulder against the wall, his back to her. He had known this place, known where to find it when they needed a hideout. How many lonely nights had he spent here, waiting for his pursuers to give up and move on... or to find him?

The mountains were riddled with caves. Time and again she had seen them as she had ridden through the Apaches, the

Diablos, the Guadalupes. Who could search them all? Who could discover this one out of many?

But that wasn't the question.

How long could they exist here? Who would last longer, the hunters, or the hunted?

"You're awake."

His voice was soft, low, melancholy.

She moved closer to him and he turned and pulled her under his arm. The bare skin of his upper body was cold, yet he seemed unaware of the night's chill.

"You never seem to sleep."

He didn't answer, just continued to stare at the sky. Tonight, there were no shooting stars.

The inner cave would have been warmer, perhaps. But sitting in the mouth of the cave, the distant canyon covered by darkness, the sky touchably close... it suited both their moods. Yet, he didn't reach to hold her again. He sat alone, staring out into the night, dredging up the demons he'd been fighting for too long.

No, not alone, for she wouldn't let him. She moved closer, and he groaned and pulled her toward him. Though the darkness hid his face from her, she felt him with her senses... smelled leather and horse and man, felt rough beard against her cheek and hard sinew wrapping her body, heard his breath coming harsh and heavy, tasted the salt of his skin against her lips.

"Coulter," she leaned into him, her arms sliding up his bare back. "Love me, again ..."

When she awoke a few hours later Elizabeth walked to the cave opening and stopped, stunned.

Below her spread a panorama of rugged rock and mountain, and a jagged canyon green with trees and vegetation lining the narrow river she occasionally caught glimpses of through the morning mist.

"Water?" Coulter's voice came from behind her.

She nodded, accepting the tin cup in her hand. He stood apart from her, his legs planted wide as he surveyed the terrain.

He hadn't touched her since they had awakened. Not to brush a wisp of hair from her cheek, or even brush against her as he reached for his holster. In fact, he seemed determined not to touch her at all, and she felt a sadness deep within. So quickly he returned to his former self.

He squatted, bearing his weight on his boot-clad toes, his eyes narrowed and brow furrowed. "No rain today. It's gonna be a scorcher." Already the mists were burning away, revealing more of the canyon and the rugged slopes surrounding it.

And suddenly she remembered. She crossed the pebbly floor of the cave to the saddlebags and untied the rawhide knot, raised the leather flap, and pulled the heavy canvas mailbag out.

He didn't even bother to turn and look to see what she was doing, and that's when she knew the source of his tension, his anger.

"I'll have the horses saddled and ready shortly." He stood up abruptly, his wide shoulders rigid, sparing her not even a glance before leaving her there alone in the cave. She knew a moment's remorse, but only a moment. Now, more than ever, she knew the importance of whatever money this bag contained.

Their chances at freedom were slim, and without money, impossible.

She struggled with the knotted hemp that held the opening closed, cursing inaudibly when it resisted her efforts to open it. Her jaw clenched with frustration, she found a sharp, thick stick and forced its point between the twines of stiff rope, working relentlessly until the knot slipped a bit, then finally loosened. Her fingers worked with frantic energy, and her breath expelled with relief when the bag gaped open before her.

She grabbed the bottom with both hands and upended it, showering the floor with its contents. Mail, many cards and more envelopes, poured out into a small mound.

Crouching on her heels, Elizabeth gazed at the pile, her heart pounding. So many secrets, hopes and sorrows before her, each envelope pulsated with energy. Yet she cared not for the secrets; her eyes had no desire to pore over private words.

She raised a large envelope to the light, but could discern nothing about its contents through the heavy paper. Nor could she tell by its weight whether it hid crisp bills from her eyes. Her fingers poised to tear, but she couldn't do it. She laid it aside.

The next she lifted was flimsy, obviously unable to contain money of any kind. She tossed it back into the bag along with a card picturing hearts and flowers and bearing sentimental verse. And so she continued, putting off the moment when she would actually open someone else's letter, perhaps see someone else's heart laid bare.

Finally the small, neat pile beside her was complete, the bag heavy with its contents once again. She reached for one heavy parchment envelope, promising due to its weight. This time, she didn't hesitate but forced her fingers to break the seal and slide the contents onto her lap before she lost her nerve.

The weight seemed to come from several pages of closely spaced, spidery writing folded in half. But when she opened them, two ornately decorated greenback dollars fell out. Two dollars. Her heart leaped into her throat. It was so easy. Food, good hot food, and, if her luck held up, different clothes to conceal their identity. Relief pumped through her veins as she mouthed a silent thank you to the unknown sender.

Her fists and her mouth clamped shut. The sender couldn't remain unknown to her, nor could the recipient. She must look, she must remember, for indeed, she must repay them every penny. But without a pencil or paper, how could she keep records?

A shadow fell across her, and she looked up to see the outlaw staring down at her.

She sighed. "I know you don't approve, but I intend to repay every penny. If only I had something to write with, so I could keep records of it all."

This time it was his turn to sigh. With a weary shrug, he crossed the cave in long strides to rummage through his saddlebag. He finally emerged with a stub of a pencil.

"No paper?" she asked.

He stared at her, then dug back into the saddlebag. When he dropped the neatly folded paper into her lap, along with the pencil, she started to thank him, but before the words formed, she had opened it and had seen what it was: A wanted poster.

The crude line drawing looked little like him, but his name itself was enough to curdle the blood in her veins. Two thousand dollars... so much reward money. No wonder he was hunted by so many.

She closed her eyes and gathered herself. She couldn't let it show, couldn't let him see the horror she was feeling. Hands unbelievably steady, she spread the page face down on the cave floor and drew a firm line down its center. Once divided, she marked the two columns, AMOUNT, and DUE TO, and went back to the letter. $2.00 to... Carroll Davis, Circle D Ranch, New Mexico.

She refused to acknowledge the guilt, refused to allow it to bubble into her consciousness. She had no choice.

One by one, she opened the envelopes. Six more proved barren of currency. The seventh, however, weighed heavy in her hand, and was sealed with wax not once, but three times, flat globs without any impression.

She reached into the missive and touched something solid and flat and paper-wrapped. Trembling, she pulled it out, unwrapped the object, and gasped at the glint of gold. Two twenty dollar gold pieces faced up from her palm. "My word!"

She closed her hand around them, heart pounding. So much money to be sent through the mails. More than she'd ever expected. She probed into the envelope again and pulled out the letter that accompanied the bounty. All she wanted was a name, not a story. No faces or emotions to get in the way, only a destination for when she repaid the "loan." But against her will, her eyes followed the crude script, and read the loving words, a mother's savings to the son who'd left her for the glory of the new territory. It ended with a final plea, both simple and pathetic: Buy yer horse and com home. Make it a good one. We need you boy. Com home.

Her fingers felt lifeless around the gleaming gold. "How can I?" she asked softly.

She folded the coins back into their individual paper covering, tucked them and the letter back into the envelope. By the time the bills, too, had been replaced, and the letters were all returned to the bag, her heart was heavy.

The crunching of Coulter's boots, the clink of his spurs, told her he was returning to the cave for her. Quickly, she jerked her head up and wiped her face with the corner of her skirt. By the time he rounded the narrow ledge and entered the hollowed rock room, she was standing, with the mailbag at her feet.

"If you're ready, Mr. Coulter, I would appreciate your carrying this bag for me. I'm afraid I might drop it and scatter the U. S. Mail to the wind."

He snorted. "You have so much respect for the mail," he remarked, lifting the bag by its rope handle. "How much did you end up with?"

"Quite disappointing," she responded evenly. "Not a cent in the entire lot."

He shot her a suspicious look, and she met his gaze without flinching. "Not a cent?"

"None."

He let a disgusted sigh escape through his lips. "All that for nothing."

She nodded, her throat tight. She clutched her skirts in tense fingers and started for the exterior of the cave and the dazzling sunshine. But before she'd taken three steps, his hand closed over her arm with a stubborn grip. She stopped, her chin high. "Did you want something?"

"You couldn't do it, could you?" he asked softly.

"I don't know what you're talking about."

"And you thought you could kill a man."

She stiffened and met his gaze. But she found no scorn, only pity, and that was worse.

"I'm glad you didn't do it." He released her arm, glancing guiltily at the spot he had gripped. "I have a little money. We can live off the land, stay out of their way. I've done it before, plenty of times."

More running. Dear God, would it never end? Of course not. Wasn't that what he was telling her, had been telling her from the beginning? No respite, no solace... but he had found a place. Foolishly, she had left it, but what was to stop them from going back. "What about your cabin?" she asked, suddenly hopeful. "They'd never expect us to return to Texas."

He shook his head. "We can't go back. It was fine for a while. But more people are moving in—ranchers and folks passing through. It's a matter of time before somebody comes along and claims that cabin, and has a land grant to prove it."

"But for a while, at least. Until they stop looking."

"They won't stop looking this time."

The finality of his words shook her. This time, everything was tightening around them, squeezing the breath out of their lives. The leaden feeling in her heart told her that it was all her own doing.

"I have never been an impetuous woman," she began, but couldn't finish. How could he understand? "I... I know it doesn't seem that way. But the way you've known me... the things I've done... they are so alien to my nature." She felt her ridiculous eyes filling, blinked rapidly, and continued. "I just wanted you to know that I feel an immense guilt for the harm I've brought you. It was never my intention. You were right from the very beginning. I should never have forced you to help me."

His shoulders squared as he directed his piercing gaze out into the clear blue sky. He hooked his thumb into the holster, loose and low on his hip. Were it not for the tension straining each tendon, each vein to strut beneath his skin, he would have appeared not to care. But so stiff, so strained was his body, she could feel the heat of his intensity stretching between them. Keeping his eyes averted from her, he finally spoke.

"And you're sorry you came with me."

"No. Never that ..." She reached to touch him, but he pulled away.

"There's no reason to lie to me, lady."

His voice was weary, so weary, and she found herself swallowing back a lump in her throat. "I'm not lying, Mr. Coulter."

"If you're not, if you really don't regret riding with me... more's the pity." His eyes pierced hers, studying her. "It's a hell of a life for a lady."

"It's a hell of a life for anybody, Mr. Coulter. Are you going to tell me it's what you want?"

"It's what I chose."

"It's what I chose as well."

His harsh laughter broke the air. "You hardly knew what you were getting into."

"And neither did seventeen-year-old John Wesley Bridges."

He jerked at that, his anger flaring in his eyes, dying just as quickly. "We'd better be moving on."

She stared at the narrow ledge, the sheer drop below, broken only by outcroppings of rocks and boulders, an occasional gnarled, dwarfed tree clinging to the limestone cliff. If she'd known the night before, she never would have made it into the cave.

Now, she stepped forward without hesitation, the outlaw at her back.

Chapter Twenty-four

DORALEE LAY ON the feather bed, one leg pointed ceiling-ward. She rolled a silk stocking down its length and slid her new gift from Danny, the lacy, green garter, over it and high onto her thigh. Then she enjoyed a long, cat-like stretch that tingled from the back of her neck to her pointed toes. She gazed languidly at her bare, upturned breasts and pursed her lips. What she needed was a nice nap, not another night in El Paso on Dan P. Jennings' arm.

But she didn't dare refuse him. The news that his editor had declined to run her story had done nothing to improve her status with the reporter, though he hadn't seemed to hold it against her. As each day passed, she worried more and more that he was growing tired of her. Didn't they all, sooner or later?

The image of Wendell Crutcher popped unbidden into her head. She hadn't thought of him in a long time. She closed her eyes and shuddered. She didn't need to be thinking of him or his silly proposal now, either. Besides, he was no different from the others. A little younger, a little sweeter, maybe, but he'd have grown tired of her, too. Only difference, he'd have been too polite to let her know, and too married to do anything about it.

She sighed and was reaching for the other stocking when she heard a commotion in the hallway outside the door, then footsteps, quick and purposeful: Danny.

She rolled to her side and pasted a pretty smile on her face, anticipating his expression when he opened the door and found her posed on the bed in nothing but a stocking, for all the world like a picture hanging behind the bar in a saloon. Not as fleshy as some, maybe, but few men had complained.

The door slammed open and Jennings entered, his face flushed, eyes snapping with excitement, but not taking nearly the notice of her appearance that the gentleman passing on down the hall did. Before she had the chance to savor that stout man's shock, Danny slammed the door shut with as much force as he'd opened it and was crossing the room toward her.

"Get your duds packed, sweetheart. We're leaving in an hour." Already, he was snatching his own things up and flinging them into his small traveling bag.

"What's going on?" she sulked, more than a little peeved that he so easily ignored her enticing charms.

"Come on, sweetheart." He reached across and popped her bottom, then grinned. "Hot story, and I'm probably the only fellow within five hundred miles to get it, that is, if I get to it first."

She pulled to a sitting position and tugged the other stocking over her toes with a disgruntled sigh. "What is it, this time?"

Jennings picked up her corset and tossed it at her. "Our gunslinger and his kidnapped lady have just announced their presence in New Mexico. They're both wanted for holding up a stage there. Somewhere near a town called Seven Rivers,"

"Both?" Doralee turned an astonished face to the reporter, and he laughed outright.

"Both. It seems the very lady-like Mrs. Joel Dougherty not only robbed the Star Line Stage, she even left her calling card to assure that she be given proper credit."

"Miz Dougherty?" Doralee stared at him, her mouth gaping open.

"There seems little doubt, and I intend to get the story first hand." Jennings grabbed a fistful of petticoat and bustle and deposited it unceremoniously in the prostitute's lap. "Get a move on, unless you want to be left behind."

Doralee glared down at the profusion of ruffles, her pert breasts thrusting above them. Left behind! He wouldn't dare. But she felt a sharp tug of annoyance that he found it so easy to overlook her obvious display of femininity when confronted with nothing but another of his infernal newspaper stories.

She stood, spilling the undergarments to the floor around her, and snatched up the corset. Damn the arrogant bastard for ignoring her, threatening to leave her. Damned if she didn't wish she'd thought of robbing a stage herself. Imagining some rich sons-of-bitches at gunpoint, handing over their money, helpless to raise a finger to stop her... she felt a surge of defiance. Damned if the lady didn't have the right idea. Stooping over, she stepped into the corset and tugged it up her legs.

Smooth-palmed hands closed over her hips, and she would have fallen flat on her face if Jennings hadn't steadied her against him. "Get your hands off me," she snapped. "We're going to be late." She straightened, her legs hampered by the whalebone contraption around them.

He chuckled, his breath whistling hot and whiskeyed in her ear. "We'll never make it anywhere if you keep wiggling that dainty little ass of yours in my face."

Slightly mollified, she allowed him a moment to roam his hands down her body before slapping them away. "I wouldn't want to be the cause of you losin' your little ol' story."

"I knew you'd understand," he said, releasing her with a tweak on one of her round, white globes. "If you hurry, maybe we can grab some food to eat to take with us on the stage."

Doralee turned a look on him guaranteed to fry, but he'd already turned his attention to his suitcase.

Robbing stages and leaving a calling card, all proper-like. She wished to hell she'd thought of it first.

The ebony-haired beauty lifted a handful of flyers off the bar of her saloon. "I'll be damned," she said after reading the message. "Wanted posters. What are they doin' in here?"

The bartender shrugged, tugged a soiled rag out of his waistband, and began wiping the polished surface of the bar. "Some feller left 'em here afore he went upstairs with Katy. Says he's sendin' 'em on their way to every town in this part of the country. Mean-lookin' sumbitch."

The woman dropped the papers back on the bar. "Get rid of 'em. Leave the law-keepin' up to the law."

"Yes ma'am, Miz Mona." He swept them onto the floor and proceeded to walk on them as he made his rounds up and down the length of the curving bar.

Miz Mona propped a red-booted foot on the brass footrail and leaned against the mahogany counter. "Tell me more about this fella, Reggie." she said, and inhaled a thin cigar.

He filled a jigger glass with rye and slid it toward a customer, then returned to her side. "Like I said, he's a mean-lookin' one. Big fella' with black hair, drinkin' pretty heavy. Some salesman came in for a drink, said there was a stagecoach robbery over in New Mexico. Said some lady did it, if ya' can believe that. Said it was the one that outlaw took off with a while back. They's callin' her La Desperada in the papers now, the lady desperado. Anyways, this feller's been drinkin' 'n all, and when he hears what the salesman has to say, he gets all riled up 'n excited, says this is just what he's been waitin' for." He shook his head and frowned. "Katy had him pegged fer a spender from the time he walked through the door. Offered herself right off, but he was ornery with her, told her to leave him be. But after hearin' about the stagecoach robbery, he changed his tune. Funny thing, he kept callin' her Elizabeth, but you know Katy. She'll answer to anything if there's a dollar in it. I don't know, though. Didn't like the looks of him. Mean-lookin' sumbitch. Side of his face had been cut up pretty bad. By the time he 'n Katy took off fer her crib, he was mean-drunk, though it didn't seem to affect his walkin' none, nor his itch neither. Plumb near dragged her up the stairs."

"Katy can handle him," the woman replied, her eyes sliding over the crowded room for signs of trouble.

"Reckon so," the bartender replied doubtfully. "Didn't like the looks of him none."

The woman sighed, dropped the cigar stub to the floor, and pressed it out beneath her toe. "How long they been up there?"

The bartender paused in his polishing to consider. "An hour maybe. Maybe a little longer. Busy night like tonight, I lose track."

"Guess I'd better go up and check on her. Make sure she's not giving away her wares, again. The little bitch is liable to give them twice what they pay for if I don't keep an eye on her."

She had made her way through the noisy, smoky throng of customers to the foot of the stairs when a scream split the air. At first, no one reacted. When the scream came again, the room silenced uneasily.

But before anyone moved, a half-dressed girl appeared at the top of the stairs, her face a mask of horror. "Miz Mona!" she wailed, twisting her skirt in her thin hands. "Miz Mona—there's blood everywhere—oh, God ..."

She slipped to her knees, rocking and moaning hysterically. "Katy's dead!"

Wendell crossed the valley alone, the heat radiating from the wound in his shoulder and searing into his consciousness, probably the only thing that kept him upright in the saddle. The slightest shift in his position made the pain knife through him. Don Obregón had tried to stop him from leaving before it was better healed, but to no avail.

Ahead was the towering El Capitan mountain, and the Guadalupes, behind him were the dark, brooding cliffs of the

Diablos, and behind that, the gentle Apaches he longed to return to.

But he couldn't. Turning back was impossible now... now that he knew the truth... the truth about Clayton Dougherty.

The bitter gall rose again, the pain of betrayal, the confusion. Each jog of the horse sent a painful reminder to his brain. He was as big a fool as everyone thought he was, believing in a man like that. If he could just get word to somebody who could do something about it...

Doralee's reporter.

He squeezed his eyes shut and gritted his teeth against the pain. Her blond perfection danced before his blurred vision like an angelic promise. And the reporter would tell the story, the whole story.

Wendell had a story to tell.

The sun was high overhead, just starting its downward slide toward the mountains when Coulter reined in atop the last steep hill outside Lincoln, his eyes scanning the town, such as it was.

The road twisted through the settlement, lined haphazardly by a dozen or so substantial dwellings, though all were the typical flat-roofed adobe of the region. Only two structures were more than a single story in height, the Murphy-Dolan Store and the torreón, the old watchtower, stood taller still. Since it was the heat of the day, he wasn't surprised to see the streets empty.

Satisfied that they could enter in relative safety, he motioned to Elizabeth, and moments later she was beside him, the paint mare prancing restlessly by Sage's side. The horses were a good pair, both strong and with great endurance, a fact for which he was increasingly grateful on this long trek. Sage flicked a straight brown ear at a fly trying to bite its vulnerable inner flesh; Coulter slapped it away.

It had taken them close to three days to reach this small town, a site he'd selected with a specific purpose in mind. But now, so near their destination, he found himself hesitating, his shoulders tight with apprehension.

He watched Elizabeth, her hands sure on the reins, her thighs beneath her divided skirt gripping the mare's sides controlling the animal's restless stirring. Straight-spined with upthrust chin, she rode with confidence, and he felt a sting of pride. Never had her spirit flagged. In fact, her determination seemed more staunch than when they'd begun.

Of course, she didn't know his purpose in coming to Lincoln, New Mexico, after all the towns they'd avoided.

"You're sure there's no danger?" she asked, raising her hand to shield her eyes as she studied the layout below them.

"Sheriff's up in Santa Fe, trying to collect his reward money for capturing Billy the Kid." Coulter swung off the horse and approached her, continuing to hold the stallion's reins. The stallion followed him with a minimum of head-tossing and snorting as Coulter dragged the heavy mailbag from Elizabeth's saddlebag.

A fallen pine tree, toppled recently, judging by the fresh, green needles, provided sufficient camouflage for the bag. He broke a limb to cover it better, then proceeded to mount Sage and pull closer to Elizabeth again.

"Nobody around here's interested in causing trouble. They're too busy slapping each other on the back for sending Pat Garrett after the Kid. If people had any idea how hard it is to get the government to fork over a reward, they'd think twice before going after a bounty."

"Of course. I'd forgotten." Her lips parted, her eyes darkened with emotion, and he cursed himself for mentioning the reward. He was used to living with a bounty; she had become obsessed with the idea that he was hunted. "It seems like a lifetime ago that I heard they'd gotten Billy the Kid."

"A little over a month, that's all. I doubt if anyone will be concerned with us passing through. We can find out what we need to know ..." His voice faded as the reality of what he'd planned sank in.

"And then we'll go on," she finished firmly "I suggest we proceed."

He nodded curtly. She kicked her heels into the mare's side and started down the hill. He stilled his misgivings and followed.

As they approached the first of the homes, his attention was drawn to a smaller shelter behind the larger adobe. In the yard was an horno, an outdoor earthen oven, and the aroma of bread baking and of pungently seasoned food cooking carried to him on the slight breeze. His stomach tightened in response. He turned to Elizabeth; she gazed longingly at the thin wisp of smoke drifting upward from the rounded mound of earth. But then, as if feeling his eyes upon her, she dropped her gaze to her hands clenched over the saddle horn. Always the lady, never complaining.

"Hold on," he said, reining in. "Maybe they'll sell us something. It's bound to be better than the grub at the hotel and cheaper to boot."

She had the mare whipped around in an instant, though her posture was so erect, her manner so cool, most would not have recognized her eagerness. But most hadn't spent the last days observing her, memorizing her every move, storing up memories against the time when she'd be gone.

"You're certain we can afford it?"

"I'll take care of that." He guided Sage closer to the simple adobe hut. When a young Mexican girl appeared in the doorway, he held two coins aloft. "Food, por favor?"

She seemed to understand, and spewed a flurry of Spanish into the interior of the casa. Moments later a younger boy and an older woman appeared, each bearing clay dishes of steaming food.

Coulter's own body was almost trembling at the sight and smell of the hot, pungent beans and fried cabbage. He gestured toward Elizabeth. Her smile encompassed everyone, her hand steady as she accepted a flat bowl, nothing about her or her actions indicated the extent of her hunger. But he knew.

He knew by the hollows in her cheeks, the quick intake of breath when she brought the beans near her face. Her reaction surpassed pleasure and hinted at desperation as she scooped the first bite into her mouth with a flat, corn tortilla.

Her deprivation was reason enough to continue with his plans. How long could he continue to subject her to a hell of desert heat and hunger without hope of getting better? Then he thought of the other reason... the death that was hovering over his head, growing closer each day. The death he refused to let her witness.

"¿Señor?" The boy was holding a dish toward him, and he took it in numb fingers, his eyes blinded to all but the woman, his senses blocking out even hunger as he watched her eat.

The young girl held up a bowl of cooked chiles, redolent in oil and garlic, but he had no eyes or taste for them. The beans in his mouth were as tasteless as dust though his throat protested their fire, his hands nerveless to the heat of the container. He forced the food down quickly and returned the dish.

Elizabeth did the same, then flashed them a wide smile. "Delicious," she said, then added haltingly, "Deliciosa."

How ladylike, Coulter thought wryly. She tried to fit in everywhere. And damn near succeeded more often than not.

He watched her return the bowl. Her sun-streaked hair was tousled, despite her attempts to control it with coils and combs. One long strand had worked its way loose, feathering down her neck and over her shoulder. Others wisped around her face in loose tendrils. So delicate, so fragile was she, yet so deceptive, for beneath that skin of golden-hued satin was a framework of delicate steel.

She adjusted the dark wool scarf over her head, the better to protect herself from the increasing heat of the sun and he wanted to snatch it away, the better to see her.

"Mr. Coulter?"

Even her voice was velvet brocade, soft, with the gentlest of rasps as she spoke his name.

"Are you unwell?" She pulled the mare closer, and the thighs he dug into the stallions were tense with more than an effort to control his fiery mount.

"No. Of course not. We'd better go on into town and see what we can find out."

He tossed the coins and watched the boy and girl snatch them in midair, giggling at his generosity when he added a third for good measure. The mother bobbed up and down in a gracious bowing motion, beaming at him and the Señora.

"Do you know Carlos De Luna?" he asked. At the name, the older woman nodded and pointed down the crooked street toward another of the angular adobe buildings.

The daughter stepped forward. "Señor De Luna is not at Lincoln. He is at Santa Fe with Sheriff Garrett. They collect reward money for the Kid."

Carlos with Pat Garrett. It was a happenstance he had not considered. His momentary dismay quickly flared into unreasoning relief. It was a reprieve. He couldn't send Elizabeth away now, not alone, not without protection. The protection Lucius Merriweather could have given her, or Carlos. He couldn't send her away now.

But he didn't dare let her stay with him.

"Come on," he ordered, forcing his voice to remain calm despite the stranglehold he held over his emotions.

Chapter Twenty-five

THE TWO HORSES paced the crooked, deserted street slowly, Coulter ever watchful for suspicious movements. The mare was two paces behind when he stopped at the hitching rail at the corner of the sole two-storied structure in town. Coulter cast a wary glance at the building, his eyes registering shock when he realized that what had been the Murphy-Dolan Store was now identified by an official-looking sign as the Lincoln County Courthouse.

He let out a low, nervous whistle. Things had changed since he'd last passed through three years before. Every instinct warned him to turn around and ride, to put this place behind them.

Instead, he swung his leg over the horse's back and dismounted. He grunted a caution when Elizabeth started to do the same.

"Wait here," he said, then ambled down the length of the covered porch to the steps in the center of the building and mounted them slowly, his spurs clinking dully against the splintered wood. But when he would have gone inside, he stopped dead in his tracks, staring at the adobe wall beside the open doorway.

His blood ran cold, draining from his face. Wanted posters, some old and tattered: one for Billy with a crude death-sign scrawled against the Kid's solemn face, one for himself for murder and quoting a new, higher reward figure. His was the same inadequate line drawing that had always failed to portray his features with any reliability at all.

The wanted poster that stole his breath was the new, bold, and clear. There staring out at him was a photograph of an Elizabeth he'd never known, an Elizabeth he'd sell his soul to have protected from the hell that awaited her on the day this portrait was made. It was her wedding picture.

Half-smiling, her chin raised in anticipation, her features animated, her expression eager, she appeared the joyful, expectant bride. With a heavy heart he read:

KIDNAPPED
Elizabeth Cooke Dougherty
$5,000.00 Reward
payable by Mr. Clayton Dougherty
upon her safe return
Cavendish, Presidio County, Texas

Across the top of the poster was a handwritten message: WANTED FOR STAGE ROBBERY.

The word "kidnapped" had been carefully crossed through, as had the phrase, "upon her safe return."

There was no attempt at description, nor was there any further description of her crime. There was no need for any, for the photograph would serve to stir up more interest than the exorbitant reward money or any amount of heinous detail of her perceived crime.

Elizabeth waited restlessly as she watched Coulter's attention trained on the posters outside the courthouse. Gradually she sensed something wrong. Her awareness of his tension charged every fiber in her body with electricity and she stiffened in the saddle. Her brow knitted in concern, she swung her leg to dismount, the saddle leather creaking and the bridle jangling softly.

Coulter faced her then, his entire body relaxed, his expression void of emotion. But his eyes... his eyes pierced the heated air between them, stilling her in her tracks before she could take a step toward him. "Mr. Coul—"

"Susannah." She angled her head in confusion, and stepped forward.

"Susannah, there's no need for you to come in. Wait out here."

She bristled at his tone and moved forward despite the scowl that formed on his face. Abruptly, he descended the three steps in two strides.

"What is wrong?" she implored, extending a hand toward him.

He clasped her hand in his own, a certain urgency in his touch transmitting itself to her. "Get back on the horse."

His voice rustled over her like a hissing flame of warning, and she pulled back in dismay. When she did, her gaze shot over his shoulder and she spotted her poster.

"My God," she whispered, her knees threatening to buckle beneath her weight. She swayed forward, and only his grip tightening on her hand steadied her as her wedding picture swam before her disbelieving eyes. "My God ..."

"No," he said sharply, yet low-voiced. "Behave as if nothing is wrong. Get back on the horse. Sit tall, hold your head high. Don't fiddle with your scarf or act like you're hiding yourself in any way."

She felt the blood draining from her face as she fixed her eyes on his, desperate, terrified. "We've got to get out of here."

"I'm going inside—"

"No. They'll recognize you," she begged, her voice cracking.

"Shut up, and quit acting like a fool." He released her hand and strode to the courthouse.

His words stinging in her ears, she forced herself to follow his orders, too numb to disobey. In the saddle again, she longed for the mare to begin her usually impatient prancing, but the animal remained obstinately placid, guzzling water from the trough. Even the stallion seemed more interested in drinking than in fighting against the rail that anchored him so ruthlessly in place.

Elizabeth sat with her spine straight and chin raised, praying that the scarf sufficiently shadowed her face from prying eyes. For if she were recognized, if someone were to match that innocent bride on the wall with her, she would have finally accomplished the very thing she feared most.

She would have led the man she loved straight to his death.

Inside the courthouse, three men played poker around a desk while a fourth, older man squatted in the corner whittling a piece of soft pine. Four faces turned in Coulter's direction as he entered; two hands went to holsters; no one spoke.

Coulter removed his hat and nodded. "I hate to disturb you, but I was hoping you could help me."

"Sheriff ain't here," one of the card players growled, tossing a card onto the desk. "Hit me."

"I know," Coulter said. "That's what has me worried. My wife and I are headed up toward Albuquerque so she can be with her sister when she has her baby, and we got wind that there was a gang workin' this road farther north. With no sheriff around, she's pretty scared."

"Ain't no gangs workin' any roads 'round here," the card player remarked, spitting a brown stream into the crockery cuspidor at his feet. "But if you're really worried, there'll be a stage through in two days."

"We can't afford a stage." Coulter stared the man straight in the eye. "From the sounds of things, the stages around here haven't been too safe anyway. When we heard about that outlaw and that lady holdin' up a stage south o' here, we thought it was just a wild tale. But that wanted poster outside..." He shook his head. "You just can't trust anybody any more."

"You ain't got nothing to worry about from them folks," wheezed the old man in the corner. "They've already robbed another stagecoach, right up near Cimarron, so's I hear tell."

"Cimarron?" Coulter held himself carefully in rein. "When?"

"A couple o' days ago. Shee-yit!" The card-player tossed his hand into the middle of the desk. "These cards ain't worth buffalo dung today." He shoved away from the desk and stood up, his trousers hanging low beneath his bulging middle. "Tell your little wifey she ain't got nothin' to be feared of from that lady outlaw and Boone Coulter. They know better than show up in Pat Garrett's territory."

Coulter forced a thin smile. "I'll be sure to tell her."

The man followed him to the doorway and squinted out at Elizabeth. "Reckon it would help if I explain the situation?"

Coulter's fist balled at his side.

"Ransom," hollered one of the men, "git back in here. It's your deal."

"There's no need to trouble yourself over it, I'll tell her what you said." Coulter replaced his hat in a slow, deliberate motion, his arm blocking the man's view of Elizabeth. "I thank you for your time."

"Good luck. Hope it's a boy."

Coulter could only nod, the movement dislodging a bead of sweat on his forehead, sending it trailing down his temple to his jaw. He didn't dare brush it away, didn't dare do anything but stroll to Elizabeth's side.

He adjusted his bandana, finally allowing himself to look at her. Her face was white beneath the edge of scarf, her lips compressed in a tight line.

He stroked the mare's silken mane. But his low words weren't for the animal. "Sweet lady ..." he whispered. "Hold on. Just a little longer..."

Sage shied away from him as he unwound the reins from the hitching rail. "Don't you start now, you son-of-a-bitch," he growled, grabbing the bridle and yanking it toward him. The stallion's eyes showed wild white, and his rear hooves kicked out.

But Coulter was mounted before the stallion could continue with his display of temperament.

"Come on." The horses moved forward at a steady pace. His gaze swung from side to side, but no one witnessed their departure other than a few children playing.

A small boy raised his head from the pile of dirt between his legs and extended a forefinger at them. "Bang!"

Coulter twisted in the saddle and saw Elizabeth's reaction, her eyes closed, lips in a tense, straight line. She quickly recovered and gave the child a soft, tentative smile.

Coulter prodded Sage north, leading Elizabeth out and then around Lincoln in the direction they had entered, south; in the same way they had entered, unnoted.

When they topped the hill again, he felt a surge of relief from a near brush with disaster.

"Mr. Coulter, the mailbag."

Instantaneously, the relief coursing through his veins boiled into a torrent of frustration and anger. "Lady, forget the mailbag," he ground through clenched teeth. "There's no way to return it without getting caught."

"But we must," she pleaded. "Maybe if we just leave it out in the road?"

"The next stage isn't due through here for two days. Besides, if this mailbag turns up, they'll know we've been here. Right now, we're safe enough, but if we leave that mailbag in the road, you may as well leave another one of your goddamn calling cards with it."

"I gave my word."

Grumbling a curse, he shifted his weight to his left foot and stood in the stirrup, then jerked his right leg over the stallion's back. Each step toward the fallen pine tree was punctuated with the crackling of dried sticks beneath his boots, his anger quelling his usual instinctive efforts to muffle his noises.

He flung the brush away, and seized the rope handle. With one mighty heave the canvas bag came free. He took a half-dozen angry steps back toward her, then he remembered ...

"Lady, do you know what we've done?" he called out as he lugged the bag to her.

"Dear God, what now?"

"We've robbed another stage!"

"What? What are you talking about?"

He took a perverse pleasure in her shock. "We held up one in Cimarron. Two days ago."

"Mr. Coulter, now I know you're quite mad. Cimarron is at least five days from here."

His hands closed over her waist to lift her from the mare's back. "I know that. You know that. But the people in Cimarron think we robbed their stage."

"That's preposterous! I would never do such a thing!"

"There's no sense in ruffling up like a wet hen. You did do such a thing once, so you may as well realize that we'll be accused of more."

"But we didn't! We wouldn't!" she sputtered. She tilted her head up at him in confusion. "If they're accusing us of that, there's no telling what they'll accuse us of next."

"Exactly," he murmured, his eyes filling with the stunning vision of her anger.

"Next thing you know, they'll be accusing us of every stage robbery from San Antonio to Laramie!"

He pulled her gently into his arms, watching the light of knowledge slowly transform her features from indignation to amazement. "That means they don't know where we are."

"They don't know where we are," he repeated softly and the humor ebbed from him as his arms embraced what he so nearly had lost.

"You think I don't know, don't you?" She pressed her cheek against him, her lashes dark and soft against her cheekbone. "It's been in your eyes for days... you're trying to find a way to get rid of me."

He dared not try to deny it.

Elizabeth pulled free. "Some things don't change, do they?"

"If you're talking about me getting you to safety, no, some things don't change." He was tired, so goddamn tired.

She whirled at him, her hands clenched. "I'm talking about you running! Running away from me, from life!"

"Oh, come on, Elizabeth! This isn't some Philadelphia garden party; this is New Mexico, where the only law is who holds the gun, and right now I've got at least a hundred aimed at my head!"

He grabbed a gnarled limb and flung it into the brush, his muscles bunched with anger. "You think I don't know that it'll only take one—just one—to take you down with me? You think I ever spend a minute of the day without seeing you with a hole in you, bleeding with a bullet that was meant for me?"

He moved closer, tendons standing out on his neck, the veins at his temples throbbing, rage seething in his eyes. "I've seen death, Elizabeth! I've seen it too many ways, and I'm not going to see it on you!"

"Then that's where we're different," she whispered. "Because I've been seeing the same things, the guns aimed at your head, the blood—I know exactly what's ahead of us, Mr. Coulter. The difference is, I'm not going to let you die alone. If I have to hold you in my arms and watch the life drain out of you, I will... but you won't be alone."

"Oh, lady," he groaned helplessly. "I'm not worth it, can't you see that?" He dragged his fingers through his hair, fighting for words to make her understand. "If I get you out of this alive, I'll have done something worthwhile for the first time in a very long time. I, don't suppose there's much else good that can be said for my life, but it's better than nothing."

Her slender hands fell limp at her sides and she stared into the dense forest.

"Whether you realize it or not, lady, I gave you everything of value I possessed before I even knew your name. My pa's cross... and my word."

"But it's not yours, Mr. Coulter. You gave your word to me, so that makes it mine, doesn't it? And I don't want it anymore. I don't want to be saved, if that means we'll be separated."

"You're talking foolishness."

"Am I?" She turned slowly to face him, her eyes large and haunted and filling with shimmering moisture as she raised her chin to meet his gaze head on. "I gave you my life when you didn't want it. I held you at gunpoint and trusted you with it. And then, I gave you my love... And again, I had to force you... because you truly don't act as if you want it."

"Don't say that. Don't ever say that." He placed a hand firmly under her jaw and his lips took hers with a devouring need, drinking sustenance from their sweet well, sliding his other hand around her back until his arm circled her, his fingers brushing the swell of her breast.

He caught her soft whimper in his mouth and molded her body against his. Her hands climbed his back until they reached his shoulders, pulling him closer, closer.

"Don't let me go," she said softly. "Don't ever let me go."

To let her go would save her life. To hold her, to keep her with him would seal her death.

He couldn't answer.

Instead, again he captured her lips with his, drowning in the wellspring of her love, hating himself, despising himself for his weakness.

Yet he couldn't stop his hand from cupping the fullness of her breast, his body from responding to her gentle moan when his fingers rubbed against the firm peak. He fumbled with the buttons, and then the dress gaped open, revealing her camisole-covered breasts to his hungry eyes. Her head fell back, exposing her neck to his lips, and he trailed them downward to the salty crevice between her breasts. He dragged his tongue down to the spot where the skin ended and the white linen began, tormenting himself, yet refusing to slide the strap from her shoulder.

She shrugged the offending garment away with a restless movement on her shoulders; her hand cupped her breasts to his lips; her voice whispered a tortured sigh even as she arched against him.

His arms circled her, caressing the silken skin of her back, his fingers dancing down her spine until she was writhing in his arms.

Only the utmost control gentled him when the grinding need coursing through his body drove him to a response that was primal, unreasoning. There was no blanket to protect her back, no time to prepare a place to love her, even if his body would let him. Desperate, he jerked at the buckle of his holster until it swung loose in his hand. He dropped it to the ground beside them.

She reached and rubbed the evidence of his desire and found him hard and pulsing and ready. More hurried movements and her drawers slid to the ground and his trousers were tugged down over his thighs. Her tongue stroked his lips and he started in surprise, then drew it into his mouth.

When he slid his hand up her leg she parted her thighs willingly, and finding her moistened nest, he could hold back no longer. He knelt before her. She bent low to kiss him again, and he lifted her onto him, leaning back and groaning in exquisite agony when she settled onto him, sheathing him. Her quick intake of breath raised her taut breasts to his lips once more and he filled his mouth with them, suckling the life-giving force like a newborn babe. He lifted her hips, supporting her as she moved over him, each descent pulling him higher and tighter inside her.

Her breasts swayed before him, their dusky rose nipples tantalizingly close. He was torn between two pleasures: the desire to capture the sweet peak again and feel her contract around him in response to his suction... the desire to let her continue her movement without interference, the long strokes, now quickening, now torturously slow...

He felt her tension mounting, and concentrated desperately on the languid expression of her face, her moist lips parted and panting. He trained every thought of her satisfaction in an attempt to slow his own raging, distending need, but when her pace quickened frantically, he felt himself losing control and a guttural sound escaped his throat.

And then she was gasping, whimpering, tightening around him and milking him of his fluids. She fell forward and his lips seized a luscious nipple, his tongue laving it, his teeth rasping against it as his pleasure pumped from him, and she writhed against him until the ecstasy was more than either could bear.

I love you... The words formed, but wouldn't come, and he knew shame and guilt. He had nothing to give her but disgrace and pain and ultimately death. Death had been his partner for many years, but not hers. Please God, never hers...

Then she raised her face, and he saw it was wet with tears, and he felt something black inside him tearing open and spilling its anguish to meld with hers.

"Please," she begged, her chin raised in defiance even as she was his supplicant. "Stop trying to drive me away. Please don't send me away."

"Elizabeth, sweet Elizabeth ..." He pulled her against him, his arms tangling in the hair that now tumbled down her bare back, and before he could stop them, the words pouring from his lips were those of his heart, not his mind. Words that his guilt told him must be sweeter to his own selfish ears than they could possibly be to hers.

"Elizabeth... don't cry... I won't make you leave. You can stay with me... you have my word."

Chapter Twenty-six

"WE MUST CAMP by water, and camp early," Elizabeth said a few hours later as they skirted a hill several miles west of Lincoln. The mare's easy pace soothed her nerves, and she held the reins loosely in her hands.

Coulter shot her a wary glance. "Any particular reason?"

She didn't answer, just continued to study the trail ahead of them. He'd find out soon enough, she thought.

Coulter wiped his brow with his faded bandana, then pointed ahead to a flat, grassy valley, its center split by flowing, tree-lined stream. "May as well stop down there."

An hour later camp was made and Coulter went to hunt their dinner. Elizabeth loosened her hair around her shoulders and brushed it to a golden sheen. She rummaged in her carpetbag, idly thinking what she wouldn't give for a nice roasted hen, potatoes, perhaps a tart blueberry buckle with sweet cream...

Now stop that right now, she admonished herself.

Her fingers closed over the small tin of henna. She cradled it in her hand, its black paint flaking, the tin rusting at the corners where the weather had gotten to it. This gift of scorn had become a gift of life.

There were no directions. She pried the lid off and poured a sprinkling of a surprising green powder into her palm, its odor pungent, earthy. As she rubbed it into her damp skin it left an orangish stain.

Oh, God.

At the moment she wished Coulter were a drinking man. A stiff belt of whiskey would certainly be appropriate before she got on with this task.

The water in the coffeepot was just beginning to steam on the flat stone at the edge of the fire. For lack of a better idea, she tipped the can and poured the powder into the tin pot. When it hit the hot water, the scent was magnified tenfold and a tremor of panic swept through her. She picked up a stick from the ground and stirred the concoction, now a strong- smelling emulsion the consistency of thin mud.

She touched it tentatively, found it hot but not scalding, and carried it to the stream bed where she sucked in a deep, strengthening breath, filling her lungs with courage. Bending over from the waist, she poured the mixture into her hair, rubbing it in with her free hand. When the pot was empty, much of her hair was still dry and panic rose in her throat. Frantically, her fingers worked the muddy substance until every strand was coated.

She was growing quite lightheaded from being upside down. Yet if she stood up it would drip all over her.

She dropped to her knees and knew a mild relief, then slowly, slowly raised her head. After a moment's hesitation she finally deemed it safe to remove her hands from her head, and almost squealed when she saw their bright orange hue.

Only one thought managed to keep her from total panic: They'll never recognize me now.

Coulter picked up his pace when he realized the campsite was just around the bend in the river. He felt inordinately proud of the young pronghorn antelope slung across Sage's rump. Tracking the herd had taken him longer than he'd anticipated, but once found, they were easy to kill. Tragically attracted to any shining object, they responded immediately when he had flashed the gleaming blade of his knife. He had taken his pick, choosing this small one because there wouldn't be much waste of its tender flesh.

He was anticipating the expression on Elizabeth's face when he emerged from a more heavily vegetated stretch beside the river to the campsite.

"What the hell?" Even Sage, sensing Coulter's shock, stopped. Elizabeth's pale face stared at him, visibly shaken, from under a fiery halo of hair.

His mouth worked but no sounds would come.

She stood abruptly, her cheeks suffusing with color to rival her hair. "It's... bright, isn't it?" she asked, her voice quivering.

He nodded mutely, still frozen to the saddle.

"I don't believe anyone will recognize me from the poster now, do you?"

Laughter rumbled up from deep within him, from some private place he'd forgotten existed.

"Mr. Coulter!"

By the time his laughter erupted, he had slid from the horse, and dropped the antelope to the ground, never drawing his eyes away from her, and finally, when his legs gave way, he sat right there on the ground, his chest heaving with laughter.

"It's dreadful, isn't it?" Her hands flew to her hair and her lips quivered. "Oh my God, what have I done?"

He could only shake his head as tears welled in his eyes.

She seized him by the shoulders and began shaking him, until finally in self-defense, he was forced to grab her in turn.

She stood very still, her hands on his shoulders, her eyes filled with fear. Her mouth gaped open, and he wanted nothing so much as to capture those full lips in a kiss. But before he could act on the impulse, she was moaning, "I'm a fright, aren't I?"

"No. You're definitely not a fright." He nuzzled her cheek and she angled closer, giving him a clearer shot at the slender column of her neck. "You're an amazing woman, Elizabeth Dougherty."

He felt her skin shiver under the soft pulses of breath that accompanied his words. She stilled in his arms, her breasts rising and falling more slowly with each calming breath.

"You're sure it's not dreadful?" she asked, sounding unconvinced.

Her hair spilled over his hands like liquid fire, shards of sunlight bouncing off it that spanned every fiery shade of the spectrum. He traced her face with his callused thumb, stroking the fine red line around her temples where the dye had stained her skin. He lifted a handful of hair to his face, and it smelled of fresh-tilled earth after a rain shower, rich and heady and filling his senses with memories of a Missouri springtime long ago.

He tilted her face to his and whispered her name. Then, as if in a trance, he bent closer until their lips touched, parted, and his tongue sought her moisture like a man dying of thirst. And he was, day by day, becoming more and more dependent on her. The thought of losing her was the equivalent of losing the will to live.

Her body fitted against his, her softness against his hardness, as if two parts of a whole. She brought light to the dark recesses of his soul. She stirred him with a power that went beyond her physical touch. With her in his arms, at his side... he hoped, he believed.

That night the stream calmed them with its cool breezes, its gentle lapping noises, though it was little more than a narrow black ribbon in the moonlight. A green log popped in the fire, spraying a shower of burning embers into the air. With night hawks crying overhead and crickets chirping in the tall grasses, it was easy to pretend that everything was normal. But Elizabeth was past pretense.

By the flickering light of the campfire, she broke open her gun and examined it carefully. The chambers were empty; it held six bullets when loaded. She snapped it shut, then broke it open again. Each time her hands were a little more sure, a little less hesitant.

"Is that for anybody I know?" Coulter drawled from the blanket where he reclined, his arms folded behind his head.

"You." It snapped shut again.

"What have I done?"

"I just want to be ready when you tell me I can't stay with you again."

"I gave you my word," he grumbled.

"Under duress."

"That never stopped you from holding me to it before." He reached across the space between them and grabbed her hand. "Put it up, Elizabeth. I don't like you fooling with that thing."

"I'm not going to let it misfire. It's not even loaded."

His voice tense, his grip tightened on her. "You heard me. Put it up. You don't need it."

"You never know what I may need," she said gently, easing his hand from beneath hers. "I'm just getting accustomed to it. I don't want to be caught unaware."

He sprang up and knelt before her, bracing her shoulders with his hands. The firelight gilded half of his face with flickering gold, leaving the other half in shadow. "I'm not going to let anybody catch you unaware. I'm not going to let anybody hurt you."

The same sweet languor that had filled her, that had overridden the desperate voices in her mind ever since his promise, coursed through her at his touch. How precious those words, I won't make you leave, to her ears. She hadn't felt the full impact of her fears of losing him until those fears were relieved. Now she closed her eyes, letting his voice, the night air, the gentle currents emanating from his hands to her shoulders to the innermost places of her being soothe her with their presence.

"Hold me," she whispered, and when his arms circled her, the coarse sprinkling of hair at his neck rasping her cheek, she knew a blessed balm of peace. The night hid many terrors, the world waited with its threats, but in his arms she had no thought of anything but him. Nothing dared intrude on the magic she found there. Was it any wonder that she wanted to stay in his embrace forever….

Then he spoke, his voice rumbling in her ear, and the peace was shattered. “I’m going back to Lincoln.”

She pulled away, her heart pounding. “We can’t go backward, they’ll find us for certain. We need to keep moving ahead.”

The lines of his face were rigid with tension. “I’m not running any more, Elizabeth.”

“Of course not. We’re not running, we’re just... protecting ourselves the only way we can.”

He shook his head slowly. “You know I planned on going back after I got you to safety. You know I have to go after Clayton Dougherty.”

The blood froze in her veins. She strained to keep her voice steady. “I thought you had changed your mind.”

“Elizabeth.” His voice was hard. “What did you think you were asking me when you made me promise not to send you away? Did you think I was promising to keep following your lead, to keep running until I’m gunned down in the back like a coward?”

“No. Of course not.” But that was exactly what she had thought, had hoped, and had prayed the bullet would never come. She knew a sharp pang of bitterness. It was funny how one’s attitudes altered after one goal was won, and a new one emerged.

“Say the word, and I’ll get you on a stage headed out of here even if I do have to steal. I’ll do anything now, but then I’m going back.”

“I’ll never say that word.”

He let out a harsh breath. “You’re a damned stubborn woman, Elizabeth Dougherty.”

Her hand tightened around the pistol. “Too stubborn to let you die alone.” She shoved away from him and broke the firearm open one last time. He knelt silently, watching, understanding as she slipped the bullets in, one by one. When she snapped it closed, five chambers were filled.

He slipped it from her fingers. "You constantly surprise me, lady. From the time you first held a gun on me, I wondered if someone like you even knew what to do with it. Something told me you might."

"Joel taught me. He insisted I have a gun of my own for protection... the gun he killed himself with."

Darkness swirled around them. She waited for him to stop her, as always, to refuse to listen. How could she blame him, when her story was a mocking echo of his own, a reminder of the men who had destroyed his life?

But this time he didn't. "You were so afraid... afraid enough to turn to me."

She closed her eyes, and unbidden, the black and white nightmare reappeared. "Why did he have to use my gun? Wasn't it bad enough without that?"

Coulter pulled her toward him and wrapped his arms around her. "Damn him to hell for what he did to you."

"He must have loved Susannah very much."

"That's no excuse for what he did to you."

"He was lost. I wanted to help him, I tried, but he just got worse and worse... and when I heard the gunshot, I ran in and I saw him with my gun in his hand—" She broke off, burying her face against him. She was past tears, but not pain.

He took one of her hands in his, chafing it gently between his rough palms. She hadn't realized how cold it was until it was encompassed in his warmth. He raised it to his lips and pressed them against the flat of her hand.

Then, Coulter pulled away in shock, and knelt tensely before her. "The bastard!"

"What?"

"The son-of-a-bitch."

"Who are you talking about?"

"The gun was in Joel's hand?"

She nodded mutely.

He shook his head. "If he'd turned that gun on himself, the recoil would have torn it from his fingers."

"I don't understand ..."

"Joel Dougherty didn't kill himself."

Her voice was nothing more than a hoarse whisper. "Clayton."

"The son-of-a-bitch killed his own brother."

"But why? His own brother? He even was crying right after it happened!"

"Crying because he had to kill his brother?"

"I still don't understand."

"You're not that innocent, lady."

She shook her head in confusion.

"Think about it," he pushed. "You lived in the same house with him for a year. How did he treat you? I'll lay you odds it wasn't like a sister."

Her cheeks burned and she remembered the heat of Clayton's gaze following her every move, the sting of his taunts when Joel wasn't around. Months of it, and she was going mad with the pressure... and so was Joel... and so was Clayton.

As if reading her thoughts, he seized her shoulders and pulled her face closer to his. "What did he do? Did he ever—"

"No!" she choked. "No, he didn't. But the night Joel died... the night I came to the jail and set you free... he was going to."

"How the hell did you stop him?" Coulter demanded.

She lifted her shoulders. "I hit him in the head with a lamp. He chased me, but I knocked him down the stairs."

Coulter rubbed his cheek. "There may be more." He ran his fingers through his hair, distracted. "Somebody knew who I was and where I came from. Somebody got in touch with that reporter, Dan P. Jennings of Harper's Weekly, and I couldn't figure out who, or how they knew. ..."

"Oh, God." It was all coming clear. "Joel was obsessed with all the eastern newspapers and magazines... especially Harper's Weekly."

"Joel wrote Jennings. It was his way to bring me to Cavendish. He wanted me to kill Clayton."

"Justice," she whispered, an echo of a distant plea.

"And Clayton found out, and killed Joel with your gun."

She knew the twisting pain of the vortex of killing she'd been swept into. Where did it end?

"I'm not running any more, but I'm choosing my own ground. We're staying here until he comes"

He. She didn't have to ask who. "What makes you think he'll come here?"

"Everybody's going to be searching between Cimarron and Seven Rivers. I'm sending a wire that only Clayton Dougherty will understand. He'll come."

Wendell rode into Seven Rivers in the early afternoon. Pale beneath his weathered tan, his left arm in a sling, he would have drawn sympathy had his expression not been set with such steely determination. Instead, the glances he drew were mostly just plain curious.

He dismounted in front of the hotel, bigger and finer than the one in Cavendish, though that wasn't saying much. He removed his hat before entering, holding it at his side in his good hand.

The hotel lobby was a large plank-floored room. A narrow staircase with ornate banisters climbed up one wall; in the nook beneath the stairs was a desk with a sign-in book for guests. Standing in the doorway however, he faced a wide bar backed by a large painting of mountains and sky that was pleasing to the eye, even if it didn't look like any mountains and sky Wendell had ever seen. Evidently the bar wasn't open yet, for the six tables of assorted sizes were stacked with chairs and a young girl was mopping the floor.

The girl raised up and wiped her hands on her apron. "Were you lookin' for a room, mister?" She wet her lips nervously, her eyes widening as she saw the spot of blood soiling the bandage on his shoulder.

He managed a stiff shake of his head, but he didn't feel any too steady on his feet. "I'm looking for the telegraph office."

"It's through that door in the corner."

Wendell cut between the tables to the corner doorway she indicated. The Western Union office was little more than a small closet. Wendell stepped up to the window and looked through the metal bars. A thin man with a potbelly dozed at a small table, one hand resting near the telegraph key, the other cupping a small flask against his thigh.

Wendell rapped his knuckles against the wall and the man jumped, spilling a small amount of liquor on his pant leg.

"What? What?"

"I need to be sendin' a wire, please."

The little man eyed him through bloodshot orbs, then nodded. "Where to, young feller?"

Wendell shifted uneasily. "I ain't really sure. To a magazine in New York City... I forgit the name."

The man aimed a disgusted look at the ceiling and sucked in his cheeks. "There's a lot of magazines in New York City."

Wendell felt the color creeping up his neck. "This one's got a man's name. Harkey. Harber. Somethin' like that."

"Mm-hmm. Wouldn't be Harper's Weekly would it?"

"Yeah! That's it! Gee, mister, that's it exactly!"

The old man chewed on his lower lip. "Do you know who you're sendin' this wire to up there at Harper's Weekly?"

"A feller by the name of... Jennings. I think."

"Mm-hmm." The balding head bobbed once or twice. "Wouldn't be Dan P. Jennings, would it?"

Wendell's mouth dropped open. "That's it! How'd you know that?"

"Well, young feller. Guess you've put me in a pickle. You see, as an employee of the Western Union Telegraph Company, I should just take yer wire and let it go at that." He angled his head and squinted at Wendell from beneath a pair of bushy eyebrows. "Fact of the matter is, I'd feel purty low if I didn't tell you to jest save your money and see if you can't find him in town somewheres."

"Here? In Seven Rivers?" Wendell's heart jumped into double-time. "Are you sure?"

The man took a healthy swig from his flask and wiped his nobby thumb across the corner of his mouth. "Reckon that man's sent more messages out o' this town than we've had in a month of Sundays. Damn near never runs out of words. Pretty excitin' ones at that, what with the stage robbery and such. Things have really been firm' up something fierce betwixt bounty hunters and everybody else that's roamin' through."

Wendell didn't bother to question the twist of fate that had brought the reporter to Seven Rivers. Nor did he question that his knees plumb near turned to jelly at the thought of seeing Doralee again. "Thank you, mister," he said, already halfway out the office door.

"What did you say your name was, young feller?"

Wendell paused, his hat clenched in impatient fingers. "Crutcher. Wen—" He stopped short, then stood a little straighter, showing off his badge. "Sheriff Wendell Crutcher out of Cavendish, Texas."

"Well, hell's bells, why didn't you say so to begin with?" The old man dragged himself out of the chair and reached toward an array of messages pinned haphazardly to the bare wood wall above him "Let's see... yeah, here it is." He yanked one down and frowned. "Well, here's a fix. This is for the sheriff of Cavendish, Texas all right. But it ain't fer you, it's fer a feller named Dougherty."

"Sheriff Dougherty ain't sheriff no more," Wendell said, his knuckles turning white and jaw working. "I am."

"Well, since it particularly said sheriff, I suppose it's official." The man shrugged and shoved it through the window. "This come in Tuesday. Nobody 'round here knew of any sheriff's in town from Texas. I'm just glad somebody showed up fer it."

Wendell fingered the folded paper in his hands. It wasn't meant for him, and he knew it. He probably shouldn't even take it.

But he did.

He shoved it in his pocket. “Thanks,” he said, and stepped into the comparative brightness of the hotel lobby. The girl had finished her mopping and was setting up the chairs.

“You ready for that room, now?”

He admired the way her pretty brown hair pulled back with a blue ribbon, the way her apron nipped in her waist to make it look even tinier, the way her ankles showed pertly when she reached up for another chair and he felt a fresh stab of longing, but not for her, for Doralee.

“Can you tell me if someone I know is staying here?”

“Who is it?”

“Dan P. Jennings.”

Her face lit up and she spun to face him. “Mr. Jennings? Oh, yes, he’s got the nicest room in the hotel, number 10. If you’re looking for him, he’s probably out lookin’ fer somebody new to interview, lookin’ for someone who remembers something about that lady outlaw everybody’s so all-fired interested in.”

Wendell swallowed hard. “Is he… is he alone?”

Her lips pulled into a disapproving line. “No.” she sniffed. “That hussy he has staying with him probably hasn’t even stirred out of bed yet.”

Wendell charged toward the stairs.

“Where do you think you’re going? You can’t—”

Wendell jabbed a thumb at his badge without even slowing down. “Official business.”

She stood gaping as his long, lanky legs disappeared up the staircase, two steps at a time. “Well, I’ll be.”

Chapter Twenty-seven

EVERYTHING WAS TURNING out just fine, Doralee figured. Her worries were for nothing, it seemed. She stretched a pointed toe toward the ceiling, drawing circles in the air as she considered her good fortune. Most importantly, Danny's excitement over his story only stimulated his interest in the commodity she was offering.

Commodity. A smile curved her full lips. He sure did love teachin' her those big words.

Her smile melted into a frown as a knock sounded at the door. Danny would have just burst right in. The maid should know better than to bother her this early in the morning. Yesterday a well-aimed boot had convinced her to wait until afternoon before even thinking about bringing the fresh linens Danny was paying through the nose for. Doralee yawned and slid a finger between her breasts to scratch an itch.

The knock sounded again.

If it was that damn maid, again... She slid from the bed, snatching her new wrapper and slipping it over her bare body. She was tying the bow at the waist when she called, "Come in."

The door squeaked open, but no footsteps entered. Giving the bow one last tug, she raised her head....

They stood in silence, her mouth gaping, his Adam's apple bobbing. "Wendell?"

"Doralee."

"Where on earth did you come from?" A ghost couldn't have scared her more.

"Doralee, I need to talk to you."

"Well, come on in and shut the damn door before people start talkin' more than they already do." Her heart was thundering in her breast. She gave him a sidelong glance as he entered and closed the door behind him. The kid looked like a scarecrow, bandaged and sunburned... but there was something different about him, too. Something she couldn't put her finger on.

She'd never noticed he was so tall. Or maybe he'd never held himself so tall before, not even when she'd given him his first taste of femininity.

She hopped onto the bed and sat up against the pillows. Lordy, she hoped he wasn't aiming to pick up where he'd left off before. A tumble with the kid wasn't worth risking getting caught, even if he did look like a good tumble might heal a good part of what ailed him. One thing about men. They figured a good tumble would improve almost any situation.

"Well, go ahead and say whatever you've got to. If Danny comes back, he'll kill us both."

"Does he treat you good, Doralee?"

Confused, she gave a half-shrug. "Better than most."

"Then he's a good man? Somebody you can trust."

"In his own way, yeah. And he's smart, too. A real change from the fellas I'm usually around."

Wendell nodded sadly, apparently not even offended. "I need your help, Doralee." His good hand had a grip on his hat that would have strangled a rattler. He didn't meet her eye.

Here it comes, she thought, shooting a quick glance at his crotch. Her mind was already thinking up as sweet a refusal as she could muster when he spoke.

"I need to talk to Mr. Jennings."

"Danny?" Her mouth hardened and her breath came in short snorts as the insult hit her. "What the hell do you want with Dan P. Jennings?" She didn't move, not even to pull her robe closed higher on her bosom, especially not to pull her robe closed higher on her bosom.

"He's a reporter, isn't he? Doesn't that mean that if he thought somethin' was important, he could write about it, 'n everybody would see it? And they'd know the truth, and ..." His voice faded. "Those people in Cavendish appointed me sheriff when Sheriff Dougherty resigned. They made me sheriff until they could hold an election, 'cause they didn't have time to pick someone better. I know that, just like I know they probably had somebody new elected before I'd been gone a week."

Doralee's aggravation at Wendell faded a bit, but she didn't bother denying what he was saying. The kid was a fool sometimes, but he wasn't stupid. "Sit down, Wendell," she said, wondering if she sounded as weary as she felt.

He eased onto the straight-backed chair Jennings had used to bar the door the night before. His shoulders hunched and head down, he stared at the hat he held dangling between his widespread knees. "I get so confused sometimes, Doralee. I don't know what's right and what's wrong. I mean, a sheriff is supposed to know right, 'cause people depend on him But I don't know. I don't know, Doralee. I don't know what's right."

"And you're askin' me?" she asked, her voice rich with irony. "A lot o' folks would say you were barkin' up the wrong tree, askin' a whore to explain what's right and what's wrong."

His head snapped up, his jaw rigid. "Then a lot of folks would be wrong."

She felt a sense of shock when she saw the hard look in his eyes. Like a bolt, it hit her what had changed about Wendell Crutcher.

His innocence was gone.

"There's some wicked people in this world, Doralee. Some folks that seem good ain't, and some that seem bad... maybe they ain't, either. It's easy to look at folks like you and say what's wrong. I reckon it's too easy. If you can see the wrong and point it out then that makes you feel like you're right. It seems that there's so much wickedness in their world, that people have to point their fingers and call names at you to convince themselves that they're keeping things under control. I know why you wouldn't marry me, and I don't blame you. But I just want you to know…" His voice cracked, and he wiped his face with his sleeve.

Suddenly Doralee felt her own damn throat clog up.

"I really did love you, Doralee. And I wouldn't have cared what people said or if they pointed or if they called names. You see, people have been laughin' at me and calling me names all my life. I figgered we had that in common, that we kind of understood things other folks didn't."

She crossed the room and cradled his head against her bosom. Soon his tears were soaking her breasts, and her tears were soaking his hair.

"If you don't stop cryin' like a durn fool," she sobbed brokenly, digging her nails into his hair, hating him for making her cry like one, too, "I'm gonna slap the shit out of you!"

He raised his face to her and she saw the pain of self-loathing in his eyes. "You always did think I was a fool, didn't you?"

"Yeah, I guess I did. But we're all fools, Wendell. Every damn one of us is fools. You're just a different kind of fool."

"But why? What makes me so different?" he pleaded, and she wanted to hit him, to throw something at him, to scream until her throat was bloody so he'd stop looking at her like she was supposed to have the answers. Instead, she shoved at his shoulders and stepped back from him, but her legs seemed barely able to hold her up. She was shocked to realize her hands were cold, clammy. She wanted to sit down. She sank down on the corner of the bed, her back bumping against the iron bedframe. And still, he waited for her answer.

Why did she feel like what she said next was so damned important? Why couldn't she just send him packing, get him out of her life once and for all?

But she couldn't. She clenched her shaking hands in her lap, and thought with all her might. Why was he different?

"I suppose," she said finally, her voice hoarse with frustration, "it's because you're so goddamned young, Wendell Crutcher. I ain't talkin' about years. I'm talkin' about your heart. You're young in a way most of us never are. I guess that's what drove the sheriff plumb crazy most of the time. He needed you there lookin' up at him and making him feel important and believing in him, 'cause the rest of us knew him for what he was, a mean son-of-a-bitch who was no good and bound for hell like the rest of us. But he kept the peace, and that's a mighty tall order out here.

"He needed you, but he couldn't hardly stand to be around you because he couldn't look at you without knowing what he was supposed to be. You say you don't know the truth, Wendell, but that ain't so. The truth's a part of you, shinin' out, bright as a new penny, and you can't hide from it like the rest of us. I reckon that's what makes you different."

"But sometimes the truth hurts somebody you never wanted to hurt," he mourned softly. "I wish I wasn't different, Doralee."

She felt old, so old. She had been many things to many men. But for the first time in her life, she was looking at a man and wondering what he might have been to her, wondering if he might have been someone who could have actually lessened her pain, instead of adding to it. For the first time, she found herself wanting to hold and be held, wanting to open herself and feel love without shame. And she knew she wouldn't do it. It was too late.

"I always said you were gonna make a fine man, Wendell Crutcher. Don't let me down."

He nodded. "I guess I need to talk to Jennings."

It was after one in the morning and Clayton Dougherty had been sitting alone at a table at the back of the saloon in Seven Rivers for quite a spell, cleaning his nails with the edge of his knife blade. When one bottle'd emptied, he'd demanded another one, and the replacement had been done with speed and caution. Other than that, nobody had bothered him, not even the whores.

He rubbed his hand against his trousers and glared, then held his fingernails up to his face. There were still traces of brown around the edges. He whistled low and worked on picking out the dried blood a little more.

A weasely little bastard, half-bald and pale-skinned with the look of a drunkard about him, sidled up to him. "Don't figger you'd share a friendly sip with a stranger, would you?"

"Hell no, you thievin' son-of-a-bitch," Dougherty snarled.

The man backed off, but not far. "You have the looks of a bounty hunter to me. I've been helpin' a few along, for a little compensation," he continued, his words coming on a wave of rotgut whiskey stench.

"What's it take to get rid of you, a bullet between the eyes?" Dougherty tipped the bottle to his lips, but the man stood his ground, his bulging eyes watching the liquor greedily. Wiping his mouth on his sleeve, Dougherty eyed the man thoughtfully. "What's a little bastard like you know that anybody'd pay for?"

The corner of his mouth twitching, the man folded his shaking hands over his small pot belly. "I'm the telegrapher. Ain't much that goes on that I don't know about."

"You said you been helpin' bounty hunters." Dougherty pinned him with a long, suspicious gaze. "You know somethin' about Boone Coulter and Elizabeth Dougherty?"

Nose quivering, the man grabbed a chair from a nearby table and straddled it. He wet his lips, watching Dougherty's hands caress the long neck of the bottle. "Reckon I do. Reckon I know a mighty lot."

"I want to know everything."

"Sure, mister. Sure, anything you say."

Dougherty motioned for another bottle.

The man grinned, showing his rotten teeth. "Good, good. I knew you were a generous man ..." He rubbed his hands together in anticipation, almost snatching the bottle from the bartender's hand when he delivered it to the table. He uncorked it with his teeth, spit out the cork, and took a long drink. When he lowered the bottle, he let out a noisy, fume-filled sigh. "That's good stuff. Thank you kindly." He thrust a thin hand out. "Mick Flanagan, at your service."

Dougherty ignored his hand and gave a curt nod. "Clayton Dougherty."

The man wheezed and turned pale. "Dou—Dougherty?"

Misunderstanding his reaction, Clayton nodded. "The lady was my brother's wife."

"You ain't sheriff of Cavendish, Texas, are you?" the man asked, his expression almost desperately hopeful.

"Used to be."

The man tilted the bottle to his lips and took another long draw. When he'd had his fill, he lowered it to his thigh, and red-faced and red-eyed said, "Shit."

"What the hell is your problem?" Dougherty snapped.

"I think somebody sent you a message last week. And I think I gave it to the wrong person yesterday."

His voice deadly calm, Dougherty asked, "What kind of message?"

"Weren't much to it," Flanagan babbled. "Just tellin' you that somebody was planning on meeting you in Lincoln. Shit, I can't remember his name ..."

His face expressionless, Dougherty grabbed the man's neck, his thumb digging into the jugular. "You'd better remember."

"Hey, pleeease," he wheezed. "Bridger. That's it. Bridger!"

"I don't know any Bridgers." Dougherty shook the man until his head bobbled. "You'd better think hard, or I'll snap your miserable little neck."

"John!" the man moaned, his eyes bulging, "Wesley... Bri—"

"Bridges." Clayton grunted and released him. After a stunned moment, Flanagan started to rise but Dougherty's knife flashed under his nose. "Why don't you get back up here and tell me everything you know?" he asked, his voice calm, lethal.

"Yes—yessir." Flanagan gasped, his eyes near to popping out of his head when he saw the dried blood on the rusty blade.

"Blood moon." Coulter leaned back on his elbows beneath the moon that floated low on the eastern horizon.

The wind had picked up in early afternoon stirring the air with red dust, giving the moon a crimson glow, Elizabeth thought calmly. She rolled onto her stomach, and cupped her chin in her hands. "I don't think Clayton will ever get the message."

"He'll get it. If he hasn't already." Coulter stretched out flat on his back, folding his arms behind his head. "I'm going into town tonight."

His words startled her. "Must you?"

"I think so. It's been two weeks since I sent the wire. There may be a reply, or …"

"Or he may already be there." She completed the sentence for him.

He nodded, his face lined, his expression weary.

"And what am I supposed to do?"

"Wait."

"No."

"Elizabeth," he sighed, and raised up. He reached for his boots but didn't put them on.

She noticed all over again how he had hollowed, drawn tighter, the waiting taking its toll on him as it had on her. A time of waiting, a time of loving, the days had followed one after the other, a golden idyll. If she tried very, very hard, she could picture them together, like this, without end.

Except when reality crept in by way of a certain hollowness in his voice, a tension that never left the sharp creases around his mouth. Had they once upon a time been dimples, before life had erased the laughter from his face? And with that reality came not the panic, the fear that had been a part of her for so long. A body could only take so much panic, so much fear, before it ceased feeling. Instead, she would find herself surreptitiously feeling for the comfort of her gun, checking and rechecking the chambers, never letting it far from her sight.

Even now, her eyes strayed to the spot where it lay, beneath her folded shawl.

And even now, knowing the direction of her thoughts, he touched her chin, pulling her focus back to him. He traced the pulse at the base of her neck with a roughened fingertip. "Kiss me, Elizabeth."

Like steel filings to a magnet, she inched closer, bringing her lips to his, and at the moment of their bonding, his arm circled her with its strength, its power.

Tension vibrated between them, infecting even their lovemaking with an intensity so desperate, so sensitive, so absolute, that for hours afterward her body felt like a finely strung instrument, still humming with remembered harmony, but already tensing for the discord to come.

How different his strength was from hers. His fought to shut her out, hers fought to make them one. He was the armed warrior, steeling himself for battle, taking what she offered for sustenance, but afraid to accept it completely, afraid to risk absorbing her "weakness." She too was armed, but with a different kind of strength, quieter perhaps, but more dogged, more determined, more patient.

And so, each time he pushed away, she retaliated by drawing nearer. Each time he closed her out, she swept him in. Until finally, he had stopped pushing, had stopped closing, and began to take her so completely, she felt herself sucked into the vortex of his passion, felt it tightening around her, spinning her beyond knowledge of anything but him.

Her hand crept into his shirt, finding the hard ridge of his collarbone, stroking, memorizing every detail about him, his taste, wild mint and sage; his smell, pine and juniper; his voice, soft and rustling even in anger, especially in passion. She stored these memories against the end that she prayed would never come, or if it did, would come to them both. For she could not imagine life without him.

Again, he must have sensed her thoughts, for again he demanded her attention, her total attention, his hand tightening at the base of her neck, his mouth devouring the recesses of hers, his breath blending with her own. He would not let her think, only feel.

"Love me," he whispered.

Doralee frowned at the paper under her foot and stooped over and picked it up. Some durn fool had written her a note, and her not able to read more than the few letters in her name. It wasn't from Danny. His figures and writings were pretty, polished.

It must be from Wendell. He'd been casting cow eyes at her ever since they'd gotten to Lincoln. Wouldn't it be just like him to try something, now that Danny's promises to take her to New York seemed finally to be coming true. Well, she wasn't letting anything get in her way now. She crumpled the note into a ball and kicked the door shut.

She and Danny shared a room on the back side of the L-shaped, one-storied adobe hotel, as far from the noisy dining room as they could get.

She was relieved to see the warm amber glow of the oil lamp and the rumpled bed. She began unbuttoning the jacket of the demure gray suit Danny had bought her. It was too dad-blamed hot for so many layers of clothes, no matter how pretty.

A knock sounded at the door.

"Shit," she hissed. Danny wouldn't have knocked; it had to be Wendell. Poor Wendell. She tried to stifle the pang of regret, and as usual, had a hard time of it.

"All right, all right," she muttered, yanking the door open with an exasperated sigh, but instead of Wendell's lanky form, the large, hulking figure of Clayton Dougherty filled the doorway.

"Well, well, well ..." He stepped forward, and the amber light illuminated his dusty apparel, his scarred face, the large knife held lovingly in his hand.

"If it ain't our prissy-assed little whore, Doralee." He slung the door closed with one hand, brandishing the knife with the other.

"No!" But her scream was cut off as he slapped his hand across her mouth. Before she could react, he'd grasped her hair and slammed her head against the wall. She felt her cheekbone snap at the impact, pain shooting throughout her head.

"You gonna tell me what's goin' on here?" he growled. "What that reporter bastard of yours is doin' sniffin' around Boone Coulter?"

God help her, she would have told him anything, but he rammed her head against the wall again before she could respond. His face grew fuzzy, and she uttered a low, guttural moan. "What's Wendell Crutcher doin' here, slut? Tell me!" His hand dropped to her throat, the point of his knife grazing the skin beneath her ear, stinging. "What's everybody doin' here?" His eyes were wild, blood-shot and glazed.

No matter what she told him, he was going to kill her. And after her, Danny, and then... Wendell.

Please God, not Wendell. She shook her head feebly, despite the knife he pressed into her neck. Wendell. If he found out what Wendell knew, what Wendell had told Danny... "No," she gasped.

It was the last word she ever spoke.

Chapter Twenty-eight

COULTER FLEXED HIS fingers over the reins, feeling the tendons and muscles in his forearms tense and stretch. His back was stiff, shoulders taut, eyes almost burning as he scrutinized the surrounding terrain. Sage moved under him like an extension of himself. This was where he and the horse became one, why he never considered finding a more controllable mount. Together, they were alerted to the faintest sound. They would not be caught unaware.

Elizabeth rode beside but a few paces behind him, her henna-red hair covered beneath a scarf and a shawl that shielded her from the night's chill. Later she must remove them, he realized. She must show her hair in town, for that's what people would remember later, and that detail might help save her when—if he didn't come out of this alive.

Dread tightened his gut. The thought of her so vulnerable to danger, riding into Lincoln at his side... but what else could he do with her? He'd known better than to leave her behind, for she would have followed, increasing the risks with her impulsiveness. No, he had no choice but to bring her along.

He slowed when he saw the town stretched before them, a double band of diffused lights lining the crooked road. Night dimmed the image, hiding details, but he remembered them precisely. On the far end of town was the courthouse, of little use to him. The hotel, saloons, homes... He suddenly stiffened in his saddle.

The torreón.

Unlighted, the tower was barely visible from this vantage point. But located in the center of town and designed as a watchtower for Apaches that had long since ceased to be a threat, it provided exactly what he needed: a refuge for keeping her safe, an excuse for making her stay there.

She rode beside him now, and he stared at her profile, gauzed and softened by moonlight, and felt the bittersweet pang of loss he'd been wrestling with for days. He reached across the open space between them and took her cold hand, pressing a small, cloth-wrapped object into it. He watched her as she unfolded the cloth and found the coils of gold chain, the cross. He heard her soft intake of air.

"You don't have to do this. It was never really mine," she whispered. "It means so much to you. You should keep it."

He shook his head, and when he spoke, his tone was gruffer than he'd intended. "It's yours now. Just put it on."

Her movements were hesitant, yet graceful, as she slipped it over her head, and he knew a strange peace knowing that it was nestled against her skin, a talisman of what he felt for her.

"What are we going to do?" she asked, her voice strained.

"I'm going to see if I can slip in a couple of saloons unnoticed." She startled to interrupt, but he silenced her with a sharp shake of his head. "Listen to me, Elizabeth. One man alone is easy to ignore. But if you walk into any of those places, every eye will be on you. If Clayton Dougherty is there, no red hair is gonna keep him from recognizing you."

"But if he's there, he'll recognize you!"

"If he sees me, he'll follow me out. Clayton Dougherty isn't going to do anything in front of witnesses. He's built a life these last ten years on the illusion that he's an honest man. He sure as hell hasn't come this far to blow everything open."

"But —"

Coulter nodded, his heart in his throat. This was the part he had to make convincing. "I can take Dougherty in a fair fight, and he knows it, so he won't fight fair. I need you to go to the top of the tower and watch out for me. You can see everything from up there." He took her cold hand in his. "I need you Elizabeth. For God's sake, don't argue with me over this."

He could feel her staring at him, trying to find a flaw in what he said. She didn't want to believe him, didn't want to believe that she could better serve him by hiding in a watchtower than by being at his side. But finally, she agreed and he felt a slight loosening in his throat.

"He might not even be there yet," he said.

She didn't respond, but her expression told him she held out little hope.

"If anything happens to me—if I get wounded—remember, you mustn't fight him. Promise me right now, Elizabeth Dougherty, you won't do anything foolish. Promise me you'll cover me, but if he gets me, you'll take off and head for the mountains and stay there until it's safe. Clayton Dougherty's the only one who would know you, and I guarantee you, if I go down, he'll go down with me. Break into the mail bag, if you have to, and get the money, and use it to get on the first stage that comes. Get as far away from here as you can." She didn't answer, and he applied desperate pressure to her fingers.

"Promise me, Elizabeth. I want your word."

"I can make that promise, but I can't promise that I'll honor it," she said softly.

He squeezed his eyes shut. "Make it anyway."

"I promise."

He tried to convince himself that it was enough.

Wendell stared at the mug on the table in front of him. The thin rim of froth was gradually disappearing as the beer went flat before his eyes. He'd been listening to the reporter's sharp, nasal voice from across the room for hours.

Jennings was nice enough, as far as Yankees went, but that didn't mean he deserved a gal as sweet as Doralee. What if he took her off to New York and got tired of her and dumped her? She'd be lost and afraid, so far away from home.

Wendell didn't bother to look up as Jennings slid onto the stool beside him. "You've been nursing that same beer all night."

Wendell met his gaze for a moment, then shrugged and forced a few swallows down.

"I agree, I've had better," the reporter said, his own manicured fingers lightly caressing a scratched jigger glass.

"It tastes like horse piss," Wendell muttered, shoving the mug away.

"You've got it bad, don't you?"

Again, Wendell shrugged.

"I wish I could say something to make it easier for you. I imagine you'd take a punch at me if I told you you're better off without her, so I won't say it."

Wendell shook his head. "She's better off without me, that's what counts."

"What are you going to do when this is over?" Jennings asked.

"It's already over for me."

The reporter raised his heavy, black brows in question.

"I ain't got no more reason to be here. I've done all I can. Now that you know about Sheriff Dougherty ..."

"No, Dougherty isn't sheriff, any longer," Jennings corrected. "You are, Sheriff Crutcher."

Wendell snorted. "I ain't no more a sheriff than you are. When I ride back into Cavendish, I won't even be a deputy. Sheriff Dougherty was the only one crazy enough to pin a badge on me, and that's just because he needed somebody foolish enough to believe his lies, somebody stupid enough not to ask too many questions. When I go back—"

"Then don't."

"What?"

"Don't go back."

"I ain't got nowhere else to go."

Wendell shifted his weight on the stool as Jennings studied him with a relentless gaze.

Finally, the reporter spoke. "You've lost your woman, you've lost your hero, you've lost your youth, and somehow you managed to do all that without developing the grit and the callousness to protect you from what life's gonna throw at you next. I don't know what it'll take to bring it out in you, or how long it'll take for it to happen, Wendell. You've already been through more than most men could take and still be honest. But somewhere deep inside you, you've got what it takes, Wendell Crutcher. I don't know where you're going next, but I just don't believe it's going to be Cavendish, Texas."

The unaccustomed alcohol, scant as it was, had blurred Wendell's mind. The muscles in his cheeks and in the corners of his eyes and mouth felt numb, dragged down, and suddenly he knew that he had to get out of this place, this town. Maybe the reporter was right. Maybe he shouldn't go back. But he sure wasn't staying here either.

He slid off the stool, his eyes darting around the smoky room. Yeah, he was getting out of here tonight. There was nothing else he could do here.

"Tell Doralee goodbye before you leave, Wendell."

He stared resolutely toward the door. "I left her a note."

The reporter smiled. "Wendell, Doralee can't read."

Wendell's eyes popped open, flaring with a moment's brief hope, that died just as quickly. "I don't think she wants to be bothered."

"Believe me, she does. You've given Doralee something nobody else ever could. Maybe it wasn't enough to hold her, but you came closer than anybody else ever will. Tell her goodbye."

Wendell nodded, and turned to go.

"Oh, yeah." the reporter added, the corner of his mouth twitching. "She'll be expecting me. Sometimes... well, don't be too startled if she greets you with a surprise. She likes to do that sometimes."

Moments later Wendell approached Doralee's door. He could just guess what kind of surprise Jennings was talking about, but even though he felt himself stirring, he knew he wasn't going to do anything about it. He knocked once and the door gave way under his hand and it swung open. His brow creased in a frown; he was wondering if her silence was part of the surprise when he stepped inside.

Dougherty held his hands in the cold, cold water. Beneath the shallow, rapid river's surface, his fingers grew numb as he tried to wash away the feel of hot, sticky blood on his hands and forearms, the telltale traces under his nails. He had to cover his tracks.

The slut hadn't told him a thing but it didn't matter. She deserved it, every bit of it. It didn't matter anymore why they were all here or how much any of them knew. In fact, it was a turn of luck. It would save him the trouble of hunting them all down. He'd never have to look over his shoulder again.

Together in the same place... and somewhere nearby, Coulter.

He'd get rid of the reporter, the deputy, the outlaw. He'd take pleasure in killing them all.

Especially the outlaw.

Ten years he'd been regretting not shooting him and his daddy in the wagon after the torching. He'd spent ten years building a new life, had had it in his fingertips until... until Joel had brought Elizabeth Cooke to Cavendish.

Dougherty licked his lips as his breath came faster.

He'd have his brother's bitch wife at last.

A light mist clung in the air, but the street below Elizabeth was visible. She knelt, her hands propped on the edge of the wall that encircled the flat roof of the tower, clutching the gun. She watched for Coulter's quiet, easy-gaited walk as he emerged from the shadow of the tower below her. When he was nearly across the street, he cast one last look over his shoulder toward her, then disappeared into the first saloon, to watch, to listen. She prayed no one would recognize him. She prayed Clayton was not there.

A shadow appeared in the saloon's open doorway, and she watched, restless, breathless, as Coulter emerged. He didn't glance up at her this time, but strode north toward the next building. Quickly, she scanned the scene below, watching for any sign of someone following. Another shadow peeled away from the doorway, large and hulking—she cocked the gun and aimed at the figure as it hurried south: a woman, a large woman. She relaxed, trembling, against the wall, swept with temporary relief, as Coulter passed safely through the doorway of the second saloon.

Minutes that seemed like hours passed. She quivered when he reappeared. Thank God, no one followed him. Her hands began to shake uncontrollably. She could hardly breathe, so intense was her fear.

After he entered the hotel, she slipped the gun into her pocket and clenched her hands to stop them from shaking. She was forced to admit Coulter had been right. No one could watch him from behind, not with her watching from this excellent vantage point.

The night breezes blew a little harder, a little colder, on the roof of the torreón. She leaned against the three-foot wall, pulling her shawl tighter around her shoulders, her skirt weighted down on one side by the pistol in her pocket. Maybe Clayton had gone back to Cavendish. Maybe he hadn't gotten the message.

Her mind was numb with maybes.

She watched a couple stroll by the entrance to the saloon, willing time to pass, willing safety upon him, the man she loved. She regretted a dozen times over that she couldn't be two places at once, here as well as there. She heard the mare neigh, and then a thumping sound. Glancing over her shoulder at the deserted rooftop, she hoped the horse would quiet down. As if the mare had read her mind, there was silence.

But if Clayton were in Cavendish, she thought, it wouldn't change a thing. It would buy time, yes, but only that. For whatever Clayton Dougherty was, Boone Coulter intended to track him down, and finally, finally put an end to their running.

All she could do was watch and wait. She rubbed her hands together vigorously. They were warm and steady none too soon—Coulter would be coming out any time. Her hand lowered to her pocket to pull out the gun.

A hand slammed over her mouth, and she was hurtled forward. Her elbows crashed into the tower wall, her knees ground into the roof, and the butt of the pistol jammed into her hip. There was a whirring in her ears, the loud booming of her pulse, and her eyes filled with the image of Coulter walking unprotected into the street. She tried to scream, but the hand muffled her attempt to a grunt. Then her attacker yanked her, flipping her to her back, then fastened his hand over her throat, squeezing until there was only a tight, painful passage for air.

Clayton Dougherty hovered over her, his face twisted in a mocking, horrid smile, and even in the dim moonlight, as if through murky water, she saw the way one eye glowered beneath the scar she'd inflicted.

She tried to speak, but his hand tightened on her neck.

"Bitch," he hissed. "You're gonna pay ..."

Black dots swam before her eyes, flashes of color and explosions of pain; her lungs screamed for air... cold, so cold... the pain. The world was receding, when suddenly he let go, and all she could do was lie there and whimper as she drew in air in quick, icy gulps.

"Not here," he rasped, rising over her and grabbing her arms. He wrenched her roughly to her feet. "Not yet."

She looked down into the street, it was empty. A sob of frustration tore from her throat, and Dougherty laughed.

"Is that what you want, bitch? You wanna wait up here until your lover comes back for you? Even with a pistol, I could pick him off from up here. Nice little spot you've got here." He laughed again, and fingers of ice closed over her heart. "Or maybe you wanna wait until he comes up here, let him see you... and me... right before I blow his head off, right before your eyes. That what you want?"

She shook her head, closing her throbbing throat against the sickening, mewing cries that were trying to escape.

"Then you listen good, and do what I say," he snarled. He twisted her arms behind her back, and she arched in pain, and he twisted harder until she thought her shoulders or elbows or both would pop through her skin. He tugged, and she could do nothing but what he wanted. He forced her across the roof with him to the opening where the ladder waited for their descent. Her pistol bounced against her thigh with each step, and she prayed he wouldn't notice.

"Now listen, and listen good. I'm gonna step down on that ladder, and then you're going to follow. Nothing funny, you hear? Just nice and easy."

"It's not strong enough," she croaked desperately.

"You let me worry about that."

He was behind her, and his grip tightened on her wrists as she felt him take the first rung, the second. She tensed, ready to kick him through the opening, but he stopped her with a vicious squeeze. "You now," he ordered, and she felt for the rung with her foot and found it.

And so they descended to the tower's inner room and down the next ladder that took them to the ground floor where the mare was hobbled and waiting, as mounts had waited years past to carry the warning of Apaches. Only tonight, the enemy had crept in unnoticed. Tonight, the mare whickered restlessly, but then quieted, and Elizabeth knew a deep despair.

He pushed her forward, his breath hot in her ear, "We're gonna take a little walk by the river."

She knew only the small comfort of her gun bouncing against her thigh, out of sight, but never out of her mind.

Chapter Twenty-nine

COULTER HAD ONLY one saloon left to check.

He entered the White Elephant, the noise and smoke and stench rolling over him. He wanted nothing more than to turn around and leave, fill his lungs with night air and freedom and take Elizabeth and run. But he knew as long as he was running, there was no freedom. He squinted against the stinging smoke and moved to the bar, eyes seeing all while seeming to see nothing. No man even remotely resembled Clayton Dougherty, and he knew relief and frustration.

At the bar he ordered a drink that he didn't plan to drink and slouched over it, listening. Most of the attention seemed to be focused on a stranger, a Yankee regaling the saloon's occupants with tales of faraway places, stretching the imagination to the point of incredibility, and yet the men, hungry for entertainment, believed. But no one mentioned the stage robbery. He gathered no new information to enlighten him.

So Dougherty hadn't come yet. Coulter's shoulders slumped, more fatigued than relaxed, while his mind raced ahead. He would get Elizabeth and head back into the mountains to wait.

Frustration punched him in the stomach, recoiling through his body. How much goddamn longer till he was free?

Or dead.

And then a name rose above the babble of voices, jolting him. Jennings. Dan P. Jennings. The reporter who wanted to pay him for his story... Coulter steeled himself, waiting a dozen heartbeats to angle his head slowly toward the Yankee stranger. What the hell was he doing here?

And then he knew, his message must have gotten out. Why else would Jennings be here? Unreasoning panic raced through his veins, panic that he squelched from long years of control. Slowly, he pushed away from the bar. Slowly, he wove his way through the crowd toward the door. And stepping into the street, he managed to walk a dozen yards before he finally lifted just his eyes to the top of the torreón.

His heart skipped a beat. Sometime during his stay in the saloon, the moon had been swallowed up by clouds, the watchtower swallowed up by rising fog; he couldn't see her.

She was there. She had to be.

He just wished he could see her.

The narrow river flowed quickly, noisily beside them, the water shallow, the current chattering in the night, drowning out their words. If she screamed, maybe someone would hear, but she would be dead and Clayton gone before any one came.

He circled her, the knife tip grazing her jaw, dragging down the nape of her neck, scraping over her ear, finally resting at her temple. "Lookin' mighty purty, Miz Dougherty. Mighty purty. Saw you and Coulter come into town and couldn't believe my eyes. Him puttin' you up there on that tower was smart, too. I couldn't get him without you seein' me. So I had to go for you first."

"What do you want from me?" she demanded.

"Reckon you know that already, don't ya', Miz Dougherty?" The knife point pressed into the tender spot under her jaw. He leaned closer; the point jabbed at her skin. Then the knife fell away and he grabbed a fistful of her hair and jerked it closer to his face. "What the hell is this? What have you done to your hair?"

She refused to answer.

He gave it an angry twist. "You little whore," he snarled, and even in the dim light, she could see the wildness in his eyes, the anger newly-fueled. "Joel ate himself alive wantin' you, thinkin' he wasn't good enough."

"No!" His words pounded into her, bringing back the old nightmare.

"Thinkin' he wasn't good enough for a whorin' wife who ran off with his murderer!"

"Boone Coulter didn't kill Joel, and you know it!"

Dougherty shook his head slowly, his low chuckle sending streams of fear into her veins. "Everybody knows Boone Coulter killed my brother, and now they'll know you for the whorin', lyin' bitch that you are!"

Elizabeth clenched her hands in her skirts. Close... the gun was so close... "Joel killed himself." She flung the words at him despite her doubts.

"You're stupid, too, you know that? Stupid! Joel didn't kill himself. He thought he had it all! He thought he'd found a way to get rid of me and his guilt, so he could love you like a man, and have my money, too! You stupid bitch!"

Her rage overcame her fear and she blurted, "You killed him! You killed your own brother!"

"Yeah, I killed him," he growled. "Joel wasn't man enough to face me, so he saw to it that Coulter would find me, and Joel would never get his lily-white hands bloody."

His fingers dug into her shoulder as he pulled her to him. "I killed him, and it's your fault! If it hadn't been for you, he never would have turned on me! He thought his darling Libby was an angel on earth. Then he got the bright idea to let Coulter take his shot at me and kill me like he did the others... Joel must have spent years followin' that Coulter's trail, watching him get closer, and closer, and then it stopped. And I was still alive. Then he met you... and he wasn't man enough for you, either, was he?"

He reached for her skirt, gathering it up in his fist, raising it to expose her legs. "Got anything for me, Miz Dougherty? Got anything left for me? Or did you give it all to that goddamned gunslinger?" His hand slid up her thigh, his ragged fingernails scratching her tender flesh, and she fumbled for the gun, bunched in the folds of her skirt. There was no way she could get into her pocket.

"Whore!" He spat the words at her, dropping her skirts to jerk his gunbelt off one-handed while his free hand held the knife to her temple. He tore at his clothing, exposing himself, and with a quick kick, he swept her legs out from under her. She hit the ground, and he landed over her, crushing her beneath his weight.

She twisted beneath him and freed the hand nearest the gun. He cursed and pressed the tip of the knife against her neck, broke skin, and all she could do was swallow, blink back tears as she felt the warm blood drip slowly down her neck. She groped for the pistol and her hand found the butt; it was pinned between them. She felt him tense, knew he felt the gun too, heard his savage snarl. She squeezed the trigger, knowing that it was aimed too low.

The gunshot seemed to be followed by a late echo, and she knew only confusion and wonder as she saw his head snap back at the impact of the bullet, and felt the sting of the knife slicing into her.

And then she knew nothing but red-hazed pain. She tried to reach for her neck, but her hands were weighted down by Clayton's dead weight. Whimpers, sobs, bloody gasps, bubbled from her throat as she cringed away from him. She was swimming in blood... Her blood was draining from her, her life ebbing away, and she heard a distant voice keening... her own voice, floating pure and empty... and she felt as if her spirit were leaving her behind in this pool of hot blood.

Elizabeth wasn't there.

Coulter descended only four rungs from the roof before dropping the remaining distance to the floor he scaled the next ladder, and landed in a crouch, sprang up and scrambled toward the door.

From the direction of the river, he heard a muffled gunshot followed by a second.

His heart exploded in his chest, and he sprinted toward the sound. No other gunshots followed; no one appeared to investigate what he'd heard. His feet pounded into the hard earth as he ran behind the buildings, then cut toward the river, following the sound of gunfire ringing in his ears.

The fog was swirling, misty fingers wrapping ghostly fingers around trees, bushes, and still he dashed alongside the river, slipping, stumbling toward... he knew not what. Only that the gunfire echoing in his mind wrapped cold icy fingers of fear around him. Gasping, he broke out of the underbrush, his gun drawn.

"Help me!"

For a moment he paused, trying to make sense out of what he was seeing. The deputy from Cavendish crouched over a large body on the ground a few yards away. Without feeling, he recognized the body. Clayton Dougherty. And he didn't care, couldn't care, not until he found Elizabeth.

"For Pete's sake, help me! I only got one good arm, and I can't lift good," the kid choked. "I think it's Miz Dougherty!"

Coulter sprang forward and saw her, pinned under Dougherty's massive form. He jammed his gun in his holster and grabbed Dougherty's shoulder. With one desperate heave he slung the sheriff's body aside.

"Is she alive? Jeezuz, he cut her bad."

Coulter shoved him aside and knelt beside her. "No …" he moaned. He ran his hands over her body, his stomach recoiling at the blood, so much blood, her dress so sodden, so sticky. He reached for the pulse at her neck, and instead his fingers found the wound, still oozing her lifeblood in a thin, steady stream.

"I... I killed him." Wendell's sob broke the night. "God damn him to hell, I killed him... but I was too late."

Blinded by fear, by rage, by tears, Coulter snatched the bandana from his neck and wrapped it around her slender throat, his fingers fumbling with the knot—how tight, how loose? Desperately, he sought the pressure to stop the flow of blood without cutting off the flow of air.

"Elizabeth, listen to me!" he begged, pulling her into his arms. "For God's sake, listen to me! I was wrong..." He choked on the acrid scent of gunpowder and blood and death, rocking, clasping her against him like a child. "Don't die, lady." Tears coursed down his cheeks. "Damnit! Don't you give up on me!"

A litany of fear and panic, of grief and love, his pleas continued.

Dawn broke clear and bright the next morning.

He had failed her; he had weakened and let her come into town with him, let her risk her life for him. He rode into Lincoln with the bundled body on a crude litter behind him. Head erect, skin drained beneath his ruddy tan, jaw clenched, he rode. As he made his slow way down the long stretch of winding, dusty road, faces appeared in windows, people in doorways, silent, curious, gaping. Even the mighty Sage was subdued, the mare following, riderless.

When he arrived in front of the courthouse, a small group of men had already assembled, and in their midst, the young Texas sheriff, Wendell Crutcher.

All eyes were on Coulter, and he reined in, his right hand raised with his gun aimed skyward. "My name's Boone Coulter. I'm wanted in three states and two territories. I've killed seven men; His voice cracked; his eyes glimmered with moisture. "I'm turning myself in."

"It's a trick!" one man shouted. "He's lying!"

Coulter shifted in the saddle, and trained his pain-dulled eyes on the speaker.

"She's dead," he said quietly. "This is Elizabeth Dougherty, and she's dead. Please give her a Christian burial," His voice broke, but he went on, "and erect a stone fitting for a brave woman, a good woman, a lady."

A low murmur spread through the crowd, and despite his confession, perhaps because of it, several men shrank back, but not the young sheriff. "Surrender your arms."

Two pistols, one pearl-handled, one smooth ebony, hit the dirt along with a rifle.

Unarmed, his threat lessened, the caustic voice repeated, "How do we know he ain't lyin'?"

The stallion held perfectly still as Coulter slowly eased from its back. Wendell stepped forward, and as he drew near the litter, his face turned ashen.

He raised the edge of the blanket, and the morbidly curious strained forward to catch a glimpse of the lady outlaw. He swallowed hard, his eyes caught by death's image. Finally he nodded. Blinking back tears, he covered her face again. "It's her."

Coulter turned to Sage, his face lined with fatigue, etched with pain, and removed the saddle, the bridle. For the first and last time, the horse stood still as the outlaw stroked its long head.

"Get out o' here, you son-of-a-bitch," he rasped; he slapped its rump and the stallion snorted and reared, its hooves flailing the air. Then Sage galloped toward the mountains, alone.

"It's over," Coulter whispered as he watched the stallion disappear from view.

CHAPTER THIRTY

VOICES BUZZED, THEN faded, then buzzed again. One of them sounded familiar, yet it wasn't the one she strained to hear. So tired, so weak... she slipped back into the darkness. But the light wouldn't leave her alone. She tried to turn her head away from it, but a sharp pain assaulted her, shooting up and down her neck, and so she stayed still, refusing to open her eyes to the glare.

"She's better. Much better. But she lost so much blood ..."

A strong, thin hand smoothed over her brow, and then an arm slid under her shoulders and she felt herself being lifted. It hurt. Why wouldn't they leave her alone? Tears stung her eyelids and her throat ached. When a warm object pressed against her lips, she couldn't turn her head away.

"Come on, Miz Dougherty, just a little bit."

She opened her eyes, and was too tired to wonder why Wendell Crutcher was spooning broth into her mouth, too tired to care. She swallowed because she couldn't do anything else, her eyes trained on his kind, homely face. After he'd dabbed the last drip from the corner of her mouth and eased her back onto the pillow, she succumbed to sleep.

The next time she awoke, a new voice rumbled over her. She opened her eyes and realized it was night. Now only a candle illuminated the room. The man at the foot of her bed was a stranger, and she wanted to pull the sheet higher over her body, but her arms felt leaden, too heavy to move. He arched a heavy, black brow and smiled ruefully. "So, at last we meet, Mrs. Dougherty."

She closed her eyes in confusion and was grateful to hear Wendell's voice again.

"Miz Dougherty, are you feelin' better tonight? I don't want you to strain yourself, but Mr. Jennings here wanted to talk to you before he leaves."

Jennings. She'd heard his name before, but he was a stranger, and she had no interest, no energy for strangers. She turned her head painfully to find Wendell beside her. "Coulter ..."

Wendell's eyes darted guiltily to the stranger's, then met her gaze again. He didn't pretend not to know who she was speaking of. "He's in jail."

She squeezed her eyes shut.

"He turned himself in, ma'am."

She inched her head sideways toward Wendell, ignoring the pain that knifed through her at the movement. "I don't understand."

"There's a lot you don't understand," the stranger said in his clipped tones, moving to stand beside Wendell.

"Who are you?" she asked.

"Dan P. Jennings, with Harper's Weekly."

"Joel sent for you?"

"We don't know for sure, but, yes, it seems likely that he wrote me about Boone Coulter."

"And did you get your story?" she asked bitterly.

"I got two stories. The one I reported to Harper's that's being read all over the country even as we speak... and the real one."

She stared at him wearily. "What?"

The two men exchanged cautious glances. "Ma'am, are you up to hearin' all this?" Wendell asked softly.

Wendell seemed paler in the candlelight, his expression grave. "I went into the Diablos lookin' fer y'all. I... I was pretty scared, but I just had this feelin' that Coulter had taken you there, Miz Dougherty. I stumbled across a fresh grave, and thought maybe it was Coulter's or yours. That's when I got caught by Obregón's guards and shot—not bad, just winged in the shoulder. They took me to Don Obregón. He told me about Sheriff Dougherty. About Missouri, about you and Coulter ..."

"And he let you go?" she asked, amazed.

Wendell hung his head. "I was kind of delirious right after I got shot. They gave me some medicine for the pain, and I guess I was talkin' a blue streak, 'cause later Don Obregón knew all about... this... this lady that I had feelings for." He gulped, not meeting her eyes. "Don Obregón said he felt sorry for me and let me go. And I'm sure glad he did, or Sheriff Dougherty would have killed you, too." His voice faded to a whisper.

She frowned. "You... you were the one... you killed him?"

"Yes ma'am. I knew he was there. I was lookin' for him, and I heard his voice. I took off runnin', my gun ready, but I almost got there too late. You shot him in the belly, and I got him in the head."

"Thank you." Her throat was raw and aching, but still, she forced the words out. "Don Obregón did us all a great service when he spared you ..."

"You were pretty lucky, Miz Dougherty. The doc said if the artery had been cut, you would've died before Coulter'n me got you back here to my room. Even as it was, you almost didn't make it. Coulter stayed with you, prayin' over you all night."

The room seemed to fade from her vision. Closing her eyes, she could almost see him there with her. She gave up to sleep.

After she had rested again, she learned the details of Coulter's sacrifice, and of Wendell's sacrifice. Jennings had withheld part of the truth, submitting a story that was just as useful to him perhaps, but incomplete all the same. Wendell had led Coulter to Doralee's body, and together they had planned to substitute one woman's body for the other's to have Doralee buried in a grave with Elizabeth's name. Coulter had sacrificed his freedom, his life, to win her safety, to stop the manhunt and allow her to truly escape.

When all the facts were known, she brooded silently, victim of a thousand tortured thoughts. How could he do this to her? How could he have turned himself in? He had promised she could stay with him. Angry tears stung her eyes. Her hands were cold, her feet, and she shivered beneath the covers. Her eyelids grew heavy, and it was harder to concentrate, yet she must. "And exactly what has been in the newspapers?"

"The whole story, until the end. No one knows you're alive."

"Miz Dougherty," Wendell said nervously, "there's more." When she didn't respond, he cleared his throat and plunged forward. "We had to explain somehow who you were... are. Mr. Jennings was traveling with a... friend ..." His voice broke and he couldn't continue.

Jennings took up smoothly where he left off. "I'm afraid what he's trying to tell you is that you'll be traveling under false pretenses when you're strong enough to leave here. Since Elizabeth Dougherty is dead and buried a mile up the road, I had to tell the doctor that you were my female traveling companion. A... whore," he finished sheepishly.

"Then you must be an accomplished liar, sir, for I can't imagine anyone believing you." But his gaze shot to her hair, and she remembered. "Good lord," she whispered.

"I am an accomplished liar," he said with a low chuckle. "But you'd already provided some pretty convincing evidence."

"Elizabeth Dougherty is dead. ..." She should have felt something, but she didn't. No remorse, no shock, only wonder. "My family?"

The reporter's face showed crimson for the first time in the painful interview. "We were afraid your family would insist on having the body returned to Philadelphia. They didn't."

"I'm sure they didn't." An unreasoning desire to laugh sprang bitterly to her lips. From dried-up spinster to notorious black sheep. How far she had come.

"Mr. Coulter said to take care of you till you're strong enough to travel, then Mr. Jennings will ride with you to San Francisco, or anywhere out of New Mexico," Wendell offered helpfully.

"All in good time," Elizabeth snapped. "First, tell me where Mr. Coulter is."

"He's still here in the Lincoln jail, but the governor's sending a whole slew of guards down to take him back to Santa Fe."

"When will they arrive?"

"In two days, ma'am."

Jennings spoke up. "My sources tell me Pat Garrett's personally recruiting them."

She turned a stern gaze on the reporter. "And when do you plan to expose my existence, Mr. Jennings?"

"It would serve me no purpose," the reporter said brusquely. "I have no intention of following this story any farther. I give you my word. It's over."

"Is it?" she murmured. "I wouldn't be so sure, if I were you." She tried to raise up, but could barely lift her head. Wendell jumped forward and helped, propping pillows behind her so that she could see them better.

"Well, gentlemen," she said wearily, "now that you've gotten me in this fix, I hope you intend to get me out of it. I think you'd better get me something to eat. I'm going to need my strength, aren't I?"

Midnight.

The wind howled outside the courthouse, but the air in the second-story room was still, oppressive. In the corner, Coulter sat pressed against the wall, his arms clasping his knees, his haggard face void of expression.

At first, he ignored the footsteps ascending the stairs, the rustling noise of someone approaching. Keys rattled in the lock, and his door opened. Slowly, he raised his eyes to his captor and saw a cloaked figure holding a gun that was trained on him.

No.

The hood of her cloak fell open, and her hair gleamed russet and gold in the dim light, her skin too pale, yet so goddamn beautiful he wanted to cry. But his relief was short-lived, supplanted by panic and frustration. Heart pounding, he pulled to his feet, balling his fists. "How did you get in here?" he demanded, sending a desperate glance over her shoulder to the empty staircase. "Elizabeth, you've got to get out of here! They'll hang you if they catch you here!"

She could keep up her pretense of calm no longer. She crumpled into his arms, and he buried his face in her hair, clinging to her as she clung to him, drinking in her scent. "My God, my God, what are you doing here?" he rasped. "This is crazy."

She pulled away from him then, her eyes lit by an inner fire. "I'm going to release you," she said. "If you agree to my terms."

"What the hell are you talking about? What goddamn terms?"

"I'm going with you."

"You can't! There are guards, and the whole state of New Mexico will be looking for us, this time. Elizabeth, for God's sake, leave while you have a chance."

"Coulter, listen to me! Everything's arranged. I'm getting you out of here."

"But —but how?"

"There's no time for that, now. We have to hurry. Everything's arranged." And then she was tugging him forward, and he could do nothing but follow her down the flight of stairs. His hand went automatically to his hip, then fell away empty.

Elizabeth was already halfway across the room to the desk where Wendell sat, an untouched cup of coffee in front of him. "What are you doing?" she demanded. "Drink it!"

"Beggin' your pardon ma'am, if they're going to blame me for a fool again, at least this time I want some evidence that I really was tricked." He held his gun out to Coulter and sighed. "Don't hit me too hard. Just put out my lights for a little while. I won't raise an alarm till daybreak, anyway."

Coulter stared around the empty office, stunned. "Where are the guards? What the hell is going on?"

Wendell shrugged sheepishly. "Well, nobody thought it strange when I said I wanted to guard you tonight, seein' as how I've already lost one reward off you already. So I took the shift, and they were out on the porch playin' cards, and then I offered 'em a little coffee..." Wendell motioned at the closed door on the other side of the room. "They're all tied up purty good. They ain't gonna raise a ruckus fer quite a while, I reckon."

"Coffee?"

"It was Miz Dougherty's idea."

Coulter's jaw clenched, a muscle twisting. "I'll just bet it was." He snatched a rifle from the wall rack, his holster from the desk top. "You thought of everything, it seems."

"Somebody had to get you out of this mess you got yourself into," she bristled.

Their gazes locked.

"We've got a long road ahead of us, lady ..."

A slow smile curved her lips. "I'm banking on that, Mr. Coulter. I'm banking on that."

EPILOGUE

Lincoln, New Mexico—1906

MICAH STOOD AND watched the stage disappear around a bend in the crooked road. He fought down an uneasy urge to call after it to stop, but it was too late. Now that he was here, he'd best have a go at it.

Lincoln seemed to be just another western American town with its angular, adobe buildings and hot, dusty air. He'd come miles out of his way, and once more he questioned his sanity for doing so.

He approached the courthouse, where an old, stoop-shouldered man was perched on the corner of the porch.

"Excuse me, mate."

The old man stopped in mid-stroke, leaving a long strip of curled pine attached to the limb he was whittling. He glanced up at Micah through one squinted eye.

"Could you be telling me where to find the lady outlaw's gravesite?"

"English, are you?" the man asked.

"No." A half-smile pulled at the corner of Micah's mouth. "My folks were Yanks, but I was raised in New South Wales." Reading the man's confused expression, he added, "Australia." He rubbed his damp palms on his trousers.

The old man studied him a moment, then returned to his whittling, indicating a large oak tree with a thrust of his chin and a snort. "The lady's buried over there. There's a marker; you can't miss it. That New York feller that wrote the book about her 'n Boone Coulter paid fer it. Folks is always acomin' to see it, but I c'n tell you, no decent folks around here wanted it, anymore than we'd build a monument for Billy the Kid. We're better off without any reminders of the likes o' them, I say."

Micah clenched his fists at his sides, his lean cheeks suffused with color. Stifling the urge to respond, he pivoted briskly on his booted heel and strode toward the tree.

This detour was a waste of time, anyway. He could've been almost to New York, if he'd ridden the train straight through as he had originally planned. But his mother would have never forgiven him. He'd promised her that he'd visit the grave. Yet, with each dreaded step toward the small, grass plot, his feet felt heavier.

A few feet from the stone marker, he stopped, swallowed, then forced himself ahead. The sight of the name weakened his knees and made his heart pound. The thin air he inhaled seemed too scarce to fill his lungs, though he was high-country bred and raised. Again, he wiped his hands on his nankeen trousers and tugged the turned-down brim of his hat farther over his eyes.

He read the inscription once, twice, slowly assimilating what he saw there.

La Desperada
Elizabeth Cooke Dougherty
1857-1881
"Like the Phoenix from the ashes,
Her legend will live on."

There was no denying the words carved in stone, no way to dismiss them as a fanciful story devised to lull a young lad to sleep at night. Suddenly, it was all real. He dropped to his knee, stunned. His heart was filled with the chilling reality of a fate so narrowly missed.

A half-hour later he rose, and as his mother had asked, picked a handful of wildflowers and scattered them over the grave. The sun began to dip behind the mountains, and for a moment, he felt a bittersweet pang of familiarity: For a moment he was back on their station in the Snowy Mountains, hearing his sisters and brother echo his mother's voice as they recited their lessons, seeing his father on horseback, herding a mob of wild horses from the uplands.

The wave of homesickness passed. Perhaps he understood why his mother had insisted he come to this place, understood why his father hadn't wanted him to return at all. For good, for bad, what had happened here was a part of his history as well as theirs.

Micah Bridges walked slowly toward the hotel, his mind whirling, his fingers already itching to write home.

He'd go to New York, he'd work for this Dan P. Jennings, all in good time. But first he'd see for himself this strange land that had given him his heritage, and perhaps his destiny.

Author's Note

Upon entering the Trans-Pecos region of Texas for the first time, I realized that I had discovered the true Texas, the Texas of the imagination. Crossing the Pecos River is crossing a barrier in time to a forgotten corner of the world that few people know exists, much less take the time to explore.

In setting my story in these mountain regions of West Texas in 1881, I took certain chronological liberties. 1881 was a time when the region (other than El Paso) was only beginning to be inhabited. I have escalated the settlement of the region by several years in order to include certain aspects of history that are integral to the heritage of that area. For example, the camp meeting that Boone Coulter witnessed did not actually occur until 1890. Today, almost a century later, the Bloys Camp Meetings still draw hundreds of ranching families to a week-long ecumenical revival every August. The Sierra Diablos were not settled until the early part of the twentieth century. Even the Mescalero Apaches only entered them sporadically, so Don Miguél Obregón's presence there was purely part of my fictional dream.

And that brings me to the point of this note. Many hours of research went into this work, and those familiar with the times and places I depicted will recognize most of the historical details as accurate. However, it is first and foremost a work of fiction, and is not meant to be a scholarly representation of the era.

ABOUT THE AUTHOR

PATRICIA BURROUGHS (Pooks) is a fifth-generation Texan who lives in Dallas with her husband and near her three sons and their families.

Her earliest memories are of long afternoons spent soaking up the drama and laughter of the silver screen, and of long nights absorbing the magic of the written word—by flashlight. As a teenager, she sang, danced and acted in community theater productions.

These influences, she believes, are the foundation of her lifelong ambition to write, to spin the dreams that ignite imaginations—to repay the debt to those who reached through the klieg lights, flashlights and footlights to touch a young girl's heart.

Find out more about Pooks, her books and other projects, and where she will be appearing at conferences, classes and readings, on her websites:

http://patriciaburroughs.com
http://planetpooks.com

ABOUT BOOK VIEW CAFÉ

Book View Café is a publisher and professional authors' cooperative offering DRM-free ebooks in multiple formats to readers around the world. With authors in a variety of genres including mystery, romance, fantasy, and science fiction, Book View Café has something for everyone.

Book View Café is good for readers because you can enjoy high-quality DRM-free ebooks from your favorite authors at a reasonable price.

Book View Café is good for writers because 95% of the profit goes directly to the book's author.

Book View Café authors include Nebula and Hugo Award winners, Philip K. Dick and RITA award winners, New York Times bestsellers and many other notable book authors.

http://bookviewcafe.com

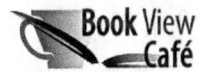

Book View Café

www.ingramcontent.com/pod-product-compliance
Lightning Source LLC
Chambersburg PA
CBHW070837260626
47170CB00007B/2405
* 9 7 8 1 6 1 1 3 8 3 0 8 9 *